MW01016492

TH GIFT

of the

RAINBOW

SERPENT

JOAN GREENLEES ABRAMSON

Joan Greenlees Abramson

ELTON-WOLF PUBLISHING

THE
GIFT
of the
RAINBOW
SERPENT

To Mary,
Thank you for your
interest and support.
Best wishes!
Fondly,
Joan Abramson

01 02 03 04 05   1 2 3 4 5

ISBN: 1-58619-034-2
LOC: 2001092803

First Printing September 2001
Printed in Canada

Published by Elton-Wolf Publishing
Seattle, Washington

ELTON-WOLF PUBLISHING

2505 Second Avenue Suite 515 Seattle Washington 98121 (206) 748-0345
e-mail: info@elton-wolf.com   Internet: http://www.elton-wolf.com
Seattle • Los Angeles

DEDICATION

THIS BOOK IS DEDICATED to my husband, Walter Abramson, whose zest for adventure enabled us to spend two fascinating years in the Outback of Australia. I am grateful for his patience and encouragement upon our return, insuring that The Gift of the Rainbow Serpent *went from dream to reality.*

ACKNOWLEDGMENTS

I AM DEEPLY GRATEFUL for the unwavering support of my daughter and son-in-law, Kathy and Robert Gately, who never ceased having faith in my novel. I appreciate the constructive suggestions and unfailing optimism of my friend Jane Livezey. I am indebted to my editor, Aviva Layton, for her fine critique and helpful advice. My heartfelt thanks to the Vista Writers' Roundtable and to Raymond Hug, who guided me through many dark hours with my computer and encouraged me to keep writing. Special thanks go to John Abramson and to Kathy and Jerry Turner for their interest and help. To all our wonderful friends in Australia, I send a fond greeting for opening their hearts to us and sharing some of our most memorable experiences.

CHAPTER ONE

ERIC CHRISTIANSON had driven on plenty of rough roads back home in the States, but this track undoubtedly was the worst. It had started in Kingoonya, 185 kilometers to the south, and there would be no relief until he reached his final destination, the opal-mining town of Coober Pedy. He dreaded to think of the damage that must be occurring in the interior of the caravan he was towing. Little corrugations inside of big corrugations tossed his rig up and down like a puppy shaking a slipper, and surely there was no part of his body left undamaged by the jolting of the road. Twice his head had hit the roof of his utility truck, hard! He still had a headache and there were over 100 kilometers ahead of him. The shuddering and vibrating never ceased; no variation of speed lessened the incredible pounding, and no part of the road was superior to another. The track was very wide, for new lanes had been made on each side of the original by drivers hopeful that another pathway would be an improvement. Eric tried them all without success. He had read about the "gibber plain," that rock-strewn land in the outback that continued on and on in all directions, but he was not quite prepared for the relentless pounding and bouncing from which there was no escape. When the big road trains roared past, spitting up rocks, he was glad he had bought a windscreen protector for his ute. Broken glass along the "highway" testified to the fate of windows of less farseeing drivers.

Uncomfortable as the traveling was, at least it afforded him time to reflect on his purpose in coming to Australia. Unlike others driving this wretched stretch of road, he did not seek the precious fire opal that lured so many to Coober Pedy. His was a far more complicated quest.

When he had parted from Anne in Sydney that last day of his R and R, sixteen years before, it was with the promise of marriage when he was mustered out of the army. The Korean War was winding down, and he soon would be released. When he presented her with the opal mosaic koala pendant, he had whispered, "I love you, and I'll be back for you." She had lifted her beautiful auburn hair so he could fasten the gift around her neck; both knowing it was all he could afford, but that it represented total commitment. They spent their final moments together watching the sailboats in the harbor. The beauty of the scene would stay in his mind forever: Anne at his side with her hair blowing in the breeze, the sun sparkling on the bay, the little sailboats darting in and out like dragonflies. The bright sails billowed out, and caught the morning light, spangling the water with gypsy colors. He had looked into her eyes and repeated, "I promise," and they both knew he would keep his pledge.

He would have kept it, too; if a combat injury hadn't sent him stateside to a hospital, and from there he was transferred to another one. Anne's letters were delayed in reaching him. When they finally arrived after a circuitous route, her news shocked him. She was pregnant, had lost her job and had nowhere to turn. Her folks were too straight-laced to approach. He tried to arrange a proxy marriage but authorities refused him. In her next letter she told him she planned to marry a man who was willing to take on the baby. She pleaded for Eric not to contact her again, and although devastated, he had respected her wish. But since then his life had changed dramatically; now finding the child had become an obsession. After traveling over 2000 kilometers, he had learned that Anne was dead, but he finally had obtained the name of his son from her husband. The lad, Sandy Blackwell, was somewhere in Coober Pedy. Eric's visa was good for another ten months, so he had plenty of time to find him. The place couldn't be that big!

As he neared the town, the landscape gradually changed to occasional low undulating hills, and he could see big heaps of opal clay where the miners had brought up the discarded material.

A few of the piles had trucks parked near them, but many claims appeared to be abandoned. When he could see buildings in the distance on the higher parts, he breathed a sigh of relief and ran his tongue around his mouth to see if any teeth had been jarred loose. The dirt track changed to a sealed road, and he drove into the town in comfort. He pulled into the caravan park, the "park" being a barren expanse of dirt on which no blade of grass or shrub was visible. The slightest puff of wind raised swirls of fine dust that settled on everything. A glance into his caravan confirmed his fears. Unlike the utility truck, which had arrived relatively unscathed, the interior of the caravan was a scene of chaos. Drawers had tumbled out and emptied their contents, canned goods and utensils were scattered about, and his clothes lay in tangled heaps. He was thankful he had not brought salad oil or mayonnaise to complicate the mess. No door hinges had held against that incredible road. Tired as he was, he gathered the energy to put things right before relaxing in a warm shower in the amenities building. Relaxation couldn't last long, however, as the shower was coin operated, and a sign stated that even with a sufficient deposit of money, the water might stop suddenly. Water was in short supply in Coober Pedy.

He decided a walk into town to buy some fresh meat would relieve the pain in his cramped muscles. He had almost made it back to the caravan park when a dog attacked him. It happened so suddenly that he had no time to fend it off. The emaciated creature snatched the parcel of meat from Eric's hand, ripping his flesh with sharp teeth, and then dashed away. Eric recognized that hunger, not viciousness, precipitated the act, but that didn't lessen the shock. He bound the wound with his handkerchief and made his way to the hospital, a modest wooden building he had passed on his way to the caravan park.

The nurse made a quick examination. "You'll need stitches. Doctor will see you shortly—he's setting a broken arm now." She gently cleansed the wound.

Eric tried not to wince. "I'm lucky there's no rabies here."

"Yes, that's one deadly thing we don't have in Australia. This isn't a pleasant welcome to Coober Pedy for you, especially after driving that road."

"How did you know I just arrived?" For the first time he looked closely at the nurse. He had expected to find a matronly woman, but to his surprise, he was attended by a slim, golden-skinned girl. Her soft voice seemed familiar. He knew he had seen her somewhere before, but the circumstances eluded him.

She didn't answer his question. Eric forgot his pain in the pleasure of seeing such an attractive face. Her eyes were large and dark, full of compassion. Her curly brown hair, cut short, formed an interesting frame about her features. Her chin was rounded and firm, her lips almost voluptuous, and yet, there was something different about her. He decided it was the nose—it was not quite the nose one expected. There was a slight incongruity in the way the nostrils flared. Yet it wasn't unattractive, Eric thought. It just added an exciting dimension to what seemed rather mysterious. Her skin was petal-smooth, but the color appeared to be natural rather than from a tan acquired under the Australian sun.

The nurse looked down at him and smiled. She smiled with her eyes as well as her mouth, and he strained for recognition. He had seen her in a crowd somewhere, dressed differently, but where? Suddenly he knew. It was at the Yunarra Lutheran Aboriginal Mission the week before, where she had humiliated him. He stared at her, hoping their present encounter might embarrass her, but she seemed oblivious to anything but caring for his injured hand.

"I'm giving you a tetanus booster and an antibiotic," she said.

The doctor arrived and examined the wound, closing it with a dozen stitches. "Drop by in a week and the sister will take them out."

"The sister?" Eric looked at him, baffled.

"Over here we call a graduate nurse 'sister'."

"Oh."

"Be sure you file a report with the police. There are too many dog bites here. The damn Aborigines keep five or six dogs, and they're always hungry. Sorry."

Eric didn't know whether the doctor was talking to him or to the nurse, but her heightened color answered his question. He tried not to look at her directly.

"I was lucky," she said. "I flew in with Opal Air. You had to drive here." After a moment's hesitation she added, "Pastor Holmgren said you'd been a teacher."

"Yes." He flushed with anger at finding he had been under discussion at the mission.

Out of curiosity he had taken an afternoon off from his

traveling to visit the mission. Eric remembered hearing his Sunday school teachers talk about missionaries in Africa, but he had never heard of any in Australia. He was shocked to encounter some semi-civilized natives on his way in who were begging for candy and beer. They were dirty and unkempt, and a baby in a woman's arms was almost covered with flies. He was so revolted that when he arrived at the mission and found a young crowd of half-dressed Aborigines on the steps of the pastor's bungalow, he assumed that they were of a similar type. They tricked him by feigning ignorance when he had tried to communicate with them in limited English. This girl, who concealed her face with a broad-brimmed hat at the time, was involved in the prank.

After the crowd left, the pastor's daughter invited him in to meet her parents, and Pastor Holmgren advised him that several of the youths were attending college. Although he mentioned that his foster daughter, Molly, was a nurse, Eric never had expected to meet her again. He resented that she had played him for a fool, and his past was none of her business.

"Most people who come to Coober Pedy are interested in mining. Are you planning to get involved?"

"No," he answered abruptly.

"I'm glad you're not."

Molly's reply irritated him. She had no right to pry into his affairs, and he could care less about her opinion. He deliberately turned his back on her and addressed the doctor.

"Have you heard of a young lad here named Sandy Blackwell?"

The doctor shook his head. "People come and go all the time in Coober Pedy. Unless they need medical treatment, I never meet them. Ask at the police station."

Eric didn't thank the nurse after she finished bandaging his hand but stalked out with what he hoped was some semblance of dignity. From the corner of his eye he caught her look of amusement, which only added to his discomfort. He knew he had acted childish, if not churlish.

He found his way to the police station and entered with high expectations.

"Do you know of a young man here named Sandy Blackwell?"

Upon hearing the American accent, Sergeant MacDonald leaped to his feet and slammed his fist on the desk. "Do you think we have nothing better to do than run a bloody missing person's bureau?"

Eric stared at the officer. Since his arrival in Australia two months before, he had been received with civility and sometimes with amused camaraderie, so this hostile reception baffled him.

"I just thought—" he began.

"Well, you thought wrong! We're not baby sitters here. Coober Pedy is a workingman's town. I can't keep track of every no-hoper who travels through. Miners come and go. Maybe this fellow doesn't want to be found. Maybe he changed his name. Did you think of that, Yank?"

Eric's shoulders sagged. "In that case, I'm wasting my time here." He started toward the door.

The policeman's voice boomed out again. "Aren't you the bloke the nursing sister just phoned about? The dog-bite case?"

"I guess so."

"Then why didn't you report it?"

Eric shrugged. "The dog's long gone by now."

"But you were told to report it. Can't you follow orders?"

Eric's face darkened. A faint scar running from his left eye down his cheek became more visible. The policeman thrust a paper at him and snapped, "Fill this out."

The two men glared at each other. Then Eric snatched the paper with his left hand and struggled to write with his bandaged right hand. Twice the pencil slipped through his fingers and dropped to the floor. Each time that he picked it up he avoided looking at the policeman—not wanting to give him the satisfaction of knowing his sardonic smile had been observed. Eric continued filling out the report. NAME: Eric Christianson. DATE: He couldn't remember the day and wasn't about to ask. He glanced at a calendar on the wall — March 18, 1972. ADDRESS: none. His hand throbbed as he continued to write.

MacDonald sat back and folded his arms across his chest, waiting. His sunburned face reflected antagonism as he gestured to the stack of papers lying before him. When the American finished writing, the sergeant's lips twisted, and hot words boiled out.

"Do you realize all that goes on in this town, including your little dog bite incident? We've got thefts, knifings, poaching, public brawls, and yes, even murders! I have to file reports on all of them. There are only two escape routes out of town—north to Darwin or south to Adelaide, and after a rain they're impassable. So we're all cooped up here together, and I have to maintain law and order." His pale blue eyes narrowed. "We've got a lot of nationalities working here: Germans, Hungarians, Greeks, Italians, Yugoslavs. And then you 'new-chum' Yanks show up here expecting a red carpet reception."

Eric looked the officer in the eye. "I don't want special treatment. I just asked a simple question. Whatever your grudge is, don't take it out on me!" He flung the report on the desk and stalked out.

He was still chafed about the incident when he returned to the caravan park. That confrontation, on top of the humiliating encounter at the hospital, had put him on the defensive. He decided to open a can of stew for supper and then go to bed. What a day! His last impression before drowsiness overtook him was how inconceivable it was that he had come to this place deliberately. Only his mission to find his child would have driven him to a mining town.

CHAPTER TWO

AFTER THE AMERICAN LEFT, Molly sat at her desk and pondered her reaction to him. At the mission, she had assumed he was a typical tourist who had come to look down his nose at the Aborigines as so many did. When he spoke of the wild-looking natives he met coming in to the mission, she felt he was equating them with her and her friends. Actually, they were all students enjoying the last of their holiday from school, and it seemed only fitting to play a joke on him.

The scene was set when her foster sister, Beatrice, said, "These people are quite gentle. They won't hurt you," and he had replied, "Do they speak English?"

He had sat down next to her and attempted to converse, but she pretended not to understand. Her hat concealed much of her face, so he couldn't see her expression. When he asked if she liked music, she spread out her hands as though she didn't understand, and then, incredibly, he began to sing a few bars of "Waltzing Matilda." The group could scarcely contain their laughter. To complete the charade, Danny asked him if he had a wife, and his emphatic, "No!" led to a new opening.

Andrew said, "That is good. Not good for white woman when willy-willy come." They all had nodded solemnly.

Apparently forgetting that she couldn't understand English, the American had asked Molly, "What does he mean?" and the boys all chorused, "Tell him, Molly!"

Molly had answered in a soft voice, "Some Aborigines believe the great wind brings a baby spirit ... and the woman becomes pregnant." The American knew then he'd been the butt of their joke, and as the group chortled, his face reddened. When they shouted, "We go walkabout now!" and scattered, he prepared to leave, too. Beatrice restrained him and urged him to come into the bungalow for tea and to meet her parents, Pastor and Mrs. Holmgren. "You know," she said, "they recognized your American accent the minute you spoke. Let me make it up to you. Please."

Molly slipped into the house by the back door, uncertain whether to join the family or not, when she overheard her foster father explaining the purpose of the mission. "You may think it's a hopeless task here, but all is not what it seems." Molly knew the pastor had felt the American's chagrin and wanted to clarify some misconceptions. Not wanting to intrude, she waited. "I know you encountered some of our less disciplined natives when you drove up the track, but they are only part of the picture. My wife and I have been here for thirty-five years and in that time we have learned tolerance and practicality."

"Thirty-five years!" the American echoed.

"I know what you're thinking. You feel we've wasted our lives, but that isn't so. I have seen other missionaries in their misguided zeal put a heavy yoke on these simple people, constricting them with shame and fear. We work with them through love and hope. We don't try to take away their old ways—some of them are very good. We try to show them better ways when we can and work from a positive approach."

Molly was surprised to hear the American say, "It's all a matter of education, isn't it?" and Pastor Holmgren's reply, "You're a teacher, aren't you?"

She could barely hear the reply, "I was." She felt guilty for eavesdropping and wanted to enter the room, but curiosity held her back as the pastor continued, "Those young people you saw outside are our successes. Some are in college now, and Molly, my foster daughter, has just completed her nurse's training. I'm very proud of them."

She was glad that the American had the grace to say, "I really insulted them, didn't I?" After he left, she felt somewhat contrite about enjoying her role in the escapade.

Now that she had encountered him again so unexpectedly, she felt confused. She had hoped he might have approached her with a sense of humor, but he had been downright cold and apparently unforgiving. Well, she would be just as cold as he was when she saw him again.

Dismissing Eric from her mind, Molly turned to Sister Elizabeth Thomas, the supervising nurse, who had come to relieve her.

"How is it going, Molly? You've hardly had time to get settled in. Keeping busy?"

"Not too busy. Some respiratory problems, broken arm, dog bite."

"Be thankful for a light day. When the Aborigines get their dole, look out! Oh, I am sorry! I didn't mean ..."

"It's all right," Molly assured her. "I may be only one quarter Aboriginal, but I don't deny my heritage. I know about their problems, and that's one reason I'm here—to help if I can."

"That's a big order. You know they get their money every fortnight and the first thing they do is pay last month's food bill and then head for the liquor store. Since they got their drinking rights, it's been really bad for them. You'll see some of them lying around drunk or fighting, and when their money is gone, they charge the next fortnight's food. We get a lot of action during this time. It's a sad situation. People try to help, but ..." She shrugged.

"I hope I can do something while I'm here."

"You'll be kept busy with all the other ethnic groups living in Coober Pedy. Most of them get along fine, but there are some problems. They tend to be a little clannish, but that's understandable. They each have their own language and customs, and some don't assimilate as easily as others."

"There haven't been any patients overnight since I arrived."

"No, we don't have many. The Flying Doctor Service

takes the more serious patients to Adelaide. Also, our kitchen facilities here aren't much—just good for warming things up or making a quick sandwich. When we do have overnight patients, the German couple who runs the "Hofbrau Café" sends over meals."

"Are there many mining accidents?"

"Well, Coober Pedy's main industry is opal mining, of course, and it's dangerous work, but we see relatively few accidents—one or two a week maybe. Most of the miners are careful, but there was one bad cave-in last spring. It was a real tragedy. Our usual cases are from personal conflicts, fights and such, and of course, respiratory problems—people noodling under the blowers and dust storms."

"I can see that there's rarely a dull moment."

"At times that's right. But on the whole, it's fairly peaceful. Sergeant MacDonald keeps a tight rein on the town. I think you'll enjoy it here. There are lots of amenities. I guess you saw the Greek store when you came in to town. They have stocked just about anything you would want. And there's a general store as well as an Italian restaurant. And the Opal Inn, of course."

"It sounds very cosmopolitan."

"It is, Molly. Just be careful in picking your friends. A word of warning—don't accept a date with Peter Bagley. His nickname is "Peter the Con" and he's notorious for his underhanded deeds. He's a handsome devil, and unfortunately the girls fall for him."

"I have no intention of dating. My work here will keep me busy, and on my off days I plan to help at the Aboriginal reserve."

Elizabeth laughed. "We'll see. Girls are in short supply in Coober Pedy. A few brave women come with their husbands, but most miners leave their wives in Adelaide or Sydney. It's a pretty harsh place for a woman. I feel so sorry for that Yugoslav woman who lives out in a horrid tin shack at the Eleven Mile. She and her husband will have to move into town during summer, of course. The heat gets pretty bad here, Molly. A lot of people leave."

Molly shrugged. "I have no illusions about comfort. I'm just here to do a good job where I'm needed. It will be wonderful to put into practice all the things I've learned and trained for during the past two years." She smiled at her friend. "I've never lived a life of luxury, Sister Thomas. Conditions were rather primitive at the Yunarra Mission, and I've learned to compromise."

"Then you should do very well here," the nurse answered.

The first week had passed swiftly, and there was little time to look back. Her new routine kept her busy with paper work, patching wounds, assisting the doctor, and doling out medicine. Each day brought different activities. She learned that the doctor had a mining claim, too, and when business was slack, he would take a few hours to do a little work with his partners. Everyone in Coober Pedy was involved in the opal industry in some way. Well, she knew she would not be.

She had too much of her grandmother in her to like all this tearing up of the land.

Although she had been only six years old when Pastor Holmgren took her to visit her grandmother, she remembered everything vividly. She knew that many people scoffed at the idea that a child as young as she could recall so much, but it was true. Everything about the encounter was so exciting that she had treasured every detail. She could close her tired eyes now and recite their conversations as though it were yesterday. She could remember how Niboorana had embraced her and told her to call her "Kabbarli", which was "Grandmother" in their tongue.

"Kabbarli," Molly had repeated. "That's a funny name, but I like it. I'm glad I'm here."

Tears streamed down Niboorana's dark cheeks. She hated to release Molly but finally did so with a gentle squeeze. She gestured down the track where her small shack was located, and Pastor Holmgren lifted Molly's small suitcase from the Land Rover.

"I'll be staying with the McCurdys," he told the child. "You'll have tonight and tomorrow night with your grandmother, and the next morning we'll have to go back. I'll be right here if you need anything." He gave her a hug, reluctant to relinquish her. He shook hands with Niboorana. "Take good care of her."

Niboorana looked down so the pastor would not see the

angry flash in her eyes. Take good care of her! As if she could cause one moment of unhappiness or permit the slightest injury to this girl for whom she gladly would exchange her life. On second thought, she realized the man standing before her loved Molly, too, and had given her a fine home. He had honored his commitment and had brought his foster daughter to visit her, if only for a short time. She raised her eyes in gratitude. Without this man's dedication, she never would have seen her granddaughter again. Her appreciation must have been evident, for Pastor Holmgren smiled and then turned to his hosts. They watched as Niboorana led Molly down the road.

Niboorana's house was little more than a 'humpy', a one room dwelling constructed of boards and galvanized iron. She still preferred to sleep outdoors, but in deference to Molly's upbringing, she had moved her cot inside. She herself would sleep on the rough plank floor. A small woodburning stove was in a corner. It was sufficient to cook on or to warm the dwelling in the cold winter, but was seldom used. Niboorana worked six days in the big house for Mrs. McCurdy—cleaning, washing clothes, helping prepare meals and tidying up afterwards. She often ate in the kitchen after her employers and their three children had completed their meals. When she cooked for herself, it was done over a small campfire. A blackened billy and two pans were all she had for utensils. A weathered outhouse stood in the back at a discreet distance from her dwelling.

Molly stared around the sparsely furnished room. Cupboards made of wooden crates were stacked on top of each other, providing ample space to store her grandmother's meager belongings. A few articles of apparel were folded and placed on the makeshift shelves along with some personal items: a comb and brush, a toothbrush, a small jar of ointment, and a cracked mirror. A shabby, cold-weather coat hung on a nail driven into the wall. Niboorana stood stiffly, her skinny hands clasped tightly as she waited for the child's reaction. Her anxious eyes followed Molly's gaze while her heart pounded with uncertainty. Was this visit too late for her to connect with this offspring? She had faced many uncertainties in her life but none with greater consequences. The possibility of rejection was all too real, and she could not bear the thought of losing this child again—it would signify the end of any meaning in her life.

Suddenly Molly laughed with delight as she spied some toys on the bed and rushed over to them. One was a rag doll, cleverly dressed in a flowered gown adorned with bright pink ribbons. The other was a little lamb made from bits and pieces of discarded fleece. Molly cuddled them in her arms, her eyes shining. "Are these mine?" she asked—an unnecessary question for it was evident that she had already claimed ownership. Niboorana smiled in assent. Relief flowed over her body like a caressing hand.

"Thank you, Kabbarli." Molly snuggled the lamb against her neck and then asked unexpectedly, "Do you like me?" She tipped her head to one side as she observed her grandmother.

"You haven't seen me for a long time, have you?"

"I love you, child, and it has been much too long. My heart is filled with happiness that you are here now. You are everything I hoped for."

Molly beamed. Then she said, "Tell me about my mother."

Panic swept over Niboorana. The old taboo of never speaking the name of the dead lingered deep in her consciousness, but she could not resist the pleading in Molly's eyes. With an effort she composed herself. "Your mother's name was Ashira. She was a beautiful, loving woman with a kind spirit. You have her eyes, Molly. It is sad that she did not live to know you. She would be very proud of you." She gestured to the makeshift table. "We will eat now. Mrs. McCurdy sent down supper for us."

After the meal Molly asked, "Will you tell me some stories, Kabbarli? I have heard people talk about the Dreamtime. Was it like dreams at night?"

"Ah, no. It was a sacred time before man walked on earth." How could she explain to this little girl about "timeless time" when totemic beings wandered about on the land involving themselves in adventures and mysterious activities? About how they had been in many places and left evidence of their being on special rocks and mounds and water holes where their spirits still resided. Niboorana believed these spirits were alive and influenced life in the present. Her own people's totem was the goanna; other tribes were emu or kangaroo people. Each animal on earth had a counterpart in the Dreamtime. She had heard of the Valley of the Winds in the sacred Olgas in the Center, where the breath of the powerful Serpent could become a vengeful hurricane if anyone transgressed the tribal laws. She did not want to frighten her granddaughter, so she would choose carefully which stories to tell.

She started with a light-hearted story about Old Man Kangaroo, but Molly was fast asleep, clutching the doll and the little sheep in her arms, before she had finished. Niboorana smiled and sat quietly watching her granddaughter's expressive face relax into slumber. Each moment with Molly was precious. She was a wonderful gift from her vanished father— a man who had honored a dead woman's memory by keeping his word. Niboorana was indebted to the kindly pastor and his wife who had taken Molly in as their foster daughter. She wanted to instill her people's values in Molly but did not want to alienate or confuse the child during this short, impressionable visit. She knew she must tread carefully. Niboorana sighed. Time was so short.

She looked again at Molly's golden skin and delicate features. You are a fine girl, she thought, and I hope you are strong enough to survive. She closed her eyes and concentrated on transferring her strength to Molly. She became rigid and upright, and did not change her position as time passed. Determination made her tireless. Hours slipped by before she finally stretched out on the floor. She was at peace with herself.

What pleasure Molly found in wandering around the McCurdy station! Everything had fascinated her: the shearing shed, cool and dark; the blacksmith building with its great bellows and forge; the schoolroom where the children studied their lessons. It was like a small town. Much to her delight the jackaroos had put her up on one of the less spirited horses and led her around. She ignored the sulky boy who stuck his tongue out at her as she passed by. She didn't understand when Mr. McCurdy said to Papa Holmgren, "A pretty little thing, but neither fish nor fowl." Nothing mattered except the thrill of being there.

As they wandered around, her grandmother told Molly more tales of the Dreamtime. That night Niboorana began her favorite story about the rainbow serpent. "She came from the far north and created valleys and hills. She made deep pools of water for our refreshment and brought the wet season that renewed life. Some say the serpent lay down in the moist earth and wherever she pressed her body, rivers formed. She is very special to the Aborigine."

Molly had said, "I saw a carpet snake once, and it had lots of colors. Do you suppose it was one of the rainbow serpent's children?"

"I don't know child, but it is possible. I do know that all things in this world are one. We are the land and have kinship with all other living things now and those that lived in the Dreamtime. We have been given this earth to care for. It should not be changed or altered. We must live in harmony with it.

What it is made of, we are made of. We are part of it."

This discussion had puzzled Molly. "But people dig in the ground and plant things to eat. Mrs. McCurdy has a nice vegetable garden."

"Yes, that is so."

"And people cut down trees and burn the wood to keep warm, and they make furniture and houses."

"Yes, that is so."

"And they dig up pretty rocks and wear them on their hands and neck."

"Yes."

"And they dig deep holes to get water. Are these things wrong, Kabbarli?"

"No, Molly, they are not wrong because people no longer live the way they used to, taking only what was needed and leaving the land unspoiled. But it is wrong to be greedy and take more than enough. If the earth is made ugly, then the spirit of the earth will be unhappy and will abandon us, and without spirit we are nothing."

"Is 'spirit' the same as 'God'?"

"I ... I think it may be."

"What does 'abandon' mean?"

"It means ... to go away from us ... to leave us ..."

"Then everything's all right," Molly smiled. "Papa Holmgren says God is always with us."

She gave her grandmother a big hug.

Molly roused herself from her reverie. What precocious questions she had asked! Her understanding grandmother must have been taken aback trying to answer them. Molly recognized that Niboorana had never tried to undermine her granddaughter's innocent faith, yet she continually had armed her with the strength of her own ideals. Molly knew she would live in this town and render it service, but she never would accept the ruthless tearing apart of the land. Let others succumb to the lure of opal—she would set her sights on healing.

CHAPTER THREE

ERIC TRIED TO SHAKE OFF THE ANGER and disappointment he felt on the first morning after his arrival: anger at the arrogant policeman he had tangled with the day before, and disappointment at finding no information about Sandy. Coupled with the resentment he felt toward the nurse and the throbbing of his hand injured from the dog bite, he knew his dour mood needed to be lifted. A brisk walk into town would help relieve his tension, but upon reflection he thought "brisk" might not be the right adjective—heat, already oppressive, caused him to jerk back when he opened the door.

He had left the States in late January, with snow deep in upper Michigan, and had arrived in Australia at the end of summer there, missing springtime entirely! It was a strange feeling, this reversal of seasons. Although it was technically autumn now, it would probably feel like summer much longer here in Coober Pedy.

As he walked along, he was struck again by the difference between this place and others he had visited. Yesterday in the late afternoon there had been a preponderance of men on the street going in and out of the shops, carrying away provisions. He had been intrigued. In other places it was the women who did the shopping. At first he couldn't quite distinguish what set the men apart from those he had seen in similar country towns, and then he realized it was a dearth of the fair-skinned, lean, blue-eyed Anglo Saxon he associated with Australia. The men here were of different nationalities, many appearing to be from southern Europe and Asia, round faced, brown-eyed and darker complexioned. On his drive into town the previous day, he was aware of a casualness in their general demeanor and dress, but noted an inquiring, almost sharp, expression in their gaze. There were few men on the street now. He assumed that most would be working in their mines, emerging like nocturnal animals when the heat dissipated at the end of the day.

Coober Pedy seemed to offer every amenity: a general merchandise shop, a miners' store, two food markets, several small restaurants, petrol stations, a hotel and motel, a school, the hospital, and an underground church. This could hardly be called a typical outback town!

He strolled through both markets, one from which he had bought the meat that attracted the hungry dog. Apparently it was owned by what the Aussies called "New Australians." The proprietor looked Greek, as did his pretty daughter at the counter. The shelves were stocked with as many cosmopolitan goods as could be found in Sydney to accommodate every taste. The building itself, while apparently fairly new, had an old-establishment rustic charm. It was dark, cluttered and emitted exotic fragrances.

Eric found himself increasingly attracted to Coober Pedy, in spite of his initial revulsion at finding himself in a mining town. It had a raw, frontier character that he appreciated, a welcome change from the staid college atmosphere he had left behind. He could have ended up in a much less interesting place, he decided.

He bought some supplies and visited with the friendly shopkeeper. "Do you know of a young man named Sandy Blackwell?" This had become his standard question wherever he went.

"No, but Coober Pedy is a big place—it stretches for miles, and Sandy is a pretty common name here. I know a couple of Sandys myself, but not with that surname. A lot of the Aussies have reddish hair and beards, you know—the Scotch or Irish in them, I guess." He smiled, his strong teeth white against his dark face. "We're a real mixture of nationalities here, but I guess you've figured that out."

"I don't quite know where to look for him," Eric said. "The policeman didn't give me any advice—in fact, he gave me a real dressing down."

"I'm surprised. He's usually helpful to tourists. Sergeant MacDonald is all right, but he has too much to do, and I guess sometimes he's a little short on patience. We have a bulletin board over there on the wall for people to put up advertisements and inquiries. Try posting a notice. It might bring some results."

"Thanks. I will."

The storekeeper assumed Eric was interested in mining and obliged him with some pertinent information for unasked questions. "Always ask before you go on a miner's claim. Most are friendly, but if they're not, they'll soon let you know. It's not safe to trespass."

Eric agreed silently. That was the last thing he intended to do.

He learned several more pieces of information from the storekeeper. "No one works for wages in a mine. They all work on shares. The opal fields are named for special reasons. Here's a booklet with some maps you might want to read. The Olympic Field was started by some Greeks, and they did real well, too. Some are named for their distance from town, the Four Mile, the Eleven Mile and so on. Like I told you, Coober Pedy stretches a long way."

Eric returned to his caravan to compose the notices he planned to post in several areas. The message was brief: "Would Sandy Blackwell or anyone with information about him please contact Eric Christianson at the caravan park. Important." There was nothing more he could write at this time. If Sandy didn't see the notice himself, perhaps one of his mates might spot it and tell him.

After posting the cards, he was drawn to an opal shop that had a wide variety of precious stones on display. Sensing a potential customer, the owner bustled about showing off his wares and acquainting Eric with techniques distinguishing quality. Although Eric had some background in geology, he had learned long ago that being a good listener was the best way to acquire knowledge and win friends. The shopkeeper shoved a piece of milky, glassy looking material toward him. "Know what that is?" he asked.

"It's common opal, isn't it?"

"Out here, we call it 'potch.' There's no fire in it."

Eric looked again at the display. Some stones were opaque and some were translucent, but both exhibited bright spectral colors, which shifted and changed as they were rotated.

"What makes the color? Minerals?" Eric asked.

The proprietor beamed, glad for the opportunity to expand on the latest scientific discoveries. "No. Researchers used an electron microscope and found that opal is composed of silica spheres. In precious opal the spheres are generally larger and packed together in an orderly arrangement. When light passes through them to the spaces between, it's scattered, like a prism. It's a member of the quartz family but has higher water content. It's a very delicate stone, you know."

Eric hated to leave the fascinating display; each piece was so distinctive. He could understand a miner's thrill in extracting the opal from deep underground. He thanked the shop owner, slightly embarrassed that he hadn't bought anything. But with many months to go before his visa expired, he had to be careful with his money. Besides, he had no one to whom he could give such an expensive gift.

By the end of the day he had acquired much knowledge about the local inhabitants. The information varied with the nationality of the storytellers and their attitudes. Eric sifted through a rich mosaic of facts and innuendos before arriving at some of his own generalities. He learned that the Greeks were considered well-behaved and hard-working, as they struggled with a strange alphabet and an unfamiliar tongue. They were known to keep a restrictive watch over their women. They were pious in their religious orthodoxy, but not to an extreme, and clannish in their mining and business operations. The Greek Club was their main recreational place.

It was painstakingly evident that the Croatians and Serbians kept their lives completely separate, each having their own social club. Sometimes fights erupted between the two groups, exposing in their new lives the old hatreds of their previous homeland. There was an inexorable distrust that never seemed to lift, although several people confided to Eric that the children of both nationalities got along very well in school, which augured well for the future. The native Australians lumped both groups into the heading of "Yugoslavs" which embittered them, but the locals refused to be drawn into their battles and shrugged them off.

The Italians had their own club, too, and it was a lively place. They were a volatile people, usually happy, who enjoyed life and expressed their feelings physically as well as vocally. There was nothing inhibited about the Italians! Mama Ciano was a warm woman with a heart as big as the surrounding desert, and fearless when scolding her husband for being sharp with the Aborigines who came to trade in their store. The Italian restaurant was a popular eating-place with its festive wax-dripped candles on the tables, the red and white table-cloths and hanging strands of garlic and gourds.

The Germans and the Hungarians were a different breed, Eric was told. They were of a more serious nature, ambitious and efficient, thrifty and cautious. They arrived with very little and soon owned stores, garages and restaurants, becoming a visible power in the community. They worked well with the old-time Australians, as both sides put aside the past when they shot at each other during the war.

It felt good to be walking, but Eric realized just walking would not be sufficient to bring his body back to top condition. He had lost muscle tone and needed something more vigorous to compensate for his slackness. For the first time he cast about for something else on which to spend his time and effort. His visa forbade him from working at a regular job. But surely he could find something to do. Not mining, of course, that would be his last choice. But something.

As he returned to the caravan park, he noticed some nondescript dogs coming along the road and with them straggled a group of Aborigines. Mick, the young man whose caravan was parked next to his, was sitting outside, and Eric struck up a conversation, indicating the approaching parade and explaining about his bite.

"The dog that bit you must have been a stray," Mick said.

"When you see a pack of dogs, they're usually with Aborigines."

Eric found the young man's company pleasant. Mick usually drifted down to one of the pubs after work, but this afternoon he had chosen to sit outside and visit. "The Aborigines want to get back to the reserve before dark. It's a couple of miles from here. They always take their dogs with them. They used to keep them for hunting and also to keep warm during their walkabout days. You've heard of a 'three dog night' or a 'five dog night'? That meant really cold weather! They wore no clothing, you know, so the dogs kept them from freezing. Of course they built fires—not big ones that wasted heat, but small ones they could get close to. Sometimes when they slept, they rolled into the hot ashes and got horribly burned. You can see scars on some of the older ones."

"They're an interesting people," Eric observed.

"They were fond of their dogs," Mick continued. "Treated them better than their wives most of the time!"

"Everything was for survival, wasn't it?" Eric said. "We wouldn't last two days in some of this country on our own."

"They're terrific trackers, you know. Actually, they do have keener eyesight than ours. Been tested by doctors. Also they have an inborn sense of time and place. They have fantastic memories and can find their way back to a place they haven't seen for years."

"Have you known any personally?"

"Oh, yes. There's an old man they call Walatta. He's still the most respected of his tribe. He can tell some wild tales, but the booze is getting to him. It's their ruination."

"It's a shame." Eric sighed. "They must really feel displaced in our so-called civilization."

"You wouldn't like to eat what they did in their primitive state—wichety grubs and snake and roots—when they were lucky." Eric made a face. "But scientists say they had a balanced diet and were healthy. Now the soft drinks and lollies are doing them in. They love sweets, you know."

Eric enjoyed his voluble, young neighbor. He was beginning to look forward to his stay in Coober Pedy, however long it might be. He was glad to be part of such a vibrant, egalitarian society.

The next day was somewhat cooler, so Eric decided to investigate the surrounding area. He picked up a map and headed out toward the Shell Patch. Since the entire area had once been a great inland sea, he was not surprised to hear about the opalized shells and fossils that were found. He located points of interest as he drove—Kenda Flat, the Four Mile, Stony Hill, Han's Peak. He stopped at the Eleven Mile. There was no sign, just a corrugated track leading off the dusty road he was traveling.

He parked his ute out of the way and just wandered about, marveling at the scene. The entire area with its dozens of conical heaps of white opal clay resembled a moonscape. The symmetrical piles rose up in all directions and although Eric had been told that a claim was fifty meters by fifty meters, it seemed as though every foot of this territory had been mined. Some mines had obviously been deserted, while others still had blowers parked adjacent to them. Some had the less sophisticated windlass poised over the opening.

Unlike a natural moonscape, this one was filled with sound. Many blowers were working, and their noise added to the din made by the compressors, blasting, drilling, shouting and mechanical winching. Occasionally, as though there was some predetermined signal, it was quiet, and then the sounds continued. A few workers glanced at him curiously but most paid him no heed, and none objected to his presence.

Eric came upon a working claim. The miner, who was checking his equipment, waved to him in a friendly fashion. Eric walked over to him, introduced himself and explained his quest.

"Sorry, mate," the sunburned Australian said. "I've not heard of any Sandy Blackwell, but this is a pretty big place. He'll see your notice and turn up sometime if he's here. You're a Yank, aren't you?" He laughed. "You can't escape that accent. Are you going to be around long?"

"As long as necessary. It depends on finding Sandy. If he doesn't show up, maybe I'll hang around a bit. I don't relish driving back over that road very soon."

The miner laughed. Strong teeth showed white against his reddened skin. "You're right on there, mate. It's a bloody mess, isn't it? When we have a bit of luck, we fly instead. What happened to your hand?"

"Dog bite. It's healing."

"Damn dogs. They're always hungry. Say, if you want to noodle, go ahead. We don't mind."

Eric hated to show his ignorance but decided bluffing would be unproductive. "What's 'noodling'?" he asked.

"Hunting through the opal clay the blower dropped. If we let any good stuff get away from us down below, it's our own bloody fault, and you're welcome to anything you find." He grinned. "Nothing's too good for a Yank. My dad told me what your guys did for us in the war. My name's Bill," he added. "If you stay here very long, you'll get 'opal fever' like everyone else."

"Oh, I don't expect to do any mining," Eric said. He was silent for a minute and then commented, "I see some miners aren't using blowers."

"No. Some use a windlass. It's cheaper. Most miners work with blowers. They're made from a truck and compressor and other equipment. They are very costly, but you can cover a lot more area with one. My partner and I blast, pick out the opal and examine it down below, and then the blower sucks up all the debris like a giant vacuum cleaner and dumps it. We miss a little, but we work on quantity."

"How are you doing?"

"That, my friend, is a question you never ask out here."

"Sorry. I guess it's like asking a Texas cattle man how many steer he has. I'll take you up on your offer and do a little noodling if you don't mind."

"No, we don't care. But some miners do, so always ask.

If they hit a good pocket, some bits and pieces may show up on top. The miners don't want some poacher to move in while their backs are turned."

"Does that happen often?"

"Too often! And it doesn't do much good to complain to the police when it's over. There's no way you can identify your opal after it's been snitched. You have to catch the thief in the act, so my partner Ralph and I built our shack over there. One of us stays here all the time when we're on to a good find. Well, enjoy yourself." Bill grabbed the metal bar resting across the opening of the shaft and lowered himself down the ladder.

Eric walked over to the hole and stared down. A convulsive shudder passed over him. He turned his back on the mine and began to sift through the loose clay, trying to keep his bandaged hand clean. He found a few slivers with good color and pocketed them. He heard the sound of the motor change just in time to jump away before the canister opened and dumped a large quantity of material on the spot where he had been working. He realized that noodling on an active mine required a good sense of timing.

As the morning wore on, the heat became uncomfortable, so he walked back to his truck and sat in its shade while he ate lunch. He noticed a young miner working on an adjoining claim and admired the frequency with which he climbed up the ladder, winched up a five-gallon bucket of opal clay and dumped it on the growing pile. The miner then pulled through the debris, evidently searching for any opal overlooked down below. A second miner never surfaced, and Eric wondered idly about their working arrangement. The man on top seemed to be expending an enormous amount of energy, which struck Eric as odd, because most of the miners seemed to have a more relaxed attitude. He assumed the partner below must be doing an equal amount of work, which accounted for the almost frenzied activity of the man he was observing. He realized that every situation had its own special arrangements and outsiders would do well to keep their speculations to themselves, so he dismissed the questions from his mind. He wandered about later, inquiring about Sandy Blackwell and receiving only negative replies.

He explored some deserted heaps, found them picked over and returned to Bill's mine. A different man stood outside the opening. He was a tall, lean-faced fellow who gave Eric a big smile. The guy's bright blue eyes crinkled up at the corners as he greeted him.

"You must be the Yank."

"Right, and thanks for letting me noodle. I've found a few pieces that whetted my appetite." Eric retrieved them awkwardly from his left pocket.

"A dog got you, eh? They're a menace—all skinny and hungry. Damn Aborigines! Let me see your opal." The miner glanced and then passed judgment. "Mostly rubbish; a little pinfire; some potch and color. This one is almost a harlequin pattern—it has patches of color—too bad it's so small. The best stuff is crystal, but it's found mostly in Andamooka. If you get crystal with good color, you have a real gem. That kind of opal is few and far between in Coober Pedy, but we've been lucky enough to get a little. Paid for our blower. By the way, my name's Ralph."

"I'm Eric. Do many miners make it big out here?"

"Well, I'll tell you. A couple of years ago roughly ten million dollars worth of opal was sold out of Coober Pedy. But remember, mate. That's what is *known* to be sold."

Eric whistled in admiration.

"But there were over 3,000 miners working here," the Australian continued.

Eric made a quick calculation. "That's less than $3,500 per person. Not much for a year's wage."

"That's an average. Many didn't make that much. That's why you see a lot of hungry miners around here. Some don't stay. Some stick it out until things get better. A few get rich, but a lot go broke. The ones who make it give hope to the ones who struggle." Ralph grinned. "We manage!" He returned Eric's paltry pile of opal chips and began to climb down the shaft. "By the way—don't noodle on that claim to the south. And, if you see a pretty woman walking around by that tin shack, don't look at her twice. Her husband is a mean one, really jealous, and likely to stick a knife in your back if he even thinks there's any hanky panky. He's a brute to drag a woman out here. His name is Duro. Stay clear of him."

Again Eric stared down the hole, which had been shored up with wooden planks and timbers to protect it from crumbling. This time he did not turn away but stood for many minutes, a set expression on his face.

The following day he returned to his new friends' mine and tried noodling once more. Again, he uncovered a few pieces of opal as he pulled through the loose clay. Bill surfaced from the mine to check the blower and gave him a friendly greeting.

"Would you like to come down into the mine and see where we work?"

Eric evaded the invitation. "I'd like to, but my hand still has stitches, and it might not be the best thing right now. I get them out at the end of the week."

"Of course. Later, maybe."

"Yes, later."

"Tell us if you strike it rich! That'll mean we're being very careless down below."

"No worries, mate!" Eric laughed.

"I see you've learned our favorite expression! Have you also learned our Australian salute?"

"No, not yet."

Bill waved his hand across his face. "That's to chase the flies off! I don't know how they find us way out here, but they do. You'd think they'd all cook in the summer."

"How involved is it to put down a shaft?" Eric said. He'd been curious to know but hesitated to ask, not wanting to get too personal about finances. Bill and Ralph had been uncommonly patient and helpful, which he appreciated. Although he feared he might be out of line, he decided to risk a rebuff.

None came, only a good-humored chuckle.

"Opal fever got you, eh? Thinking of starting your own mine? The permit's easy—fifty cents will get you a Miner's Right. That means you can mine on an area fifty meters by fifty meters."

"That's certainly reasonable."

"That's the easy part. You have to make a survey and put your pegs in at each corner, standing three feet above the ground, three inches in diameter. Then you have to decide where you want the hole drilled. That's the hard part. There's no way of telling where the opal lies below the ground. You may come up with some indication, maybe not. You can miss a seam of opal by a foot or a mile in this game. There are no guarantees. Just because a neighboring claim has found good opal doesn't mean you will. You're supposed to work your claim eight hours a day, five days a week. There's some leeway, especially in summer or if you're sick."

Eric absorbed the information and asked, "How deep are the shafts drilled?"

"The auger goes down eighty feet, but if you hit opal before that, you stop. That's called 'the level' and you begin making your lateral drives from there. It's hard work—don't let anyone fool you about that."

"Doesn't blasting shatter the opal?"

"Not often. We're careful where we blast. Some use gelignite; we use nitropril. We drill a hole into the wall about six inches deep and two inches wide, and fill it with a 'sausage'.

That's a paper packet filled with nitropril. You need plastic wire, detonators, cordex—it all costs money. Mining isn't cheap. After the blast, we pick out the opal seams by hand and send the refuse up by the blower."

"How much does a blower cost?"

"In the neighborhood of $6,000. Then you need ladders, drills, picks and petrol."

"Wow! How can men do it unless they're pretty well in the money to start with?"

"You'd be surprised how much can be done by hand. Take that Greek bloke over there—Dimitrios. He uses a hand winch and buckets. Rumor has it they done all right but the partner skipped with the parcel. Too bad. Doesn't happen often. Most important thing in mining is getting a good partner. Me and Ralph've been together for four years. He's fair dinkum." Bill scrambled over the side of the opening and disappeared down the ladder.

Eric glanced over at the neighboring mine again and saw a young man standing at the top of the shaft. Although he could not read his expression from that distance, he had the distinct impression that it was one of suspicion, even anger. He shrugged off the thought, and after noodling a little longer, found one sizable piece of opal that had good color. He turned it around and around in his hand, watching the colors flash and change position as the light hit it from different angles. He felt the urge to get involved in opal mining, if he could just conquer that unreasonable fear. He had something to prove to himself, and if he found Sandy, he didn't want his son to think his father was a wimp. He and Sandy could work together. They would make a great team. And, if he didn't locate Sandy, well, there would be something challenging to do during his stay. The proposition of sinking a new shaft sounded complicated. Perhaps it was too much to take on right now, but maybe he could find someone with an established mine who needed a partner. By sharing with a partner, he wouldn't be "working" in a technical sense, and thus perhaps he would avoid the legal restriction of his visa. He would give this idea some thought.

CHAPTER FOUR

ERIC RETURNED TO BILL AND RALPH'S MINE the next morning and walked over to the opening. He stared down, again with a feeling of revulsion. Would that horrible childhood experience always underlie his consciousness? It followed him like a curse. As the oldest son of pious Swedish Lutherans, his had been a happy life in the mining town of Iron Valley. He had been reared with a firm hand and much love. When he had asked his father why his hair was dark instead of light like his brother's, his father told him one of his ancestors must have been a Spanish princess! Eric loved his father's tall tales and yearned to see that mysterious place called "the mine" where he toiled such long hours every day.

His mother had a small flower garden in front of the house, but the big garden in back was for vegetables. Enough potatoes, onions, carrots, cabbage and squash were raised for the entire winter. The root cellar, a pit dug into the earth, had enough head room for Eric to stand upright. It was first covered with timber; then, with a thick blanket of straw and dirt, which helped protect the contents from the intense winter cold. The domed top insured that rain would run off. After the first snow, Nature became the great insulator. Always cool and pleasant in summer, the cellar was a favorite place to go when the sun beat down. It emanated a faintly musty smell that Eric enjoyed when he went down to collect vegetables. He imagined that "the mine" was somewhat like the root cellar: pleasant and comforting.

While the family never went hungry, even when work at the mine slowed, sometimes there was little variety. Eric didn't mind the sameness of the bland Scandinavian diet. It took little to please him. A bowl of hot potato soup with a slice of homemade bread made a satisfactory repast. The family did not talk much at mealtime. Eating was a necessity, not a social occasion.

One evening when Eric was eight years old, he broke the quiet by announcing, "Papa, I want to be a miner like you when I grow up."

His father laid down his fork and looked directly at Eric. "So, you want to be a miner when you grow up?"

"Yes, Papa."

"Have you given that idea a lot of thought?"

"Yes, Papa. Will you take me down into the mine with you some day?"

His father speared a chunk of meat and ate slowly without answering. Then he scooped up a gob of mashed potato on his fork and rolled it onto some peas. Continuing to eat, he appeared to be oblivious to his son's request. Then he wiped his heavy mustache, laid down his fork and sighed.

"All right, Eric. I will take you down with me tomorrow. Mama, cook an extra pasty. He can be excused from school one day."

His mother raised her eyebrows but said nothing. Never would she demean his authority in front of the children. Hulda cleared the table and helped prepare tomorrow's noontime meal. Although only three years older than Eric, she had already assumed much responsibility for household chores. Eric was fond of his sister. She read stories to him when he was younger and slipped him little tidbits when she was cooking. She gave him a conspirator's smile now, and he smiled back, unable to contain his joy.

He didn't sleep well that night, tingling with anticipation. He awakened several times expecting it to be morning, but the room was still dark. When daybreak finally came, he rushed downstairs, completed his chores in record time and bolted his breakfast. He picked up his lunch bucket, noticing that it was heavier than when he carried it to school. Hulda's eyes twinkled. She must have put in an extra treat. He gave his mother a quick hug and tried to match his father's long stride as they walked down the street. The sun was just peeping over the horizon.

The men gathered at the entrance to the mine greeted Eric and his father, laughing good-naturedly at the pair.

"Hey, Blackie, who's the giant with you?"

"Do we have a new miner today?"

"Better look out for your jobs, boys! We got competition!"

Eric stared at his shoes, embarrassed, but his father just patted him on the back and said, "My boy wants to be a miner."

The lighthearted laughter ceased, and the men nodded. They understood. Eric was presented with a hard hat that was much too big for him, and they walked through the main tunnel and entered the elevator. He'd never been in such a structure before. As the men crowded in, the space around him seemed to be shrinking until he feared he would be crushed. Sweat and grime permeated the walls from decades of use. The smell—acrid and penetrating—revolted Eric. He tried to hold his breath.

He would remember vividly the ensuing hours for the rest of his life. The old elevator creaked and jerked as they descended. He clutched his lunch bucket to his chest, partly to try to still his hammering heart, partly to give himself some space. As the elevator light flickered, panic almost overcame him. Everything was too dark, too crowded and too cold. Tears started to form, but he forced them back by sheer will. He would not disgrace his father by showing fear.

They went down and down. It seemed as though the elevator would continue forever. His anticipation was replaced by a dull dread. When the elevator finally stopped, the men got off and his father squeezed his arm.

"That was quite a ride, wasn't it?"

"Yes, Papa."

His father noticed the greenish tinge on his son's face.

"The first time is always the worst."

"Yes, Papa."

Eric was aghast at what he saw. The walls of the mine oozed with mildew and slime that dripped down onto the footpath, making balance precarious. The reinforcing timbers in the tunnel were encrusted with iron rust. Eric groped his way through the dim passage. The intermittent light scarcely broke the darkness. Mold and dampness were pervasive, and a terrible stench hung in the air. Eric felt nauseous but tried hard not to show it. He put out his hand to touch the wall, quickly drawing it back as though he had touched something dead. He shivered and again tears threatened. He hadn't cried since the day he first saw the scar the spilled hot coffee had left on his face. But, emotion overcame him. Poor Papa—to have to work in the mine all day and never see the sun! He surreptitiously wiped his face and hoped his father had not noticed. When they reached the track with the ore cars, the men rode to their individual destinations. Eric and his father spent the rest of the morning inspecting the timbers and making note of needed repairs. Eric was cognizant of his father's tremendous responsibility. Lives depended on a timber boss's judgment. Even as he shrank from his surroundings, he was engulfed by a wave of pride.

They stopped for lunch at noon. Eric's pasty was still warm and gave him a small degree of comfort. He took big bites, trying to shut out the desolation. The afternoon seemed endless, and his legs ached as he followed his father around.

The hard hat pressed down on his throbbing head.

The day finally ended. Eric drank in big gulps of fresh air as they left the mine. Never had sunlight been so welcome. The walk home was silent until Papa asked, "Do you still want to be a miner when you grow up?"

"No, Papa."

"Good."

Nothing more was said.

Memories of that horrible experience from years ago surfaced again. He knew there was only one way to dispel the devil that was tormenting him. He would have to go down into a mine again! He shuddered at the thought. If only he could rekindle his belief that the mine was like the root cellar, unchallenging and cozy.

That afternoon Eric returned to the opal shop that he had visited before. The proprietor liked the Yank—besides, an American accent usually implied there was money.

"Could you show me which of your opals came from the Coober Pedy fields?" Eric asked.

"Almost all of them. I have a few boulder opal from Queensland, just for variety, and some crystal from Andamooka, but the rest are local. Oh, yes, here are some pieces of Mintabie, just to show you the difference. See? It's a darker background. That field is much farther north."

Eric examined the various pieces with a more practiced eye than he had on his original visit. "Which color is most desirable? Does it make any difference?"

"Depends on your market. Color, any color, is an important factor, the greater the variety, the better. By itself, blue isn't much good. The color tends to disappear when you cut it. Green is valued next, then gold, orange and red. The more red, the better. Once in a while you'll find violet. Orientals prefer the cool colors, but red usually brings the highest price. The best opal has all or most of the colors."

"What's a black opal?"

"That's a stone that has a dark background, containing all the colors of the rainbow. It doesn't have to be black, deep gray will do. The background really sets off the colors. A good one is very expensive—one the size of my thumbnail can cost many thousands of dollars. You're talking big money when you talk about black opal."

The owner showed Eric some cut stones with different patterns. "This one has pinfire. It's fairly common, so it's not so pricey. This one is a harlequin—it has patches of color that change with every angle when you rotate it." Eric nodded, remembering what Bill had told him. "Then you've got some with a 'flash' that lights up when you move it from side to side." He demonstrated and the green flash seemed to leap out of the stone and then subside.

Eric looked longingly at the exhibit and thanked the owner. He had a lot to think about. That night he and Mick sat outside in the balmy air after supper. He enjoyed talking with the amiable and knowledgeable young man. It helped to pass the time.

"I saw some Aborigines out on some of the opal heaps today," Eric said.

Mick nodded. "They enjoy going at their own pace. They can see opal better than a white man, but they don't go after it the way we do. Most of the miners let them noodle. They're inoffensive and can pick up some extra money that way. They come around to the caravan park sometimes with bottles of good opal. Some people cheat them. It's not fair, but if the natives are desperate for drink, they'll sell cheap." Mick stretched out his long legs. "I've been here about a year, except for the summer. It's almost time for me to move on. I'm working my way around Australia."

"What work do you do?"

"I'm a mechanic in a garage in town. Never got into the opal business—too risky for me. The garage pays good wages, and it's steady work and no worries."

"I suppose you have a lot of repair work after people drive that road up here," Eric laughed.

"Too right! We keep plenty busy. Even the local roads beat up a vehicle."

"I was a mechanic in Korea," Eric told him. "I think I could still take a Jeep engine apart and put it together blindfolded."

"You don't look old enough to have been in the Korean War."

"I'm thirty-five. I enlisted when I was eighteen. And Swedes don't usually show their age!"

"I was wondering what work you did. A mechanic, eh?"

Eric did not correct him. He found that when he said he was a teacher, some people started watching their grammar and felt uncomfortable. The night had deepened. Mick leaned back and stared at the bright stars overhead.

"There are two things I'd like to see in the States," he confided. "Constellations like the Big Dipper and Orion, and I'd like to visit the Grand Canyon. It must be beaut."

They sat in comradely silence for a while, and then Mick broke the mood with his garrulous enthusiasm. Eric didn't mind—he liked the young fellow. "You know, Coober Pedy is really a beaut place, all in all. Outside of summer, of course. Weather is usually good, unless the wind blows, which is too damned often for some folks. People either like it here or hate it—there's no in between. Me, I like it. People are friendly; there's even a drive-in movie and pubs—everything you'd want in a city except all the bloody people! There's a shortage of girls, but I'm doing all right. I've got my eye on a little red-headed waitress at the Opal Inn. Nice sheila."

"You said it was time to move on. If you like it here, why don't you stay?"

"I don't know. Nothing's too permanent with me. I hate to be tied down. I've been on my own since I was fifteen, and I've just been moving from place to place, seeing the country. Great place, Australia, except for the bloody politicians—but you got them everywhere, don't you?"

Eric nodded but didn't interrupt the flow.

"I really do like it here. I'll see what chance I have with that waitress. I might even settle down and get me a dugout. They're beaut—cool in summer, warm in winter. All the comforts of home. Ever been in one?"

"Not yet, but I hope to."

"Where are you going from here?" Mick asked.

"Oh, I thought maybe I'd go on up to Alice Springs and see Ayres Rock on the way. Have you been there?"

"Yeah. The Rock is beaut, but Alice is getting too citified for me. Lots of Americans there because of the Base. You'd feel right at home."

Eric winced. "I'm not trying to find my fellow countrymen," he confessed. "In fact, I'm rather avoiding them. I'd like to see the 'real' Australians, not just the city folks. Big cities are pretty much the same all over."

"Too right." Eric smiled at Mick's repetitive vocabulary. "Out here people can be themselves. Everything's on a first name basis and no questions asked. I like that. Too many bloody rules in the city."

Eric agreed. He tilted his chair back and studied the unfamiliar sky. He located the Southern Cross, surprised that it was not more prominent. He was in a reflective mood tonight and glad to have someone to talk with. All inquiries about Sandy had proved fruitless, and he realized each day with growing certainty that his quest was a fool's errand. There was little hope of finding the lad in this vast land, but he felt no urge to move on. It was as though something else com-

pelled him to stay. He thought of the mines all around him—
men were climbing down into them every day with no fear. It
was as normal for them as walking on the surface. Since his
disturbing talk with the nurse at the hospital that first day and
his subsequent visit to Bill and Ralph's mine, the thought of
getting down into a mine enticed him, and not only just once
but to do it over and over. Maybe conquering his peculiar fear
would put his nightmare behind him forever.

CHAPTER FIVE

DIMITRIOS SCOWLED AS HE LEFT THE POST OFFICE. Why hadn't Sophia written? He received her last letter more than a month ago, and in the meantime he had told her about the wonderful find—the "pipe," so cherished by opal miners. It had formed millions of years before when liquid opal rose into a vertical opening in the matrix, taking on a cylindrical shape. This would not have interested her, but the fact that it had extraordinary beauty and represented thousands of dollars, would. He had been so excited that he just had to share the good news. Now that Aristotle had betrayed him and stolen it, he was beside himself. He would not tell Sophia about the theft. He could never imply that he was not doing well because her father read all his letters. Any suggestion that Dimitrios could not meet his commitment to Sophia would throw her into the arms of old Papadopolous.

What an awful bargain he had had to make! He loved her so—it wasn't fair. Even now Dimitrios felt anger rising. He had never been truly attracted to any of the local girls in his village until he first saw Sophia that evening at her window. But to have hope of marrying her presented tremendous obstacles.

A vision of her was always before him—her long, blue-black hair, a lustrous cascading over her shoulders as she undressed. Not that he should have observed her in such an intimate situation, for Greek girls were too well chaperoned to get even a peek in advance. But as the night was hot and sultry, the window was open, and she just happened to be standing there as he passed. Their eyes met, and she instantly withdrew from his sight. That one glimpse was enough to inflame him so that he was unable to sleep that night. His body ached to have her, and because he knew she was chaste, she was all the more desirable. His passion could not be stilled. He made some quiet inquiries and found that Sophia's family was respectable but poor. Her father was partially handicapped and had difficulty finding work. Sophia had one older sister and three younger ones, a large brood to provide with even a pittance of a dowry. Dimitrios, certain his suit would be well received, entreated his father to make the first formal approach. The family received Nicholas Mylonas cordially but deferred any commitment.

"Sophia is too young to consider marriage," was the polite response.

"But of course my son will wish to wait until Sophia has completed her schooling."

Mr. Skourus shook his head. "No, we can make no commitment at this early date. I'm sorry."

Dimitrios found this hard to accept. Other girls married at her age and a poor family was usually glad to have one less mouth to feed. Then one Sunday at a rendezvous with Sophia after church, he discovered the real reason for the stall.

"My older sister must marry first," she whispered. "It is the custom. But my family is so poor there is only enough money for Christina's dowry."

"But I won't expect a dowry for you!" Dimitrios protested. "I wouldn't want it unless it's just a token to satisfy convention. It's you I want. Can't your father understand?"

"I know that, but still Christina must marry first. And ... and you see Christina is not pretty." She blurted it out. "She is a lovely girl, but she is not pretty. No one will marry her without a big dowry."

Dimitrios remembered seeing her—a skinny girl with a large, unattractive nose that seemed to dwarf her face. His shoulders sagged. "Then you can never marry! It is an impossible situation. Your father cannot hope to keep all of his daughters unmarried until a suitor comes along for Christina."

"He doesn't. He has another plan." She looked down at her feet, a slow embarrassed redness tingeing her beautiful features.

"Well, what is it?" he prompted. "Maybe we can overcome it some way."

Still she hesitated and then raised her agonized gaze to his. "My father has been approached by his old friend, Mr. Papagopolous. He is very wealthy. He has told my father that he wishes to marry me and will help with the dowries of Christina and my other sisters. Do you see why I am so unhappy?"

"But he is older than your father! I won't permit it to happen. Just because he is rich, he can't buy you with his bribes!"

"I don't know what we can do. Father and Papagopolous came from the same village. He lost his wife last year. I guess he wants a new, young one."

"Then let him marry Christina!"

"He wants a young *pretty* one," Sophia corrected with bitterness.

"I have prospects!" Dimitrios shouted, and Sophia cautioned him to lower his voice. "I'll go to your father and beg for time. He said you were too young. I'll ask for two years. I'll find a way to make more money lots of it. My little tourist shop is growing, and I can get other jobs. He'll have to listen to me. I love you so, Sophia. We'll not give up."

She slipped away and joined her family. Dimitrios returned home, almost overwhelmed at the thought of losing her but determined to proceed with a plan. But what plan? Without doing something illegal, how could he raise a large sum of money?

After he had composed his thoughts, he remembered his friend Alexander, who had emigrated to Australia the year before. Alex had written his parents that he was going to the opal fields at Coober Pedy, where he hoped to make his fortune. It would be hard work, but the rewards were great. That night Dimitrios made up his mind. He would apply for emigration to Australia, and if accepted, he would approach Sophia's father himself and ask—yes, *demand*—that he wait two years for Dimitrios to prove himself. If he hadn't done so by then, Sophia would be released from his claim.

Asking and receiving were two different matters. Mr. Skourus was visibly antagonistic to Dimitrios' proposal, even though the youth had proffered it with calmness, almost deference.

"But my dear Mr. Mylonas," Sophia's father countered, "my good friend Papadopolous is not a young man like yourself. He will not be willing to wait for two years for you to 'prove yourself' as you so optimistically phrased it." He brushed his heavy mustache and almost glared at Dimitrios. "My eldest daughter, Christina, is eighteen. In two years she will be twenty—almost an old maid. She must marry first. Two years is too long."

Dimitrios bowed his head at the finality of the words. When he looked up, Skourus saw the naked agony in his eyes and softened a little. He was not a hard-hearted man nor an unreasonable one. He loved his family and wanted only the best for them. He sincerely believed the less freedom women had, the better. A marriage with a dependable older man would be more advantageous than allowing his beautiful daughter to throw herself away in a possibly unstable relationship. Arranged marriages were more enduring than those based on shallow romantic notions of love. But the boy had stated his case so strongly and was reputed to be such a diligent worker that Skourus felt himself relenting on his harsh stance. "I will give you the two years you ask for," he began, "on one condition."

Dimitrios leaned forward, ecstatic. "Anything, sir. Just tell me."

"At the end of the two years, or before," continued Skourus, "you will have the sum of $10,000 Australian, converted to Greek currency, in the bank here. Sophia will be eighteen then and through school. That's the best I can do. I will inform my friend that I cannot promise Sophia's hand in marriage until that time. He wants her so badly that I know he will wait. In fairness, I will tell him that he has a rival and apprise him of the conditions." He shrugged. It was evident that Sophia's father did not expect Dimitrios to succeed, and he had nothing to lose in the bargain he had just concluded.

The young man reeled. $10,000! It was a staggering amount. Old Papadopolous was rich—he owned orchards and vineyards and a villa. How he had accumulated such a vast estate was a source of gossip, but no one really knew. Dimitrios boiled with anger at the unfairness in the disparity of their situations, but he would try. Never could he save that much money by staying in Greece. Australia was his only hope. As soon as his papers cleared, he would fly to that vast continent "down under" and go to Coober Pedy to attempt the impossible.

He was not allowed to see Sophia alone before he left, but he spent an hour with her in the presence of her family the evening before his departure. Her eloquent eyes shone with devotion, and he carried the image of her lovely face with him when he boarded the airplane. His determination to win her buoyed his spirits and helped mitigate the disappointment of his father in seeing him go so far away. Dimitrios resigned himself to long hours of back breaking work and self-denial, but the goal made all the sacrifices worthwhile.

The night he arrived at the dugout Alex told him, "You've come just in time." Alex introduced him to his partner, Aristotle, and continued, "We've just uncovered a new seam of opal, and it's solid and rich in color. We've dug out enough to make up a parcel, and a buyer is in town. You can come with us tomorrow to meet him."

After a simple meal that night Alexander and Aristotle discussed their future. By taking in a new partner, each would be giving up part of his share to Dimitrios who had only his labor to contribute to the undertaking. They decided to give him 20 percent leaving 40 percent for each of them. A strong addition to their labor would speed up their work, and the promise of greater production would insure a good return. They all shook hands on the sealed bargain. Aristotle departed, and Dimitrios, bone tired, curled up on some blankets on the floor in the corner. After this first night, he understood he would sleep out in their shack by the mine, giving Aristotle the opportunity to move into town.

Dimitrios felt as good as new the next morning having had a refreshing sleep. He took some cursory glances at Alex's partner, appraising Aristotle with some uncertainty. The muscular man would be a good worker, but his dark eyes seemed to flick here and there instead of giving a direct gaze. Something sly and evasive in his demeanor disturbed Dimitrios, making him wonder if his sudden appearance was not to the older man's liking. But Aristotle had seemingly welcomed a new addition to the work team and had not protested giving up 10 percent of his share, so Dimitrios dismissed his misgivings. Life was harsh out here, and everyone had rather individualistic characteristics. One took a person at face value until something proved otherwise.

The three men drove to the hotel in Alex's truck. Opal buyers rented rooms for several days, posting notices on the hotel bulletin board and in the markets. Another miner was in conference with some buyers when they arrived, so they had a brief wait.

"It won't be long," Alex informed Dimitrios. "These fellows know their business, and outside of a little bargaining, it's pretty cut and dried. I like to deal with the American buyers—they want their money's worth, but they're fair. I've dealt with these men before."

Dimitrios felt his lips curling into an involuntary sneer. He didn't want to hear anything good about Americans, but his reasons were his own. Soon it was their turn. Alex had brought several small bags of fiery opal and a larger container containing opal of lesser quality.

"He'll grade it himself, with his partner," Alex whispered.

"They each have a calculator and figure the value, then confer together and compare notes. That's when the fun begins."

Alex had already sorted the opal into size and quality, but the buyers spread it around on a tabletop and did their own sorting. After making their final examination, each worked with a calculator and then compared notes. They offered $10,000. Dimitrios was amazed at the amount and expected his friend to jump at the price. He was surprised to hear Alex refuse.

"We want $16,000. That's a fair price. You can see it's good quality."

The Americans shook their heads. "Some of it's good, some fair. There are some dead spots. That's too high." As Dimitrios despaired that the sale was doomed, the buyers offered $12,000. Alex turned it down and made a counter offer of $13,000.

The older of the two buyers, a tanned, relaxed man gestured toward the large container. "Let's see your potch and color." His partner, brisk and business-like, ran his fingers through it and nodded.

"Toss this in, and it's a deal." Alex and Aristotle looked at each other and nodded.

The Americans smiled and brought out a bottle of ouzo and five glasses. All tension disappeared, as each drank a toast to their successful business transaction. The money was counted out in fifty dollar bills, which made bulky stacks. Alex stuffed them into his pockets. They all shook hands and left, passing more miners on their way out. Aristotle would receive his share of the total when they returned to the dugout.

Dimitrios was overwhelmed. Money, large amounts of it, was easy to come by here! He would have his $10,000 in no time and could return to Greece in style. No wonder Coober Pedy was called, "The Opal Capital of the World." How exciting to be a part of it!

Alex laughed at his enthusiasm. "That parcel represents four months' work," he said. "We may not see another one like that for another four months, or longer. Opal is not as easily come by as you think, and this was split two ways remember. Some of it goes to operating expenses, which are considerable." In spite of the dampening words, Dimitrios remained elated. That was the most money he had ever seen at one time.

The next day he wrote to Sophia in spite of the fact that each letter took precious savings for the postage. He was unable to say all that was in his heart because he knew her parents, and probably her sisters, would read the letter also, but he wanted to declare his love and firm intentions again. His message was optimistic and full of description of his new life in the opal field. "Sophia, you cannot believe how bleak this countryside is—dry, barren desert as far as the eye can see. Most people live in caves or in shacks, but the more affluent have built regular houses. It rains so seldom here that everyone saves rainwater. It runs off roofs into gutters and is channeled into big tanks. Every drop is cherished. The artesian water is so full of minerals that it takes a reverse osmosis plant to make it drinkable. It's very expensive. Right now the weather is pleasant, but I'm told the dust storms can be bad." He laid his pen down and reread what he had written. What he wanted to say was, "I love you with my whole heart, and wish I could hold you in my arms. I long for the day when we will be married. I think of you constantly." Instead he finished his letter with, "I miss you and hope you miss me, too. It will not be long now. I love you very much."

The following day they drove out to the Eleven Mile. When they climbed down into the mine, Alex first showed Dimitrios the drives that had already dug out and explained how the glimmer of opal in the walls might indicate a possible seam. His instructions included the use of the pick to tear down the walls and the gouge or a screwdriver to dig around the opal and work it out.

"Never rush extracting the opal," Alex warned him. "Opal is called "precious" for a good reason. If you're not super cautious, you can cause a fracture and ruin a special piece. Easy does it."

Dimitrios nodded. Nothing would be spoiled because of any impetuosity on his part.

Aristotle showed him how they worked down the toe of the wall beneath the appearance of the seam so that a cave wasn't formed, always trying to keep the wall vertical and not pocked with big cavities. Picks and shovels were used interchangeably.

"We shovel the discarded clay into these five-gallon buckets for hoisting and dumping on top. When we have more drives cleared, we can haul the material into them to fill up the space. Only sometimes we want to leave the tunnels open, in case we want to look the walls over again. We blast at times to bring the walls down faster if there's no indication of opal."

"Is it safe to blast down here?" Dimitrios tried to control the tremor in his voice. He hadn't expected the use of explosives. "Can't the roof of the mine fall in?"

"No, there's no danger if you know what you're doing. We're careful not to weaken important supporting pillars, but these thick walls between the drives make things pretty safe. Of course," he added, "we never take chances."

They worked the rest of the day, taking time at noon for lunch and a rest. Their quest for the continuation of the opulent opal seam of the previous week was not successful. They found what seemed to be a promising potch lead, which soon disappeared into sandstone. They showed Dimitrios how they blasted, hoping to open up a better area. Alex drilled several holes and packed them with the gelignite tubes he had prepared and lit the fuse. They all ducked around the corner into another drive and a few seconds later they heard the loud boom.

"Miners always drill two shafts to create ventilation," Alex explained. "But there's always a bad odor after blasting." They cleared away the rubble, examined it and found nothing of interest. They continued picking and shoveling. Dimitrios climbed to the top of the ladder and hoisted the buckets with the windlass.

At the end of the day the young Greek was tired and

ready for an early sleep. The other two, hardened from their months in the field sat in the shack and smoked. Aristotle talked of some day returning to Greece, where he had a sweetheart. Alex wanted to own a store in Sydney. All they needed was another good find—or two or three. They laughed as they imagined what they would do with their money if they really struck it rich.

"I'd go to the Greek Club here and set up drinks for everyone," Alex said. "No one ever talks directly about a good find, but a little barbecue for friends and some drinks at the club lets everyone know you've had good fortune. It's not safe to advertise it around, and you sure don't want the government to know about it. They'd take a big chunk out in taxes you know, and you might never have that kind of luck again."

They had brought out some canned food and other supplies for Dimitrios, and showed him how to work the stove. A barrel outside the shack held water from a previous rain.

"I'll get along fine," he assured them. All he wanted now was to eat something and fall into bed, but the other two were inclined to talk.

"The next time we have a little luck, we'll take you to the Greek Club to celebrate. It's always a pleasure to play host on occasion, but we're cautious about gambling, and you should be, too. The card-playing opponents are very skillful, and you can lose your shirt if you're not careful."

"I have no intention of gambling," Dimitrios assured them. He did not reveal his purpose for saving money. The less other people, even friends, knew of his private business, the better.

And now he stood by the post office, frustrated and bitter. He would have had almost enough money if he had agreed with Ari to sell the opal, but he had demanded that they wait in the hope of making another lucky find. He wanted to return to Greece with more than he had promised. He had left Sophia as a boy—he would return as a man, a man of means ready to claim his bride. But Ari, not willing to wait, had betrayed him. Dimitrios was sure he could find more good opal, perhaps not of the same quality, but enough to give him a new start. But he was almost penniless and would have to get a new partner. He cringed at the idea of another one cheating him, but he could not continue to do all the work alone. Strong as he was, he felt the strain, and he sensed that emotionally he was near the brink.

If only his friend had not broken his leg and returned to Sydney. The ironic thing was that it was not an injury in the mine—Alexander had tripped over a box in his dugout! He had given his mine to Dimitrios and Aristotle, but the work would only be done by two men now. Dimitrios didn't mind—he was used to hard work, but Ari was lazy. He had seen his chance to escape from the drudgery, and he had, leaving his partner with no transportation and little hope.

Now there was no letter from Sophia, which added to his frustration. He would write again and tell her things were going well, but he begrudged paying the postage. He glanced down the street and saw his mining neighbor, Duro Sulecic, going into the market. Dimitrios wondered about Duro's surly manner and sour expression when he had such a pretty wife. Dimitrios rarely spoke to Duro and would never ask him for any favors. He appreciated that Bill and Ralph at the next mine gave him rides into town occasionally to buy supplies. His needs were few, he didn't expect comfort, and he could live by the mine until next summer. By then he hoped he would be on his way home to Greece. But first he would have to find a trustworthy partner—one with a little money. The possibilities were very slim.

CHAPTER SIX

ERIC WAS IN POOR SPIRITS when he walked to the hospital to have his stitches removed. The lack of response to his inquiries about Sandy concerned him. He just hoped that the nurse he wanted to avoid would be having a day off. But as luck would have it, she greeted him at the entrance.

"I need to have my stitches out," he said.

"I know. I've been expecting you."

"Oh." Feeling he had been a bit abrupt, he added, "I wasn't sure there would be a nurse on duty this early in the morning."

"There is always a nursing sister on duty here, Mr. Christianson," she answered crisply, deliberately distancing herself from him.

He floundered about for something to say. "How many nurses work here Sister ..." He paused. "I don't think I heard your name?"

"Riley. My name is Sister Riley. There are three of us here. We work twelve-hour shifts and rotate each week for night duty. We get some time off each week, but we're always on call in case of emergencies. With only one doctor, we have to be versatile." Her professional attitude tinged on coldness. Gone was the playful teasing of the week before.

"Those are long hours you serve."

"Yes. We are very conscious of our duties." She deftly removed the stitches and examined the healed wound. "How has your hand been? Painful?" Her questions, asked without looking at him directly, were in a tone that indicated medical, not personal, interest. He observed her covertly, surprised to see how attractive she was.

"It hasn't hurt much, and it gave me an excuse to relax a bit and look around. This is quite a place."

"Yes, it is." The lack of small talk left him groping for something to stimulate the conversation. For some unfathomable reason he found himself wanting to prolong his visit. "There are some interesting shops—you can buy almost anything here."

"Yes."

Eric was annoyed. If she was deliberately trying to freeze him out, she was close to succeeding. He would try once more. "I've been out to the mine fields for a few days trying my hand—my good hand—at noodling." He smiled. A tentative smile crossed her face but was quickly replaced with a frown.

"Are you planning to go into mining?" she asked, concern reflected in her voice.

He almost said, "It's really none of your business," but something held him back. He didn't want to spoil what might develop into a potential friendship, and there was an unusual quality about the nurse that he wanted to learn more about. He admired her directness, but he was baffled by the irrelevancy of her question. Didn't everyone who came to Coober Pedy want to go into mining?

"I haven't given it much thought," he answered.

His easy answer did not placate her. "It's very dangerous," she said. "I've treated several mining-related injuries in the short time I've been here."

Eric couldn't resist a barbed comment. "And that makes you an expert on the subject?"

Her face reddened, and he wished he could retract his flippant words. He felt in order to justify himself he had to plunge on, so he said, "There are many dangerous jobs—police work, firefighting, even fishing has its perils. There's no work entirely danger free."

"Yes," she flashed back, "but those kinds of work are productive. There's a benefit that comes from them."

"You don't think opal mining is productive?" he countered.

She gestured in frustration. "I've seen so much greed ... so much betrayal ... Some men seemed to become obsessed and lose their perspective."

"Like 'gold fever'?"

"Yes. You know the old expression, 'When men find gold, they lose God.'"

He couldn't help replying, "My, you've observed a lot for your tender years."

She bristled. "It doesn't take long to see avarice."

"Don't you think there's a place for beauty in this world?" He waited for her answer. He could see the veins stand out on her hands as she clenched them in front of her.

"Of course I do. Opal is a lovely stone. I'm sure it brings happiness to a lot of people. But the getting of it can be so ruthless, and all this tearing up of the earth ..." She stopped. Her intensity made him uneasy, and he was relieved when she regained her composure.

"You've healed so well that I don't think the doctor will need to see you."

"But I would like to see you again, if I may," Eric found himself saying. "Could we call a truce?"

"A truce? Have we been at war?" She was momentarily startled at the thought, her eyes widening, and then she began to laugh. Gone was the tightness around her lips, the puckered lines between her brows. "I guess we have been at war," she admitted.

"I'm afraid I was the belligerent one," Eric apologized. "I'm waving a white flag. Will you accept my surrender—on my terms, of course?"

"And what are they?" She tilted her head back so he could look directly into her dark eyes, which had the same impish look he observed when he first met her.

"I'd like to take you to dinner some evening soon," Eric said, "as a pledge of my good will." He observed her hesitation and added, "After all, we're almost old friends, aren't we?"

She gave him an enchanting smile that charmed him. He found himself waiting for her answer like a schoolboy.

"Well, it will have to be some time next week, of course, when I'm free."

"I understand. I'll be back later to make a definite time." His words seemed stilted. She nodded with dignity, and extended her hand as if sealing a formal bargain. Now that she had made a commitment to see him again, Eric felt uncharacteristically shy.

On his way back to the caravan park he wondered how it all had happened. He had gone not wanting even to see her again, and now ... The strong attraction he felt toward her left him uncomfortable. Actually, the entire episode was unreasonable—he scarcely knew her. She was a complete enigma. It was as though she had put a spell on him.

Eric drove out to the Eleven Mile to compose his raddled thoughts. He noodled a bit on Bill and Ralph's mine with little success and then wandered over to the neighboring claim. As he approached, a young man climbed up the shaft and lifted himself over the side, preparing to hoist up a bucket of opal clay. He confronted the American.

"What do you want?" he snapped. "You can't noodle here."

"I'm sorry if I'm trespassing. I'm just interested in different methods of operation."

"You're a Yank!" Dimitrios spat the words out, which

were both a statement of fact and a denunciation.

"Yes, I'm from the States." The nonchalant tone did not diminish the hostility in the youth's eyes. "I'll leave now." Dimitrios turned his back and began winding up the windlass, his thoughts in turmoil. Desperation caused him to wind faster and faster, until he broke into a heavy sweat. He surmised that the American probably had money, and it might be his last chance to get help. He couldn't continue working like this. Even though he had developed strong muscles with the hard work he had endured these last few months, the pace was killing him. A broken man, even a rich one, would not be an acceptable suitor for Sophia. The long hours in the mine helped him work out his emotions relating to Ari's duplicity, but the present situation could not continue.

He grasped the bucket and poured out its contents on the irregular cone surrounding the opening. A flash of color in the loose clay helped him make up his mind. The stranger had walked halfway back toward Bill's mine when Dimitrios called out, "Wait!"

Eric turned around, puzzled. He didn't understand the young miner's antagonism. The hostility was present before they had even exchanged words, and unless the fellow was unduly suspicious of anyone who approached his mine, there must be some underlying cause. He shrugged and began to walk away again when the miner shouted louder this time, "Wait! Please."

Eric took his time returning, hesitant to become a participant in a row, wondering what had changed the Greek's mind. He stood silently, waiting for Dimitrios to speak. He was surprised to hear the young man say, "Look what I just found," as he held up a piece of opal in the sunlight. Eric could see a flash of color from where he was standing. He walked over and examined the stone which was small but gleamed with bright fire. The miner said, "Do you want to noodle? It's okay." Eric wondered why the Greek had changed his mind and become so willing to share his good fortune. He shook his head in refusal. "Thanks, but I'm really just looking around the field. I'm new at all this. Bill and Ralph have let me have some fun noodling on their heap. One day I worked at a different mine, but there were too many of us!" Eric laughed. "We divided up the territory, but no one did very well. I think you have to work hard down below for the good stuff."

Dimitrios tried to smile in return, but Eric could sense that it was forced. The young man's change of personality made him edgy, and he took a step back.

"My name is Dimitrios Mylonas." The miner made a conciliatory gesture. "You are welcome here, and you can work over my heap now if you want. I don't miss much, but I'm alone now, so sometimes a little gets by me." Dimitrios pointed toward the mine, his voice rising a pitch. "I've had bad luck. We found a 'pipe', but my partner stole it." His voice now tinged on hysteria.

Eric wondered what on earth he was talking about and began to edge away. "I'm sorry he stole your pipe," he said. "I don't smoke, but I can imagine how—"

"No, no! You don't understand! A 'pipe' is special opal, very fine quality. He stole it! He ran away. There's no way I can get it back. I need money so bad. I don't know what to do. I'm broke. I'll kill him if I find him. I can't believe he'd do that to me. A fellow Greek!"

Eric didn't reply to the almost incoherent torrent of words. He's after my money, Eric thought. He thinks I'm a rich American. I better get out of this one quickly. He turned, determined to leave, but Dimitrios grasped his arm. Eric tensed, anticipating a struggle.

"Please, sir, hear me out! I have something important to say to you." Dimitrios almost choked as the words tumbled out, his eyes blazing with a wild light. He was pleading now, all hostility gone, and he knew how much pride it was costing him to humble himself before this tall American. "I told you, I'm broke. I do not hide that. I've got to get money. My life depends on it. I must get help to keep working. I have a good seam going, but it takes too much time to do it alone. I tell you the truth. I don't even have enough money to buy gelignite and fuses. I'm not trying to trick you. I'll make a good deal with you."

He still clutched Eric's arm, but his eager face seemed less fanatical now. Eric decided it could not hurt to listen. Rather than discouraging him, the nurse's warnings about opal mining had made him want to explore the possibility all the more.

"Well?" Eric was curious but noncommittal.

Dimitrios presented his proposition. "In return for your buying the necessary supplies for the mine and helping me with the work, I'll give you half of any opal we find. You can do physical work, can't you?" Eric thought he detected a faint sneer in the question, but Dimitrios' expression was bland. "You can come down into the mine now and look at the area where I'm working if you want. I'd like you to see exactly what the conditions are."

Eric felt the familiar agonizing horror sweep over him. He realized if he didn't conquer his fear soon, he never would. He just wasn't ready to descend into the mine, so he temporized. "I'm interested," he said, "but I want to think about it." He would check with Bill and Ralph for their opinion first. He was in no hurry to invest in a venture that might be a lost cause. But on the other hand, the thrill of anticipation was an emotion he had not experienced for a long time. Dimitrios lowered his gaze but not before Eric saw the look in his eyes that branded him as a coward or a liar, and he cringed. The last time anyone had looked at him like that was after his father died.

That winter had been especially long and hard. Eric could hear his father coughing for many hours during the night. A bout of influenza further weakened him. Eric watched him leave for work each day in trepidation, noting the sputum flecked with blood as he hacked and spat. His father drank too much lately and his hands shook. They looked dry and old, like the twigs that rasped on the window pane at night. Eric could not dismiss from his consciousness the picture of the damp, smelly mine. It was always there—gray and specter-like—each morning when he told his father goodbye.

That last day Eric had cried, "Papa, I wish you didn't have to work in the mine!"

"Then who would put food on the table and buy your shoes for school?"

"I just wish I was old enough to work, and then you wouldn't have to."

His father smiled, ruffled his hair and embraced him. Now that Eric was older, hugs were not as frequent. Both surprised and pleased, Eric felt his uneasiness lift a little. As he watched the older man stride down the street, he thought, Papa is so strong. He will be well as soon as the weather gets warm.

When the warning siren broke the stillness of the icy afternoon, his mother turned pale and ran to get her heavy coat and hat calling out, "I am going to the mine. Hulda, watch the boys."

"No, Mama! I am coming, too!" Eric grabbed his own warm jacket and caught up with his mother. Although she shook her head, she didn't order him to return, and he clutched her hand with all his strength. Together they tried to run, but the frozen ridges on the road cut into their shoes and slowed them down. They arrived breathless at the entrance to the mine. Many others were huddled there, commiserating together, voices quietly exchanging the latest information. Then a silence fell on the group as fear robbed them of speech. The bright colors of hats and scarves were incongruous against the white faces. They waited with numb patience and desperate optimism.

Eric held on to his mother's hand, and from the pressure with which she returned his grip, he knew she was glad for his presence. Hours passed before the crushed and broken bodies were finally brought to the surface. Each stretcher brought a rush of women to peer at the wounded and dead. Some stepped back with a shake of the head while others issued heart-rending wails of recognition. Eric's father was one of the last to be brought up. He lay gasping, barely alive.

He and his mother had spent the long night waiting by his father's bedside. At 5 a.m. Eric had looked at the clock. If it were a different situation, he and Papa might be getting up to go hunting. There was almost always venison to eat, in season and out. It had been a joy to go hunting with Papa, a special masculine companionship—the older man cautious and silent, young Eric proud and excited. There had been so many happy times.

Eric looked at his father and saw that his breathing had stopped. His bruised face held a hint of peace. Eric put his arms around the still figure and held him close, as he himself had been embraced that terrible afternoon in the loft after he broke the mirror. He gave way to deep, racking sobs that awakened his mother, slumbering in a nearby chair. Nothing would ever be the same again.

All day neighbors came calling to express their condolences, bringing food to help relieve the extra responsibilities the family would now face. Their kindly gestures of love were an attempt to assuage the family's grief. Pastor Anderson came to help them with arrangements for the funeral, but he could not stay long. Others needed his comfort, too. Many other men had been lost that day. As the evening drew to a close and all their well-meaning friends had gone, the family sat silent and uncomprehending around the big black stove. From time to time Eric added small logs to keep the room warm. Hulda had busied herself during the day with household chores. Now, exhausted after her all night vigil, the full impact of her father's death hit her. She clung to her mother weeping and then climbed the stairway to the loft. Lars slumped in his chair, fighting sleep, and Eric ordered him to go with his sister.

Eric turned to his mother with defiant eyes.

"Mama, in Sunday School I was told, 'Ask and it will be given unto you.' I prayed, Mama, I really did. I asked God to let Papa live. I prayed with my whole heart, and He let Papa die. I don't think He cares."

"Hush, Eric. There are things we don't understand. I don't know why this happened, but I know that God will give us the strength to endure."

"But why are we told to ask if it doesn't do any good? It's not fair."

Tears rolled down his mother's face. "I don't know, Eric.

We just have to believe there are reasons and that prayers are answered in God's good time."

"I'm not going to pray again, ever." Eric's lips tightened. "Not ever."

"Oh, Eric, don't say that. That grieves me so."

"Papa worked for me in that awful place. I'm not worth it, Mama. I'm not worth it. He wanted me to have new shoes ..." His words choked in his throat, but tears would not come. She put her arms around him and held him tightly, but she felt his withdrawal.

That night he experienced the nightmare for the first time. He and his father were in some murky, unfamiliar place. Eric was holding a rifle, but his father was unarmed. Something threatening approached. He couldn't make it out. He tried to shoot, but the bullets just rolled out of the barrel and dropped to the ground. Then he felt himself falling into a pit. It was cold and slimy. He caught hold of the rungs of a ladder, and somehow his father called from below. As he reached down to help him, his fingers became limp, and he felt himself giving way. A terrible blackness enveloped him, and he grew colder. As he started to fall, he awakened screaming, his heart thudding as though it would burst. Lars and Hulda, exhausted, slept through the noise. Intuitively he knew this was not the last time he would have that dream.

All the older mines, abandoned when the iron ore became depleted or proved too costly to extract, had their entrances boarded up to discourage trespassers, but Eric's friends discovered one such mine where the weathered wood had deteriorated.

"Hey, Eric. We found a neat place to do some exploring." Rusty Larson, always game for some new experience, often led his friends to the brink of foolhardiness. With some concerted effort the doorway was pried open, and the boys stepped cautiously inside. The darkness engulfed them, and they laughed self consciously. Eric hung back, overcome with a foreboding dread. Rusty urged him to accompany them, but he could not move. The boys advanced a few feet into the darkness, feeling their way along the sides and taking one step at a time.

"Come on, Eric." Rusty's voice boomed out. Still Eric could not move. His companions, looking back, said nothing more, but their expressions read cowardice. Eric desperately wished to join them. He stood transfixed for what seemed an eternity, and then he turned and ran home.

That night the dream came again.

The next day he walked by the old mine deliberately, noting that the old door had been repaired and bolted. No one could go inside now. Relieved and tormented at the same time, he castigated himself for not going in with the others. He was restless and unhappy, taking foolish chances, challenging fate, swinging from branches like Tarzan, diving from dangerous heights into the lake. He often walked by the old mine and stared at it with brooding eyes. The following winter he skied down precipitous slopes and walked on dangerously thin ice. He came through it all unscathed—little disappointed to have acquired no battle wounds.

Each week, weather permitting, he accompanied his mother to the cemetery. He pulled weeds from around his father's grave and brushed the accumulated dirt from the headstone. Finally he stopped walking by the mine, but the contemptuous look in his friends' eyes continued to haunt him.

Eric knew he had met a watershed in his life. He turned to Dimitrios and took a deep breath. "All right, I'll go down now."

Dimitrios wondered how the American would react to the climb—it was forty feet down. The panic that crossed Eric's face at the suggestion that he check out the working area below revealed deep dread, which pleased Dimitrios. He needed to look down on this Yank, and since he couldn't do it literally—for Eric was at least three inches taller—he would have to find other means of attaining psychological superiority. Dimitrios would find some way to put Eric into an inferior position, even though he might become his benefactor. The American should never know that his Greek partner held him in contempt, however. He would be very careful to hide his feelings. It would be a privately sustained pleasure—a grudge nurtured by years of festering resentment.

Eric felt a cold fear as he peered down the mine shaft—heart pounding, frantic fear and gut-chilling terror. He had been in situations far more dangerous, but he could not control this terrible apprehension. As he stared down into the blackness, he recalled the descent into a mine so many years ago with his father. The feeling of pain and loss hovered just below the surface of his consciousness. He sensed that Dimitrios watched every move and every expression. When he grasped the iron bar that lay over the opening, his fingers were white with tension. The moisture increased the probability of slipping, but there was no turning back.

He swung his body over the hole, planting his feet firmly on a rung of the ladder. If he let go now, it would be a long drop, insuring that he would be killed outright or be left a hopeless cripple. The iron rungs were hot on his hands—the Australian sun seemed to work overtime here in Coober Pedy. As he descended the metal became cooler, the air smelled damp and earthy. His hands and feet moved mechanically in perfect coordination. He felt almost relaxed. He didn't look down into the total blackness at the foot of the shaft. He glanced up and saw the round area of daylight slowly diminishing in size. He could barely make out the face of the Greek now.

Eric tried not to think about the story Ralph had told him the previous afternoon. He and Bill had found a deadly king brown snake in their mine last year. Even a snake, however agile and balanced, could misjudge conditions and fall victim to a small cave-in of the surface dirt. Would such a venomous creature be lying at the foot of the ladder now? He could visualize it, hungry and implacable, alert to the sounds his hands and feet were making on the rungs, and very sensitive to the temperature change as his body reached the bottom.

The ladder was a series of ten-foot sections hooked together. It swayed back and forth as he descended, and little spurts of dirt and pebbles fell on his head as he descended the bored shaft. Eric closed off thoughts of snakes and cave-ins. He would not again show the young Greek any sign of distress. Something in his manner disturbed Eric. It was as if Dimitrios wanted to humiliate him, but he didn't know why. He had done nothing to warrant such an attitude.

In a few minutes, Eric had reached the bottom of the ladder. He moved his hands to a lower position and stretched his leg down until he felt the hard clay surface below. He let go and groped around for the bucket that Dimitrios told him would be there. He located the flashlight and turned it on, pleased with the small beam it projected and the fact that no unblinking eyes reflected back. He spent only a moment taking in the central room with its large supporting pillar. He walked around to inspect the column, noting some bright flashes of color here and there. Like spokes of a wheel, three drives led from the main room, but he did not follow any. He walked back to the opening and shouted, "I'm down! It's all clear!"

Bits of gravel spattered down the shaft as Dimitrios quickly descended. Eric smiled with contentment. His hands were dry, and he was comfortable knowing that he had overcome his terrible fear. He could now show the Greek a genuine acceptance of the task at hand, not just a facade. Eric was determined to win his respect. He had decided to become a partner in this mining venture—hoping for success but steeling himself to possible disappointment. He remembered Mr. Sorenson's advice about failure being no disgrace if one learned from it. He often had passed that same advice on to his students, and he reflected for a moment on his teaching days. They had been good, rewarding times, and he missed the students and the challenge they gave him. But now he had a new challenge, and he would put his full effort into making it meaningful.

After Dimitrios indicated various areas that showed the possibility of opal veins, Eric nodded in what he hoped was a professional acknowledgment. They climbed back up to the surface, and Eric was struck with the young man's pallor. Dimitrios did not look well. "How much have you eaten lately?" Eric asked.

"What concern is it of yours?" The words were out before Dimitrios could retract them. He was uncertain about the American's plans, for although Eric had nodded and looked interested, nothing definite had been discussed. Dimitrios feared Eric would back out, finding some easy excuse to leave with vapid words of coming back after "thinking it over." He would not allow the man to patronize him. He drew himself up with another stinging retort but the American spoke first.

"If I'm going to have a partner, I'd like a healthy one."

The impact of Eric's words was slow, and then Dimitrios' lips began to tremble. He almost lost control. The American held out his hand to solidify the business arrangement, and Dimitrios shook it with ill-concealed fervor.

The joy of it! He could hope again.

CHAPTER SEVEN

"Duro, I cannot stand living here another day!" Maria screamed. "How can I keep this shack clean with a dirt floor? The cracks in the walls let in all the dust and the mice! Even the cat can't eat another mouse. And it's so hot! You're down in the cool mine all day!"

"Stop whining and put my supper on. I'm tired."

"You don't ever listen to me! I'll go mad if I have to live here any longer."

"No, you won't. You'll go right on doing what I tell you to do. Now shut up and let me eat in peace."

Maria glared at her husband. "If you would just let me drive into town once in a while. I like to talk with Anastasia. She's my only friend."

Duro's face darkened. "You know why I can't trust you out of my sight. You are never to go anywhere alone. Wherever you go, I go with you." He grasped her arm so tightly she began to whimper. "Don't even think of taking the truck into town while I'm down in the mine."

"You know I wouldn't, Duro. That's why I'm asking. Please."

"Forget it. You'll stay right here."

He devoured the food in minutes. Maria watched him in disgust leaving her food untouched. How different Duro was from his brother! Back in her Serbian village, everyone knew Lejos. His wife always extolled his considerate nature, and Maria had mistakenly attributed the same qualities to Duro. Her friend had hinted at a dark side when she told how the two brothers had avenged their sister's rape by disguising the murder of the guilty man as an accident. She had finished the account by saying, "Whereas Lejos helped reluctantly, Duro enjoyed it."

This disastrous marriage was her own doing, and there was no way she could escape. She had learned to tread cautiously when it came to the past. Now she had provoked her husband and feared repercussions.

Duro threw down his fork and looked at Maria suspiciously. "What have you been doing today? Walking around the other mines and talking with the men?"

"Of course not, Duro. Besides, they're all underground, just like you."

"Not all the time. Not that young Greek fellow."

Maria began to panic. She sensed that his old hostility would soon surface, and she needed to deflect it. "Tiger makes me laugh sometimes. He likes to play. I made a little toy out of scraps— "

"He'd better start catching more mice or I'll throw him down an empty mine shaft!"

Maria held her breath but said nothing. The cat gave her much needed comfort and affection, and she wished now that she had never complained. Duro punished her when she made him angry. He turned on her, eyes blazing.

"You deserve to be here. You wouldn't be in Australia if you hadn't tricked me. I didn't want to bring you, but before we were married you said you wanted to come here, and after I found out about your lie, it was too late to change the application."

Maria sat quietly, saying nothing. She hoped his bad mood would pass, but his hostility was so strong. Against her better judgment she pleaded, "Duro, please don't bring that up again! I can't bear it."

She knew she should never have tricked him into marriage by telling him she was pregnant with his child, but she was desperate. Her lover had deserted her, so she had permitted Duro liberties in order to finalize their relationship. She closed her eyes and tried not to think of that terrible day when Duro had paced up and down, waiting for the birth, his fists clenched, his face contorted with doubt. The midwife finally had sent him outside, and as the sun began to set, he heard a baby's cry. The midwife came to the door, smiling, holding the infant in her arms.

"A fine boy," she told him, "but your wife had a hard time."

He glanced at the baby and then stared at the woman. She held out the tiny bundle, but he didn't move. "The baby must have been premature," he stated.

"Oh, no. Full term. That's why it was such a difficult birth. He's a big baby." She cuddled the infant, who was crying lustily.

Duro's dark eyes never left her face. "The baby was premature," he repeated. His words were cold and implacable.

She began to remonstrate. "No, I didn't say that," and then his hand grasped her chin and forced her head up. She tried to lower her head but could not. She remained stubbornly silent, and he increased the pressure.

"The baby was premature. That is what you will tell the village. The infant was born too soon and mercifully died."

He relaxed his hold on her chin and reached out for the baby. She turned white, clutching the baby to her breast, shaking her head in desperation.

"No, you can't—" she protested, and then she recognized the diabolical look on his face. "Please, for God's sake, no," she whispered.

"The baby was premature and did not live," he said. "If I hear differently, your daughter will meet with a terrible accident." His eyes seared her with their intensity. "Do you understand?"

"Yes." She choked on the word and lay the baby on the table. Then hastily gathering her materials into her basket, she rushed to the door, crossing herself as she ran. By the time she had reached the porch, the newborn had stopped crying.

Duro had stood by the bed and watched Maria silently for a few minutes. Sensing his presence, she opened her eyes.

She tried to raise herself to a sitting position and put her hand to her breast then fell back weakly.

"I'll never forgive you for this," he said. "Who was he?"

She didn't answer, and he struck her hard across the face. A great welt appeared on her pale skin. "I'm asking you again. Who was he?"

"He was a stranger." Her mouth moved, but he scarcely heard her words. "He forced me!"

"You're lying!" Duro's eyes held a savage light. "Tell me his name." He raised his hand to strike her again.

"Please don't hit me! Please. I tell you I don't know his name. I'm telling the truth. I don't know!" Her voice ended in desperation.

He lowered his hand and looked at her carefully.

"I was afraid to tell anyone," she sobbed. "No one would have believed me. You don't believe me now! I prayed that I would not be pregnant, but when I found out, then I ... I did what I had to do. My father would have killed me. But I did love you, Duro. I did." Again she tried to sit up but fell back, exhausted.

"Would you recognize him if you saw him again?"

"Yes! Of course. I could never forget his face! Now let me be ... Where's the baby?" she asked suddenly.

"It died."

"But I heard it cry!"

"It died."

As comprehension set in, Maria's eyes filled with horror.

She tried to pull the thin blanket up to cover herself, as though somehow it might offer some protection, but her fingers refused to move. For a moment she lay rigid, then she turned her face to the wall and whimpered, "Beat me. Kill me, too. I just don't care."

Duro stared down at her, and then thrusting his fists into his pockets, he turned abruptly and left the room. He sat in the darkness, brooding. There was nothing for him now in Yugoslavia.

He looked with increasing impatience for his acceptance papers from Australia. The day the approved application arrived, he approached his mother in the kitchen, where she was preparing the noon meal. "The permit came, Mama. I must go."

She nodded and continued to peel potatoes.

"Lejos said he could find some kind of work for Papa and you in the city. He will look after you."

Tears came into her eyes but did not fall. She held her head high, the years of privation giving her strength. "We will be all right. You do what you have to do."

Inexplicably he felt a modicum of concern. He stared at her, realizing that he had not really looked at her for a long time. She suddenly appeared gaunt and careworn. "If things work out well, I could send for you."

"No." She was emphatic. She gave him a quick embrace, which almost unnerved him and left the room.

Maria's reaction to the news was more emotional. She

grabbed the papers from his hand, scanned them and let out a cry of joy. "Thank God! Now we can leave here. Any place will be better than this." The two years of torment under Duro's and his mother's domination had been enough for her. She hoped that moving to a new country would produce some good changes in Duro, too.

The Australian government paid for their passage and guaranteed assistance in finding work, conditional on their promise to stay at least two years. Duro had gladly signed the necessary papers. He had no desire to return to communist Yugoslavia, even though conditions had relaxed from earlier times. There was more freedom now than in some of the other iron curtain countries, but privilege went with party membership and he lacked the stomach for complete involvement. Too much of a loner, he resented authority and desired to work for himself.

The flight to Australia was long and uneventful. As the airplane's wheels left the tarmac, Duro felt exhilaration tinged with sadness as he realized he was cutting his ties with the old country forever. He would miss his brother Lejos, who had helped him through the terrible war years that shrouded his childhood. Sometimes at night the dreams of bloody bodies and cruel faces caused him to awaken screaming, but then Lejos would hold him. Only three years older than Duro, Lejos served as both brother and father while their father was away fighting with the partisans under Tito. His mother, a strong woman, had little affection to offer the family, using her energies for survival. While he had felt a measure of dutiful respect for his mother and father, warmth among them was absent. The brutal war shriveled them emotionally. Duro had felt a closer kinship to the land itself, but since it did not actually belong to him and never could be passed down to his children, he left it with small regret. Children, he thought bitterly. Maria had been unable to conceive again. Somehow it was her fault. He looked over at her, asleep on the seat beside him. How tiny and frail she seemed. It would have been so much better if he had followed his mother's advice about selecting a wife of sturdy peasant stock. Everything had gone wrong in his life, including this disastrous marriage.

Sydney Harbor was an unforgettable sight as they flew over the famous bridge and looked down at the circular quay with its ferryboats. The opera house, still under construction, stood out on the promontory like a fantastic ship, the succession of arched tiled roofs rising like billowing sails. Duro pointed out hundreds of boats in the harbor, and Maria joined his enthusiasm. It was truly a heady sight.

"Some day," he said, "I will live there and own a house and a boat."

"We will live there," she corrected him, with some trepidation and was relieved that he didn't take offense.

The days that followed were busy with more paperwork, medical examinations and hours of waiting. Finally they were released. Duro was placed with a construction firm, mixing concrete and pouring footings. He worked with men of many other nationalities. The cacophony of languages, plus the Australian slang, "strine" as it was called, bewildered him. He rapidly learned swear words, followed by idioms and a few nouns and verbs. At the end of a year he could speak passable English, and although his accent was heavy, he was pleased that he could communicate.

Maria did not fare so well. She worked in a bakery owned by Hungarians and was slow to learn their language. When the only other Serbian kitchen helper left for a better job, she was devastated. She didn't understand directions given in English. Her employers and her co-workers—all Hungarian— ignored her as they chattered amongst themselves.

"My work is too hard," she complained to Duro. "They give me the worst jobs and get angry when I don't under- stand. They all shout, 'Learn English!' but they don't even speak it themselves. Why couldn't I have been placed in a Serbian business?"

"Then learn English! It's the only way to get ahead."

"It's too difficult. I can't remember the words."

"Just try. You have to keep working at it."

They never went out for pleasure. Duro took all her money and added it to their savings. Disillusioned and unhappy, she complained to Duro. He did not retaliate. He mostly ignored her.

After listening to her continual complaints, he finally snapped, "You can go back any time you want. I'll pay your passage. There are plenty of other girls here to choose from."

She recognized the reality of his threat and drew her resentment around her like a heavy cloak.

Duro found city life oppressive—it was crowded and noisy. Their small living quarters were expensive, and they lacked the money for the carefree, boating weekends enjoyed by the regular Australians. But they had more than enough to eat, for there was great variety of reasonably priced food in the shops. Duro was finally able to buy a second-hand truck. When he was out of work because of strikes, he felt at the mercy of the unions—they were all-powerful and made decisions for him. It gnawed at him that he was not in charge of his own life.

When a fellow Serbian invited him to work in his opal mine in Coober Pedy, he jumped at the chance. Marcos told him, "My partner's wife finally convinced him to quit and move back to the city. She was unhappy there. It's not an easy life for a woman. Maybe you'd better talk it over with your wife first."

"That's not necessary. Maria will do as I tell her."

Traveling on the paved road across the Blue Mountains was an unexpected pleasure. They made good time at the beginning of their journey, and enjoyed the forests and foliage. As they continued westward they noticed the terrain becoming drier, the grass shorter, the gum trees more sparse. Sheep country became cattle country; the stations became larger. Flying doctor centers became apparent; towns were smaller and farther apart. It was all so different from Yugoslavia—Maria began to feel some trepidation and soon missed the green and humidity of Sydney. The sun relentlessly beat down on them. The dry air parched Maria's skin. Mile after monotonous mile, the landscape was harsh and alien, with scarcely the sight of another human being. Maria began to dread their destination and wished that Duro had left her behind. But she knew he would never let her out of his sight for any length of time and would keep her with him even if Coober Pedy proved to be an inhospitable place. She had no choice but to continue the journey. Since their relationship was less strained lately— in fact, it was almost amicable—perhaps their new home would be better than she thought.

Marcos had flown back to Coober Pedy to greet them after their exhausting trip. He took them to his dugout for refreshments. The rooms, carved out of the native clay, had ample space for furniture and kitchen equipment. Maria looked about in wonder. How pleasant to live in an underground dwelling with such a comfortable temperature. There was even bottled gas for cooking and a generator that produced electricity. She smiled in spite of her exhaustion.

"That's quite a road from Kingoonya, isn't it?" said Marcos, almost enjoying their discomfort. "Driving it is everyone's baptism to Coober Pedy. I've done it several times, but I've had a run of good luck so now I can fly. I hope my wife doesn't put pressure on me to quit mining. She won't live here, so I have to go back to Sydney from time to time. You won't have to drive it again, Duro. You can stay here as long as you want to."

"What about summertime? I've heard it's terrible."

"You heard right. Most miners leave and go down to Adelaide for the summer. By law, we're supposed to work our mines every day, but, we feel we can leave when the weather gets unbearable. The law understands and looks the other way. We take it up again in the autumn."

"We're here to stay," Duro said emphatically.

Maria spoke for the first time. "It wouldn't be too bad living in a dugout like this one."

"That's why you can stay here in the summer if you want to. Then Duro can keep an eye on the mine. It's good to let people know someone is watching it, although we don't have much trouble during the hot season."

"You mean we won't be living in a dugout the rest of the year?"

"No. Your place is next to the mine. It can't be left un-attended during our working days—too many poachers if you're on to something good. Someone has to stay there to protect it."

That night Marcos fixed a sleeping area for them in a corner of the room, explaining that in the morning he would take them to the mine where they would live. While Maria slept, Marcos showed Duro several small piles of opal and told Duro to study them. "What do you see?" he asked.

"Well, this pile doesn't seem to have any color at all. It's kind of glassy looking but nothing more."

Marcos nodded. "That's called 'potch'. Sometimes when you find potch, it's a good indication that there might be better opal eventually, but it's not worth anything by itself. Now look at the other piles."

Duro examined them more critically. "They all have some fire, but this pile has the most. It's quite bright and there seem to be many colors."

"Right. This is our best opal. If we're lucky, it has every color in the rainbow and no dead spots. What about the other two piles?"

Duro turned over several pieces from one pile and compared them with pieces from the last pile. He frowned for a minute and then said with some hesitation, "They both have some fire, but this pile doesn't have very much."

"Correct. That's what we call 'potch and color'. Sometimes we just throw it into a sale to sweeten the pot. Overseas buyers can use it in cheaper jewelry or sell it in the rough. They may put a couple of inferior pieces in with some good stuff in small bottles and sell by the ounce."

"And the last pile?"

"It's pretty good opal, better than potch and color, but not the best quality. Believe it or not, there are several grades of opal better than my best, but so far I've not been able to find them. I'm talking about opal that sells for a couple of thousand dollars a carat."

"Wow!" Duro sat back amazed.

"So you see what the rewards can be." Marcos smiled

and poured out wine for them both. "To our new venture!"

They drank heartily, then Marcos gestured toward the opal. "Now I'm going to scramble the four piles together and have you separate them again."

Duro spent a few minutes sorting the stones into four piles and then sat back. "How did I do?"

"Very well for a beginner. The potch is easy, isn't it? Sometimes we find blue potch, which has some value. The really good stuff is pretty easy to spot. It's the in between stones that are the hardest to identify. You'll do very well. It just takes a little practice."

The next morning Duro followed Marcos out to his mine. Maria slumped in her seat, eyes closed. Marcos turned in on a side road, winding his way through other claims until he stopped at his own mine. He pointed to the corrugated iron shack where Duro and Maria would live. Maria's heart sank.

The hand-over-hand descent down the iron-rung ladder to the mine bottom forty feet below did not bother Duro—he seldom feared anything. Marcos showed him the drives that had already been gleaned of opal and the new one that was just begun. Marcos pointed out the faint line of opal that was exposed—the area where they would be working next.

"It could lead to something good, or it might disappear. It's always a big question. The important thing is that you have to be very careful." He showed Duro how to gouge above and below the line in such a way as to not fracture the seam. "It looks as though it might be continuing and widening. That's good news."

It was pleasant down in the mine, and Duro found it good to be using his muscles again. He was glad to be in the comfortable, moist air underground where he was shielded from the intense heat of the sun.

"I'll show you how the blower works to save on cleanup time in the mine. It's like a giant vacuum cleaner and just sucks up all the loose clay. It sure beats loading five-gallon buckets and hauling them up with the windlass. We used to shovel the debris into an unused drive sometimes, but this is a lot better. I invested in the blower after a lucky find last year, and it's paid off. We can get a lot more work done."

The day sped by faster than Duro anticipated. The closeness of the walls did not oppress him—on the contrary, for the first time in many months he felt free.

"I'll teach you about classifying opal," Marcos said to him at the end of the day. "There's a lot to learn, but you'll catch on fast."

Maria glared at Duro when he came into the shack after work. She spread her hands to indicate their abject living arrangements. Their two room shack had a dirt floor; there were no closed cupboards for food, no electricity, no refrigeration. The lingering days of summer still held heat and dust with tenacious fingers. The surrounding area was devoid of a bush or even a blade of grass, let alone a tree to provide some shade. The privy was a corrugated iron stall, surrounding an abandoned fifty-foot mine shaft, with a crudely constructed toilet seat resting on top. Maria dreaded using it. She took a can of insect spray with her, and used it liberally. In Sydney she had laughed at the rollicking Aussie song, "The Red-Backed Spider Beneath the Toilet Seat," but she found nothing humorous in the song now. The bite of the venomous creature could be worse than that of a black widow.

Her voice took on a harsh note as she looked at her husband defiantly. "I can't stay here! I won't stay here!"

"You'll have to," he answered curtly. "It's not so bad. We'll get by. There's bottled gas for cooking, and Marcos will get us a small compressor that we can use for electricity. He's going to take us to his dugout tonight and teach me about opal. We'll eat out this time. From now on, you'd better have dinner ready for me. Now let's go. He's waiting."

Maria's anger turned to hopelessness. There was no escape.

CHAPTER EIGHT

GOING TO THE MINE each day rejuvenated Eric. On clear days the sunrise turned the sky into brilliant opalescence, and he reveled in the clean air. On windy days the color of the sun changed to a dirty mustard, and thick, powdery dust blanketed the ground, but he had no complaints. He remembered a Bible verse he had memorized for Sunday school—"This is the day the Lord has made—let us be glad and rejoice in it." He knew that many of the men here would scoff at him if he quoted it. Eric recognized that, as in most other places, there were a variety of attitudes and beliefs in Coober Pedy. Long ago he had adopted a "live and let live" outlook.

He knew some Australians were antagonistic to any semblance of "churchiness," possibly from long-held resentment of their ancestors' treatment by the clergy in the nation's beginnings. Eric had met several men of that type in pubs and always avoided them. For whatever their reasons, some people simply enjoyed castigating others and belittling their views. He often wondered what his own deep-down beliefs were. He wasn't sure what he would say if it became necessary to define or defend them. He acknowledged that he did not have the unquestioning faith of his parents. He even considered at times that he might be an agnostic, although he was aware that many sincere believers had conditioned his moral approach to life and still exerted an influence. He thought of the women in Iron Valley who had brought food to his home after his father's tragic death—quiet, unassuming women whose mere presence comforted his mother. He recalled the neighbors who deco-rated the altar for Hulda's wedding when their step-father, Sven, was too stingy to do so. They had been generous with their homemade refreshments for the reception, unpretentious people putting their faith into action. He had not thought about them for a long time.

In general he found the miners to be rebellious and unsentimental, but he noticed they had a grudging respect for clergymen who lent a helping hand and practiced what they preached. Eric was convinced that deep down they admired anyone who was willing to stand up for his convic-tions. They just didn't want "Bible thumpers," as they called the more aggressive evangelists, pushing religion at them. They ridiculed phonies and despised hypocrites, and Eric hoped he was neither.

Weather changed from day to day. Yesterday had been a day for shorts, while today Eric needed a jacket. The sharp wind battered his back. The wind must be coming right off the Antarctic, he thought. "The Land of the Unexpected" was a good moniker for this land down under. He blew on his hands to warm them. He hoped the temperature would rise during the day.

Although life had slammed the door on him several times, Eric never indulged in self pity. He had become more wary in his maturity, but that did not preclude the hope for a meaningful relationship. He was lonely, and Molly's response to his invitation had been encouraging. He was not seeking intimacy at this time; he would settle for companionship.

He dropped by the hospital in the late afternoon and found an unfamiliar nursing sister in charge. She gave him an indulgent smile when he inquired if Molly was off duty. When Molly appeared, she was wearing a light cotton frock that made her look like a schoolgirl.

"I was hoping you would have dinner with me tonight," he said. "The Opal Inn is featuring roast beef, or steak, if you prefer."

"I'd like very much to go."

"You don't mind going out with an old man?" Oh, God! he thought. Why on earth did I say a stupid thing like that? I'm ruining any chances I may have with her.

She wrinkled her nose. "If you're fishing for a compliment, I won't give you one! I don't consider a difference in age important."

He hadn't either until he saw her again and was struck by her youth and vitality. She couldn't be much more than twenty. Her acceptance of him so naturally pleased him. The temperature had risen, and her dark brown hair lay in waves about her head, damp from perspiration.

"I'm glad my hair is short," she said. "Long hair and hot weather don't mix."

"Did you ever wear it long?" For a moment he was caught up in a fantasy of brushing her long tresses away from her face in candlelight. She quickly destroyed the image.

"Yes. I kept it long for a while when I was growing up, but it got tangled with all the wind and dust. It was too hard to wash and became a real nuisance. You must understand that when there is drought and water is scarce, it's a luxury to use it on hair. Sometimes I looked like a lubra from the wilds."

"What's a lubra?"

"An Aboriginal woman."

"Oh." He shifted his feet and glanced away, remembering the natives he had seen on the road to the Yunarra Mission with their filthy, matted hair.

"It's much easier to care for now."

"It becomes you very well," Eric said. He felt as awkward as a schoolboy.

He had chosen to go to the Opal Inn because he enjoyed its special atmosphere. The walls were painted with subdued earth colors, and pictures of the Australian outback were prominently displayed. The room emanated a distinctive air that was pure Australian. Opal buyers from overseas always stayed there, enjoying the relaxed comfort and attractive decor. Eric had looked forward all week to this date—not that he dressed up for it, for casual clothes were totally acceptable and expected. The Aussie working man disdained anything "flash."

The restaurant was not crowded, and the waitress brought their menus promptly. He ordered a bottle of good wine and raised a glass to Molly.

"Cheers," she said.

"Here's mud in your eye!" he replied.

Her face registered shock. "What a terrible thing to say!" she protested.

"That's just an American expression meaning, 'Good Health' or 'Good Luck'," Eric explained hastily.

Molly laughed. "That's really funny. I guess you think we have some odd expressions, too." A comfortable feeling settled over them, and they grinned at each other.

"This is very nice wine," Molly observed. "We never had any alcohol at the mission, of course. I learned to appreciate it when I was in Adelaide, not that I drank it very often. We have some wonderful vineyards in the Barossa Valley. You may not know that Australian wine has won prizes all over the world." She sighed. "I think this might be my last drink for a while, though."

"Oh? Why is that?"

"I've seen what alcohol does to my people—I say 'my people' even though I'm only a quarter Aboriginal. I've never tried to hide my racial background, Eric. You must understand that. Alcohol is destroying the Aborigines. I should be an example to them. I go over to the Aboriginal Reserve as often as I can, to help."

"That's very commendable, Molly, but you do have a life of your own, you know."

"You don't approve?"

"I admire your sincerity. I guess I'm just a little intimidated by your dedication."

"But *you* must be dedicated as a teacher!" she cried. "Are you on sabbatical leave from your school now?"

"No, I'm just traveling." He didn't want old wounds opened.

"Do you plan to teach when you return?" she persisted.

"No, I don't."

"Why not?" She looked at him curiously.

He wished she would stop her inquisition. "I ... I just got burned out, Molly."

"That's hard to believe!" she said indignantly. "I can't imagine your not wanting to work with young people. I'm sure you have a lot to offer."

"I'd rather not talk about it." He was not being truthful. He did want to talk about it, but not at this time. He did not know Molly well enough to confide the details of the unsavory Debby Sue Markham mess.

His was the misfortune of having Debby Sue in his ancient history class. Her father was not only a member of the board of trustees but also a generous contributor to the endowment fund. Debby Sue was intellectually challenged, personally undisciplined, and her sole interest in college was becoming a cheerleader and reigning as "Queen of the Campus." Using every wile and sexual innuendo to achieve her purpose, she found many admirers of her dimpled smile and attractive figure. Eric was not among them. She would sit in the front row of his class in her tight sweater and short skirt with her shapely legs crossed, hoping to disconcert him. He ignored her.

When Debby Sue turned in a paper, *Jewelry in Ancient Greece*, he recognized it as having been submitted three years previously by a far more talented student. He remembered it particularly because the writer had shown considerable insight and originality of presentation, and the research had been impressive. Debby Sue hadn't even tried to rewrite it with some of her own ideas but had submitted it verbatim. Eric tossed it aside with disgust—she must think him a fool. He confronted her with the facts after class the following day.

"Debby Sue, this paper is not your own work. I cannot accept it."

Her eyes blazed. "But it is mine. I wrote it myself."

"No, you didn't."

She adopted a seductive pose. "But Mr. Christianson, I did write it. I may have gotten some ideas from other work, but lots of students do that."

Eric didn't change his frosty expression.

She flounced out of the room, calling back, "It is my work!"

He gave her an "F" on the paper and wrote a curt comment. Coupled with her poor grades on tests, she would receive a "D" in the course. The upshot was that Debby Sue would not have a high enough grade point average to qualify for cheerleading the following semester or to accept the title of "Snow Queen" during the winter festivities after the Christmas holidays. Furious, she plotted his destruction.

One afternoon she dropped by his office, ostensibly for a conference. "I must talk with you, Mr. Christianson," she told him. "It's important."

Eric sighed and put down the papers he was grading. "All right, Debby Sue. Come in."

She glanced down the hallway before entering, noting that Mr. Hurley, dean of students, was approaching. She quickly stepped inside, closing the door behind her.

"Leave the door open, please," Eric told her. It was his policy never to be alone with a female student behind a closed door, especially one like Debby Sue. She didn't comply with his request, instead she advanced toward him with a venomous look on her face. He had an instant premonition, but it was too late. In a flash she dropped her books, revealed a ripped blouse and pushed her hands against Eric's chest, shouting, "Stop it, Mr. Christianson. Let me go! Let me go!"

She slapped Eric's face as Dean Hurley threw open the door. He gasped. The sorry looking vignette might have looked contrived to anyone but him. Unfortunately his authority entitled him to track down all wrong doing, and his sanctimonious nature relished uncovering even the appearance of evil. Debby Sue stood crying, gathering together her torn cloth-ing, and then fled past him.

Eric hastened to explain the malice of her scheme and the non-coincidental timing, but the dean's sense of outraged propriety was not mollified. The scene appeared too intense, too real to be fabricated.

"We'll discuss this in my office later, Mr. Christianson," he said coldly. "I must inform the members of the board about this unfortunate situation and meet with them." By the time the dean returned to his office, his righteous indignation had cooled somewhat. He called other members of the board and heard them express some doubt about the circumstances, enough to make him wary of making the wrong decision.

In the meantime Debby Sue appeared disheveled and distraught at her dormitory. Her cohorts gathered around her, consoling her in her distress and exulting vicariously in the titillating news. She immediately notified her father by phone, and within ten minutes the campus buzzed with the news.

Mr. Markham contacted the college president and pre-sented him with an ultimatum. "That teacher has got to be dismissed immediately," he stormed.

The president called Hurley, demanding action. No delay in determining Mr. Christianson's guilt would be tolerated. The dean was caught in a dilemma. Action of some kind had to be taken, but the wrong move might imperil the institu-tion. If the story were true, of course he would have to see that Christianson was fired, but even then a criminal complaint might be leveled against him by the parents of the girl, and that would be devastating publicity for Crestmore College. If the story was false and the teacher was retained, they were in danger of losing considerable financial backing, because, of course, Mr. Markham would believe his daughter and withdraw his support. If the story was false and the teacher was dismissed without cause, he might sue the college. The dean again discussed the matter in further detail with the board members and received their advice. He summoned Eric to his office.

"Mr. Christianson, the board recognizes the delicacy of this situation and the unpleasant position it puts you in." Eric detected a slight conciliatory attitude by Hurley which heartened him momentarily but was disabused of any optimism after the dean had cleared his throat and begun to address him again. "In view of the seriousness of the accusation and because of the Annette Bower incident earlier, we feel we must take action."

Eric frowned, puzzled. "I don't know any girl named Annette Bower." He searched his memory. "I've never had anyone by that name in my class. I don't know what you mean by 'incident'."

The dean brought his handkerchief to his lips in a delicate gesture and coughed. "She says you made improper advances to her in the library basement a few months ago. You recall you discussed something about that with me."

"Oh, that!" Eric laughed with relief. "I told you some girl came out of the ladies' room just as I left the men's room.

I was hurrying because it was closing time, and we almost collided. I started to apologize, but she turned and ran upstairs. Although I tried to catch up with her and explain, she had disappeared. The light was dim, and she was bundled up against the cold. I couldn't have recognized her even if I'd known her, which I didn't. I told you so there could not be any misunderstanding about the situation. A male teacher can't be too careful."

"No, he can't, Mr. Christianson. But unfortunately, Annette has come forward and declared that you were trying to bodily assault her."

Eric's eyes narrowed. "Is Annette Bower a friend of Debby Sue Markham's by any chance?"

"That is beside the point."

"No, Dean Hurley, it is very much to the point. When did this great revelation take place?"

The dean stared at the papers on his desk. "This afternoon. She said she didn't come forward at the time, not wanting to make trouble, but in light of the attack on Debby Sue today—"

"Attack!" He stood up, leaning on the desk with whitened knuckles. He could predict what was coming.

"We are in a very precarious position here, Mr. Christianson. Neither girl's parents are anxious to press criminal charges with all the notoriety that accompanies that sort of thing, but obviously some sort of resolution to this problem must take place."

"Dean Hurley, I am innocent of both charges, and I'm not going to back down. I've never avoided a fight yet when I was in the right. By God, no spoiled, malicious girl is going to ruin my reputation. I'll haul my grade book into court if I have to and expose Debby Sue as the lying little cheat she is. And as far as the preposterous charge by Annette Bower ..."

The dean sighed. He was afraid of this. No matter how it turned out, the reputation of the college would be called into question. He spoke carefully, not wishing to antagonize the man hovering opposite him. "Mr. Christianson, believe me, I sympathize with you. But perhaps you don't understand. Mr. Markham is prepared to hire lawyers right now and follow through with all the vigor necessary to bring the case to trial. But of course it will take several months of preparation after charges have been filed, and you know how much lawyers enjoy prolonging the legalities. We will have to suspend you until the trial is over."

Eric felt an impotent chill engulfing him like a tide of cold water. He said nothing.

Hurley continued. "Both parents are willing to drop the charges if you tender your immediate resignation."

Yes, Eric thought, the girls will be vindicated, and my reputation will be sullied beyond repair. He hastily considered his finances. His divorce had not been cheap, and his share of the money from the house sale would be sufficient only to sustain him for part of a year, without lawyer fees. He sat back in his chair.

The dean droned on. "It is possible that both girls are fabricating their stories and we are doing you a great injustice, but ..."

Eric saw the inevitable reality. He was expendable; the endowment fund was not. With Debby Sue on the stand, displaying all her histrionic talents, and her father's money backing a smart lawyer, he wouldn't have a chance. Anything he brought up against the girl would be construed as persecution. A sexual misconduct charge would follow him the rest of his life. He recognized the subtle blackmail, but he would turn it to his own purpose. The college would wish to avoid a trial at all costs. Just the undercurrent talk of scandal must be making the trustees tremble.

Eric looked directly into the eyes of the unhappy dean and spoke with a resolute voice. "My first desire is to have this case taken into court, no matter what the cost. I am not without funds to defend myself." He could see the pallor creeping across Hurley's face. "But on second thought, I feel some allegiance to this institution—after all, I have always devoted myself to its best interests since I came here." He sensed the dean relaxing. "I will be willing to avoid confrontation in court if I can resign quietly with no mention of this on my record. You will, of course, give me a recommendation on the strength of my past work and enumerate my diversified valuable services."

Hurley nodded reluctantly. Eric continued. "You will also give me my full salary for the remainder of this semester, which is soon to close, and all of the next semester."

Hurley's intake of breath was so noticeable that Eric feared he had overstepped the bounds, but though the dean was taken aback by the audacity of the proposal, he was visibly relieved. He asked for time to confer with other members of the board, and Eric returned to his office to gather his personal possessions. Within an hour the dean phoned—the board had approved. The necessary papers would be drawn up early the next day and brought to his apartment.

"But my classes ..."

"A substitute teacher has been arranged."

"But the kids—I'd at least like to say goodbye."

"We feel that would be inadvisable, to save us both embarrassment. We are simply saying you requested leave which has been granted, without explanation."

"But of course everyone knows why," Eric said bitterly.

"I'm sure many of your students will understand the situation and hold you in high regard."

Eric thought he detected a tinge of sarcasm in the dean's voice. Even if he were sincere, the words bore small consolation. Rage almost choked him—he was being forced to sneak away like a thief in the night. For a moment he almost changed his mind and decided to fight, but he knew the cards were stacked against him and resigning with his conditions met was the best possible choice.

That night as he surveyed his few possessions in the apartment, he was surprised at how little he owned or cared about. He packed the car with his clothes, books and a few mementos, and sat down and wrote out his resignation. That night his nightmare returned, more terrible than before. He awakened from it drenched with sweat, and an appalling sense of failure and futility clung to him. The next morning a courier from the college brought a portfolio of legal papers to be signed. He read them carefully and found them to be as he requested—there were no loopholes. He retained the originals and handed his resignation to the courier and then phoned his realtor. "I'm leaving unexpectedly. You can use my first month's deposit if you need to tidy up the apartment. It's really in good shape, except for a little food left in the refrigerator." He cut off any questioning and then headed for Northern Michigan.

How could he possibly explain the whole sordid mess on a first date with this lovely young woman? He sensed that he had alienated her with his abruptness. She was very quiet and gestured "No" when he offered to refill her glass. He attempted to recapture their earlier conviviality, but the atmosphere was strained. "Where do you plan to go when you leave here?" she asked after a long pause.

"I'm not leaving soon. I have several more months on my visa."

"I know I'm repeating myself," Molly answered, "but I hope you're not planning to mine."

"As a matter of fact, I'm mining right now."

An expression of disillusionment swept across her face.

"I'm working with a young Greek fellow. It's been good

for me."

"The exercise?"

"That ... and other things."

Molly raised her eyebrows. Suddenly he found himself confiding in her about the need to conquer his deep-seated fear. He had never told anyone about this before, and he knew that if she laughed at him, it would be the last time he sought her out. He waited for her reaction. She didn't rebuff his revelation but first looked concerned, and then relieved.

"I'm glad you told me. Confronting a fear takes a lot of courage. Now that you've solved your problem, you can quit mining, can't you?"

Eric hesitated before answering. "It's not that easy, Molly. You see, I've invested in equipment, and I'm a full partner now."

She looked at him for a moment, and then it was as though a shadow blocked the light in her eyes. "I'm sorry you've become involved. I'd be a hypocrite if I said anything else."

"I'm glad you're honest with me, Molly. I still hope to see you again."

When she didn't answer, his hopes plummeted. The slight lift of one shoulder told him more than words. When he stopped at the hospital, he turned to her for a goodnight kiss and was discomfited by the look of wariness that crossed her face. It lasted only a moment, but it was enough to cause him to withdraw his embrace. He thought about the look on his way back to the caravan park.

CHAPTER NINE

MOLLY FOLDED THE TOWELS MECHANICALLY as she tried to push Eric Christianson out of her mind. She found him attractive, even with that faint scar on the side of his face, but there were so many uncertainties about him. She had not dated many men. She had been far too busy during nurses' training, and even if she had wished to go out, she realized her mixed parentage had kept most prospective boyfriends at arms length. She had never denied her background, but it had restricted her social life. In fact, the only boy she really had cared for had been Wilanya back at the mission, but that was more of a sisterly attachment on her part. She thought of him now because she had been folding towels in the mission infirmary the last time she had seen him.

A small sound had caused her to turn around, and Wilanya was standing in the doorway disheveled and dirty. For a moment she was taken aback and she then rushed toward him with a big smile and outstretched arms.

"How good to see you!" she exclaimed and then hesitated. His dark eyes were staring without expression, and he began to back away. She watched him carefully. His hair, obviously uncombed for weeks, was full of bits of leaves and twigs. His soiled shirt and pants hung loosely on his gaunt frame, and his feet were caked with dirt.

"You look ill, Wilanya. Have you been in the bush all this time?"

He shook his head and again took steps backward. She grasped both of his arms and restrained him. "Don't go, please! There's so much to talk about. I've been worried about you, Wilanya."

The youth shook himself free and finally spoke. "You are so clean here at the infirmary. The towels are so clean. I'm just a dirty Aborigine. I don't belong here."

"That's not true, Wilanya. I'm always glad to see you, no matter what. I wondered how you were and where you'd gone."

"Did you? I would have thought you had other things on your mind." He thrust out his lower lip.

"Like what?"

"A boyfriend, maybe."

She smiled at his suggestion. "No. There's no boyfriend."

"Then ... Going away to school. You've decided to go, haven't you? To nurses' training? You were talking about it when I left."

Molly took a deep breath. "I'm considering it, Wilanya. I've thought about it a lot. Working here in the infirmary has made me realize I have a vocation. I ... I want to try."

"Then there's no place for me in your life," he said, bitterness vying with self-pity. "I think I knew it when I went away. I'll always be beneath you."

"Oh, no, Wilanya. I'll never be better than you. I just have this goal that I must try to reach. It shouldn't come between our friendship."

"Friendship! You know I've always wanted more than friendship! You're friends with everyone here at the mission. I want to be special!"

"But you are special to me, Wilanya. We've grown up together, shared our thoughts and feelings. I always hoped that you would want to go on to school, too."

"You know I'm no student, Molly. I could hardly get through the tenth grade, even with your help, and you passed all your exams with flying colors."

"There are other paths to follow. You could take up some mechanical work. You have abilities there. Pastor Holmgren said so."

"I don't give a damn what Pastor Holmgren said!" Wilanya lashed out. "I'm tired of being advised and told what to do. I want to get away from this place for good. We're treated like children here. I've seen something of the rest of the world, and I want to be part of it. You'll feel the same way when you leave."

"I hope not. I think my heart will always be here, no matter where I might be sent."

He reached out suddenly and tried to kiss her. She pulled

back and held him at arm's length. "Not this way, Wilanya," she said firmly.

"Which way, then? Do you remember what I told you down by the billabong that last night?"

"You didn't know what you were saying."

"I meant what I said. I told you that you belonged to me and would always be mine. I'll never let anyone else have you, Molly. I swear it."

"Wilanya, this is foolishness. I don't belong to you. I'm not a piece of property. I'll never belong to anyone."

He tried to put his arms around her a second time, and again she pushed him away. An ugly look smoldered in his eyes. "You're too high and mighty now for my kisses, aren't you?" he sneered. "And I'm too dirty. You're mostly white—you don't want a dirty Aborigine touching your nice, clean, white skin, do you?"

"Wilanya, stop this! You're insulting me. You know I have never denied my people."

Suddenly Wilanya let out a choking cry. "I'm so miserable, Molly! I don't know what to do. I couldn't find work. No one wanted to hire me. I started drinking. I couldn't stop. I found myself lying in the gutter one day, stinking drunk. Then I went into the bush. I just don't belong anywhere." He began to sob, his hands covering his face.

Molly put her arms around him and held him tightly. "Go have a good wash. I have to stay here until my helper comes because we have patients. I won't be long. Mother

Holmgren will fix you something to eat. She'll be so glad to see you."

He stumbled out of the room as Molly watched him with concern. He had forgotten his bush ways and was unprepared for life away from the mission.

Wilanya loitered about the infirmary each day, seldom smiling, sometimes scowling. He made no effort to engage other young men in conversation, even though he had known them most of his life. He refused to join them in the necessary communal work that kept the mission in food and repairs. He was glad some of the advanced students had gone on to higher education; now they would not be rivals for Molly's affection. At times he felt impotent and useless, at other times he felt strong and able to court Molly. He did not want her to go away. If she stayed at the mission, he would be secure. He and Molly could marry and live here at the mission and be safe.

Wilanya hung his head when he thought of the words "safe" and "secure." His people never had known security in the outback. There was always uncertainty—lack of food or water, sandstorms, drought, enemy tribes that might attack them. Life was always a challenge, but they had survived. His parents had come to the mission when he was a young boy, so all he knew of life outside was from the tales told by the elders. He had scorned the ways of his parents, but secretly wished he could have experienced their hardships and acquired their lore. He had not been circumcised, had never gone through the painful initiation rites, had never had to prove his manhood. He knew he was not a man. He was a frightened, unhappy child, and he didn't know what to do.

"Please don't go away, Molly," he pleaded. "If you stay, I know I'll do better. I'll take the shop courses. I'll learn to farm. I'll even paint those damned boomerangs for the tourists. I know we can make it together. I know we can. Please stay."

Molly placed her hand over his and squeezed it. "I don't know what to say, Wilanya. I don't know what's best for either of us. I want to see my grandmother. It's been a long time, and I must talk with her. I can't give you an answer now."

"If you go away, I will too, and you'll never see me again."

"Oh, Wilanya—you can't keep me by threatening me. Don't you see? This must be right for both of us, and we're so young."

"We're not too young according to tribal law."

"Wilanya," Molly said gently, "we're not living by tribal law any more," She smiled. "If we were, we'd be out on the desert eating witchety grubs and running around naked!"

She had hoped to coax a smile in return, but instead he flared.

"There's more to tribal law than that!"

"Of course there is. There is a lot that is good, and I appreciate it, but there are many things we cannot accept today. Besides, we're not a tribe any more— we're a ... people. Don't you see that? I'm trying to find the best in both worlds."

"Good luck, then!" He jumped up and ran down the road, leaving Molly standing on the steps, disturbed. That

Joan Greenlees Abramson

night she asked her foster father for the use of the Land Rover
so she could make a quick trip to Wiluru Station to see her
grandmother.

"You are troubled in your spirit," Niboorana observed.
"Yes, Kabbarli. I don't know which way to turn."
"It's Wilanya, isn't it?"
"How did you know?"
A smile of ancient understanding crossed Niboorana's
face. She sat back on her haunches—a position she had used
since childhood. "You are fond of him?"
"Oh, yes. We've been friends for years. But I don't know
if I love him. He seems so lost without me. He wants me to
give up nursing."
"You are no longer bound by tribal law."
"I know."
"You may marry whom you wish."
"Yes."
"You want to help your people."
"Yes, Kabbarli. That has always been my wish."
Niboorana sat quietly. Molly did not press her. Patience
was everything to an Aborigine. Time had no significance.
Then she spoke again. "One person cannot give strength to
another. Strength comes from within."
"Yes, Kabbarli."
"And the male must be stronger than the female. That is
the way of life."

Molly wasn't sure she agreed, but she kept silent.

"The male makes the decisions, and the female follows."

Molly bowed her head. This was not what she wanted to hear, but she had come for advice and would listen.

"But the male is dominant because he has earned the right," Niboorana continued. "He has been trained from boyhood to endure hardship and to learn from the wisdom of the elders. The responsibility of the future of the tribe is his. The wife must be subservient to him and accept his judgment. It is the way of our people."

Molly felt a knot tying up her insides. She respected her grandmother, but her words were distressing. Niboorana read the conflicting emotions on her granddaughter's face and spoke again.

"Wilanya has not gone through initiation. He has not earned the right to be a leader. He is in a different world now and must earn the right by his own conduct. It is shameful for a man to take his strength from a woman. I did not have a choice in my life, but you do. You must do what your heart tells you. I cannot tell you what to do."

Molly put her arms around her grandmother and held her close. "You have helped me, Kabbarli. I know what I must do."

She stopped briefly at the big bungalow to pay her respects to Mrs. McCurdy, who gave her a big embrace. "Molly, what a lovely young lady you've become. Bert is out in the north paddock. He'll be sorry he missed you."

Molly laughed. "He's always away when I come. I think

it's deliberate. I haven't seen him since I was twelve, and we didn't part on very good terms then."

Mrs. McCurdy laughed, too. Then her eyes narrowed as she examined the pretty girl more closely. Perhaps it was just as well that Bert was away working. If she had advance notice of Molly's visits, she just might arrange for her son always to be somewhere else on the station. That way there would be no complications.

When Molly arrived at the mission, she found that Wilanya had gone. His sudden departure did not surprise her. She felt mild disappointment and tremendous relief as she prepared for her eventful trip to Adelaide.

Now, two years later she was here in the little hospital at Coober Pedy, folding towels and wondering about her long-lost childhood friend. She hoped he had adjusted well and was happy in his new life. She knew that she had chosen the right course for herself.

CHAPTER TEN

PIETRO BAGNINI was the third child born to a hard-working Italian immigrant couple. Their first two children, daughters, had been born in the old country, but Pietro was a native-born Australian. Two daughters and another son had followed Pietro's birth.

"We have been blessed with more than our share of daughters," Papa Bagnini often said, shaking his head. He needed strong sons to help with the labor in the vineyards of the Barossa Valley, begun long before by pious German vintners. The Bagninis worked long hours, were scrupulously honest and gained a respectable place in the community. All except Pietro.

"I do not understand our son," Mama Bagnini told her husband many times. "He is different. He doesn't listen to our advice. He has wild ways. What did we do wrong?" She spent a great deal of her time worrying about her recalcitrant son, wondering if they had been too busy after they first settled to give him the attention he needed. All of their children had been raised with the same firm hand, applied indiscriminately when necessary, but Pietro had reacted differently from the others. While his siblings had accepted correction without deep resentment, Pietro maintained a smoldering defiance, causing his father to lay on an even harder hand. The uncurbed violence that lay lightly beneath his nature frightened his mother, but the sly, mean streak was not always apparent to others, many of whom were taken in by his smooth manner, good looks and glib tongue—especially the girls.

One evening he returned home late with a bruised face, refusing to answer questions. "I got into a little scrape. Nothing to worry about."

"You can't go on like this!" his father protested. "You must settle down. Your work in the vineyard with the rest of the family is only half-hearted. Even young Carlos works harder than you. You're eighteen now, old enough to take responsibility. Some day we'll be able to have our own vineyard, but it takes effort."

"I'm not interested in being a vintner. I have other plans for my life."

"Then you'd better forget them. You live here, you work here."

"Then I'll leave!"

"You can't! We need you."

Mama Bagnini hovered in the background during this altercation, clutching her rosary. How would it all end? She loved her son, but she didn't know what to do. They went to mass every Sunday and observed all the holy days, but nothing seemed to affect Pietro. She prayed that no harm would come to him—or to anyone else, by his hand.

One evening he came home late. Close behind him was an enraged neighbor brandishing a knife, screaming, "I caught him in bed with my daughter! He'll either marry her or I'll kill him!"

Bagnini, covered with shame, endeavored to calm the aggrieved father with reassurances that of course a wedding would be arranged. Pietro stood sullenly, arms folded, animosity flashing in his eyes.

"Gino," said the neighbor, "we will finalize this conversation in the morning. There is my daughter's honor to be upheld. We will go together to see the priest and make the arrangements." The two fathers shook hands, sealing the agreement. Pietro said nothing, not even after his father berated him for bringing disgrace on the family.

"She's a nice girl! Why couldn't you wait?" Bagnini shouted after his son turned his back and stalked to his bedroom. His voice echoed through the small house, and his wife cowered in her bed, trying to shut out the unsavory episode. What dreams they had for their first-born son! Now this. But perhaps good would come of it after all. Other marriages begun under adverse circumstances turned out well. She prayed that this one would, too.

While his parents made plans concerning his life, Pietro was making plans of his own. He had no intention of marrying anyone, especially that dull, bovine girl next door. He was at fault of course, at fault for getting caught. It was not his responsibility if a girl made herself available to him. He would not be forced into a ridiculous wedding. The sooner he left the better.

He lay down for a short time to be sure his brother was asleep and that the house was quiet. When he heard his father snoring, he got up quietly, gathered together his few clothes and personal possessions and slipped out the back door. He would not be missed until dawn when his parents arose early to begin the tasks of the day. By then he would be miles away.

He changed his name to Peter Bagley and never communicated with his family again. After drifting from place to place for several years—often one step ahead of the local police—he arrived at Coober Pedy. He was nicknamed "Peter the Con" behind his back; he had no friends. He played every rascally trick in the book and just managed to keep out of reach of the law. He was suspected of "borrowing" equipment while the owners were temporarily away and managing to return it just before they returned. It was strongly believed that he had poached in mines but he was never caught in the act. He set tourists up to mining opal in abandoned mines that had no trace of fire, but he made a good profit on equipment rental.

As he sauntered through the Greek store one day, he chose a few provisions for the following week. As always, several small items were slipped into his jacket pockets unseen. His purse was a little lean at the moment, so he would live abstemiously until his fortunes improved. They always improved sooner or later.

He gave Anastasia a seductive wink, which brought color to her cheeks. He knew she was pleased although greatly embarrassed by his attention. He was sure no one else made her feel desirable as she sat behind the counter, a long sleeve concealing her deformed arm. Her virginal shyness fascinated him, and he speculated on how delightful it would be to lead her into the pleasures of lovemaking. He had enough sense to ravish her only in his imagination. He could imagine the punishment that would be meted out to any man foolish enough to tamper with her.

Peter's eyes wandered idly to the bulletin board covered with notices—for sale signs, shacks to let, lost dogs, spectacles found—then his gaze stopped at a neatly printed notice concerning information about Sandy Blackwell. He didn't know any Sandy Blackwell, but he never let the possibility of an opportunity pass him by. He recognized that Eric Christianson was the Yank staying at the caravan park, and Americans meant money. He hesitated a moment, looked casually around, unpinned the notice and thrust it quickly into his pocket. He stopped at several shops and confiscated each like notice.

That evening he knocked briskly at Eric's door, and when the American opened it, Peter waved the notice in the air. "I know Sandy Blackwell," he announced.

Eric grasped his hand excitedly. "That's great! Come in. I was hoping my sign would bring some results." He gestured for Peter to sit down, his face aglow with pleasure. "Is he still in Coober Pedy? Where can I find him?"

Peter gave Eric a thoughtful look. "It depends on what you want him for."

"Oh. I understand. I'm not after him for any wrong doing, that's for sure. I'm not with the police. He's ... he's a friend of a mate of mine. Asked me to look him up."

"Oh. I understand. So if you can't find him, it's no big deal, right?" Peter watched Eric's eyes, reading correctly that this was a very important, personal matter.

"Well," Eric hedged, "I promised my mate I'd find him, and I like to keep my word."

"Of course. Did this friend of yours have an address for this Sandy character?" Peter kept his voice almost impersonal, knowing the American was anxious. He wanted to slowly draw Eric into his trap.

"No, he just said 'Coober Pedy.' That's why I put the notice on the board. I suppose he's mining here, but this is a pretty big place, and also he's rather young to be working."

"How old is he?"

"Oh, in the neighborhood of sixteen, I guess."

"That's old enough to work. I started younger than that."

Eric began to squirm, tapping his fingers on the table. "Can you take me to him?"

"I didn't say I could take you to him," Peter countered. "I just said I knew him, and I'm fairly certain I can tell you where he is."

"Well, where is he?" Eric demanded.

Peter sat back, relaxed and smiling. "Not so fast! We're not in such a hurry about things here in Australia. You've heard, 'No hurries, no worries'?"

"Well, what do you plan to tell me?"

Peter was pleased that the American was visibly trying to restrain his impatience. "How much is the information worth to you?"

"I should have known money would be involved in this," Eric said, his voice tinged with suspicion.

Eric recognized the precariousness of his position and didn't want to press his luck. He waited.

"I'll give you ten dollars for his current address," Eric offered.

Peter gave him a pitying look. He was sure the American was good for more so he would toy with him a bit longer. "You can't be in any hurry to find this bloke," he said and stood up. "Maybe someone else can help you."

"What's your name?" Eric asked abruptly.

Peter shook his head. "It's obvious you don't trust me. Why should I tell you my name?"

"Because I'd like to know whom I'm dealing with."

"And I'd like to know that you're serious about finding Sandy Blackwell. He's a good lad. I don't want to create any problems for him. Why should I trust you?"

"All right. But first describe him to me."

Peter felt the American was simply fishing, but he had to

be careful. Maybe Christianson did know what the fellow looked like and was testing him. Well, he could play the game, too. "Oh, he's about my size, reddish hair—that's why they call him 'Sandy'— blue eyes, nice smile." He shrugged. "If you don't want the address ..."

"Okay. Tell me more. How long has he been here?"

"A couple of months. I met him in a pub. He was down on his luck, couldn't get a job, needed some money. I gave him fifty dollars. He told me he'd pay it back when he could. I'm sure he meant it at the time. I think it's only fair I get some of it back, don't you? Like I said, he seemed like a nice bloke. Something came up, and he moved on."

"Tell me where he went." Eric's eyes seemed to bore into Peter, and for the first time Bagley became uneasy.

"He told me he was going to go back home."

"And where is that?" Eric studied him carefully.

Peter chose a place he was sure the Yank had never heard of. "He came from Menzies, Western Australia."

"You bastard!" Eric said in a tight voice. "I know a con job when I see one. You see, I know where he came from. Get out of here!"

Peter drew himself up with great dignity. "Hold on there, mate! That's a serious accusation." He bit back a hot response and tried to keep his tone conciliatory. He had never achieved anything with precipitous moves. "You'll welcome me back the next time I come. I know more than I said, and the price will go up." He silently kicked himself for trying to run a bluff without more facts, but he would get them. Someone on the field must know about this bloke Sandy Blackwell. The situation smelled of money, and he wasn't about to give up. Besides, he had other tricks up his sleeve.

His most lucrative job was in hiring himself out as a guide to the opal fields and entertaining the gullible visitors with flamboyant tales of the mysterious "outback." Many American travelers returned to the States and spoke with authority about experiences which had been conceived in the fertile imagination of Peter Bagley. ("We met the most interesting chap over in Coober Pedy, Australia. He'd been everywhere and could tell the most incredible tales of dangerous exploits in the *outback*. He was born in the *outback* and knew it like the back of his hand. A real down-to-earth Aussie.")

His careless charm coupled with a bold manner made him particularly vulnerable to the ladies, especially to those whose own attractions were somewhat deficient. In addition, his warm brown eyes seemed to spell both affection and adventure, and to the unwary female he was wickedly exciting.

"The bloody bastard," Sergeant MacDonald swore more than once to his deputy. "If we could just catch him in one of his schemes." To his chagrin, he couldn't. The policeman never gave up hope that the wily fellow would let his guard down, but Bagley was too conniving to overstep the line. His activities were always just barely legal, which made him safe. He was too shrewd to be taken by surprise.

One of Peter's specialties was his "Moonrise over the Opal

Fields Tour" with a lovely, or less than lovely, young tourist as companion. If the girl was really unattractive, he gathered a group together and charged a fee—a flexible amount depending on his financial circumstances. If she was at all presentable, he took along a bottle of wine and a blanket, making it an exclusive session. His strong personality usually insured that even the most reluctant girl would submit, and he seldom entertained an unappreciative client. On the rare occasion when he overcame timidity by force, the girl was usually too embarrassed to tell anyone.

On one particular night he felt fortunate in having made the acquaintance of Miss Lily Hampton, a recent arrival from England. Lily was twenty-two, passably good looking in subdued light, and had just been jilted. She arrived with a busload of other tourists taking a safari tour of the "Red Centre." She found Peter quite dashing with his Aussie side-swept hat and engaging banter. She attended the small group he guided around town and its environs that day, and Peter approached her about the possibility of slipping away for the evening. She accepted with enthusiasm.

They drove out to the Four Mile because this was one field that Peter was sure would have no distractions. Most of the mines had been worked out long ago or were abandoned as unproductive. He had a particular place he always frequented on these excursions where he had dug out a large shelf on one of the heaps of opal clay. The full moon soon would be rising, casting enough glow to add to the mystique and stir the senses.

He parked behind the opal heap and helped Lily out of his car, squeezing her arm affectionately as he did so. He spread the blanket gallantly on the shelf and smiled down on her with what he hoped was a deliciously enchanting smile.

"This is a special night for me, Miss Hampton," he said.

"Oh, do call me Lily," she responded, gazing at him with admiring eyes.

"The Aborigines have many legends about the night," he fabricated, "how the spirits enjoy coming into one's body and making the blood flow faster, the skin get warmer, the pulse beat stronger." He put his arm around her, and she snuggled closer. He opened a bottle of wine and poured a large amount into two glasses he had brought for the occasion. The wine brought a flush to her cheeks which even in the half light he could see. The moon began to show a tiny bright curve that continued to grow, its fecundity bathing them in creamy light.

"The moon looks just like a gorgeous ripe melon, doesn't it?" He wasn't looking at the moon as he spoke.

"You're so poetic, Peter," Lily breathed. She drank some more wine and cuddled closer. Then she began to giggle. Peter put his hand on her back and pulled her gently toward him, certain he would meet no resistance. Her eyes looked blurry and unfocused. He slipped his hand down the opening of her blouse and began to whisper in her ear.

Suddenly she stiffened and pulled away from him. Her rejection angered him and he was about to become more forceful when she wailed, "I'm going to be sick!" and vomited down the front of her clothes. Peter leaped back in disgust.

"Oh, my God!" he said. "What a bloody mess! Let's get out of here!"

He threw her some tissues, and she desperately tried to clean herself up. He pulled her roughly to her feet and steered her to the car, hating the thought of her riding with him. He wished he could just leave her out on the opal heap but knew he could not abandon her.

All the way back to town he fumed with anger. Wasted time. Wasted wine! Next time he'd pick a local girl. Maybe that good-looking new waitress at the Opal Inn. Anyone would be better than Lily Hampshire. God, what a night! He dropped her off where the safari bus was parked and sped away as quickly as possible.

After going to his dugout to change clothes, he drove back to town. He went into one of the pubs to listen to the chatter at the bar for anything pertinent, any little scrap of information that might lend itself to some scheme. The few untalkative men at the bar yielded nothing. Next he went to the Opal Inn to look over the busload of new tourists that were enjoying the amenities of the hotel. He didn't see anyone promising. His eyes drifted over to the new waitress who looked attractive in spite of being harried. Yes, he recognized distinct possibilities there.

CHAPTER ELEVEN

ERIC SLUMPED IN HIS CHAIR. He was so sure his notice would bring positive results, and now this con man almost played him for a sucker. Sandy Blackwell had lived in Victoria, not Western Australia, and what a terrible time he had had locating that address! And after meeting Ben Blackwell, he knew Sandy would never return there.

Eric had the surname of Anne's father, a butcher by trade, in Bathhurst, New South Wales, but that was over sixteen years ago. How could he start out with that meager information? He had debated with himself all the way across the Pacific Ocean whether he should go through with his plan. However, his determination to locate his child, not to reveal his relationship but simply to lay eyes on him, had won out. Instinctively he felt he had a son, and increasingly he found himself mentally referring to "him." He daydreamed about the boy's physical characteristics—would he be a "dark Viking" like himself or have a lighter complexion and blonde hair like Eric's mother and Hulda? Or might he be more like Anne with her bright auburn hair or perhaps a combination—fair skin, maybe freckled—with sandy or rust-colored hair? Would he be tall? He hoped he would—height had certain advantages for a man. But of greater importance, he wondered what standards and aspirations the boy would have. He had read that many youths in Australia left school at the end of the tenth grade and found work. Jobs were plentiful now, which was an attractive alternative to going on for further education. As a teacher he felt this was misguided policy. As a former teacher, he corrected himself. He didn't ever plan to go back.

Curiosity about Anne's parents led to further reflection. If Anne and her mother resembled each other, the older woman would be beautiful, even in her later years. He wondered how he would introduce himself without giving himself away. After long consideration he decided he would pass himself off as brother to a girl who had served with Anne in Tokyo and had requested that he look her up. It was rather flimsy but the best he could conjure up.

He spent the first few days buying a utility truck and a small trailer, reminding himself to call it a "caravan." He stocked up on necessary food supplies, which he found reasonable, but the high cost of the vehicle and petrol made him realize he would have to spend conservatively as he faced possible long distances of driving in uncertain conditions. His visa was good for a year, as long as he reported in quarterly at a capital city. But he had to make sure his money would last that long. He had been required to purchase a return ticket before being admitted to the country so he had no worries on that score.

"No worries!" He laughed out loud. That was the Aussies' favorite expression and one he knew he would hear many times again.

He found Bathhurst to be a thriving town with many shopping areas. Undaunted by his task, he began checking out all butcher shops. By the end of the second day he had personally visited almost every shop with the question, "I'm looking for a butcher named Evans. Have you heard of him?" and was disappointed by the negative answers which usually ran, "Sorry, mate. Wish I could help, but I don't know him," followed by, "Try Garrity's down the street," or another name.

It was with a sinking heart that he entered the last shop on the outskirts of town. The butcher was a grizzled little man with hands that seemed incongruously large for his size. He rested them on the butcher block before him and stared at Eric. "What can I do for you?"

As Eric explained his mission, the old timer's watery blue eyes lit up. "Well, stone the crows!" he cried. "A Yank!" Then he shook hands, and Eric almost winced at the strength of the man's grip. The butcher laughed. "Surprised you, didn't I, laddie? I always get a reaction." He held his hands out in front of himself and examined them. "Been hoisting carcasses of beef and sheep so long, that my hands outgrew my body."

Eric joined the good-natured man's laughter and waited. There were no other customers in the shop, and he anticipated a rambling story about the meat business. Tired after a long day and anxious to glean as much information as quickly as possible, he didn't relish garrulity.

He looked benevolently at Eric and said, "I'm always glad to see an American—they saved our necks in World War II. I was in Singapore when it fell, and for all we knew, all of Australia was gone. What was the name again of the bloke you're searching for?"

"Evans," Eric prompted

The butcher scratched his chin, pondering. "I remember working with a fellow named Evans at least ten years ago. He wasn't here very long. I think he moved away, but I don't know where. I never saw him again. I'm sorry I can't help more. Nothing's too good for you Yanks. We don't see many out here."

"Well, thanks anyway." He turned to go, shoulders drooping.

"Wait. Maybe the Union could help you." He wrote down an address with directions on how to get there. From that organization Eric learned that Evans had not paid dues for the previous eight years, so evidently he had quit working or had changed jobs. The last address on file was in Toowoomba, Queensland. Before he left, Eric found the telephone numbers of all the people in Bathhurst named Evans, and called each one, asking if they had a daughter or relative named Anne. None did.

Eric started for the "Sunshine State" hundreds of miles away, remembering to shift with the left hand and to drive on the opposite side of the road. "Remember, mate, it's the "opposite" side, not the "wrong" side," the salesman had told him with a wink, jabbing him lightly in the ribs. "You bloody Yanks think you own all the roads over here." Eric had automatically thought in terms of miles—now he would have to reorient his thinking into kilometers.

After looking at his map, he decided the quickest way was to take the main highway up the coast to Brisbane and turn westward. If his mind had not been on his quest, he would have enjoyed the scenery as he passed back over the Blue Mountains and up the coast. He noticed the change to semi-tropical vegetation, banana plantations and a profusion of flowering plants. He wished he could linger at some of the scenic spots but was driven to keep moving. The long stretches of beautiful white sand beaches with so few people on them amazed him. Back home, he thought, there would be thousands of people swimming on a sunny day. Then he remembered two things—the entire population of the continent of Australia would fit into the Los Angeles basin, and many dangerous sea creatures lurked in the ocean here. He had seen pictures of the blue bottle jelly fish and the deadly scorpion fish, both terrifying for anyone venturing into the water. Photos of the bathing beaches around Sydney showed shark nets to protect swimmers.

The new address was of no help. The current occupants had bought the house from a man named Flannery three years before. No, they didn't know where Flannery lived now and had never heard of Evans. Eric checked with the postal authorities, real estate agents, the telephone company, the markets—all without results.

Then he found the answer while interviewing the Episcopal priest.

"I remember the Evans case," he said. "Very sad."

A chill swept over Eric as he waited.

"It was about seven years ago. I didn't know them personally—they weren't of my church, but I was struck by the tragedy of the situation."

Eric's mouth was so dry he could hardly speak. "What happened?"

"They both were killed in a head-on collision on the Gold Coast Highway. Drunken driver in the other car. He survived, of course. Always seems to happen that way. It makes one wonder at times, doesn't it?"

"Then ... it was just the two of them? No family with them?" He held his breath.

"No. I guess they hadn't lived here in Toowoomba very long. Maybe he found there was too much work to do on the place they bought so they sold it and moved to Maryborough. I wouldn't have known about it except I was visiting my niece there when it happened, and I read about it in the paper. So sad."

"Was anything said about next of kin?"

"Not to my recollection, but of course that was seven years ago. You might try the newspaper office. They keep back copies of stories."

Eric set out once more, hoping there might be some conclusive facts to be gained in Maryborough. The old obituary notice listed one daughter, Anne Blackwell, of Victoria. There was no other address. Victoria! That was the state from which he had received her last communication. Her friend Margaret had rented an apartment in the city of Geelong, and Anne had shared it for a short while. Eric had thought of starting there when he first arrived, but it seemed like hunting for a needle in a haystack. He didn't even know Margaret's surname. However, before he left Sydney on his wanderings, he had attempted to communicate with the apartment owners. He spoke with a helpful long-distance operator who connected him with the managers, but this turned out to be futile. No, they had no recollection of the girls he referred to. A lot of people had come and gone since then. Sorry.

His pursuit of the elusive Evans couple had seemed a better way, but now he was faced with retracing his steps for a thousand miles and adding many hundreds more to those. He would go personally to the apartment house and stir the memories of the managers to try to find something they might have remembered. It was a long shot, but what did he have to lose?

This visit, too, seemed to be a dead end. The managers of "The Sunny Side Flats" were negative in their responses.

"Look, mate," the husband said, "like I told you on the phone, I'd like to help you, but the flat those girls rented sixteen years ago has been rented by a lot of other people in the meantime." He thought for a minute and then continued. "I have a faint recollection that one was dark-haired and the other a redhead; both pretty."

"You would remember the pretty ones," his wife snorted. The couple reminded Eric of Jack Sprat and his wife. The husband was stringy and weatherbeaten, the woman plump and complacent. She sat back and worked some macrame as they spoke.

"They didn't stay too long," the husband said. "I don't know where they went. I think the dark one went up north some place. Didn't leave a forwarding address with us—maybe they did at the post office, but they don't forward mail over a year. Hell, it's been a long time. What do you expect?"

"Wait!" his wife cried with a note of triumph. "I remember something. The redhead got married. A little rushed, if you asked me. Just went down to the registry office one afternoon, got married and left the next day. I felt sorry for her."

"Her married name is Blackwell," Eric prompted. "Do you recall her husband's first name?" Eric's heart pounded, hoping for another scrap of information.

"No, but you could probably find it in the registry office."

"Of course." He felt like a fool. Why hadn't he thought of that before? He just wasn't using clear judgment any more. Now if he could just get hold of some tangible information!

The wife's protuberant eyes stared at him for a moment, filled with suspicion. "What do you want to know for?"

"My sister worked with her in Tokyo and asked me to

look her up if I could," Eric replied glibly, surprised how easily the lie sprang to his tongue. "They were close friends but somehow lost contact after Anne moved here. Do you remember anything else about them? Any information would help."

The woman shook her head. "I don't remember anything else. They sure didn't confide in me. I didn't like him. He seemed rough and crude, not her type at all." Eric cringed. "Oh, yes—he had a property out west—a sheep station." She laughed at the recollection. "I called him a black sheep behind his back—a combination of Blackwell and sheep, you know," She explained it as though her American visitor were too dense to make the connection. "It struck me as funny."

"It is funny," Eric agreed quickly. "Can you remember anything more about the property—like its name or where it's located?" Eric found himself holding tightly to the arms of the chair as he stared into the woman's eyes, as if he could will her to recall some little detail.

She looked off into space, her fingers rubbing her chubby cheeks. She began to shake her head and then said, "Wait now. There is something else. I haven't thought about this for years, but it was odd, and I guess it just stuck in my mind."

"Yes?" Eric leaned forward, scarcely daring to breathe.

"It had to do with sheep, or wool—something like that. Yes, it was wool! Wooloorama Station. Now why would I remember that after all these years?"

Eric shook hands with both of his benefactors, thankful that the wife had such a penchant for gossipy details. He went to the registry office and obtained a copy of the marriage certificate. The groom's name was Benjamin Blackwell, age thirty-eight, the bride was Anne Evans, age nineteen. The address given was the flat in Geelong. Eric's shoulders drooped. He was close, so close, and yet so far. There must be some way he could get a current address. Then another idea occurred to him—sheep stations must be recorded somewhere. Wool was sold at auction; checks were processed through the Wool Board. He would make further inquiries in that direction—some new information would surely turn up.

His hunch proved fruitful. Wooloorama Station was listed via Dimboola, Victoria. He took out his map and studied it, plotting his itinerary. Dimboola was considerably off the beaten track, farther north and west toward New South Wales, so he would need to stock up on extra supplies. Some of these stations were huge, and amenities infrequent. The last lap of his journey loomed ahead, and optimism and anxiety alternated.

The countryside yielded no surprises. Rolling grassy terrain stretched on either side of the dirt road as far as he could see. Sheep grazed placidly until he drew near, and then they bolted. The lushness of the landscape indicated that rain was plentiful here, close to the seacoast. He found the grass shorter and in some places sparse, the farther he traveled northwest. Homesteads were less numerous, road traffic infrequent. Fences separating paddocks enclosed larger and larger areas. The land became less desirable than that which he had passed through earlier, and Eric wondered what he would find at Wooloorama

Station. He was gratified when he saw the sign indicating the road to the town of Dimboola. He was nearing the end of the trail now.

As he approached the last gate into Wooloorama Station, he wished with his whole heart that he had never started this quest. He recognized that his own selfish needs had driven him to this, and the potential of bringing distress to all concerned was great. He could not realistically presume a past acquaintance between his sister and Anne unless conditions were just right. Anne could not acknowledge any tie with him, and at best he could see the lad and be on his way. He would have to pretend he was a lost traveler, which in itself was far-fetched. What American new to the country would be wandering so far from the beaten track? But Americans had a reputation for daring and adventure, didn't they? Maybe he could get away with a combination of excuses. He would just have to use intuition.

Two men were replacing posts on a section of fence as he drove up: one a leathery-skinny fellow and the other a grizzled, burly, red-faced man who stared at him with questioning eyes. He realized this older man might be Blackwell and feared that his pretense of being lost would be recognized instantly as a fabrication. He quickly chose a different approach.

"I'm a writer," he said. "I know I'm far from the main track, but they told me in Dimboola about your property, and I thought I might pick up some local color." The barrel-chested man appraised him without comment. "I arrived recently, and I'm generally just wandering around, avoiding the big cities." The man let Eric talk on without replying. "I've never been on a working sheep station, and I hoped you might let me explore." Still there was no response. "I don't want to take you from your work," Eric added lamely.

"A Yank, eh?" The man finally answered. "We don't see many out here." There was no welcome tone in his response. Eric walked over to the fence. The man laid down his shovel but did not extend his hand. "The name's Blackwell." He waved his hand at the surrounding area. "You can see we've got our work cut out for us. Haven't had enough rain, and the sheep are thin."

"Yes, I can see that. Weather sure can play hell." Eric wrinkled his brow. "Blackwell? My sister knew a girl who married a fellow named Blackwell. They worked together for a time in Tokyo. Only her name was Anne Evans then. They lost contact after awhile." He waited, hoping to pry out additional information from this surly man.

Blackwell stared down at the ground for a moment as though debating whether to offer the customary hospitality to a stranger and then said, "I can spare a few minutes. Come on up to the house. We can have a drink and a yarn."

"I wouldn't want to put your wife out," Eric began solicitously, but Blackwell cut him off.

"She's dead. No problem."

"Dead!" The word leapt from Eric's lips involuntarily.

He felt the color draining from his face and could not control it. He had never anticipated this, not even with all his planning. Blackwell stared, baffled at his stricken countenance, and then comprehension set in.

"You're the bloke who knocked her up, aren't you? She never told me it was a Yank." Blackwell spat, and his small pig-like eyes blazed with smoldering intensity. "You've got a hell of a nerve lying your way in here. I'd get out of here fast if I was you. On second thought ..." He advanced toward Eric with doubled fists.

Eric took a step backward. "Yes, you're right about that. I did come here under false pretenses, and I deserve anything you might do. But believe me, I would have married Anne if I could have—the damned war came between us." His eyes pleaded for understanding. "I've never stopped wondering about her. I just wanted to know how she and the child were."

"Oh. The child, eh? So she wrote you about Sandy, did she? Then Anne was a real slut, keeping up with you behind my back."

"No! You misunderstand. I never had any communication with her since ... I just ... Oh, God, what's the use?" He turned away, miserable and humiliated. "Just tell me what happened to Anne." His words almost constricted in his throat.

"She died of a burst appendix three years ago." Blackwell gloated over Eric's pain. "So you came too late to see your lover."

Lord, she must have been miserable with this man, Eric thought. Poor Anne. He turned back and stood his ground—

he'd come too far to quit now, no matter what the consequences. He faced a belligerent, vengeful man. "Is the boy all right?"

"The boy? Forget it!" A cunning expression crossed his face. "You'll not see your by-blow now or ever. Serves you right."

"He's not dead, too?" Eric cried. At that moment Blackwell could have beaten him to a pulp, and Eric wouldn't have resisted. Blackwell chuckled, pleasure emanating from him at his opponent's dismay.

"No, Yank. Sandy flew the coop a while back, and it's no loss to me. Nothing but trouble. Now you'd better get out of here, too, if you know what's good for you."

"Can you just tell me where he went? Please." Eric was humbling himself now. He'd grovel to get the information if he had to. He recognized the sadistic nature of the man, but hoped that Blackwell might slip with some revealing fact. Anger sometimes loosened the tongue. It didn't happen.

"I don't know where he is, and I wouldn't tell you if I knew. I don't give a damn. Now get moving." He looked at the caravan. "Hell, the road's too narrow for you to turn around here. I'll have to open the gate for you or I'll be stuck with your mangy carcass." He stomped away.

The second workman had continued mending the fence, his back turned, apparently oblivious to the altercation. Now he spoke softly but hurriedly. "I heard you asking about the missus. She was a fine lady, deserved better. I don't owe Ben Blackwell any favors. There was talk in the shearing shed of Sandy going to Coober Pedy. Try there."

With a whispered, "Thanks," and a brief tilt of his head, Eric acknowledged the man's contribution and drove through the opened gate. Blackwell glowered at him as he turned around and spat again as Eric drove away.

He consulted a map when he reentered Dimboola and discovered he had almost a thousand miles to go before he would reach the opal town of Coober Pedy on this last lap of his journey. He was getting proficient at switching kilometers to miles now, but he wondered how many "last laps" he would have to go around before finding Sandy. At least he had the boy's name and a chance of finding him in Coober Pedy.

Eric clenched his fists. Yes, he had the name, and he had finally arrived in Coober Pedy, but what good was it to him if it just brought out con artists like Peter Bagley? He knew he had to get out of the caravan and walk off his frustration. Better yet, maybe Molly was on duty tonight, and if she weren't too busy, she might spare him a few minutes.

CHAPTER TWELVE

ERIC'S JUMBLED THOUGHTS GAVE HIM NO PEACE on his way to the hospital. Hospitals reminded him of his father's death and the hardship it had brought to his mother. When Molly unlocked the door to welcome him, her smile quickly changed into a look of concern.

"You're not injured?"

"No. I guess I was just a little lonely. I saw the light and ..." His voice trailed away, and he stood there feeling foolish.

"Do come in, Eric. There is only one patient here, and he's fast asleep. I was feeling a little lonely myself." She gestured for him to sit down.

He didn't know where to begin. He wasn't ready to explain his interest in Sandy yet. Eric cleared his throat. "I was thinking about my mother tonight and—"

"Eric!" The surprise in her voice and the strange look on her face took him aback.

"I'm sorry, Molly. I shouldn't presume you'd be interested in my family."

"No, Eric, it's not that. It's just that I was sitting here

thinking about my poor mother, too, and this seems more than a coincidence. Some Aborigines believe in mental telepathy, and I've seen examples of it with my own grandmother. This is truly uncanny. My thoughts were sad."

"And so were mine. My mother died from exhaustion, taking care of my step-father after he had a severe stroke. He was a miserable person. I was in the service at that time and couldn't help. She deserved better." He would have liked to tell her more, but he felt inhibited. He could only relive the next scene in his own mind.

"Mama," he had told her shortly after she married Sven Gustavson. "I can't stand to see you living in this hell house."

"Eric, you mustn't talk that way. The pastor said we must give thanks for everything."

"You can't be happy in this situation."

"Son, you are confusing happiness with joy. Happiness comes from the outside. Joy comes from within. You and Lars and Hulda give me great joy. Don't you see? I am joyful that God gives me the strength and will to endure."

Eric had turned away, moved by his mother's answer. The word "endure" struck him like a dagger. He would not argue with her again.

He shook himself from his reverie. Molly was sharing something of her own past.

"I never knew my mother. She died in childbirth. My

grandmother wanted to keep me at the station, but my father insisted on taking me to the Lutheran mission. He felt I would have more advantages there. I understand from Mrs. McCurdy that there were so many rituals for the newborn that never would be performed if he took me away, and my grandmother feared for my spirit. But she did make him promise that I would be allowed to come visit her, and my foster father, Pastor Holmgren, honored that pledge."

"Do you ever see your father?"

"No. He was a drifter. He stayed longer at Wiluru Station than any place because he loved my mother, but after her death he moved on. He sent money to the mission for the next two years, and then we never heard from him again. He named me Molly after his Irish mother." She sat quietly, contemplating her hands, wishing to tell him more but unsure of the reception. Later, maybe, when she knew him better, she could tell the story her grandmother revealed to her. It was the only reference she ever made concerning her mother's early life. Even now she remembered the comfort of curling up on her grandmother's lap while she related the incredible and sometimes frightening tale.

"Your mother was six years old and your uncle, Goonabi, was eleven when we went on this journey," her grandmother said. "We were going to a corroboree, a gathering of tribes for special ceremonies. Goonabi was being initiated into the tribe. It was such an important event that I dared to disobey my husband."

Members of the tribe had camped recently on the out-skirts of town and made contact with Niboorana. They did not come to her dwelling because she could not extend the mandatory hospitality due her people. Achmet, her husband, would not have allowed it. But they had communicated with her, informing her that Goonabi had reached the age when he should be initiated into the tribe. As the group struggled to maintain its customs, let alone its existence, each male child was of supreme importance. As with other tribes, there were fewer and fewer full-blooded boys, and each played a pre-cious part in the continuation of the sacred rites of their people. Niboorana knew this was true—to achieve manhood Goonabi must go through this initial ceremony. Subsequent rituals would continue the process, but this first indoctrina-tion was vital.

A corroboree had been called at a distant sacred place, and members of the tribe were gathered together from various parts of their territory. Soon her people would be leaving for this event. Women were forbidden to watch the actual cir-cumcision, but there would be plenty of food and gossip to share. She longed to go but dreaded telling Achmet. As the day of departure approached, she knew she could not post-pone the confrontation.

Even years later, after many repetitions, Niboorana could still feel her throat tighten as she retold the story. It would take many days journey to get to the corroboree, so she would have to take Ashira along. Ashira was too young to be left behind. She knew that Achmet would forbid her from going. But she must go. The compelling urge within her could not be denied, even by fear.

She squatted next to her husband as he relaxed in his chair after supper. She lighted his pipe and removed his shoes. For several years the government had hoped to dispense with the use of camels for transportation. But since there was not a vehicle manufactured yet capable of managing the rough outback terrain, the animals were important to the movement of scouting expeditions. As her husband was the only one who could handle the camels, this unsavory work continued to be his main occupation. The long and sometimes fruitless trips into the desert, such as the one he had just completed, left him weary at the end of the excursion.

"I saw his exhaustion," Niboorana told Molly, "so I began quietly, explaining the importance of the initiation."

"You can't go," he told me.

"Goonabi must be initiated. It is time," I insisted.

"You can't go."

"If Goonabi is not circumcised, he will be an outcast from the tribe. He will be scorned."

"If Goonabi wants to go, he can go. But you must stay here."

Your grandfather was firm, but I dared to persist. "I need to be with my people," I said.

"I am your people. Who will cook for me and wash my

clothes? Who will take care of Mohammed and Ashira when I am at work?"

I lowered my eyes, Molly, so he would not see my determination. I was so torn—it was unheard of in our culture for a wife to defy her husband's wishes.

Early the next morning before dawn had licked the tops of the sand hills, I awakened Goonabi and Ashira. I took a small parcel of food and water, and we silently stole from our little dwelling. I held your mother's hand tightly and Goonabi walked swiftly before us. When we reached the encampment, the tribe already was stirring and about to depart. I greeted them and positioned my family in line for the trek and forced from my mind the thought of home and husband and my other son. I shed all the trappings of my confinement in the settlement and became one with my people again.

Goonabi looked at me with concern and asked how long the ceremony would take. Being a woman, I could not advise him, and also I did not know all the secrets. Although it was forbidden to observe the rituals, a few women had actually witnessed parts of them and whispered to me about the arcane activities. I knew that it would be painful but decided not to worry Goonabi.

"Goonabi," I said, " I know little about what will happen, but I do know that it will take several days, and you and I will be separated during much of it. I was present only at two other corroborees where initiations took place. We women were allowed to watch the young boys being decorated with sacred signs. Red and yellow ocher pigments were used with white pipe clay and charcoal. The men will tell you what the symbols mean."

"Is that all you could see?" he asked.

"No, there were dancers armed with spears and woomeras who chanted in a circle around the initiates. We women formed our own circle some distance away where we made much wailing and stamping of feet."

"And then?" Goonabi prompted.

Molly, I dared not relate all I had been told. Carefully I chose information I could reveal safely. I told him, "The boys were hoisted onto the shoulders of their sponsors and then tossed into the air and caught before they hit the ground. This took place the first day."

Your uncle said, "That doesn't sound too difficult to go through. What happened next?"

"At dawn the men arose and formed a circle. Each initiate was separated from the group and a spear was thrust in front of him. We women could approach a boy, and oh, how we moaned and wept, but he could not speak to us. With this silent farewell the boy cut himself off from his mother and sisters. Then the men hurried him away to a secret place. The yagoo, the tribal elder, was in charge now. I cannot tell you more."

"Goonabi did not reply to my story but held his head high with pride, excited that he was one of the chosen ones. I was confident that he would pass his tests of endurance without flinching. There was more that women had confided to me that I could not speak about to him. The yagoo—a fearsome figure ornamented with stripes of ocher, feathers glued to his naked body with blood from his veins—opened the ceremonies for older youths who received higher degrees of manhood. We women shuddered when the yagoo would hold the boy tightly, then turn him so his back was facing him. An older relative would step forward as the boy was held in a viselike grip and perform the circumcision with a small stone knife. Warm ashes would be used to stanch the blood flow. The lad must not cry out during the initiation or he would be forever disgraced and cast out from the tribe. He probably would die of shame. Much of the ceremonial detail had been surmised by the women. It meant death to be caught spying, but sometimes it was possible to observe a little without being obvious."

Niboorana knew that the honored initiate would then be decorated with fresh ocher and given a special headband. Then he would receive the congratulations of his male relatives and be brought a little food prepared especially by his mother. But she could not see him yet. The initiate must stay out of sight of the women. After a specified time his mother and sisters would make a little bark bed near the camp on which he could lie. They could bring him food but could not touch him. Tears came to Niboorana's eyes as she spoke of the pain her son had endured. "I was unable to comfort him. But I had to reject such weak thinking. The ways of our people were harsh but necessary. They made possible the survival of the tribe. The men had to be able to withstand great pain, and this ceremony was just the beginning of their being hardened to the realities of their existence. I had little knowledge of future ceremonies, but some time later the carving of cicatrices, the special patterns on chests and backs would take place. I have seen the scars from these on men of my tribe many times. I have only heard rumors about the blood bathing and drinking of blood. These rituals were so secret that they could not be witnessed even by the newly initiated."

Niboorana had not told Molly every detail the first time she shared the story, not wanting to frighten her. As she told and re-told of the adventure over the years, she added more as she thought Molly could understand. Her granddaughter had particularly enjoyed the part where her mother, Ashira, had kept up, following over the rough terrain with agile steps. "I was so proud of her, Molly. At no time did she loiter or complain. Her legs were sturdy, not spindly limbs sometimes seen in Aboriginal women, and I was pleased that although not full-blooded, she fit in so well with the others. Then your mother looked at me with a puzzled frown and asked, 'Mother, will I be initiated, too?'"

"No," I told her. "Girls do not go through initiation ceremonies. It is only for boys."

"Ashira pouted in disappointment, and I knew that she wanted the extra attention that such an activity would bring and had yet to understand that a woman's life never was the equal of a man's. Always it would be different. I knew I must continually plant such information in her mind, but perhaps I could ease some of her feeling of rejection now.

"Women have special abilities that men do not have," I told her. "They have babies when they are old enough to be wives."

"Ashira thought about this and then smiled, 'That's nice. Babies are fun,' and she was satisfied. You see, Molly, your dear mother looked forward to having a baby when she was old enough, and she would have loved you so much if she had lived. She was a dear, sweet woman." At this point Molly's grandmother always gave her a warm hug, and then Molly would ask, "What happened next?"

"Molly, I had fulfilled my duty to Goonabi. Already I had spent many more days than planned and needed to return to my husband and other son. Goonabi appeared before me as I began my simple preparations."

"Mother, I have made a decision." Goonabi looked at me with new maturity; and he seemed to have increased in stature. I knew in my heart that the change portended separation.

"Yes, Goonabi?"

"I am staying with the tribe. I am not going back to the settlement."

"I bowed my head in resignation. It was right for him to do this. Had my circumstances been different, I, too, would have stayed. Ashira and I traveled home alone."

At this point Molly always asked, "What happened when you got home?" And her grandmother always answered, "That is another story, and some time I will tell you." But the "some time" never came, no matter how much Molly had pleaded. After a while, she stopped asking, but she wondered why this important part was never revealed.

Now, as she sat in comfortable silence with Eric, both lost in their own thoughts, she decided that she would write to Mrs. McCurdy for any information about her grandmother's early life. After all, whatever had taken place before they came to Wiluru Station must have been traumatic, and she wanted to know. It was part of her heritage. She glanced at Eric. No, she would wait to confide in him about such Aboriginal matters until she felt he could understand without judging or being repelled.

CHAPTER THIRTEEN

MARIA PASSED THE LONG DAYS EMBROIDERING the intricate stitches her grandmother had taught her. Sometimes she looked at magazines from the Greek store that Anastasia loaned her. She still did not speak or read English well, and there were no books here in her own language. But she could look at pictures and make out some of the information. She was the only woman staying at the Eleven Mile field, and she looked forward to the times when they drove into Coober Pedy for groceries and someone to talk to.

"Duro, I'd like to stay longer in town next time and visit with Anastasia," she said one day after they had been shopping. Fresh meat would not keep, and she hoped that by preparing a nice dinner, she could soften his reluctance. "She's my only friend."

"I don't think she has much time for visiting. Her father works her pretty hard."

"He's lucky to have her. She's very efficient and friendly."

"*She's* lucky to have *him*. Where else could she get a job with an arm like that?"

Maria felt sorry for her young friend, who was born with a malformed arm that ended in a stump at the elbow. Miniature fingers at the end of the stump made it look even more grotesque. Anastasia wore a long sleeved dress and tried to hide the deformity as best she could, but occasionally it was revealed, much to her distress. Maria, tempted to complain about her own fate, held back, rationalizing her friend had a greater cross to bear.

Duro seemed happier now that he was working at something he enjoyed and could share in the profits. He became less abrasive in his speech and manner, and life for Maria was more endurable. But she longed to return to Sydney. She wondered how she ever could have complained about it. It seemed like paradise compared to her home now. She did not mind the noise and crowds in retrospect; even her job in the bakery took on a rosy aura through faulty remembrance. How stimulating everything had been there! Now here she was, and here she would have to stay. Her resentment grew deeper as the days passed.

At the end of autumn little opal of good quality had been found, just enough to keep them in food and petrol. Marcos put down another shaft, but after the eighty-foot limit had been reached, nothing, not even potch, had turned up. There was much jasper, which the drill operators complained dulled the bits, and opal clay, but nothing to indicate a good find. Marcos staked another claim, which proved barren although it was near a productive one. Duro began to worry.

"We'll keep trying," Marcos told him. "That is how it goes—riches one day, nothing for weeks." They put down another shaft, and at the thirty-five foot level they found a seam of opal that showed promise. They dug carefully and found what appeared to have good fire. They were able to make up a small parcel and took it to town.

Before they met the Chinese buyers in their room at the Opal Inn, Marcos had warned Duro, "The Chinese are really stingy. I'd rather deal with the Americans. They're tough bargainers, but we understand each other. These fellows are the only buyers in town now, and we need the money. We'll do the best we can."

The two Chinese would not budge from their last offer, which was much less than Marcos wanted. The buyers shrugged. There was other opal to be found on the field. Take it or leave it. Marcos took it reluctantly. The buyers were not hungry—he was, and he needed money for petrol and fuses and gelignite. Soon he would be blasting to speed up the work and hopefully to expose more opal. When everything went out and nothing came in, former profits disappeared rapidly.

Duro received $1,000 for his share. He had worked for four months.

Winter with a few light rains brought a change from the heat. It also brought a mouse plague. The cat caught the first mice that invaded the shack but soon grew too fat and lazy to keep up with the horde. Maria set traps and emptied them frequently, but she became discouraged long before the mice did. She tried to plug up any entrance holes, but the shack was like a sieve and the pesky creatures found ways in. She kept all food covered and washed the tabletop so often that she lost count.

Several times a day she would call, "Tiger! Come! Here's another mouse," but the cat just stretched and then curled himself up into a ball, disdainfully ignoring the challenge. After a few weeks, the plague seemed to dissipate, as mysteriously as it had arrived.

The days could be quite nippy, and the nights sometimes surprisingly cold. The mine remained at the same temperature, and while Duro was comfortable, Maria suffered. She added extra clothing on the days when there was a weather change, but that didn't provide respite from the piercing wind. It periodically whipped the dust into cyclonic tempests that roared across the land like demons. On the days when the dust storms swept in, nothing could keep the fine powder out of the shack. It drifted in through every crack and lay everywhere in thick, stifling piles.

Fortunately there were enough pleasant days between the violent dust storms, which helped Maria keep her rising hysteria under control. Others in Coober Pedy seemed to ignore weather inconveniences and even joked about them.

"The storms are not that frequent, really," Anastasia told Maria in an attempt to comfort her. "Sometimes weeks go by, often a month, without them." Anastasia liked the opal town. "In good weather, the sky is so blue, the air is so clean, and there are many things to do. There's a drive-in movie and bar-becues and sometimes programs at the school ..."

Maria cut her short. "For you, maybe, but not for me."

"There are always tourists coming through, interesting people. You do such lovely embroidery. Perhaps you could sell some of your work."

Maria considered her suggestion. She admired the Greek girl. In spite of her handicap, Anastasia was always cheerful and optimistic, harboring no bitterness about her situation.

"I accept that I will never marry," she said.

"But you are so pretty!"

Anastasia smiled shyly at the compliment and then shook her head. "No, when men see my deformed arm, they are revolted. I try to keep it hidden when I am working in the store, but sometimes my sleeve slips back, and I see in their eyes what they are thinking. The doctors told me it was from some medication my mother took early in her pregnancy, a terrible accident. It cannot be inherited, but no man would be so convinced. They would be afraid to take me as wife and have children. So I do the bookkeeping and ordering and work at the counter when things get busy. Most of the time I try to keep out of sight, but business is picking up now, and it isn't easy to hide."

"I do not seem to get pregnant," Maria sighed. "I ... I had a baby once, but ... it died. I think it would make a differ-ence in my life if I could have a child. Duro would like a son. I know he blames me for not having one. Oh, Anastasia, I am so unhappy!" She began to sob, and the Greek girl comforted her with warmth and concern.

"If we cannot have what we want, then we must accept what we have and find some joy in it."

"I try," Maria answered, brushing away her tears, "and things do seem a little better. But I cannot bear living in that shack any more—if we just could move into town!"

"Perhaps you can find a better place before next summer. Of course you cannot live where you are then. The temperature is over 45 Celsius many days."

"Marcos will let us use his dugout during the hot weather. He goes to Sydney during the worst of the summer, but he wants Duro to keep an eye on the mine and the equipment. I wish we could go back to Sydney permanently, but Duro likes to feel independent. There is more freedom here, I guess."

"But it's hard on women," Anastasia said.

"Oh, yes!" Maria agreed. "I would give anything to be able to leave."

"Don't fret about it so," Anastasia soothed. "You can adjust if you try. Except for the summer, the other seasons are nice, and maybe in time you can leave when it's hot. It's really very pleasant here most of the time."

"Oh, you just take everything with a smile. Sometimes I hate you!" Maria cried. "No! I don't mean that. But you just can't be happy all the time."

"I don't have any choice," the Greek girl answered simply. "And neither do you."

Maria gnawed at her lower lip rebelliously and then sighed. "I guess I don't."

One day after a fruitless search for new leads Marcos approached Duro with a worried expression. "I've just come from the post office. My wife isn't well and wants me to give up the opal business. My brother has been after me to come work in his restaurant in Sydney. I guess it's time for me to move back."

"What about the mine? Maybe there's good opal yet. There are areas we haven't touched." A worried note hovered in Duro's voice.

"I've been lying here thinking. I can't go home penniless. I'm considering selling the blower and truck. Would you be interested in working the mine the old way, with buckets and windlass? That's how I started, and a lot of miners do it that way still. I'd leave the ladders and other equipment. You could live here and give me, say 20 percent of your find in return for the rent on the dugout and materials."

A perplexed frown creased Duro's forehead. He was not used to making hasty decisions of such importance. "I would need another partner. It's not safe working alone."

"You're right. There's a new man, a fellow Serb, who showed up in town a few days ago looking for work. His name is Lucas."

"I saw him at the club, and I wasn't too impressed—a lot of bragging and posturing. You know the kind. But he looks strong as an ox. I could approach him about it."

They both knew it was better to stick to one's own nationality—the risks were fewer, and who else could a man trust
in this business but one of his own countrymen?

Marcos asked, "Do you want to talk it over with your wife?"

"What for? Maria will do what I want."

"You're lucky to have a wife who's so accommodating."

"She'd better be. I don't go along with all this emancipa-
tion for women."

"Well, Duro, things are a little different here in Australia."

"Not for me."

The following week Duro watched Marcos leave with
mixed feelings. His friend had taught him many things. Duro
had become an expert with explosives and felt competent to
grade and sell any opal the mine produced. That Marcos trusted
him to share honestly gave him pride. He would not let him
down. Now he would be his own boss for the first time in his
life. Everything was working out well for him.

When he mentioned that he was getting a new partner,
Maria shrugged. It made little difference to her what decisions were made. She was never consulted about anything,
and her opinion would not have mattered if she had expressed
one. But when Duro told her they now could move into
Marcos' dugout permanently, her eyes shone. The new partner would stay out at the mine. With uplifted heart she packed
their belongings and she helped load the ute. Taking one last
look at the place where she had spent so many miserable
months, she slammed the door with all her might. That night

for the first time since landing in Australia, she felt attractive and happy.

The comfort of the dugout pleased her. The thick clay walls, hewn out of the cliff, protected from the hot sun during the day and held the warmth in at night. There was one large room, once a drive that had been enlarged in the original mine that served as a sitting, eating and sleeping room. The kitchen was in a smaller room, furnished with a bottled gas stove. Besides shelf spaces dug from the clay walls there was a cabinet for utensils and a work table. A bed stood on one side next to a wooden clothes press, and in the middle of the larger room was a table with wooden chairs around it. Two windows were dug to the outside, about eighteen centimeters away, and fitted with glass. A few rugs scattered about protected feet from the cool clay. A pipe running through the ceiling provided ventilation.

Maria was unprepared when Duro suggested that his new partner be invited to dinner some night. This was a changed Duro. He never suggested anything. He always demanded. "Would you mind?" he asked, and she scarcely believed her ears. "He's all alone and probably hasn't eaten too well. He's been down on his luck. He's a good worker, though."

"Of course I will, Duro. It will be pleasant to have company. Just name the time."

She looked forward to their first guest. Being within walking distance of the shops now, she could buy a variety of food and had the facilities to prepare it well.

When Duro opened the door to welcome his new partner, Maria froze. She would recognize that face anywhere. How could she forget the man who had used and then abandoned her? Quickly she turned her face away so as not to betray her emotions. What could she do? If Duro even suspected Lucas was her old lover, he would kill him, and then what would happen to her? For a moment she almost panicked and felt herself losing control. Duro's sharp voice steadied her.

"Maria, bring wine! Sit down Lucas. Today things looked a little better. Maybe our luck is changing, eh?"

Lucas glanced at Maria's impassive face as he accepted the glass of wine, and a brief acknowledgment flashed in his eyes. He said very little, Duro did most of the talking. They discussed new possibilities in the mine and the increasing cost of supplies. Maria sat apart, her head bowed over her embroidery, saying nothing.

When Lucas started to leave, he shook Maria's hand and stared at her with an amused smile. "Thank you for a pleasant evening," he said. "Your husband and I work very well together. It's dangerous down in the mine, and we have to trust each other."

She nodded mutely and removed her limp hand from his. "Good night," she answered. She felt cold and reached for a sweater when the door closed.

Duro gave her a playful slap on the buttocks. "You behaved yourself tonight, Maria. You're turning into a good wife."

CHAPTER FOURTEEN

JANET PUSHED THE LIMP CURLS from her forehead, sighing at the appearance of another tourist coach. It was rare to have two in one day, but rival companies were bringing more tourists to the "Red Centre," and Coober Pedy was a popular stopping place on the way to Alice Springs. The coach had been full, and everyone was demanding tea at the same time. Not that she could blame them—the road up here was frightful, and if the air conditioning wasn't operating well, the passengers usually were exhausted and cranky when they arrived. Her sympathy went out to them because she had traveled that road herself and knew its discomfort, but that didn't make it easier for her.

"Miss, bring me a menu."

"I want a beer, a cold one."

"I just want your special—whatever it is. I'm too tired to make a decision."

"Young lady, a cool drink, please. You do have ice?"

It had gone on and on, and now, bone tired and ready to drop, she had to stay alert, forcing a smile. She had been serving tables at the Opal Inn since her arrival months before. She was glad to have a job since plans had not worked out as expected. Being broke in a strange town was a frightening affair.

When a lull in serving finally came, she scurried to the ladies' amenities room and splashed some cool water on her face, careful not to waste any. As she peered into the mirror, she was not entirely pleased with what was reflected back. Her nose seemed a little sharp, her lips a trifle thin, but her hair was beautiful, and that compensated for less desirable features. "Strawberry blonde" George had called it when he thrilled her with her first kiss. He had run his big calloused hands through her curls and teased her until she kissed him.

"You're really something," he said, and then as an afterthought, "How old are you, honey?"

"Sixteen," she had lied, blissful in his arms.

When her father had caught them, he'd taken a stock whip to George, shouting, "She's only thirteen!" after which George had fled and her father had turned on her, beating her unmercifully. Janet remembered that abuse so vividly that it was some time before she encouraged another suitor.

Everything she did seemed to antagonize her father, and his partiality toward her younger sisters embittered her. Her mother used to intervene on her behalf, but her efforts had proved fruitless, and often intensified the violent atmosphere. Although her mother had cautioned her to keep a low profile when she was growing up, Janet found herself deliberately crossing her father just to get him riled. When Colin came to work at their place, she visualized him as the route to escape from her unhappy plight and was more than ready to succumb to his blandishments, which were not long in coming. She convinced herself that Colin was different from George. He was knowledgeable and self-assured, smooth and wickedly exciting. He made her feel like a woman.

"Colin, take me away with you," she begged one night after she had sneaked out of the house to meet him.

"Where do you want to go?" he laughed. "This is a big country."

"I'm serious, Colin. I'll go anywhere you want to go. I'll follow you to the ends of the earth."

"That's a big promise." He could see that his bantering distressed her, so he added, "Do you mean it?"

Her dark blue eyes looked deeply into his, imploring him. "Yes, I mean it. Just tell me when."

Colin shuffled his feet, doubt registering on his handsome face. "I really didn't expect to ..." He stopped. "I do a lot of moving around, you know."

"I don't care," she said. "I won't be any bother. I'll work, too, and be a good help."

"Look," he told her. "If we go together, your father might follow us and make charges against me. You're still under age to marry. Work's finishing up here, so I'll be leaving next week. As soon as I'm settled, I'll write you and you can join me. Okay?"

She shook her head. "No. I want to go with you now, Colin. Not later."

"It's better for you to wait. Then your father will never think we're together."

"That's for sure."

He told her where he was headed and promised to write when he got there, but as the weeks passed, she received nothing from him. Janet sulked as she did her chores, slapping at her whiny sisters when they wouldn't help her, always on the lookout for her father's heavy hand. Nothing she did pleased him, but she admitted to herself that she tried only half-heartedly. She lived with frustration and resentment. She watched each day when the mail carrier stopped at their post box, rushing out to be first, but there was never anything for her. She began to wonder if her father somehow had intercepted Colin's letters.

"Tom," she asked their old handyman one day, "do you think my father could have gotten to the mail truck sometime before I did? Have you ever seen any letters addressed to me?" He shook his head, and her frustration deepened.

Janet grew angry and defensive even now as she thought of the final quarrel. It was over a trivial matter—she had accidentally burned the scones.

"You did it deliberately!" her father shouted.

"I did not!" she retorted, and when he called her a vile name, she hurled one of the hot scones at him, hitting him in the face. He grabbed her and slapped her face with brutal strength. She shrank back from the pain and ran sobbing from the room. That night she finalized plans that of necessity had been rather nebulous until now. She was determined to leave.

She packed a small valise and caught a few hours of restless sleep. She had saved a small amount of money, which would last her only a short while, so she went to the secret place where she knew her father hid his cash. She had watched with furtive interest the first time he removed a book from the top shelf in the lounge room and placed something in an envelope behind it. Only her mother had enjoyed reading, but there had been very little time for anything recreational with the unending drudgery of her everyday life. Janet knew her father thought the hiding place was secure. She had never indicated by look or word that she knew it was there. It wasn't really stealing, she rationalized. She had worked hard most of her life without compensation or appreciation, so she was taking her just wages, that was all. After extracting a generous amount, she left some of the bills in the envelope. No one could accuse her of being greedy.

She rose before dawn and tiptoed stealthily out of the house. One of the dogs ran up to her and pushed its nose affectionately into her hand. "Good girl, Rosie," Janet whispered, stroking the dog, praying she wouldn't bark in her excitement. Rosie wagged her tail vigorously but stayed quiet. It proved difficult to navigate through the equipment lying haphazardly about the yard on the long walk to the garage. Janet dared not use the torch she had brought. The night was so dark she stumbled several times. She finally reached the garage, and slipped into the Holden. In spite of her excitement, she had had the foresight to bring the keys, which always hung on a hook in the entry of the bungalow. Her father trusted no one and never left the keys in the car, although thefts of vehicles were unheard of in their area.

She started the engine, fearful her father would hear and come running in pursuit before she could back the car out. He could chase her in the ute if she didn't have a good head start. Why hadn't she thought to take those keys, too, or at least to hide them? She backed out slowly and debated whether or not to close the garage door. If the garage door was closed, her father wouldn't even realize she was gone until breakfast time. She decided to close the door and then turned on the low beam lights, heading into the track that would take her to the main road. Her fear was replaced with cold determination. She would never go back, no matter what.

Janet knew that a bus left the town at 8 a.m. each day, barring a mechanical breakdown or inclement weather. She should be able to make it in time with two hours left to complete her trip. She looked at the petrol gauge. The tank was nearly full—a precaution her father fortunately observed, living so far out. She stepped on the accelerator. The lightening sky made each little pothole in the road loom larger, but she was afraid to dodge them for fear of losing control. The ghost gums lining the track swayed slightly in the freshening breeze, giving a spectral appearance that caused her to shiver. She would be so glad to board that bus. Each kilometer she put behind her was a kilometer closer to independence—

and Colin.

I'll leave the keys and a note on the front seat saying I'm going to Sydney, she thought. If he tries to follow me, he'll be going in the wrong direction. At least he can't accuse me of stealing his car.

So here Janet was in Coober Pedy, following an arduous journey that took most of her cash. There was no Colin and no one who knew of him. He had said, "I'm heading for the opal field in the Center," and on that tenuous information she had headed to this remote place. It was the beginning of summer and the heat was horrendous. Fortunately, one of the waitresses at the Opal Inn had quit her job to follow a miner seeking more profitable work elsewhere, and the other one had left for the cooler regions near Adelaide. Janet's arrival and need for work was beneficial to both the owner and the destitute girl, and she was grateful that with her new position came a small bedroom.

Gradually she came to the realization that Colin had betrayed her, and she accepted a date with one of the few miners who was braving the summer heat. When he found that she wasn't an easy conquest, he lost interest. Embittered, she declined further invitations from any more woman-hungry men.

She had heard of Peter Bagley by reputation and observed him curiously when he came in for an occasional meal. She gave him no encouragement but was secretly fascinated by his rugged good looks and quiet demeanor. He basically ignored her, making no attempt to engage her in conversation other than thanking her for her service. One day he raised his eyes from the menu he was studying, and the intensity of his gaze startled her. She recalled afterwards that his eyes were dark brown with an almost liquid softness about them. She began to look forward to his visits. One day he smiled, warmth seeming to flow from his lips that appeared both tender and demanding. One slow evening he put on a display of conviviality that caught her unprepared, and with a captivating tilt of his head he invited her to go to the local drive-in theater with him. Flattered but uncertain, she shook her head. He increased his charm, and she began to waver, finally accepting.

Peter was a perfect gentleman. He bought her sweets and kept his distance during the film. Following the movie, he drove her back to her room at the Inn and did nothing bolder than squeeze her arm as he thanked her for a pleasant evening. Janet, surprised and impressed, looked forward to seeing him again.

He didn't put in an appearance for another week. She wondered why he hadn't tried to see her in the meantime. Is he disappointed in me, she thought. Maybe there's something wrong with me. What do I lack? Was I too cold and unresponsive? Too defensive? He had been so nice, and I hadn't even given him an opportunity to be romantic. But how could I? He didn't even *try* anything.

Her thoughts wandered during the day. Twice her boss reprimanded her when she forgot a customer's order. On another occasion she spilled a tray and was told sharply to keep her mind on her work. She began to fantasize about Peter at night. When he walked into the restaurant one evening, her pulse accelerated. He smiled at her with great warmth and touched her hand when she gave him the menu, letting his fingers linger for a moment. Fire seemed to run up her arm. She smiled back, attempting to look seductive. She was sure all those ugly rumors about him were false.

"There's going to be a full moon Saturday night," Peter said. "I have a special place I'd like to share with you. Will you come?"

Janet couldn't believe her good fortune.

CHAPTER FIFTEEN

ERIC HOPED THE WEATHER WOULD BE PLEASANT for his second date with Molly and also hoped she had tempered her animosity toward his work. At first she had been cool to his invitation to dine out again, and when she finally accepted, something had interfered each time—her work schedule or an emergency at the hospital or weather. The last dust storm hit suddenly with such ferocity that after trying to drive to the hospital with dust smothering his headlights, he gave up and turned back. He had fumed as he sat through the evening, fine powdered clay filtering into the caravan through every infinitesimal crack.

Now he looked at the sky with some anxiety. He had told Molly he would pick her up about 7 p.m., but the grayish-yellow canopy hovering in the sky foretold of another possible dust storm. He wanted tonight to be a special evening, to repair their tenuous relationship. Her seemingly irrational swing from compassion to criticism baffled him, but recognizing that his abrupt manner at their first date might have precipitated her reaction, softened his thoughts. She had been very pleasant the night at the hospital when they reminisced about their pasts.

The weather improved, and Molly was ready, wearing a pastel skirt and blouse that again made her appear more like a school girl than a mature woman when he arrived to pick her up. She appeared blissfully unaware of his perception and contrary to his expectations, gave him a radiant smile. His spirits lifted at her positive reception. He parked the utility and escorted her toward the Opal Inn. A group of unkempt men lounged at the entrance to the public bar and smirked as they walked by.

"Pretty bird," said one, who obviously had drunk more than his capacity. "Isn't that the new sister?"

"Yeah. I heard she's a 'gin.' Think so?" asked his companion.

"Naw, too light. There's something about her, though. Watta you think?" He turned to another man.

"I dunno, mate. Got nice legs—better than a 'gin.' Those Aborigine legs are always so damn skinny. I'd like to have her legs under me!" The comment was followed by raucous laughter.

Eric's hand tightened on Molly's arm, and the faint scar on his face became more pronounced. She shook her head. "Do nothing," she whispered. "They're harmless. Just too much to drink."

"I won't let them insult you. Go inside."

"No!" she pleaded. "It's nothing, really. I ignore comments like that. Please don't make any trouble. Let it go."

He looked at her dark, eloquent eyes. "I'm not afraid of them, Molly. I can handle myself in a scrap."

"I'm sure you can, but this isn't the time. Please." She tugged on his arm, and he followed her reluctantly into the restaurant. The glow was off the evening.

He never before had hesitated to hold his own against a bully or to champion a woman. He had experienced his share of fights when he started school, as all boys did in that mixed ethnic community of Iron Valley. He had exchanged punches with Italians, Poles, Finns, and "Cousin Jacks," many of whom became his best friends later. That was not true of the bully Antonio, who had taunted him with the nickname, "Scarface Al Capone." He hadn't sought the fight, but he didn't back down from the confrontation. He hadn't won the battle because his adversary was much bigger than he was, but he had gained the respect of his peers.

After his mother had remarried, he had protected both his sister and his mother from Sven Gustavson and his sons. He had begged his mother not to marry the man, but she sadly laid the facts before him. His father's insurance was depleted, and she was unable to find work that could support three children. After a beating in which he inflicted more blows than he received, the two boys made no more unwelcome advances to Hulda. His own audacity in defending his mother when Sven struck her still amazed him. The evening meal was silent, as usual. Sven and the older son glowered, and Eric's mother sat like a frightened shadow. When she rose to clear the table, something exploded in Sven.

"That worthless son of yours plays basketball after school. A childish game! A waste of time!"

Her calloused hands picked at her apron. "He works hard for you late afternoons and weekends."

"Don't stand up for him! You baby him every chance you get. I'm sick of you both!" Sven glared at her with eyes reddened from drinking.

When she tried to pass him in order to remove the dirty dishes, he grabbed her arm and twisted her around. "Did you hear me? I'm sick of you both!" Then he struck her hard across the mouth.

Eric snatched up a knife from the table and leaped forward, the sharp edge at Sven's throat. "If you ever hurt my mother again, I'll kill you!" The words were hot, but his eyes were cold and penetrating. His hand was controlled, the knife not wavering. Sven blinked and looked around helplessly. Karl's face was suffused with fear, but he made no motion to protect his father. Olaf did not move from the opposite side of the table. Eric pressed the blade slightly so his step-father could feel the sharpness. He stared into Sven's terrified eyes and repeated his words. Then he laid the knife on the table. The scene before him was like a tableau—his mother, standing white-faced, her hand to her mouth; his step-brothers rooted to their chairs; Lars frightened but admiring; Hulda seated in anguish. Then Eric fled upstairs, his hands beginning to shake. His mother followed him, crying, and put her arms around him.

"Oh, Eric, Eric!"

"I can't stay here any longer, Mama," he said, his voice cracking. "I'm afraid of what I might do if he hits you again."

"Don't go, Eric, please! Things will be better. You'll see. You're so close to graduation. Don't quit school. He didn't realize what he was doing. He'd been drinking—"

"Stop defending him, Mama. He's a brute."

"I know, Son, but I must stay. Wait until school is out."

His mother's entreaties prevailed, partly because he recognized that he was her only protection. As the days went by, Sven simmered in silence, but there were no more physical or verbal attacks. It was an uneasy truce.

Molly cut into his thoughts. "Most of the men here in Coober Pedy aren't like the ones you saw tonight. They're hard-working, down-to-earth fellows, and basically they respect a woman. Those men out there were just loud-mouthed hooligans."

"You shouldn't have to get used to comments like that," Eric told her, anger scarcely contained in his voice. He was angry at them and angry at himself that he had permitted her to be insulted.

Molly smiled a little wistfully. "When I was growing up, I was quite protected at the mission. But gradually I realized that I was a little different from my step-sister. Visitors treated me like a curiosity sometimes. My hair was quite light when I was young—many Aborigines are almost blond when they're little."

"I've seen pictures of them. I don't understand."

"The Aborigines are a separate race, you know. We are not Negroid—our hair has a different structure, and our pigmentation and facial characteristics are different. Some people call us 'Blackfellers', but we aren't."

"You seem to have accepted your position in society with grace. Don't you ever fight back? Are you always so docile about discrimination?"

Molly laughed. "Docile? At times I'm a tiger! But it has to be at the right time so it will have some meaning. A confrontation with those drunks would be a waste of energy. At nurses' training I led a protest to grant more scholarships to Aboriginal girls. I made a few enemies, but I gained a lot of respect in important quarters. Those girls need special encouragement, and they are so effective in helping their own"—she corrected herself— "*my* own people." She gave him an infectious little grin. "You see, sometimes I'm confused about where I belong."

Janet recognized the couple from their previous visit. She waited to take their order. She tried to hide the curiosity in her eyes, for Molly—pretty and exotic, didn't quite fit into any category with which she was familiar in Coober Pedy. The minute Eric had ordered dinner the first time, she recognized his accent and became very attentive. Some American tourists left tips, even though it was not customary for Australians to do so, but he had not. Perhaps this time he would be more generous. After she brought their food, she watched covertly as Eric ate, switching his fork back and forth from left to right. She blushed when she caught him looking at her with amusement, and she retreated awkwardly to another table.

Sergeant MacDonald sat stiffly in his usual place in the corner, eating alone. Janet always waited on him promptly; it did no harm to be friendly with the police. He was always grave and correct, but she recognized the little gleam of admiration in his eyes. She had learned a great deal since she left home.

MacDonald also watched the American eat, and there was an indiscernible expression on his face—not quite detached, not quite hostile, more observant. It made Janet uncomfortable, and she was glad when Peter Bagley appeared and waved to her. She hurried over with a menu. She did not notice the sergeant's eyes narrow speculatively.

The dining room had filled up, and there was a relaxed gaiety in the room. Eric leaned back, making an effort to shake off his dark mood. "I'm glad you accepted my invitation. I really enjoy your company."

Molly put her hand on his in an involuntary gesture of acquiescence. "I've looked forward to this evening, too, and I'm not disappointed. Thank you."

There was a lapse in the conversation, and then she said, "I'm trying hard not to mention mining. It's just that I'm concerned."

"I know." He was determined to change the subject. "Have you had any interesting cases lately?"

"Yes. Two days ago a six-year-old boy fell down a mine shaft! Only a broken arm. It's a miracle he wasn't killed."

"Incredible." He kept his tone flat.

"You know," Molly went on, "the openings to the mines aren't fenced or posted with any warnings. You have to be very careful."

"I am careful, Molly," Eric answered with some asperity. "Please don't act like a mother hen!"

She blushed. He looked her straight in the eye and said very seriously, "Don't push me about this mining, Molly. It's something I have to do." He didn't tell her that his old nightmare had recurred, weeks after he had been going down into the mine. The whole thing was incomprehensible. He had mastered his fear; he had climbed up and down the ladder without hesitation, and yet the dream persisted. Even trying to explain it was impossible—he didn't understand it himself.

"I just don't want it to change you, Eric, that's all," she said simply. "I've seen what greed can do to people. It can rule their lives—all their best qualities are consumed by it."

"Look, Molly," he protested. "I've just begun mining. There's no sinister element working on me. It's just an adventure, a challenge."

"Sometime I'll tell you some stories from the Dreamtime, especially the legend of the Rainbow Serpent, and then maybe you'll understand the Aborigine point of view."

There was another silence. Molly lowered her eyes for a moment and then glanced up timidly. "At the mission one of the lads asked if you had a wife."

"I remember."

"You said you did not."

"That's correct." Eric's answer was abrupt.

Molly hesitated. "Have you never been married?"

"I was once, but I prefer not to talk about it."

"That's the second time you've said that to me."

Eric, antagonized, didn't reply. He didn't need to answer personal questions, and he resented her inquiries. But perhaps she had a right to know something of his background if their relationship were to develop further.

"We were divorced."

"I see."

Her complacent reply angered him. There was no way she could understand what had happened between him and Cynthia.

The other teachers at the collage had nicknamed her "The Ice Goddess." The appellation intrigued him. He puzzled over what made her seem different. Refinement! Yes, that was it. Coming from a rough background, he had had to acquire his polish, but her decorum was natural.

He was pleased when she accepted his proposal, although he was not without doubts about the relationship. But bachelor life wearied him, and he longed for a family of his own.

She had proved to be a cold, unresponsive wife, and it was only when she announced she was pregnant did warmth enter his house. Then came the accident.

"It's all your fault!" Cynthia screamed, her eyes wild.

"My God, Cynthia, you don't know what you're saying." Eric turned away, devastated. It was hard enough that she had lost the baby. Why would she accuse him?

"If you hadn't made me quit work, I wouldn't have been home. I wouldn't have fallen."

"Be reasonable, Cynthia. It's winter—the roads are icy, and you had an hour's drive to work each way. You were seven months pregnant. Of course I wanted you to be safe."

"Safe! If you hadn't been at a basketball game, you'd have been there to help me."

"You know that coaching the basketball team is part of my contract. This institution milks its teachers of every skill they have. I had to be there. Of course, I wouldn't have gone if I'd known this would happen. Do you think I wasn't shocked to find you at the foot of the stairs? I know you're upset. This is a tragedy for both of us, but let's not say hurtful things."

"You always want the last word, don't you?"

He walked out of the hospital room without replying, still in a state of shock. The doctor, when queried, revealed that the baby had been a boy. Eric went home and closed the door to the nursery—a room so bright and clean, so full of hope. He had wanted this baby so much, a child to love and care for. It was almost as if a piece of his own flesh had been torn away.

Cynthia soon recovered from the accident and returned to her job. Eric's despondency clung to him for weeks and only gradually dissipated after he threw himself wholeheartedly back into his work. Their routines continued as though nothing had happened. The qualities that had so intrigued him during their early courtship—her reserve and crisp, cool efficiency—now seemed to have deteriorated into cold indifference bordering on contempt. Nothing he did pleased her. Her criticism was blunt, often withering. They lived in the same house, which was kept spotlessly clean and ate the same food, which was always well-prepared, but he might just as well have been living in a boarding house. It was not a home.

He had never told Cynthia about his nightmare, and on those rare occasions when he awakened her with a scream, he would just say, "Bad dream. I can't remember it." If he had recounted the actual details of his nocturnal torment, he knew her upper lip would have curled in that special way she had as she would say, "You're a grown man. It's foolish to be so disturbed by a dream." It probably was, but he couldn't shake the implacable reality of it.

Sex was perfunctory and unrewarding. He considered divorce and broached the subject. Her answer was adamant.

"There has never been a divorce in my family, Eric, and there won't be one now. You can move into the nursery if you want to."

He did, but not to avoid her physical rejection. He had

contracted mumps when an epidemic of the disease swept the campus. The younger students who had not had them in early childhood, generally got light cases, but Eric became seriously ill. They set up a cot in the nursery, but his sickness was so consuming that he scarcely noticed the bright border of colorful animals he had put around the ceiling and the soft pastel walls he had painted. Cynthia became a reluctant but dutiful nurse, taking three days off work to tend to him—preparing special dishes to tempt his appetite, staying in communication with the college, who considered her an exemplary wife. Following a week of high fever, the doctor approached Eric with a certain reserve.

"Well, Mr. Christianson. How are you feeling today?"

"Somewhat better, thanks." He managed a wan smile. "I think I'll live. There were a few days there that I didn't care if I did or not."

The doctor hesitated before going on, uncertain whether this was the most propitious time to deliver his ominous news. "You realize of course that you have been a very sick man. Sometimes there are complications."

"Yes, I'm well aware of that."

"In your case, you have been sicker than most."

"What are you trying to say, Doctor? Out with it."

"It's very possible, even highly probable, that you have been left sterile."

"Sterile?" The word numbed Eric's lips.

"The chance of your fathering more children is, at best,

remote. I'm very sorry."

Eric lay back in bed, eyes closed. "We lost a baby last year, you know."

"I heard. I'm truly sorry." He sighed and rose to leave. This kind of message was one of the hardest to deliver. "I hope I'm wrong. You can have tests done later, but in my experience ..." His voice trailed off. Eric nodded. There was nothing to say.

When he told Cynthia of the doctor's prognosis, a thoughtful look crossed her face. She sat on the edge of a chair nearby and studied her hands. "We'll just have to make the best of it, won't we?" she said. "We both have our work."

After a full recovery Eric once again threw himself into his work. Two weeks later a special teachers' meeting was canceled because of a late snow storm, and arriving home early Eric was pleased to find lights on in the house. Cynthia had arrived home first, evidently dismissed early because of the dangerous road conditions. She would have driven her car into the garage and closed the door, but too much snow had drifted in front of it for Eric to open it now. He figured he'd do some shoveling as soon as he had greeted her. He assumed that she was upstairs changing her clothes and started up when he remembered a phone call he needed to make. As he picked up the phone to dial, he could hear Cynthia speaking. Out of respect for her privacy, he was about to hang up when her words stopped him.

"Sandra, I didn't even realize I was pregnant until Eric got sick, and then I did a lot of thinking. I didn't want this baby. I love my job, and Eric would be adamant about my quitting this time. I'm not going to stay home with a lot of dirty diapers."

A woman's voice asked, "Well, what are you going to do?"

"I've already done it," Cynthia continued. "I took care of things last week. What Eric doesn't know won't hurt him."

"Are you all right?"

"Yes, I'm fine. There were no complications."

Eric stood with the phone in his hand as Cynthia went on about a new dress. Then the significance of her words reached his consciousness—she had deliberately destroyed their unborn child, knowing it would be the last he could father. Rage swelled up in him as he slammed the receiver down and bounded up the stairs. Cynthia, realizing she had been overheard, prepared for a confrontation, but she was not prepared for the intensity of his anger. Frightened when she saw his blazing eyes and clenched fists, she stood with the bed between them and held out a supplicating hand.

"Try to understand, Eric."

He dashed around the bed and grabbed her arm. She pulled away and tried to run for the door, but he caught her again. She faced him with bravado. "Don't touch me! Don't you dare touch me."

He laughed derisively and mocked her. "'Don't touch me!' You never wanted me to touch you with affection, and now you beg me not to touch you in anger." He raised his fist, and she shrank back. "No, I'm not going to hit you, though God knows I'd like to smash your lying face in. You're pathetic." His shoulders slumped. "Just get out of my life, Cynthia. I never want to see you again."

He released her so violently that she fell across the bed. He ran downstairs two at a time, and grabbing his coat and hat, flung open the door. As he dashed to the car, his feet sank into the newly fallen snow. He started the engine and tried to back up, but the tires spun, and he struggled ineffectually to get traction. He slammed his fists on the steering wheel and cursed, then sat with his head sunk on his chest, pondering what to do next. He wanted to drive for hours, anywhere, just to get away, to get as far away as he could. Now he was stuck— the storm was intensifying. In spite of his rage, his thoughts cleared enough to recognize that his emotional condition made it unsafe to drive even if it were possible. He also knew he couldn't stay in the car or he would freeze to death. Where could he go? He would not return to the house, under any circumstances. He thought of his bachelor friend, the French teacher, whose apartment was within walking distance. Fortunately he had not removed his overshoes, and after buttoning up his coat and pulling on his gloves, he set out.

The divorce was quiet, with "irreconcilable differences" on both sides. The property settlement divided assets equally, with Cynthia occupying the house until it was sold. Eric moved to an apartment. The campus was stunned—how could such an ideal couple terminate their marriage? Dark looks were cast at Eric, and Cynthia was viewed as a pillar of virtue. The more sanctimonious members of the college board did not approve retaining Eric, but divorce was not grounds for dismissal, and how could they replace a teacher who was versatile enough to instruct in history and English and also coach basketball?

He motioned to Janet for their check, sorry that this second evening had ended on a bad note. He realized it was his own fault and could not meet the curious look in Molly's eyes. When they left the restaurant, they found the street empty of hecklers. Molly was relieved, but Eric, still seething with anger at the events of the evening, would have welcomed a physical confrontation. He blamed himself for another fiasco and was silent most of the way back to the hospital.

The wind had sharpened, and dust was beginning to swirl in the parking area. Molly hurriedly tied a scarf around her hair when he stopped the ute. She opened her door and with a quick, "Thank you!" made a dash for her quarters. He hit his fists on the steering wheel and ground the gears as he drove away.

CHAPTER SIXTEEN

MOLLY FROWNED as she read the letter from Bert McCurdy. She didn't want any more complications in her life right now. She was pleased that he had evidently changed from the surly boy she had met when she was twelve, but her last visit to Wiluru Station had propelled them into a different relationship.

Dear Molly,

I can't get over how beautiful you are! It was wonderful seeing you. I couldn't believe my eyes when you drove up to the bungalow. Mum said you'd been there before, but I must have been away working. I must see you again. I know it's a long way to Coober Pedy, but I'm going to come. Don't say 'No.' I'm determined.

Love, Bert

Molly had dressed with care before driving to Wiluru Station. Summer-like days lingered and while it might not be a scorcher, the temperatures would be less than pleasant. The visit would be a short one, for she had only a few days of vacation after her graduation and soon would be traveling to her first assignment. She would not be seeing her grandmother for quite a while, so she had arranged time for this special visit.

She chose a light pink cotton skirt and blouse and a broad-brimmed, white sun hat. As she glanced in the mirror, she was struck again at how much she looked like all the other young nurses with whom she had trained. If she had not told them she was part Aborigine, they never would have known. Sometimes Molly wondered if it had been wise to tell them, but she was not ashamed of her heritage and was unwilling to conceal it. She had not received many invitations to visit the other girls' homes after that or to double date, but she hadn't minded too much. The few friends she had made were true ones and would last. She had her career ahead of her, and she was determined never to go back on her promise to help her people.

The two years she spent at the hospital in Adelaide opened her naive eyes to many aspects of life that she had missed in her secluded, sheltered life at the mission. She learned to fend off the more amorous boys, good-naturedly when possible, with determination when not. To do so without lessening their sense of masculinity or losing her dignity challenged her, but she was unequivocal in upholding her values. True, she wasn't asked out often, but those who did invite her respected her, and several urged a closer commitment, with perhaps marriage in the future. But her studies took most of her energies, and she didn't desire a closer relationship with anyone. Sometimes she dreamed of "Mr. Right," but he was only a hazy figure in her imagination. She was content with her life and eager to plunge into the new experiences of her career.

Now she was returning to the place which had so many happy memories for her and the woman who held such a magical pull on her heart. She stopped before opening the last gate and brushed her wind-blown hair and applied fresh lipstick. As she returned to the Land Rover after closing the gate behind her, she noticed a young man repairing a vehicle in the yard next to the bungalow. He sauntered over and gave her a smile.

"Can I help you? Are you looking for someone?" Then he looked at her more closely and stared with obvious appreciation. She was the most exotic girl he had ever seen, almost Parisian. He was stunned when she removed her sun glasses and turned her beautiful dark eyes on him. She smiled, showing dazzling white teeth, and he began to turn red from embarrassment. He stood tongue-tied for a moment and then repeated, "Can I help you? It's too hot to be sitting out here. Come into the house for a cool drink."

Molly laughed at his discomfort, and the corners of her eyes crinkled with amusement. She held out her hand. "Don't you know me, Bert? And yes, I have come to see someone—my grandmother."

Bert's jaw dropped. "Molly?"

"Yes, it's me."

"Molly!"

"Yes." She laughed again. "I guess I have changed a little. I haven't seen you for a few years."

Bert, completely transfixed, did not reply. Then he remembered his manners and removed his hat. He shook her hand with obvious delight and relinquished it reluctantly. Suddenly shyness overtook him, and he shuffled his feet in the dust. "Mum would love to see you. Won't you please come up to the house?"

Molly shook her head. "Thanks, but I have so little time. I have to leave early in the morning and it's late now. I was lucky to have these two days. It takes almost a full day to come and go."

"Please, Molly. Just for a minute. Have a cold drink and see Mum. She'd be real disappointed if you didn't stop."

Molly hesitated and then agreed. "All right, if it's 'just for a minute'. Get in and I'll drive you up."

Bert climbed in beside her and noticed her soft, creamy skin, the long lashes that framed her bewitching eyes, her slender hands. She drove with erect carriage although fatigue was beginning to show in her face. Bert observed her surreptitiously, scarcely believing that this was the same girl he had teased eight years before. When they started up the stairs to the veranda, he could see the well rounded but graceful body moving beneath the loose clothing. She caught him appraising her, and he flushed and looked away quickly.

"Mum," he called. "Look who's here."

Mrs. McCurdy came out to the porch, wiping her hands on her apron. Her face was steamy from cooking supper. She recognized Molly immediately and held out her hands. "Molly! How lovely to see you again. This is a surprise!"

"I know, Mrs. McCurdy. My trip came up so suddenly, I didn't have time to notify you. My grandmother has no idea I'm here."

"You know you're always welcome here, dear. What a grown up young lady you are now!"

"It's good to see you again. I've just finished my nurse's training. I'm a graduate nursing sister now, and I'm leaving for my first assignment in a few days."

"That's wonderful, Molly!" exclaimed Bert. "Isn't that great, Mum?"

Mrs. McCurdy was aware of the excited gleam in her son's eyes, and a flicker of concern passed over her face. Then she smiled graciously again at Molly. "Yes, indeed. We're all proud of you, dear. I remember so well the night you were born—it doesn't seem possible that time has passed so quickly. Your poor mother ..."

Molly broke in. "You're very kind, Mrs. McCurdy, but I really must go. My time is so short. How is my grandmother?"

"She's well but slowing down a little. I've offered to have her move closer. There's even a little spare room in the house, but she won't have it. She won't leave her little shack."

"I know. Niboorana will always cling to her old ways." Molly turned to go, but Bert took hold of her arm.

"Molly, after you visit your grandmother, stay here for the night. You can't sleep down there ... It's ... it's not right!"

Molly smiled. "It's very right, Bert. I'll never be too proud to stay with my grandmother." She gently disengaged herself from Bert's grasp. "I hope you understand. I do appreciate your thoughtfulness." She extended her hand to each of them and then ran down the steps. Bert sighed and watched her climb into the Land Rover and drive down the track to Niboorana's shack.

"Can't we take some supper down to them, Mum?"

Mrs. McCurdy shook her head. "They'll want to be alone, Bert. I'm sure Molly brought some extra supplies for her grandmother. She always does."

"You mean she's been here often?"

"Not often, but a few times," she hedged.

"Where was I?" Bert protested.

"Out working with your father, probably." She returned to the kitchen, relieved that Molly was leaving so soon for her new position. She always worried about her youngest son. He was so restless and impetuous, often reckless, so unlike her older sons. She would not welcome a romantic entanglement between Bert and Molly. The girl was capable and attractive, but it would never do. No, it would never do.

Niboorana was waiting in front of her shelter when Molly drove up. She ran to her granddaughter, arms extended, and enveloped her in a warm embrace. "I knew you were coming," she said, emotion choking her voice.

"I wanted to surprise you." Molly's mouth turned down a little. "How did you find out? Did you hear the Land Rover?"

"I saw you before I heard it."

"But you can't see the road from here!" Molly exclaimed.

"My mind knows many things my senses do not," Niboorana said quietly.

"Of course. I guess I've been away too long. I should have realized that." She gave Niboorana an extra hug.

Niboorana was touched that Molly had brought her a large, framed picture of herself in her nurse's uniform. She hung it on the wall and stood back, looking from the photograph to her granddaughter standing so tall and lovely, flesh of her flesh. Tears came to her eyes as she remembered the day Molly's father had come to take her away. Niboorana recognized that life at the mission had been best for Molly—being reared by her white benefactors but never losing touch with her Aboriginal heritage. She knew her own subtle influence had been for the good, too. Now she would not see Molly for a long time, but the picture would be a constant reminder of her—not that she needed anything tangible. Her mental images were stronger and more vivid than any reproduction. Still, it would be pleasant to see Molly's radiant face smiling at her from the photo.

They had a simple repast from some of the supplies Molly had brought into the shack over Niboorana's protest. "I get along fine. Save your money for yourself, child."

Molly laughed and continued to put the canned and dry goods on the shelves. "You say that every time. I know the McCurdys see to your needs, Kabbarli, but these are special things I want you to have."

They went outdoors, savoring the fragrance of the gum trees. Some of the bark had peeled off, and Molly shuffled around on the dried leaves and bark, making crunchy sounds. "This is what I missed in the city," she sighed, "and I'll miss it even more in Coober Pedy. I understand it is very desolate there. But every nursing sister has to start somewhere." They sat in silence, enjoying the sounds of the night. A slight breeze rustled through the trees, bringing welcome relief from the heat of the day. How pleasant, Molly thought, to be able to sit with someone and commune spiritually and be a part of the greater life force surrounding her.

"Do you see Wilanya any more?"

Niboorana's question startled Molly from her reverie. "No. He left two years ago and never returned. No one has heard from him."

"That is sad. He is a casualty of the war between his two cultures."

"Yes."

"But yours blended and made you stronger."

"I hope so."

As they sat watching the smoke curl up from the fire, Molly could feel the pull of her grandmother's mind. She found herself thinking back to that wonderful time when she was twelve years old and met her uncle for the first time.

She had stared at the huge black man before her and turned to her grandmother for an explanation.

"Molly, this is your Uncle Goonabi," Niboorana said, "your mother's brother."

Goonabi had drifted through the station on infrequent occasions to see his mother, and while this visit seemed coincidental, Niboorana knew better. She had been willing it mentally with all her strength for many weeks because she wanted the two persons she loved most of all to meet and become friends.

Goonabi scrutinized the child. "She has Ashira's eyes," he commented, "but little else."

Molly looked at him in amazement. He was heavily built for an Aborigine, with broad shoulders and large, muscular arms. His skin was darker than Niboorana's, and his black eyes, deep-set and impassive, almost frightened Molly. She had never been ill at ease with the natives at the mission, even those who recently had come in from the bush. They were for the most part gentle creatures, and they welcomed the companionship of the twelve-year-old girl who played with their children. Now she stood, uncertain and tongue tied, not sure how her uncle would accept her. Knowing she was only a quarter Aborigine, might he not look down on her with contempt or perhaps rejection? She wanted him to like her, and being well-acquainted with Aboriginal culture and the position of women, she waited quietly for him to speak first.

He was in no hurry, and many thoughts rushed through her mind. Being a man, Goonabi would have first choice of the food and sleeping arrangements, and being kin, he would be waited on and shown every courtesy. She understood that in the olden days there was nothing that was not held in common, and the selfish withholding of anything would be an affront. How would his presence affect her holiday, she wondered. She had been given two weeks for this visit, the longest she ever had been allowed, and Mrs. McCurdy had released Niboorana from any domestic chores for that same period of time.

Goonabi examined her again. "Your skin is very light." He ran his thick fingers over her arm and smiled when she didn't flinch. "You are different, but I am glad to see you." Molly smiled in return, and Niboorana sighed in relief.

Goonabi had left his tribe some time before, aware of the encroachment of civilization and attracted by the material advantages of being with other people. He could read a little, from his early years with Achmet and the settlement school, and he had learned enough practical skills to maintain his living doing odd jobs. At present he worked on the section gang for the railroad. Except for taking an unauthorized walkabout at times, he was a reliable worker and had steady work. His employers understood the complicated mind of the Aborigines and made allowances for their primal needs.

Goonabi looked at the bed which had been moved inside for Molly and shook his head in mock dismay. "I will not take your bed," he said. "I still prefer to sleep outdoors. You are probably too civilized to sleep on the ground."

Molly realized he was teasing her and laughed. She liked this giant of a man, and all fear left her.

Niboorana picked up food rations from the workers' kitchen each day, and she cooked outside on her little fire. Goonabi watched her with amusement, commenting, "You still like the old ways, don't you?"

"There is much value to the old ways."

"You're right, and we need to teach that to Molly."

"I have tried to on each visit, but her visits are so short. She gets much knowledge from the mission. The good pastor means well, but the child is often in a state of conflict. She is caught between two worlds."

"Then we must help her see the best in both worlds." Goonabi brushed his heavy wavy hair back from his face and looked at his niece critically. She was playing with one of the McCurdy's dogs that had showed up at their hut, running and tossing a stick for him to chase, animated and laughing. "Her hair is wavy like mine but much finer. Her features are delicate, unlike our people, and she has a strong spirit. She does not seem truly Aboriginal, but I think there is some kinship in her soul."

"You will help me, Goonabi." Niboorana changed her intended question into a statement. While a woman was always subservient to her son, she knew she could assert herself to gain his help.

"Yes. I think we should take her on a walkabout. That will show us what she's made of."

"She will not disappoint us," Niboorana said with conviction.

They left the next morning with little preparation, taking only some skins of water and dried meat and fruit. "On the outside chance we can't sustain ourselves," Niboorana insisted.

Goonabi shrugged. "You have no faith in me, but we'll take it anyway, as a precaution." He took a spear, a throwing stick and a blackened billy. Niboorana took a digging stick. Molly began to leap ecstatically.

Goonabi frowned. "Conserve your energy. We waste nothing on walkabout." Molly subsided meekly.

"I won't have to go naked, will I?" she asked her grandmother with some apprehension.

"No, dear. And you must wear a hat—your skin is too fair for the strong sun—and shoes, if you wish."

Molly had run barefoot so often that her feet were toughened, but even so, the sharp rocks and spiny plants penetrated, so she left her shoes on, relieved.

"Might we get lost, Goonabi?" An anxious note appeared in her voice.

"Have you not heard of map songs?" Goonabi replied. She shook her head. "That is how Aboriginal people have always made their way. They noted every part of a mountain—a jagged top, an outcropping, a scar on the face of a cliff or an unusual depression in the land that could mean a water hole. They watched for special trees or rocks. They chanted their directions and kept them safely in their minds. As our people heard these song chants over and over, they memorized them and passed them down through the generations.

Even when they were in a different area, they could remember the landmarks in their mind as though they had traveled the road many times. It was a map that never could get lost."

"Do you have a map song for where we are going?"

"No, because this is far removed from our native territory, but we will make up our own map song as we go. In that way we can find our way back. Look around you. What do you see?"

Molly glanced at her surroundings. They had already left the sight of the buildings, and the vast outback stretched before them. "Well, I see some bushes and some gum trees. They all look alike."

"Look carefully. Do you see anything that is different, an unusual shape, an unexpected color or texture."

Molly looked again. "Well, that old gum tree over there has a broken branch and a scar on one side where the bark has fallen away. And there's a large rock at the base."

"Good. That's a beginning." In a sing song voice Goonabi began a chant, and Molly and Niboorana joined him. A little farther he stopped and again asked Molly to observe. She pointed out a small depression where some rain water had evidently created a patch of green. Goonabi added this to his map song, and as the day progressed the song became longer and longer. They all chanted the repetitive words, savoring the rhythm, matching it to their strides.

As they walked through a long valley between two low hills, Molly began to sing, "Down in the Valley." Goonabi's face registered displeasure. "That's not very Aboriginal. Where did you learn it?"

"In my school."

Niboorana touched his arm. "The best of both worlds, remember?"

His beetling brow cleared. "Well, I guess it's appropriate. We'll add it to our song map."

Her uncle's vast knowledge of survival skills impressed Molly more each day. She observed how he watched the birds for locations of water holes, how he sometimes dug under apparently dry sand to bring up water, how he tracked and killed a small kangaroo with his throwing stick. The animal's tail and a few other parts he roasted for their dinner.

One day Molly watched Goonabi catch a large goanna lizard. She had trailed behind, observing as he found some little tracks which he followed, making a shrill whistling sound. The goanna camouflaged itself by hiding in the sand.

Goonabi motioned for Molly to come forward. "It's trying to protect itself," he whispered. "It may think there's a predatory hawk in the sky, so it burrows down enough to cover itself." He crept stealthily up to the mound, stirred it and speared the creature as it tried to flee.

"Are we going to eat it?" Molly asked with a mixture of dread and anticipation.

"Of course. The good spirits have provided us with food, and we would be ungrateful not to accept it."

He built a small fire and lay the goanna on the flames,

just long enough to insure the juices would remain inside. This would strengthen the flesh. Molly watched in fascination as he broke open the lizard and pulled out the entrails, being careful to separate the gall from the liver, so the taste would not be bitter. The fire had become a heap of glowing coals, and he scooped out a place to lay the goanna. When it was cooked enough, Goonabi pulled it out, allowing it to cool sufficiently and gave each person a portion. Niboorana shook her head. She had not separated herself entirely from her early primitive beliefs—she could not eat her totem. Goonabi just laughed and ate her share while she munched on some of the dried meat they had brought with them. Molly ate hesitatingly at first, and then realizing she was really hungry, devoured her share. Her eyes sparkled with happiness. This experience was the most exciting thing that had ever happened to her.

Each night they slept in hollowed out spaces in the sand. Looking up at the brilliant stars was an awesome experience. Molly had observed stars all her young life, but never under these conditions. Goonabi pointed out certain constellations and told her legends about them and explained how they could guide a traveler in his wanderings. "Always we are watched over by the spirits of the Dreamtime, but we must never abuse what nature has given us."

Molly was already acquainted with many birds already from living at the mission, but she never failed to respond to the beauty of the galahs. She thought that with their rosy pink underside, they looked like blossoms floating in the air. As the light faded in the late afternoon, the birds came in flocks, swooping and swirling, and when they turned and only the gray upper parts were visible, they appeared to have materialized from smoke. When two or three flew together in unison, she imagined they were aerial acrobats.

She was sorry when their walkabout ended, but the encroachment of time reminded them of their duties. Reluctantly they journeyed back along their song map trail, never missing a guiding landmark.

Molly had become an avid reader, devouring books about the early history of Australia and its earliest inhabitants. She asked Goonabi endless questions, which at first he was pleased to answer, until he sensed that she was testing his beliefs against her knowledge.

"Where did our people come from?"

"We were made during the Dreamtime. We were brought here by one of our great spirits."

"Why do we have totems?"

"We were made in the likeness of the animals who watch over us."

"You mean, we look like them?"

"Of course not. We are like them in spirit."

Her curiosity was insatiable, and sometimes Goonabi threw his hands up in exasperation. "It's lucky you are not living one hundred years ago," he admonished her. "Some of your questions concern matters that are taboo for women to know."

"You don't have to answer them. I can read about them in books."

Goonabi scowled at her pert answer, his face taking on an even darker hue than his natural color. His black eyes flashed. He was no longer the patient, laughing uncle. "There are such things as spirits, and they can harm you if you challenge them."

"I'll remember," she said meekly, but her thoughts were not meek. No knowledge should be taboo. She would always look for answers to her questions.

Niboorana was worried. She observed her granddaughter's quick intellect. Molly exhibited far more insight and mental courage than she herself ever had. What would be her future? She recognized that Molly would not be content to live as she did on the station. Molly was an exception to the women of her tribe with her thoughts and keen perception. She would choose a different path in life, but where would it lead her? Niboorana knew instinctively that whatever path Molly chose, it would be a good one, so she should not be concerned. There would be many pulls on her granddaughter. She felt helpless in trying to guide her. The time with her was so short, and the rest of the world had so much power.

The day before Pastor Holmgren was to return for her, young Bert McCurdy rode down on one of the stockmen's horses and grinned at her. It was not an innocent smile. Molly stroked the horse affectionately, oblivious of any ill intent on the boy's part.

"Want to go riding?" he asked.

She looked up, delighted at the invitation. She had not been on a horse since her first visit to the station, and she accepted wholeheartedly.

"Get up behind me."

She swung herself up behind Bert and waved gaily to Niboorana as they trotted down the path at a moderate pace. As soon as they were out of sight, Bert kicked the sides of the horse and used his whip.

"Hold on!" he shouted. "We're going to go fast!" They galloped at full speed, with the boy laughing maliciously. Molly held on for dear life, her arms clutched around his waist. She tried to hold her legs against the sides of the horse, but they flew out in spite of her efforts and almost unbalanced them both. If Bert had expected her to cry out in fear or beg him to stop, he was mistaken. She just clenched her jaw and tightened her grip as the horse, enjoying its freedom from a more experienced rider, continued to gallop. Bert's face got scraped as they passed under some overhanging branches, but Molly, sheltered by his back, escaped the bruising. He tugged at the reins to no avail. Panic-stricken, they continued down the road at breakneck speed. Finally, the horse slowed down of its own volition, tossed its head in an independent gesture, and headed back to the station. Bert jerked on the reins and brought it to a halt. He turned to Molly.

"Let go, will you? I can't breathe. You're killing me!"

"That was great! Let's gallop back." She was frightened but would never give him the satisfaction of showing it. Realizing that it had not been that much fun trying to scare her and wishing to save face, he lashed out at her.

"It's all your fault. You held on so tight that you cut off my wind and I couldn't control the horse. We'll have to walk back and let it cool down." There was no more conversation on the return trip.

When Molly got back to her grandmother's hut, she thanked Bert with an ingenuous smile. The boy saw a pretty, dark-eyed girl who was perfectly composed. He resented that she wasn't disheveled and upset. He asserted his superiority and stared down at her haughtily.

"You don't look like a 'gin'," he remarked. "It'll probably show up later. It always does."

For a moment Molly was nonplused. Then the color rose in her face, and she glared at him defiantly. "And you don't look like a squatter's son," she flashed back. "Mr. McCurdy is a gentleman, and you'll never be one!" She turned on her heel and disappeared into the shack, but not before Bert yelled back at her, "You're an uppity little snip! That's what happens when they let you go to school."

That evening Molly was unusually quiet, and Niboorana waited for her to speak. After she looked quizzically at her grandmother, she said, "Kabbarli, I'm confused."

"Yes, Molly? About what are you puzzled?"

"Well, at the mission Papa Holmgren said that there is

just one Great Spirit. But you and Goonabi speak of many spirits."

Niboorana reflected before answering. "It may well be that there is one spirit greater than the others."

Molly shook her head. "The mission taught me that there are no other spirits, just the Great Spirit himself. He sent his son to earth to show his love for us, so that we would be reconciled to him."

"We know a spirit can change its form," Niboorana conceded. "It is possible the Great Spirit became a man. Our spirits left the Dreamtime and became earthly creatures. It is a comfort to know the spirits care about us."

"We think differently, Kabbarli, but it's hard to explain something you don't quite understand, isn't it?" She was silent for a while, considering their conversation. Then she asked, "Why do Aboriginal people fear death?"

"Death is a great unknown," Niboorana said softly. "We always fear what is unknown. There are evil spirits that would try to take us away when someone dies, and we must guard against them. Death is a time of darkness. It is final."

"But Kabbarli, I have been taught that after death we will live again with God. Jesus proved it when He died and went to heaven. It says so in the Bible."

Niboorana patted Molly's hand. "That is a good thought." She started to say something else but changed her mind. "It is a good thought," she repeated.

Molly smiled up at her. "The mission taught me that

love is the most important thing in the world. I love you, and you love me, so everything else is all right, isn't it? I will always be your granddaughter, Kabbarli."

That experience had been a wonderful opportunity to explore each other's beliefs and values. Molly's faith was simplistic but deep, and she had tried to assuage her grandmother's fears without disparaging her. Now, just as dawn was breaking, she and her grandmother made their farewells. Niboorana took Molly in her arms and held her closely. Molly realized that although her grandmother had aged considerably and her limbs were becoming withered, there was still tremendous power in her embrace. She clung to her, reluctant to leave until Niboorana gently pushed her away, tears in her eyes. "You have chosen well to become a nursing sister, Molly. Your new learning will be a great help to many people, including your own."

"That's why I chose this profession," Molly answered quietly. "Remember you told me that we are all one? I hope I can make a difference, whatever happens." She kissed her grandmother's wrinkled cheek. "You have been a great light in my life, Kabbarli."

On her way out Molly found Bert waiting for her, his eyes shining, his sun bleached hair neatly brushed back, his tanned face freshly shaven. She appreciated his consideration at seeing her off so early.

"Please get out for a minute, Molly," he said huskily.

"I haven't much time, Bert. I do thank you for coming to tell me goodbye."

He put his hand over hers on the steering wheel. She felt a little glow pass over her.

"Please, Molly."

The sincerity of his entreaty touched her, and she relented. She stood beside him, looking up.

"I couldn't sleep last night thinking about you, Molly. You're ... you're so pretty ... so special." His calloused hands gripped hers, and he looked intently into her eyes. She began to pull back but his grip intensified. His voice quavered. "Molly, I ... I must see you again. I must."

"I'm sure we'll meet again, Bert." She tried to detach herself without avail. "I have to leave. Please." The next thing she knew his arms were locked around her, and he was kissing her passionately. She turned her face away from his insistent lips and struggled to push him back, but he persisted. For a moment she felt herself beginning to respond, her pulse racing, warmth spreading over her body. Then the raucous cry of a magpie jolted her back to reality. Here she was, standing in the dust, miles from her destination, in the arms of a man she hardly knew.

"Bert, you must stop this. At once!" Her peremptory tone caused him to stand back. "Please let me go. This is very poor behavior on your part." Her eyes flashed with indignation.

He glared at her. He had been rejected, very firmly

rejected, leaving him angry and unrepentant. Some harsh words leaped to his tongue, but he managed to cool down and appear contrite. "Molly, I'm sorry. I didn't mean to offend you. I just couldn't help myself. Don't hold it against me."

She managed a small smile and swiftly swung herself into the Land Rover, closing the door tightly.

"I've been an ass, Molly." He hung his head. "I'm really sorry. I'll write to you, though, and I'll come to see you, too."

"Bert, it's a long way to Coober Pedy, and I'm going to be very busy with my work."

He refused to be brushed off. "I'll get there some way. That's a promise. Next time I'll be a perfect gentleman."

"Goodbye, Bert." She could see him in her rear view mirror as she drove away, his unhappy face staring after her. She was disquieted. A flock of magpies flew across her vision, a flash of black and white against the rosy sunrise.

"You saved me from a commitment I'm not ready to make, not with anyone, especially Bert McCurdy," she said to the birds. "I have plenty of time ahead."

She sat back and relaxed, taking an interest in the area she was passing. How many times had she traveled this road? The first time when she was six, everything registered on her mind because it was all so new. She never had been away from the mission before. How kind Papa Holmgren had been to bring her all this long way! On other trips she had welcomed familiar landmarks, the huge gum tree where she had seen that mob of kangaroos, the gentle hill where the bungalow stood, and the thrill of seeing the house far in the distance as they made their approach. The flocks of birds, the beautiful galahs, and yes, even the magpies. Each trip, while they had not been numerous, had intensified her love for this place. Some experiences had been troubling—her encounter with Bert when she was twelve. What an unpleasant boy he had been! Had he really changed in those intervening years? Uncertain about any transformation of character, she recognized a wild unsettled nature in him that disturbed her and yet in some unfathomable way was appealing. She wondered if she would see him again or even if she wanted to.

And now this disturbing letter had arrived. She folded it up and put it away. She'd think about it at another time.

CHAPTER SEVENTEEN

ERIC CALLED FOR MOLLY later that week before she went on night duty. The sky was clear. It was one of those lovely days of pure, sweet-smelling air and skin-caressing warmth. There would be a million stars later that evening— bright and luminous, almost close enough to touch. He loved these days where everything was etched with such clarity, and he was happy just walking with Molly. The work at the mine was gratifying; he had a sense of purpose in his life, and how- ever his relationship with this charming girl developed, he was glad to have had this much.

Suddenly Molly stiffened. A young Aborigine, reeking of liquor, stepped out of a pub and lurched toward her. The youth reached out his hand and caught her arm.

"Molly! Remember me?" His voice was thick and surly. The stench of his unwashed body assailed their nostrils, and Eric grasped Molly's hand to pull her away, hoping to avoid an unpleasant scene. She didn't move, directing her attention to a closer look.

"Of course I remember you, Wilanya," she said in an

even tone. "How are you?"

The Aborigine's gaunt body swayed slightly from side to side, and he had difficulty focusing his eyes. Then a hostile expression settled on his grimy face.

"I'm just fine, Molly. Can't you see that I'm just fine? Look a little closer, Molly." He breathed into her face, but she did not turn her head away from the foul odor. "Can't you see that I'm just fine?"

"I'd be happy to talk with you when you're sober, Wilanya." Molly started to move away, feeling Eric's insistent pull, but the youth held her arm firmly. Eric made a move to interfere, and Wilanya turned on him.

"I see she's got a nice white feller," he sneered. "Me, I wasn't good enough for her. I wasn't clean enough for her. I didn't like school ... I was a nothing ... I was ..."

Molly interrupted him. "Wilanya, you don't know what you're saying. Please go now, and I'll talk to you later. I promise. Don't make trouble, please."

"I won't make trouble, Molly. Not with you. You're my girl. Always will be. But I'll make trouble with your lover man here. How is she in bed, eh? You like having a young 'gin' in bed?"

Eric's right fist connected so quickly with Wilanya's jaw that the youth didn't see it coming. He released his hold on Molly, fell back against the wall and slumped to the ground, eyes glazed. Then he slowly struggled to his feet and tried to take a swing at Eric. Eric spun him in the opposite direction and gave him a hard shove which almost toppled him.

"Go on back where you came from," he ordered. "Don't ever let me hear of you bothering Molly again." Wilanya staggered down the street muttering curses.

Molly, stricken, cried out, "I didn't want this to happen." She stretched out a hand to his departing back. "I'm sorry, Wilanya," she called after him. "I didn't want you hurt."

Eric stared at her in amazement. "You're defending him?"

"You don't understand," Molly began. "He was a friend. We grew up together. He's changed ..."

"I thought I was doing you a favor," Eric replied curtly.

"You don't understand," Molly repeated. "I do appreciate what you did to protect me, but he wouldn't have hurt me. He'd never hurt me."

"I don't believe it. There was real hatred in him, terrible jealousy. Pure malice, Molly. I don't like him being here."

"He's harmless, Eric. I swear it. He's just lost and bitter. I don't think he'll come around me again."

Eric looked at her curiously. "Did you have some kind of understanding with this ... this fellow?" Only his better judgment kept him from saying "this animal." He stared at the retreating figure with repugnance.

Molly shook her head. "Not really. Not in a grown-up sense. It was mostly when we were youngsters. It was always more on his part than mine."

Eric was repulsed. He could not visualize how Molly— sweet, clean and winsome—could have found anything attractive in this vile youth. He shrugged. Perhaps he didn't know her as well as he thought he did. They walked on slowly without speaking. He escorted her back to the hospital and said goodnight abruptly. Molly bit her lip to keep from crying. She was glad she had a patient who required much care that night.

The next morning she wrote to her grandmother in care of Mrs. McCurdy. She described the town, the opal mines, the general atmosphere and her duties. She was very happy, she wrote. Her work was very fulfilling; she kept very busy. She sent her love to Niboorana and best wishes to the McCurdy family. She did not single out Bert for any special recognition. She reread her letter and realized she'd used "very" three times. A mask for her true feelings? She was too tired to analyze the situation. Fatigue, emotional as well as physical, closed in on her, and she fell gratefully to sleep.

The following week Molly received two letters from Bert, written several days apart but apparently mailed at the same time. The first was quite circumspect, the second rather ardent. She smiled. Absence was certainly making his heart grow fonder. She tried to recall his face—sunburned rather than tanned, some freckles, reddish coarse hair and light blue eyes. Quite a nice looking fellow at that. She wouldn't answer immediately. There was no reason to encourage him. They were a great distance apart, and she had a year's term to fill at the hospital. Besides, there was Eric. She found her thoughts returning to him often, wishing he would contact her.

Eric called on her a few days later with a contrite manner but no formal apology for his previous abruptness and subsequent absence. Molly was glad to see him. His nonaggressive manner was refreshing compared with the boorishness she had encountered with some of the locals. She had been forewarned that new girls in town were "fair game", but she had not anticipated the extent of the struggle to which she'd be subjected. Dining out or a movie at the open air theater wasn't worth the wrestling match that eventually followed. As she had laughingly confided to Eric, even Peter Bagley had tried to date her, which had been a low point in her social life in Coober Pedy. She found it easier not to accept invitations. Eric was different—he was considerate and yet manly. He had an inner strength that lent him substance. But why was he so evasive about things? She hoped Eric would open up about his past soon.

"I want to show you 'The Breakaways'," he said. "It'll be an all day trip, so we'll have to wait until your off duty day. I've already told my partner I'm taking a holiday."

He's certainly sure of himself, she thought, but decided that was unworthy. Obviously he was trying to make amends. "I'm free on Wednesday. What are 'The Breakaways'?"

"It's an ancient inland seabed where you can pick up fossil shells. Bill told me about it yesterday. It sounded interesting."

"I'd love to go. What time?"

"Early. It gets warm in the middle of the day. Is six o'clock too early?"

"That will be fine. I'm looking forward to it. I'll pick up

something for lunch. We'll have a picnic!" She gave him a bright smile. How thoughtful of him to share something special with her.

On Wednesday she was waiting for him, wearing a sun hat, dark glasses and a loose cotton outfit. The corrugated road made them bounce around on the seat, and more than once she was propelled next to him. They both laughed, casual and relaxed.

The road followed the dingo fence part of the way—the barrier that ran for over two thousand miles to keep the wild dogs from entering sheep country. Cunning and ruthless, the dingo would slaughter more than he could eat when he found an undefended herd. The dried lagoon stretched out before them, with the ancient sea cliff rising above it. It had an eerie presence, a reminder of primordial days when abundant life had existed here. Now there was a bleak, limitless landscape—a lonely yet compelling area. Eric took Molly's hand and led her to the top of the sloping sand hill. He pointed into the distance.

"Can you picture how this would have looked when there was water and sea life?"

"Yes, I can imagine what it looked like then. It must have been like a little paradise." She gave him a wistful smile. "You know, in the Bible it says, 'In the beginning ...' Did you know that the Aborigines have their own story of the beginning?"

"I'd like to hear it."

"My grandmother told me this tale from the Dreamtime

many times, and I memorized it." She stopped, self-conscious.

"Go on," he prompted.

"Don't laugh."

"I promise."

She concentrated for a minute and then recited the old legend. "In the beginning there was the mother of us all, Imberombera, who came in the Dreamtime from a place far to the north. She walked on the bottom of the sea, but she was so tall that her head was above the waves. When she came, she found a land that was flat and empty. She said, 'I will make people for this land and make trees for their shade and rivers and billabongs for their water. I will make plants and animals so they will have food.' The Great Mother carried many spirit children in her body, and as she wandered she left her offspring behind to people the earth."

Eric smiled. "That's a charming account of creation. I think every belief has some story to try to explain the creation, because it is actually incomprehensible, isn't it? I believe our ancient Biblical rendition is amazingly scientific, if you examine it: first God's energizing spirit, then the creation of the cosmos, the solar system and earth, the dry land appearing and plant life, then animal life, and human beings as the climax. That's quite remarkable when you consider it was written thousands of years ago."

Molly listened, fascinated, as she heard him saying in a different way the story of the "beginning" she had heard since childhood. "You know, Eric, I can't imagine having this kind of discussion with anyone else. It's ... it's wonderful."

He laughed. "I didn't mean to sound pedantic. Do you know any more legends?"

"My favorite one is about the Rainbow Serpent. Some Aborigines believe that this may be the most powerful and important being of the Dreamtime."

"Why is that?"

"Because the Great Serpent brings the changes of the seasons. With the wet season, there is a renewal of life and everything is green again. It's like ... like a second chance. When she first appeared, she arched her body across a river and then went into the ground. Only her tail stayed on top, curving into the sky as a rainbow, a symbol of newness and hope."

"Those are essential qualities in everyone's life, aren't they? I like that story. Do you know any more?"

"Once I made up my own story about the Rainbow Serpent," Molly said shyly.

"Tell me. What is it?" He loved to look at her eyes when she was excited.

"I'll tell you, but I wouldn't tell a full-blooded Aborigine. They believe in their legends, and it would belittle them if I made one up."

"I'll keep it a secret!"

"When I was a young girl, someone gave me a little piece of fire opal. I liked to pretend that the Rainbow Serpent came into the dry country and became very hot and tired. When she could go no further, she lay down and burrowed into the ground to keep cool. She lies there still, and we see her spirit in the opal. She's willing to share of herself, but she doesn't want us to become greedy or she will be unhappy. You know," she turned to Eric, "the Aborigine feels a close kinship with the earth. It is a part of him, so he never abuses nature. He believes rivers and springs are the resting place of the Great Snake, so he treasures each water hole. He feels the rainbow in the sky is the spirit of the Serpent and really can't understand why men mutilate the earth by digging mines."

"Careful, Molly," he teased. "You're skating on thin ice!"

"I know how you feel, Eric, but just let me finish. Have you heard what Coober Pedy means in the local Aboriginal tongue?"

"No. What does it mean?"

"White Man in a Hole! That's rather a loose translation, but it's the general idea. Originally it was beyond their comprehension why anyone would dig holes in the ground and disturb the environment. Now of course they go out and 'noodle' on the opal heaps along with everyone else. They do very well, too. Their eyesight is actually much keener than ours, according to the doctors who have tested them." Molly stopped talking and then added, "I'm sure I'm boring you. I didn't mean to sound like a fountain of knowledge. I just wanted to share something with you that's important to me— using our God-given resources wisely."

"I'm not bored, Molly, and I do understand. How difficult it must be for most Aborigines to fit into our so-called civilized life."

She shot him a quick, grateful glance. "That's why I can sympathize with Wilanya. He's so mixed up and unhappy. He can't seem to make the adjustment."

For a moment Eric's face darkened, and then he gave her a little squeeze. "Well, you're a very loyal friend, and that's important. Let's see if we can find some shells."

They hunted around and found some mud-fossilized mollusks and some that were replaced with opal clay. There were no opalized shells with color. Eric laughed. "I really didn't expect to find any of those here. There are some areas in Coober Pedy where they are found, and they're extremely beautiful. Some of the most spectacular precious opal is from shells. You'll have to see one. The color and brilliance are unbelievable."

They meandered along the ridge and then went down the slope to the mudflats, still searching. The sun was climbing higher, and they began to feel the heat. Resting in the scant shade of the truck, they shared the bread, cheese and fruit Molly had brought, contentedly watching an eagle high above. Molly was happy sitting close to Eric, comfortable just being with him, but always she sensed his restrained attitude toward her. It puzzled her. She smiled up at him, a shy invitation in her eyes, but he simply smiled back and made no advances. It took all his self-control not to take her in his arms, but he realized at that moment he could offer only a tenuous future at best, and it was unfair. When she turned her head, he sensed that she felt rebuked for being forward, and he knew it when her next words broke the intimacy.

"I've had a letter from a boy whose father runs the station where my grandmother lives," she said.

Eric stiffened a little. "Oh?"

"Yes." Molly hesitated. "He wants to come see me."

"He sounds like a very intelligent young man." She analyzed his response to detect some veiled sarcasm in his tone but decided it was just indifference. She bit her lip. Things were not going as she wanted.

"I ... I just thought you might want to know."

Eric pulled away a little. "I've never tried to monopolize you, Molly. You're free to see anyone you want." He wasn't ready to tell her that he didn't want anyone else but her. He held her hand for a moment and continued, "I have no claim on you, Molly. You should be seeing other men ... younger men."

She lowered her head, her voice subdued. "I really don't want to see other men, Eric."

He studied her carefully, aware of the implication of her answer, and she became uncomfortable under his direct scrutiny. She had not been so receptive on their last meeting, and he wondered if she was playing games with him. He just wasn't sure and decided he would let things drift for a while. He stood up, smiled and extended his hand to raise her. Her flushed face and self-conscious laugh betrayed her feelings. He recognized that she had almost thrown herself at him and that he had rejected her.

"You remind me of my foster father, Pastor Holmgren," she said. "He was always giving me advice." The faint scar on Eric's face became a little more prominent. He knew she wanted to hurt him because of his insensitivity, but he didn't retaliate. He quietly picked up the remnants of their lunch and packed them into the ute, opening the door for her with an exaggerated gesture. She slipped into the seat and averted her face, trying not to cry, but she lost control and the tears started to roll down her cheeks. Eric put his arms around her and pulled her to him.

"Don't cry, Molly," he whispered. "I don't know what's happened between us, but let's not spoil things. I do care for you. I care a lot." He found himself kissing her and brushing the tears away. "Please don't cry, Molly. There are things I haven't told you about me." He could not in conscience offer her marriage unless there was a possibility of having children. Also, even if she were willing, how could he ask her to leave this land she loved so much for an uncertain future with him? He would have to unburden himself on this matter and risk losing her, but he wanted to postpone the unhappy revelation as long as possible.

CHAPTER EIGHTEEN

"MARIA, PREPARE A PROPER MEAL TONIGHT. I'm inviting Lucas to dinner."

Maria made a face. "Why? I don't like him. There's something ... shifty about him."

Duro studied her for a moment. "You usually like having another man around."

She ignored the barb and shrugged. "Do as you like. I'll go to town and buy some fresh meat. I just don't understand why you want him here when you work with him all day."

"That's just it. Our luck has been poor, and he's starting to drink too much. I don't want any careless accidents in the mine. So do as you're told."

Duro had watched Lucas with some trepidation lately. In spite of his worry, he felt a little sorry for him. Any man living alone with rather dim prospects in his work was inclined to spend too much time with a bottle, and Duro's uneasiness had grown in the past weeks. Sloppy workmanship in a mine, even once, could make the difference between life and death. Lucas hadn't been this agitated when Duro first met him, although there was something sly about him, which he never would admit to Maria. He would extend the hand of friendship to him. Some tasty food and some convivial company might restore Lucas to his former good nature, but if he didn't straighten up, Duro would dissolve the partnership and go his own way. Not that he would do much better. He was scarcely making expenses. The opal seemed to be running out in their claim.

When Lucas arrived that evening, Duro smelled wine on his breath, but his partner was in complete control of his actions and behaved respectfully toward Maria. She effaced herself as much as possible, waiting on the table silently and retiring to the corner where she did her needlework after the meal. She had not tried to make herself more attractive, wore no makeup, and her hair was not arranged in any special way but hung loosely down her back. The whole effect, rather than minimizing her beauty, enhanced it, and Duro noticed that his guest glanced covertly at her several times. As Lucas grew more loquacious with additional wine, Duro became less talkative. Twice Lucas spoke to Maria, trying to draw her into the conversation, but her answers were brief. Duro approved of her conduct, but he watched his partner with gnawing uncertainty. Lucas became more garrulous, refilling his glass without being invited, his face flushed.

"Maria, come join us," he called. "You sit in the corner like a little mouse."

"No, thank you." Her answer was soft, and Duro looked at her speculatively. Ordinarily she would have welcomed some attention, but she averted her face and busied herself in her handiwork. He felt she was trying too hard to distance herself, and he began to brood. Why had she been opposed to inviting Lucas a second time? There was definitely tension in the atmosphere. Duro eased Lucas to the door, reminding him of their work in the morning. He debated whether to invite him back again.

"Maria, say goodnight to our guest." Deliberately he left them alone at the doorway as he stepped back into the room.

"Leave me alone," she whispered, and Lucas leered at her.

"Any time you want an accident in the mine, let me know," he whispered back.

"Good night, Lucas," she said in a clear voice, turning her back on him. Duro observed that her hands were shaking.

He and Lucas worked for two more weeks, following a small vein that produced some fair opal, but not enough for a parcel. Then Duro invited Lucas again to dinner, insisting that Maria stay at the table with them after the meal. Lucas wore clean clothes and was freshly shaved, his broad face beaming with pleasure and reeking of aftershave. His heavy eyebrows did not quite conceal the crafty look in his dark eyes, which he turned often to glance at Maria. His attention did not go unnoticed by Duro, who watched her face change from placid indifference to a slow darkening, finally to a look of desperation. She started to leave the table, but he grasped her arm and forced her back to her seat. "Stay with us so we can enjoy your company," he said. "We don't want to insult our guest."

Lucas, seemingly oblivious to the sarcastic overtone, smiled at Maria and said, "I'm sure you would never do that. You have been a perfect hostess, and I feel right at home."

Duro excused himself to get something from his truck, and instantly Maria turned on Lucas, her eyes flashing. "Get out of my life!"

"Maria, come away with me! Duro's a loser. I can arrange it. He'll never find us."

"I'm in this situation because of you. You deserted me. Do you think I'd trust you again?"

"It is different now. I'll make it up to you."

"Please leave me alone! I'm resigned to my life."

An evil grin made a slash across his face. "And if I tell Duro about us, what kind of life will you have then?"

"If you tell Duro about us, he will kill you!"

The door opened and Duro entered, appearing to sense nothing out of the ordinary but keenly aware of Maria's tightened lips. He sat down and poured wine for each of them, which Lucas drank down thirstily and Maria didn't touch. Duro let Lucas chatter on about mining matters, gossip from town, weather predictions and other trivia, simply nodding from time to time in agreement. Maria sat stiffly, saying nothing. Finally Duro said, "Another work day tomorrow. We'd better say good night."

Lucas rose somewhat unsteadily and bowed to Maria. "Thank you for a delightful evening. You're a lucky man," he added, turning to Duro. Duro inclined his head slightly in acknowledgment, leading the way to the door. Maria deliberately stalked into the small kitchen area and remained there.

"You don't seem to like Lucas," Duro said to Maria after his partner left, his tone probing for information.

"No, I don't. I told you so, remember? I hope you won't invite him again."

"He seems to be very attracted to you."

"I can't help it. I do not invite his attentions." She began washing the few dishes, turning her back.

Duro spun her around. "Don't turn your back on me when I'm talking to you!"

Fear flickered in her eyes. "I'm tired. Please let me finish my work."

A long silence prevailed during which Duro stared at Maria and then relaxed. "All right. Finish the cleaning."

She breathed a sigh of relief, knowing so well his changeable moods. She was glad that this bad one had not escalated into fury. Outside of a few slaps, there had been no severe beatings recently. Keeping her husband on an even keel dominated Maria's daily routine.

Work in the mine continued. The horizontal seam opened into a vertical one which produced some good opal, enough to seek a buyer. Although the amount they received did not adequately compensate for the hard work and many hours expended in producing it, they were grateful to have money again. Duro invited Lucas to stop by their club for a small celebration. They encountered another group of Serbs and began recounting tales of the old country. Someone started singing a ribald ballad, and they all joined in. Wine flowed freely, and there was much laughter. Duro felt much more animated and content than he had for a long time. It was almost like being out on the town with Lejos, as in former days. He drank more than usual.

Duro did not know when Lucas left. He just suddenly realized his partner no longer sat at the table. He stood up uncertainly, his thoughts muddled, gradually becoming aware that he had celebrated too freely. Wanting to clear his head in some fresh air, he went outside and breathed deeply. He thought he might see Lucas there also, escaping from the smoky atmosphere, but he was nowhere to be seen. He wandered back through the dense clouds of smoke looking for him, but to no avail. He checked the toilet room—it was empty. Again he went outside. Lucas' car was gone. It was possible, of course, that he had driven back to the mine. He had a premonition, and suddenly Duro was very much alert.

Instead of driving his truck straight to the dugout, he parked down the road and walked the rest of the way. Lucas' car was parked in front. The light in the window was dim, the drawn curtain precluding any vision of the interior. He listened and could hear muffled sounds coming from within. He tried the door handle gently—the door was locked. With one mighty kick he smashed the door in and witnessed what had been only a tormenting conjecture before. Lucas held Maria in a tight embrace. Her hair was disheveled, her skirt awry, her blouse ripped open. Maria appeared to be struggling, her face full of terror as Duro burst into the room, but whether fear of rape or fear of discovery he couldn't tell.

In that blinding moment, Duro spent no time on accusations. Without hesitation he pulled Lucas away from Maria and struck savagely at his head. Maria sank to the floor, screaming. Then Duro systematically proceeded to beat Lucas with all his strength, knowing his fists were splitting and crushing bones but, oddly, feeling no pain in his hands. He felt Lucas going limp, but he held him up and gave him one last powerful cut to the side of his smashed face and threw him down. In falling, Lucas hit his temple on the corner of the table, and his body seemed to crumple like a grotesque rag doll. He lay still, blood flooding from his broken nose and mouth.

Continuing his unrestrained rage, he turned on Maria, who crouched with her hands raised in an imploring gesture. Whimpering noises came out of her mouth as she tried to speak, Duro hit her across the face, causing a bright red welt. He raised his hand for a second blow but she managed to fling herself away, grabbing a pillow from the bed and clutching it in front of her for protection. "No, Duro, no!" she screamed. "I didn't want to! I swear I didn't! He was forcing me! Look at my blouse!" She indicated the garment, which was ripped down the front. Tears streamed down her cheeks, and she cowered, awaiting his wrath.

Duro looked momentarily at Lucas' body sprawled beside him, ready to kick him out of the way, when something about the inert figure made him pause. He stared down at the battered man, half expecting him to rise and make some belated defense. So precipitous had been Duro's assault that Lucas had had no time to protect himself, let alone retaliate. He was unnaturally still. The blood had ceased to flow.

Duro knelt down and felt for a pulse. There was none. He felt no panic, just a coldness where there had been rage a few minutes before. Then a strange feeling overwhelmed him. It was as if he were someone else, examining this scene from the outside. He was an uninvolved person observing this grisly incident, drawing conclusions, making decisions. Decisions! Yes, plans must be made quickly and carried out efficiently. There was no time to lose. Duro saw with instant clarity that he must dispose of the body. No matter what the provocation, it would be considered murder in the eyes of the law, and even if Maria testified to possible rape, he would be considered a cuckold in the eyes of fellow Serbs. He would handle this situation as he had a similar situation years ago in the old country. It would be an unfortunate accident.

He sat back on his heels and thought. There was a deserted mining area at the Four Mile. The mines had been inactive since the opal had been worked out several years before. No one would be around—the night was dark and the moon would not be up for another hour. Duro wound a towel around Lucas' head, blotting up the blood as best he could. He managed to haphazardly replace his partner's jacket. He began to lift the body and then remembered he had left the truck down the road. He lowered the dead man back onto the floor, and for the first time since he had struck her, he became completely aware of Maria. She was staring at him in horror, her mouth working but emitting no sound.

"Get dressed!" he snapped. "I'm getting the ute. Wipe up the floor while I'm gone." She watched him without moving.

"He's dead, isn't he? You killed him!"

"Shut up! Get up, I said. Get your clothes on."

Slowly she rose to her feet, the red welt standing out against the whiteness of her face. She attempted to rebutton her blouse, but the rip down the front caused her to shudder. She staggered over to the cupboard where their clothes were kept and chose a clean blouse, her fingers trembling as she put it on.

Duro hurried down to the parked truck, glancing quickly in all directions. No one else was about. The few dugouts in the area were dark, their owners either asleep or still in town. He drove carefully, not putting on his lights. When he entered the dugout, Maria was standing behind a chair, clutching the back with all her strength, high-pitched sounds beginning to well up from her throat. Duro recognized the onset of hysteria and slapped her hard, shaking her roughly.

"Clean this up now!" he ordered. "Do what I say or you'll get what he got!"

"What are you going to do with him?" she whispered.

"Better that you don't know. Just clean up the mess."

He looked out the doorway—nothing stirred outside.

He lowered the tailgate of the truck quietly and hefted Lucas' body over his shoulder, cursing the dead weight. He dropped it into the back of the truck and pushed it forward, covering it with a piece of hessian. Even if someone glanced inside the truck, they would see nothing amiss.

"I'll be back shortly," he told Maria. He headed for the Four Mile, taking a back way, looking for signs of life. A few lights glowed dimly, but the track was empty. He reached the edge of town in a few minutes and soon was on the main road. He breathed more easily when he saw no approaching headlights or any signs of a vehicle closing in on him from behind. He knew he must hurry, for shortly the moon would be rising. A quick drop down a mine shaft and the distasteful job would be over and forgotten.

When Duro returned to the dugout, he parked the ute and quietly slipped inside. He would have to repair the broken lock the next day. Maria had cleaned the floor and stood with the scrub rag in her hands, her eyes looked like two dark expressionless pools. Only her twitching fingers betrayed her anxiety. He knew she was afraid of him, but she had no cause now. His anger was used up; all his feelings had become numbed, and he just wanted to rest. He threw himself on the bed and tried to relax, but the tiredness would not drift into sleep. His head throbbed; his pulse raced. How strange, he thought, my body just won't slow down. Everything's pressing down on me like a great weight. I can't seem to fight it.

"Bring me some wine," he ordered Maria. She poured him a large glass and after swallowing a mouthful, he shook his head. "I must not drink too much. I must not lose my head. There is so much to think about, so many plans to be made."

She spoke for the first time. "What kind of plans?"

"I have to get rid of Lucas' car. Lucas' absence will be noticed. The police will ask questions. We must be ready."

He saw panic sweep across her face. "No! Oh, no!"

He observed her carefully. She never could stand up to questioning, he thought. She will act frightened and arouse suspicion. What can I do?

"I'm taking Lucas' car away. Can you follow me in the ute and bring me back?" He knew the answer before she shook her head negatively. She was a poor driver at best, and he couldn't trust her at the wheel tonight. He'd leave the ute on one of the side tracks at the Three Mile, so anyone finding it would naturally think Lucas had fallen into one of the shafts. After looking fruitlessly in several mines, authorities would probably give up. There were dozens of such possible sites, and if by chance he was discovered, a fall down forty feet would produce the same injuries he already had sustained. Lucas had been drinking heavily at the club, and his death would be readily accepted as another unfortunate accident.

The three-mile hike back home helped Duro clear his mind, and he concocted yet another plan. He would return to the club after changing his bloodstained shirt, hoping no one would have noticed his absence with all the carousing going on or his change of clothes. Better yet, he would keep his jacket on. When he arrived, the crowd was still drinking and playing cards. He slipped unobtrusively into an empty seat and ordered a round of drinks. Someone slapped him affectionately on the back. He glanced casually around and asked if anyone had seen Lucas recently. No one had.

"I hope he hasn't spent all his money," Duro remarked. "He owes me some. Come to think of it, I haven't seen him for the last couple of hours. He wasn't in any condition to drive then."

He joined a card game, and nothing more was said about his partner's absence.

During the course of the game, Duro mentioned that his wife was going to drive to Kingoonya the next day to spend a few days with friends. He had promised Maria a trip to the town for her birthday, and he couldn't leave the mine now that things had picked up. If he didn't let her go, she would nag him to death. Women! The men accused him of being too soft with his wife, and they all laughed. The card game went on for another hour. Duro didn't mind losing. He was pleased that his hands were steady. He made arrangements with a miner friend to drive him out to the Eleven Mile in the morning, since Maria would have the truck.

"Lucas is probably sleeping it off and won't come for me. When Maria gets back, I'll take my turn driving out. Maybe I'll have Lucas stay with me in the meantime." He tried to think of everything to allay suspicion. When he left the club, many others still continued playing cards. He waved goodbye, relieved that it all was easier than he expected.

Maria was in bed when he returned. He pulled off the covers and ordered her to get up. She held the pillow in front of her defensively, but he shook his head. "Pack a bag. You're driving to Kingoonya tomorrow." Her eyes widened. "You can stay at the motel there. You can't be around here for the next week."

She had applied cold cloths to her face, but the ugly welt was darkening. He was glad that he had not hit her again with the same intensity. He watched her pack, as she silently placed her few clothes into a small satchel. The night's activities had drained him, and somehow now he could not hate her. Would he ever know what really happened that night? It didn't seem possible that it was still that same night. He stretched out on the bed with his clothes on and fell instantly to sleep.

When he awoke, it was dawn, and Maria was gone. He regretted that it was necessary for her to go. That road from Coober Pedy would make a wreck out of any vehicle, but there was no choice. She never could have stood up to the mildest questioning, and the condition of her face would have produced talk. By the time she returned the queries would be over, and things would be back to normal. Maria would be more amenable, too. She surely had learned her lesson this time and would be the submissive wife he demanded.

When his friends came by for him in the morning, they joked about their night out the previous evening. "We had quite a celebration, didn't we?" They all laughed, and Duro felt relaxed and calm. They stopped at the mine, but Lucas' car was not at the shack.

"Damn," Duro exploded. "He's probably sleeping it off somewhere. I need him. We were to start a new lead today."

"He must have gotten lost last night," said one of the men. "He can't be too far away."

Duro shrugged. "Just my luck. He owes me some money. I hope he didn't skip town."

"Oh, he's around somewhere. If he doesn't show up, we'll give you a ride back to your dugout this afternoon."

"Thanks. I'll do the best I can today. I'll sure give him hell when I see him."

CHAPTER NINETEEN

"I HAVE SOMETHING SPECIAL PLANNED for you, Janet," Peter told the enraptured girl. "It's a full moon tonight, and I want you to share a spectacular sight out at the Four Mile."

"I'm so happy you invited me," Janet said. "I ... I've missed you."

After thinking it over, Peter decided not to buy wine after all. He didn't want a repeat of his experience with Lily Hampton. Actually, he didn't think he would need any wine to soften up this girl. Her obvious adoration made him confident of her easy acquiescence. Infatuation certainly simplified things.

He parked his car in the usual place behind his favorite opal heap and spread the blanket carefully on the low shelf. This time there would be no mistakes. He would take his time and build the romance carefully. He suspected Janet was an innocent, and he didn't want to frighten her. Premature action might spoil everything. He might have a virtual gold mine in Janet if she were responsive, for she could be available whenever he wanted her. He enjoyed challenge and novelty, but the idea of permanency without responsibility appealed to him.

He put his arm around her gently and told her to watch where the light was beginning to penetrate the darkness. The moon would be rising there. He nibbled her ear a little, stroking the back of her neck, pleased to feel her pulse pounding. Everything was going well.

Suddenly two headlights appeared, an unexpected intrusion into their privacy. Peter cursed under his breath. Who would be coming out here at night? No one ever visited this abandoned field, even in the daytime. Maybe they would stay on the main track and not turn into this area. He held Janet tighter and whispered, "Somebody's lost. They won't stay long."

But the truck did not falter, and the driver turned into their area as if he knew exactly where he was going. This was no place for an amateur, with all the open shafts and unmarked holes, and the unexpected visitor piqued Peter's curiosity. He relaxed his hold on Janet and narrowed his eyes. The moon had begun to rise, and he could see the outline of a dark blue ute. He had seen a vehicle like that recently. He searched his memory and quickly recalled that the vehicle belonged to Duro Sulecic, the Yugoslav who had been Marcos' partner. Now why would he be coming out to the Four Mile at night? Not with a girlfriend surely. Duro's wife was a good-looking sheila whom Peter had studied speculatively on several occasions. Strange.

The driver continued down the track alongside the opal heap where Peter and Janet sat, but in the dim light he had not seen them. Peter had parked his car on the opposite side of the heap where it was hidden from sight. The truck came to a halt a short distance away, and Peter put his finger to his lips, motioning Janet to be still while he investigated. She held her breath with suppressed excitement.

He walked cautiously around the opal heap, placing each step so as not to make the slightest sound. He stayed in the shadow, his eyes as observant as a cat's, and he watched Duro trying to drag a heavy object from the back of the truck. The Yugoslav had difficulty managing it but, finally, after pulling hard, wrenched it out of the truck and on to the ground. He tugged it about fifteen feet up the slope of an old opal heap. Peter waited, unmoving. The moon was fully risen now, exposing Duro's face. The expression was one of calmness and detachment. Peter stared at the strange scene, puzzled, and then realized—he was witness to a burial! Who? Why? Fear twisted his innards. He prayed the girl wouldn't make a sound now. He didn't move a muscle as Duro pushed the body over the edge of the shaft. A few moments later he heard a dull thud as it hit the bottom. The Yugoslav returned to the ute, for a shovel and then walked back to the opening of the mine.

Peter became increasingly nervous. What was the man waiting for? Why didn't he start shoveling dirt into the shaft? He finally decided the miner was weighing his options: if he covered the body with dirt, it would be an obvious murder. If he left it uncovered, it might look like an accident—a drunk unable to navigate at night. But the Four Mile was a long way from town for an inebriated miner to wonder out to. Duro seemingly came to a decision and began to shovel resolutely, the metal gleaming in the moonlight. At the end of five minutes he turned and ran down the slope. Without looking back, he started the car's engine.

It was only when Peter saw the red tail lights gradually disappearing that he felt it was safe to move.

Janet still lay cuddled up on the blanket and looked at Peter with an inquiring expression, half eager, half hesitant.

"What was it, Peter? What did you see?"

He shook his head, unable to speak. He realized his impending impotence. For once in his adult life he would be unable to respond to a willing partner. He took Janet by the hands and raised her gently to her feet.

"I'm sorry, luv," he told her. "I must have picked up some sort of wog at dinner. I'm feeling kind of crook, so I'd better take you home. Maybe we can try it another time."

Janet, perplexed, obediently followed him to the car without questioning him. Peter opened the door for her and he climbed into the driver's seat. He drove back to Coober Pedy slowly. He had some serious thinking to do.

CHAPTER TWENTY

SERGEANT MACDONALD sat stiffly at his desk, a small frown between his eyes. Something in the back of his mind was bothering him—an elusive idea, a fragment of identification that nearly took form and then slipped away. He had found from previous experience that direct concentration was rarely profitable, so he resorted to imagery, letting his impressions wander to and fro. He sought out different textures in the stark office: the dusty surface of his desk that had been wiped clean an hour before, the crumpled papers in the waste basket, the rough weave of his jacket, the shiny surface of the clock on the wall. His thoughts drifted to shapes and forms—everything was at right angles here, as was fitting. It was a masculine, business-like and austere place. Nothing specific drifted into his consciousness; his free association did not bring to the surface what he was summoning. Like a bothersome gnat some notion was buzzing around in his mind but it wouldn't settle.

He thought of the Yank out at the Eleven Mile, wondering what his background was. He didn't like Yanks that age; in fact, his feelings of hostility grew as he sat there. The sergeant knew why: an American soldier on R and R had stolen his girl. Although he never saw the guy, MacDonald's mates informed him that his rival was a big, good-looking bloke with money to spend, and he had scarcely a shilling in the pocket of his old fatigues. That interloper in his flashy uniform had swept his girl off her feet. MacDonald had been left humiliated and resentful. The old pain came back whenever he heard an American accent.

His current situation was his own fault. He had been too hasty to get married; too hurt to be discriminating. If Elizabeth had been different, his life would have been different. Since the accident ten years ago, he was in a trap from which he never could escape. Elizabeth had become a whining shrew, never passing up an opportunity to remind him that it was his fault that she was partially paralyzed. He had been angry with her that night, the road was slippery and he was driving too fast. He had recovered from the incident with minor injuries, but her condition was permanent. Confined for long hours in a wheelchair, she sat and brooded.

The sergeant sighed. Even thinking about his wife was painful and upsetting. Elizabeth was an omnipresent burden that never lifted, embittering him to everything but his work. He lived for his work—every case he solved, every person he brought to justice, every suspicion he proved true. Without his job he would be nothing. His uniform and authority gave him stature and the respect of the community.

People didn't like him, he knew that, but they didn't under-estimate him. He was ruthless in pursuing the guilty and absolutely incorruptible. He had discreet and reliable sources for information and kept his finger on most of what was happening in town. He didn't know everything but he knew a lot.

Sergeant MacDonald's mind wandered back to the Yank. It wasn't the American who was troubling him specifically; it was something else. He let his thoughts graze a moment before realization hit him. It was the reaction of that Yugoslav, Sulecic when the sergeant told him his wife had been killed after running head on into a road train. He had tried to soften the blow by stating that her death appeared to be instanta-neous, and that she had not suffered. The man had stared unbelievingly at first and then turned pale, crying out, "Oh my God, no!" All that was to be expected; those manifesta-tions of grief did not trouble the sergeant. It was something else, something not quite right ... What was it?

He relaxed for a moment, tipped back in his chair and stared at the ceiling. Then suddenly he realized—Duro had been expecting something else from him. When Duro had opened the door and recognized the policeman, he showed a flicker of fear, and that infinitesimal flicker preceded the sergeant's delivery of the bad news. Most men here showed silent resentment when the law intruded on their property, but Duro's reaction was more than resentment. He had been momentarily alarmed and then hastily concealed it. To

MacDonald's knowledge, the wife's accident was unforeseen. How could it have been otherwise? The information brought to him was the incontrovertible fact that she had crossed right into the path of the road train, probably blinded by the rising sun. But what could have set off that instinctive reaction of her husband? It was strange, very strange. Usually these foreign men did not entrust their wives to journeys of any distance alone. Brian MacDonald was puzzled. What could account for that spark of panic? He would file this detail in that special compartment of his brain where he stored odd information, and he would consider it again if necessary.

His thoughts wandered to the new waitress at the Opal Inn. She wasn't really pretty, but she was attractive in a wholesome kind of way. It was her trim figure and her gorgeous hair that made a man look twice. He had looked at her more than twice but knew it would go no further. He had decided long ago that celibacy was the only answer in his position. It was too easy to get involved, and in this town extra-marital affairs, unlike striking it rich, were not well kept secrets. He would not put his job in peril. Although Elizabeth constantly accused him of having other women, all his energy went into his work. Still, it didn't hurt to look. He had even looked at the Aboriginal woman who took care of his wife but was glad she was spindle shanked and ugly, offering no temptation. He was pleased to have her there for she was kind and relieved him of extra responsibility.

MacDonald shook himself out of his reverie and reached for the stack of mail waiting to be opened. Work always came first!

CHAPTER TWENTY-ONE

DURO DID NOT UNDERSTAND HIMSELF. Why had he stayed on in Coober Pedy? Partly it was his lack of money—burial expenses for Maria had taken almost everything he had—but there was something deeper that held him. It was as though he wanted to steep himself in feelings of guilt and remorse. He wandered through the opal fields, walking many miles each day, returning at sundown to sit alone in his dugout and drink. Although his friends urged him to join them, he did not go to the club again. Everyone felt sorry for him, but gradually they stopped coming to see him. Although he had often resented Maria, even hated her at times, he missed her now that he was alone, so terribly alone. He was not a religious man, but he felt that some divine punishment awaited him. He wanted to leave, but something kept him bound to Coober Pedy. He was restless. Once he even walked to the Four Mile and stared down the shaft.

If he just could know what really occurred that awful night before he arrived at the dugout. The scene was etched into his brain. Maria appeared to be defending herself against

Lucas, but was she really? Her blouse was torn, but how? He would never have the answers; he would never know if an innocent woman died in the train accident. Was it an accident, or had he driven her to destroy herself?

The policeman had questioned him twice about his relations with his partner. Lucas' car had been found at the Three Mile, and a search party had investigated several abandoned mines without any results.

"When was the last time you saw Lucas?" Sergeant MacDonald asked, noting any variation in his answer from the previous questioning.

"I'm not sure. We were all drinking rather heavily. About nine o'clock, I guess."

"Some said it was closer to ten. Would you like to change your story?"

"No, I think it was more like nine than ten o'clock."

"Are you sure about that?" The policeman noticed beads of sweat appearing on Duro's swarthy forehead.

"No, I'm not sure! I was probably half drunk. I can't remember." His voice was almost shrill.

"Did anyone else in your group see him leave?"

"I don't know. I never asked them. Why don't you?" His tone had gone from plaintive to surly.

A faint smile appeared on the policeman's lips. "I know how distressing this all is for you, but you understand that if there has been any foul play, we must follow every avenue to uncover it."

"What makes you think there's been foul play?"

"I haven't said there has been—I just said 'if'." MacDonald saw Duro's calloused hands tighten. "The law is always concerned when someone disappears. Probably Lucas just wandered about and eventually fell into some mine shaft, but there are a great many abandoned shafts out at the Three Mile, and I doubt that we can investigate them all." He watched Duro's hands relax. "That's why exact times are so important in situations like these. Now, what time did you say that you left the Serbian Club?"

"I think it was about eleven o'clock. A bunch of us were playing cards. Some left and others came in. I was there the whole evening."

"You didn't leave at all?"

"No, just to step outside for some fresh air and clear my head. I was beginning to lose."

"Ah! How much did you lose?"

"Exactly $11.50. That's when I decided to quit. The stakes were getting too high for me."

"I see. Did any of the others see you leave?"

"Oh, yes. I discussed getting a ride in the morning out to the mine. My wife took the truck so I had no transportation."

"And had your wife's trip been planned in advance?" The policeman saw Duro's eyes flicker for just an instant, just like the time he met him at the door.

"Of course, it was. We had talked about it for several days, but I told the fellows about it just that night in case she changed her mind." Belligerence crept into his voice. "I can't have my friends think I put up with a wife who runs my life."

"Quite right. Well, let me express my condolences once again, Mr. Sulecic. I think it best if you don't leave town for a while in case we need more information."

"I can't leave even if I wanted to. I don't have a car."

"I understand. Well, thank you for your cooperation."

After the policeman left, Duro sank even deeper into despair. He asked a friend to take him to his mine one morning and looked at the new lead. It showed no promise, but he stayed at the shack and continued to work for several more days without encouragement. He knew working alone would be fruitless if the opal had run out. He was desperate for money. He would have to find a job elsewhere.

CHAPTER TWENTY-TWO

ONE DAY AS ERIC INVESTIGATED A NEW DRIVE with a recently sharpened pick, a sharp pain told him what havoc a moment's carelessness could cause. The point of the pick tore into his calf and blood gushed out. He quickly bound up the wound with a strip torn from his shirt, cursing himself for his haste and stupidity. Now he might have to miss many days' work. He yelled to Dimitrios to follow him up the ladder. Every step was agony—the ladder seemed endless as the searing pain jolted his whole body. When he reached the top, he tightened the binding again, and the young Greek blanched at the sight of the copious bleeding, which had not fully abated in spite of the stricture. Eric reassured his partner that it wasn't as bad as it looked and tossed him the keys to the truck as he hobbled toward it. Dimitrios drove as fast as he could as Eric lay back, absorbing each jolt of the road with his eyes closed.

As with his previous injury, Molly was on duty. She took one look at his leg and summoned the doctor, shaking her head in apprehension.

"Oh, Eric, you wouldn't listen to me, would you?" she

chided. "You've really got a bad one this time. I don't think your climb up the ladder helped it any."

"I couldn't very well have stayed down there, could I?" he said. He was in no mood for her admonitions and winced as she removed the makeshift bandage.

When the doctor arrived, she changed her tone, and became brisk and impersonal. The doctor administered an anesthetic and probed carefully.

"You're a lucky man," he commented. "It's deep and serious, but it could have been much worse. You just missed a major blood vessel. You'll need many stitches, and you'll have to rest your leg. No going up and down ladders for awhile."

"How long, Doctor?"

"Several weeks, anyway."

"Several weeks!" Eric groaned. What a mess! He sensed his young partner was working under some time restriction, and this would be a blow to him just when things had begun to look promising. Dimitrios could not do it all alone. They would need another partner.

As the doctor stitched up the jagged wound, Eric made plans. He would look for a new man to work with Dimitrios, giving up part of his share in the mine to him. After all, it was his own fault the accident happened, and he should pay for his negligence. But what experienced miner would be available on such short notice? He had heard of the Yugoslav who recently lost his wife, and rumor had it that he was looking for work. Eric asked Dimitrios to drive him over to Duro's dugout that evening, for in spite of what the doctor said about resting, this was a matter that must be attended to promptly. As always, his young Greek partner accepted suggestions without argument, but the dormant hostility in his eyes baffled Eric. He knew he carried his share of the work in the mine, in fact, he worked extra hard at times to keep up, so Dimitrios had no right to feel he was a slacker.

When Eric knocked on the door of the dugout, a harsh voice shouted, "Come in!" As he and Dimitrios stepped inside they saw that Duro was in the process of packing what apparently were his dead wife's belongings into a cardboard box. He clutched a nightgown that had seen many washings and a rather frayed sweater, neither of which he could stuff into the overflowing container. The Yugoslav glanced at the two men, his face wearing a frustrated expression that Eric did not believe was prompted by their unexpected intrusion. He looked at Eric with antagonism, his large calloused hands still clutching the worn garments.

"What do you want?" he demanded.

Eric came right to the point. "I understand you're an experienced powder man and you might be looking for work."

"Well?" Duro threw the clothes on top of the box, his tone truculent.

"I'm looking for someone to work on shares. I'm furnishing all supplies. My partner here has a good working mine, and we need a third man since I injured myself. Are you interested?"

Duro looked at Dimitrios. "I know you. Your mine is

near the one I own."

He remained silent for a few minutes. His upper lip stretched back almost in a grimace, his strong white teeth chewing at his lower lip. Eric had second thoughts about his stability and regretted coming to him. Then the miner seemed to relax.

"I have worked only with Serbian partners," he said. "There is sometimes a ... a lack of trust between nationalities. But my last partner disappeared owing me money and bills to pay, so maybe this time a Greek and a Yank would not be too bad. I need the money. My wife's burial took all my savings."

"I heard," responded Eric with sympathy. "I'm sorry that—"

Duro cut him short. "It's past," he said sharply. "Yes, I'm definitely interested. I've heard your mine has done well."

Eric lifted his eyebrows. How can secrets be broadcast so quickly? Rumor must be a powerful accompaniment to success, but of course everyone on the field had heard about the stolen pipe.

Duro sat for some time without moving after Eric left. Maria's picture was face down on the table where he had placed it the week before, and he had postponed any decision regarding its disposal. He knew it should be displayed; convention dictated it, and visitors expected to see it in its usual place. But of course he had no visitors, so it didn't really matter. He could not bring himself to look at it—not yet. He still did not know the truth about that night, there was only dark suspicion. There was something in Maria's attitude toward Lucas that had not been natural. Could she have known him before? Could he be the one who ... Duro slammed his fist on the table. He never would know the truth because the only two who did were dead, and he was the cause of their deaths. Perhaps he meant for Maria to die, sending her out at night all alone. He had no regrets over Lucas' death. Lucas was scum and he deserved it. Duro just didn't want to be accused of his murder. He was sure that there was no way anything could be traced to him. How could it? Empty roads held no witnesses, and the Four Mile had been deserted. He had a job now and could finally relax. He was in the clear.

CHAPTER TWENTY-THREE

THE FOLLOWING WEEK Molly removed the stitches from Eric's injury but was too busy to see him socially. She worked over at the Aboriginal Reserve on her free days, she informed him. Maybe they could meet some other time. Eric was disappointed and realized he had botched a promising relationship. He was still too vulnerable to confide all the convolutions of his past and trust that she would understand. He dared not lose her completely. He waited another week and tried once more. This time she was receptive. Yes, she'd have dinner with him again.

The meal passed pleasantly with small talk.

"How's your leg feeling now?"

"Much better. I haven't been down into the mine since the accident. I stay on top."

"Good. I'm glad."

"The new man seems to be working well with Dimitrios."

"Fine."

Then Eric dropped the light conversation and reached for her hand. She didn't pull away.

"I was rude the other night, Molly," he began.

"No, Eric, you don't owe me any explanations." She sensed his need, but reluctance, to confide in her. She waited quietly.

"I'm discouraged about ever finding Sandy. All channels seem to be closed. I don't know what else I can do."

"Why is Sandy so important to you?"

He hesitated. "He's my son, Molly."

"I suspected that might be so. How long has it been since you've seen him?"

"I've never seen him, Molly." She did not appear shocked or judgmental, just interested. He went on. "It was during the Korean War. I wanted to marry his mother Anne, but she was here and I was in the States." His voice grew softer. "She married someone else and now she's dead."

"I'm so sorry, Eric."

"You can see why it's important for me to find him."

She squeezed his hand in sympathy. "I'm glad you told me."

"You asked me about teaching. I thought for awhile that I never wanted to teach again, but you made me see myself in a different light. I guess I'll never stop wanting to help kids. I was terribly bitter for a few months, but deep down I really would like to try again."

"What about your mining?"

"That's been a wonderful challenge. It solved some problems for me, but it's only a temporary thing. After my accident I realized I'd just like to make enough money so that I can have some choices about the future. I don't want to go home broke."

"There's a teacher shortage here, you know," she told him.

"I don't think the government would extend my visa. In fact," he confided, "I'm not supposed to be working now. I'm actually skating on thin ice."

She laughed. "That's such a funny expression! You've used it before. I've never skated on ice, thin or otherwise!" They both relaxed.

"We've had very different childhoods, haven't we?" Molly observed.

"Maybe not as different as you think. We both lost a parent and had to struggle to find our own identity. My ..." Eric touched his cheek, "my facial disfigurement and your racial background have made us more sensitive to the problems of others, I think. My scarring isn't so noticeable now, but it was difficult for me at times when I was a young boy.

Eric's earliest memories were associated with the big potbellied stove in the living room. It was black with silver trim, which Mama kept polished until it shone like a mirror. Eric and his younger brother Lars tried to find their faces in it, but all that was reflected back would be part of a chin or a nose or an eye. It was fun to do, and it gave them an excuse to be near the warm behemoth.

The flue stretched clear to the ceiling, and there was a large opening near the base of the stove into which Papa fed logs. The children were fascinated to see him open its cavernous mouth to throw in chunks of wood. There was something almost enchanted about the stove. Eric pretended that it would come to life and talk to him like a special companion, pleasant and comfortable. On cold winter nights when he and his brother and sister climbed into the loft, he would say a reluctant goodbye to the big iron stove and try to get warm in bed. He could see his breath in the little hollow he made around his face with the covers. Although tempted to climb back downstairs and cuddle close to the stove, he didn't, because Papa would think he was a sissy. And Papa's poor opinion would be worse than any frigid night, even if the water in the pitcher did freeze by morning. The one bedroom downstairs was not big enough to include three children. Papa was not well and needed the warmer space. Besides, all youngsters in northern Michigan learned early to put up with hardship as a normal part of life.

Eric loved to hear his father tell his colorful and exciting stories. They were full of elves and trolls, giants and talking animals. Mama would sit and smile quietly, her nimble fingers busy with darning and mending. The family gathered around the stove like it was a loving friend.

There was a little shelf on the side of the stove where Mama would set the coffee pot to keep it hot all day. When Eric was only four years old, he must have reached up and dislodged it. He would never forget the look in Mama's eyes when the hot coffee spilled down the side of his face and shoulder. The pain was so intense and the shock so great that he could not cry out at first. It was as though his breath had been scalded, too. And then the screams came. Even now, years later, he could hear himself screaming and see his mother's white, horrified face. His father had just arrived home. He snatched the boy up, covered his face with cold, wet towels and carried him to the doctor's house. The rest was enveloped in a haze of worried eyes, anxious voices, and someone saying, "Are his eyes all right?" After that, there was a merciful void.

Eric began to heal, and the household returned to normal. His parents allowed him to sleep in the downstairs bedroom until he was better. When he was fully recovered, he reluctantly left the warm sanctuary of the pleasant room and returned to the cold inhospitable loft. His sister Hulda was away at school most of the day or busy with chores, so there was no one to play with. Eric grew restless.

One afternoon while Lars was taking a nap and Mama was working in the little garden, Eric went back into his parents' bedroom. He wanted to explore the room beyond the familiar furnishings, and a spirit of adventure possessed him to climb on a chair to see what was on top of the bureau. He was disappointed at first to see only some jars, a pretty bottle and a comb and brush. He opened one jar and felt some sticky white stuff and hastily closed it. A bottle yielded the scent of lavender, which he knew was Mama's special scent, so he carefully replaced the top. A scarf and ribbon held no interest for him. Then he saw the mirror, with its fancy tortoise shell trim, a Christmas present to Mama from Papa. He picked it up and turned it over. The face of a stranger looked back at him, a face with a red, puckered scar that zigzagged down his cheek from the eyebrow to the chin. Eric opened his mouth to scream. When he realized that the face belonged to him, tears coursed down his cheeks, tasting bitter on his lips.

Eric threw the mirror on the floor with all his strength, and glass flew everywhere. He could not stop the sobbing. Suddenly, he realized what he had done and was terrified of the consequences. For a moment he stood frozen, and then he ran upstairs to the loft as fast as his small legs would take him. Lars was still asleep, looking like a cherub with his tousled blond hair against the pillow. Eric knew he would never look like a cherub. He was dark, like pictures of the devil, and he feared his heart must be dark, too. Creeping into his sister's bed, he pulled the heavy quilt over him and hoped the little swell under the covers would not be noticed.

The front door opened, and the sound of chattering of voices floated up to him. He recognized Papa's voice and his cough, which was getting worse. Eric shivered. Papa must have come home early. The sharp sound of wood being dropped into the wood box followed, and then there was a long silence. When his mother and father spoke again, it was in Swedish, which they used sometimes when they wished to talk privately. Then there was another silence, long and ominous. Eric felt the icy fingers of fear run along his spine. He wanted to be far, far away.

Would he be whipped, he wondered? Rarely had he been

spanked, but when he had, he remembered the firm hand and the stinging pain. Worse, he remembered his father's hot, angry eyes and his mother's anguished face. Which hurt more, the physical punishment or the disapproval? He decided that he would rather be beaten than face his parents' rejection, although he knew he deserved both.

He heard heavy footsteps coming up the stairs. Eric began to shake. The eighth step always squeaked, and as his father approached it, Eric frantically hoped that he would change his mind and go back downstairs. But no, there it was, the squeak of the eighth step. Papa was coming up to the loft! Eric cowered under the covers. He could not control his heartbeat. He thought his chest would burst. The steps kept coming. He tried to crawl further down the bed, but he knew he could not fool his father so he sat up and waited, putting his hand protectively over the disfigured side of his face.

He had seen his father angry before, and he expected to see wrath or at the least, disappointment. But the look on his Papa's face now was not anger—it was agony, a shared sorrow from deep within his being. His father put his arms around Eric and just rocked him silently for a long time. Eric buried his face in his father's shirt. It smelled of wood smoke and tobacco and sweat—an earthy, comforting smell. Not a word was spoken until Papa covered Eric with the quilt and said, "You rest now." He sat by his bedside until Eric fell into a deep sleep.

When Eric awakened, he was conscious of the lateness,

and hunger told him suppertime must be near. He went downstairs with mixed feelings, briefly looking past the open bedroom door. The broken glass had been swept up, and the family sat in their usual places at the table. No one said anything as Eric slid into his seat. Papa spoke the familiar blessing, and Mama gave him an extra portion of fruit soup—his favorite. Her hair and sweet smile reminded him of the angel in their church window. And Papa? Papa was Papa!

"People were both tactful and cruel about my scar, Molly," Eric said. "It's gradually faded, except when I'm cold or angry, and I've learned to live with it. Now I hardly ever think of it. How about you? Do you have to steel yourself against lifted eyebrows?"

Molly laughed a little sadly. "If lifted eyebrows were all I had to contend with, my life would be easier. Some people keep their distance until they get to know me."

"Has your background made dating difficult?"

"Yes. Men shy away from me unless they think they'll have an easy conquest. Even Peter Bagley invited me out! That was a very short conversation, I assure you." She smiled into his eyes. "I've learned to judge character pretty well."

Eric smiled back. "I hope I pass muster."

She waited to see if he would expand on anything else from his past, but he didn't. He ordered coffee, prolonging the evening as long as possible. There was so much he wanted to tell her, to justify himself in her eyes, to arouse her compassion, but he held back.

He looked at the restaurant entrance as Janet said in a strained voice, "Oh, Lord! Here comes the bus. Now we will be busy and it's so late."

A group of rumpled tourists swept through the lounge entrance, eager for some refreshment. Janet rushed over to their tables to take orders. One of the group, poised in the doorway, looked out of place in her neat, unwrinkled suit and cool demeanor.

My God! thought Eric. It can't be! Cynthia stood calmly surveying the scene before her. When her eyes met Eric's, she stared in amazement. Then her expression changed to hostility, and with the lifting of her upper lip, it became the contemptuous sneer he knew so well. Color rose in Eric's face, and he toyed with his coffee cup, trying to appear oblivious. He sensed that Molly was studying him curiously, noting the transformation and perhaps assuming it was because of her questioning.

As Cynthia approached, he hoped desperately that she would be gracious and walk by without speaking. But Molly's youthful presence seemed to bring out something deep and vindictive from within her, and she stopped at their table. Reluctantly Eric rose.

"Molly, this is Cynthia Garrett," he said. He had heard that she had returned to her maiden name. "Cynthia, this is Molly Riley."

Cynthia put on her most charming smile. "I'm happy to

meet you, Miss Riley." She turned to Eric. "She's very lovely, but so young! I would have thought that Crestmore College would have taught you a lesson, but then teachers are the last to learn, aren't they?" She studied them both with an amused expression. "It's nice to meet you, Miss Riley."

She laughed and moved on to join her group. Eric stood up to leave, and Molly stood up also, looking at his closed face with bewilderment.

"An old friend?" Molly asked, trying to ease the situation.

"Not a friend," he snapped. Cynthia's appearance had put a cloud over an evening that Eric had hoped would restore Molly's good will. He was disgusted with Cynthia and with himself. "I think we'd better go."

They passed Peter Bagley as they left the inn. Tapping his fingers nervously on the table, the young man appeared oblivious to them. Thank heaven Eric had been shrewd enough to call Peter's bluff. Now the con man was probably fishing around for a new victim, and Eric wondered what nefarious scheme he was planning. Eric noticed that the pretty waitress was casting covert glances at him in between serving customers. Eric hoped she wasn't going to get tangled up with Peter. She seemed to be a nice girl.

He didn't sleep well that night. He didn't want to think about Cynthia, but the harder he tried to push her out of his mind, the more aggressive became her intrusion. How could he ever explain that unfortunate relationship to Molly?

Cynthia was uncomfortable when she retired to her hotel room that night. It was not characteristic of her to be rude in public. Rarely had she ever lost control of the cool facade for which she was so well known. Although startled when she first saw Eric, she was completely ambivalent about talking with him. But when she realized he was with a beautiful young woman and that he was trying to ignore her, all the old animosity flared up. Before she even saw the girl, she reflected that Eric was quite a handsome man and that his scar, which had so distressed her during their years together, was barely discernible. She remembered how enjoyable it had been to have an escort to social functions and how many pleasant evenings they had spent entertaining faculty and friends. But seeing Molly, with her bewitching smile, made Cynthia feel discarded—yes, discarded. Eric was the one who wanted the divorce, she reminded herself. She wanted to wound him, and she knew she had done so very effectively.

She felt a few regrets the next morning but soon shrugged them off. Her tour was expensive and short, and she had no intention of letting anything troublesome mar it. She wondered if he was also on a tour. In that case, their paths might cross again, and that could be awkward.

As she started downstairs for breakfast, her right foot twisted in her sandal, and she was gripped by a sharp pain. She hobbled to meet the rest of the group. The tour director arranged for her to be taken to the hospital to have her ankle examined.

Molly looked up as Cynthia entered, and except for a quick flicker of recognition, maintained her professionalism. "The doctor is busy with an emergency, so we'll apply ice packs for now." She gathered the necessary supplies and secured the ice pack with elastic bandages.

Cynthia lost her composure for a moment and stared at the nurse. Curiosity consumed her, and dormant jealousy prodded her to question the girl.

"Have you known Eric long?"

"Not long. Am I hurting you?"

"No. Does he live here permanently?"

"I know very little about Mr. Christianson." Molly's tone closed the subject, but Cynthia refused to let the topic drop.

"Did he tell you about me?"

"No." Molly would not be drawn out. "Do you think you can stand on it now? Does your bus leave today? It would be best to rest your foot if you can."

"We're here until tomorrow, but I don't want to miss anything. Eric didn't tell you anything about Crestmore College?"

Molly rose to her feet. "Why should he, Miss Garrett? His life is of no concern to me." Molly gathered up her supplies with a gesture of finality. Cynthia was seized with an overpowering need to drive in a vindictive barb.

"Eric was dismissed from his teaching position because of a scandal," she persisted with a note of triumph. "A sexual misconduct charge with one of his students. No wonder he didn't tell you!"

"Miss Garrett, I don't know why it's so important for you to degrade Mr. Christianson, but if you have anything to say, I suggest you say it to him. Now if you'll excuse me."

Deflated and humiliated, Cynthia felt no satisfaction in the manner in which she had handled the discussion. She had always viewed Eric as socially beneath her, but she recognized that her behavior had been—how she hated to admit it— gauche in this situation. She was glad she would not have to see Eric again. The nurse evidently meant nothing to him, and why should it annoy her if she did? Cynthia would be happy to leave the next day; she felt old and tired.

Molly mechanically placed the ice packs back into the refrigerator. Who was this hateful woman and what was her purpose? Molly tried not to believe what Cynthia had said, but Eric was so evasive about his past. Lingering doubt began to creep in. Why had Cynthia behaved so viciously?

Molly would not pry. She would wait until Eric was ready to confide in her. She would trust her instincts, and in the meantime, she would call upon a part of her Aboriginal inheritance—patience.

CHAPTER TWENTY-FOUR

Peter Bagley sat in a pub, bought a few beers, and listened to the local gossip. As always he made it his business to sift out any information that he could use to his advantage. He spent some time contemplating the relationship between Duro and his wife and about the news of her accident. The disappearance of Lucas also came under discussion, but the consensus was that he had fallen into a mine shaft in a drunken stupor or that some thief had lifted his wallet and disposed of him. Such things had happened before. Duro himself had never commented other than saying, "My wife is dead. My partner is gone. I have no luck."

A plan began to form in Peter's mind. He would not be precipitous—time was on his side. He knew Duro could not have much money now, but he also heard that the Yugoslav had begun working for the Yank. It was generally understood that the mine was doing well. In a few weeks Duro could be in better financial shape.

One day Peter approached Janet. "Honey, would you do something for me?"

His request flattered her. "Of course, Peter. What is it?"

"A certain bloke owes me some money," he told her, "but for important reasons I don't want to be seen receiving it. The transaction has to be secret." Janet was well aware that much business in Coober Pedy was done discreetly and she knew how miners tried to keep the authorities ignorant of financial exchanges. She had learned a great deal about opal during her stay in Coober Pedy: how it was examined, graded into parcels and then sold—but never sold on an open market. No neighboring miner, government official, or interested towns person ever looked upon the gemstones except the buyers and partners. All transactions were conducted with cash. She did not think it at all odd for Peter to ask for her help in a private matter.

"Would you act as a go-between for me?" he said.

"Of course, I will," she answered, excited that he would ask her. "Does it involve opal?"

"No, just money." She looked at him with adoring eyes. She would do anything for Peter.

He had written an anonymous note to Duro and slipped it under his door: "I know what's down the shaft at the Four Mile. I will say nothing, but you must put $100 in an envelope and leave it behind the last tin of olive oil at the Greek shop." He had made the demand small on purpose. He knew Duro didn't have much money now, so he'd start the squeeze gradually. There'd be time enough for a bigger bite when the partners struck it rich at their mine.

Janet went to the Greek shop during her tea break. Distances in town could be covered in minutes. She smiled at Anastasia as she entered the store. She wandered about the cluttered aisles, chose a few small items and then went to the imported olive oil section. The oil came in large cans—and there were a lot of them to meet the demands of the cosmopolitan population. She moved a couple of cans forward a little so that her hand could reach behind the last one. She nonchalantly looked around. No one was in the aisle. She felt an envelope, slipped it out quickly, and tucked it into her apron pocket with a tingling of excitement.

She paid for her purchases and returned to work. When Peter came in for tea later in the afternoon, she unobtrusively placed the envelope under the serviette. Their eyes met, but no words were exchanged. She did not see him again for three days. She was beside herself, dropping utensils and forgetting to place condiments on the tables.

He was not smiling on his next visit. "Did you open the envelope?" he asked.

"Of course not!" she protested.

"There wasn't as much money in the envelope as I expected," he said. His eyes were cold.

"I didn't touch it!" Janet cried. "How could you think I would?"

"It just seemed strange, that's all."

"How much was there supposed to be?"

"It doesn't matter. Next time we'll open it together, and

then there'll be no question."

"Next time? I don't understand. Will I be doing this again?"

"Yes, until I get all the money that's owed me."

Janet was troubled. "It isn't anything dishonest, is it?"

"No, I wouldn't ask you to do anything against the law." He smiled at her reassuringly. He didn't want to lose her— she was much too important to him now. He would be careful not to provoke her again.

"I just don't understand why you can't meet face-to-face with your creditor," she told him.

"It's complicated, Janet. He doesn't want to be seen with me."

"Oh."

"I don't know just when he's going to make another payment, so check every day when you go into the store."

"All right." Her voice lost some spontaneity, so he gave her hand a squeeze, and her face brightened.

Another week went by. Each day Janet strolled into the store at the end of her workday, but she found no more envelopes behind the oil. Later in the week, she was about to leave the store when she noticed a miner approaching from the opposite direction. He looked around cautiously and then walked by her in haste. She didn't recognize him. She browsed in another aisle, and when she moved into the oil section, she saw the stranger turning away from that area. She waited until he left and then felt behind the last can. An envelope was there. She removed it, somewhat uneasily.

When Peter came into the restaurant the next afternoon, she told him what had happened and gave him the envelope. He smiled and put it in his pocket.

"I hadn't expected such a quick response," he said. "That's good. He's scared, and I can keep squeezing him. We can open it together at my place tonight. I'll come by for you when you're through with work."

The interior of the dugout repelled her—the floor was cluttered with papers and boxes; dirty dishes and utensils lay about, crusted with stale food; soiled clothes were heaped in a corner. She shuddered.

"It lacks a woman's touch, doesn't it?" Peter said. "You can see that I'm not much of a housekeeper."

"Oh, Peter, this is awful!" Janet set to work to put things in order, using some precious water to clean up. She had been brought up to be neat and tidy. As a young girl she had cleaned house reluctantly, but she appreciated now the training that had been instilled in her. Not for a moment would she put up with this mess—not even for Peter. She started to make the bed but recoiled in disgust. The sheets were almost black with grime.

"You don't have to make it now." He grinned at her slyly. "We'll be using it soon."

"Forget it!" Janet protested. "Where are some clean sheets?"

"They're all I have, luv." He started to put his arms around her, but she pulled away.

"Just let me be until I've cleaned up this mess!" She gathered the sheets gingerly and dumped them into a big bucket. She poured in some water, and finding no laundry powder located a bar of soap. It would have to do. She scrubbed briskly, her early frustration fading. She was happy to be of use to Peter—obviously he needed her. He sat back and watched her. He could use this girl for a long time if he played his cards right. Move slowly, he told himself. Evidently she came from good stock, and she was a willing, capable worker. He was sure that she would be a faithful lover if he was patient. He told her some fanciful lies about his youth and encouraged her to speak of her own childhood. He raised his eyebrows when she shared her background. He looked at her with renewed interest.

"Where are you going to hang those wet sheets? I don't have a clothesline."

"No worries. I saw some barrels outside, and I'll drape them over the tops. They'll dry fast in this weather." She made a face. "Anything's better than the way they were. They may not be clean, but they'll be cleaner."

He opened the envelope and showed her the money. "You're doing a good job, Janet." When he drove her back to the Inn, he kissed her tenderly and felt her quick, passionate response. Next time, he told himself ... next time ... He would let her dangle for a few days, knowing she would be frantic.

Her eyes were big with relief when she saw him walk in the doorway the following week. "I'm working late because a bus is overdue," she said, her voice trembling. "I can't come back with you tonight, Peter. I'm sorry."

Peter looked so disappointed that she hastened to add, "I'll be free tomorrow night," and when his face brightened, she smiled happily and could scarcely keep her mind on her work.

"Look for another envelope, honey, and we'll open it at my dugout tomorrow." He squeezed her hand surreptitiously and felt her quickened pulse.

The next evening when she stepped inside the dugout, she was shocked. It was as though she had never cleaned. Food and dirty dishes were everywhere. She saw two mice scurry across the floor and hide in a pile of debris. She turned to Peter with tears in her eyes.

"I know water is expensive, but can't you earn enough money so you don't have to live like this?"

"Together we can," he answered easily.

"Together?" she repeated. She stood very still, looking at him in wonder. Then she held out her hands, ready to embrace him. "Oh, Peter, are you asking me to marry you?"

"Good God, no!" he exploded. Instantly he tried to soften his reaction, but the abruptness of his reply made her withdraw.

His arms went around her, holding her close "Oh, honey, I didn't mean I'd never marry you. I just meant we can't do it now. I'm not in a position to do things for you that I'd like to."

Her face clouded. This refrain sounded all too familiar.

"Janet, you're so wonderful, and you deserve so much

more than this." He kissed her with passion, stroking her hair and tightening his embrace. He felt her begin to respond and gently led her to the bed. "At least the sheets are still clean. Please, honey. You can see that I need you."

Her resistance crumbled, and she found herself giving in to his persuasion. "I love you, Janet," he murmured, and she believed him.

When she came on the next visit, he left her with no illusions.

"You said we would be together, but I don't earn enough to help much, Peter. I just barely make my living expenses."

"But we've got something else going, luv. Let's open the new envelope." He extracted some bills. "One hundred dollars more. I hear the mine is starting to pay. No one talks, of course, but I can figure things out. I watch who visits the buyers at the Opal Inn. They've been busy lately."

"But what has this to do with me?" Janet was puzzled.

"My dear young thing, can't you figure it out? I've got a fish on my line. I know something about him, and he's willing to pay for silence."

"But that's blackmail!" She stared at him, aghast.

"You might call it that."

"I don't want any part of it!"

"I'm afraid you're already a part of it."

"Well, I'm going to get out."

"I'm afraid it isn't that easy, my dear. You were there that night at the Four Mile."

"What do you mean?" she demanded.

"You remember the truck lights?"

"Yes, of course."

"Well, you were witness to a burial—a man was murdered and disposed of that night."

"I don't believe you!"

"Well, it's true. You're in this up to your pretty neck."

She looked at him with loathing. "Take me back to the Inn or I'll walk back."

"My, aren't you hoity-toity. Just remember, you've been an active participant in this business. The law takes a dim view of—what is it called?—being a 'bag lady.' Also, you've seen the man. If you get careless and he suspects you, and if that leads him to me, neither of us will live very long. He's killed once— he won't hesitate to kill again. So you must keep your little mouth shut and do as I tell you. Do you understand?"

She nodded dumbly. She had given herself to him in what she thought was love, but he cared for her no more than any girl he might have picked up from the street for a night's pleasure. She stared at the floor, trembling.

Peter was angry with himself. Things had not gone at all like he planned; he had been too abrasive. Maybe he could persuade her back with affection. He put out his arms, and she stiffened at his touch. She edged toward the door.

"Janet, honey, it'll be all right. You'll see. This is just a temporary thing. I have big plans for us. You know I really care about you."

She continued to shrink back. His eyes grew cold. He put out a hand to restrain her, and she shook it off. He realized he had gone too far, moved too fast, and had lost her.

"Just remember, if you try anything funny, there are a lot of empty mine shafts around here. Don't get any smart ideas." He slapped her across the face, hard. "Just remember who's boss. Next time it might be worse." She walked to the car and crumpled into the front seat.

CHAPTER TWENTY-FIVE

ERIC HAD HEARD ABOUT CYNTHIA'S ACCIDENT and wondered what derogatory comments she might have made about him while Molly was caring for her. He didn't want to have to prove his innocence again. He felt reasonably sure that Molly would withhold judgment until all the facts were revealed, and perhaps this was the night to divulge them. She was on duty, she told him, but they could sit in the small waiting room and talk. He began to say. "There's so much I want to tell you, Molly," but she interrupted him and asked directly, "Eric, was that woman I treated in the hospital the same one we saw in the Opal Inn? Was she your former wife?"

"Yes, Molly." It gave Eric a tremendous sense of relief to unburden himself of these unhappy details—his failed marriage, the death of his son, the doctor's prognosis after his illness, and Cynthia's perfidy.

"I'm glad you told me, Eric. I understand so much more now." She paused and then an uncomfortable expression passed over her face. "Miss Garrett said something about why you left Crestmore College." She waited.

"Good Lord, Molly, I feel as though I'm on 'True Confessions'. You're not making it any easier for me!" He laughed, but she didn't. Her eyes held a plea that the explanation would absolve him of any wrong doing. He started at the beginning, telling her of the forces against him in the Debby Sue Markham situation. Her fixed gaze never left his face until he finished the account, and then suddenly her expression softened, and she squeezed both of his hands.

"I'm so happy, Eric. Everything's all right between us now, isn't it?"

"Molly, you know I have nothing to offer you. Since my illness— "

She swiftly pressed her hand against his mouth. "We'll say no more about that, Eric. It doesn't matter to me. Nothing is certain in this life. Now I have something to share with you." She took a letter from her desk and showed it to him. "I've received some amazing information about my grandmother, and I'd like you to read it. I understand now why she couldn't talk about her early life. Aborigines feel it's taboo to talk about the dead. That's why it was so hard for her to tell me very much about my mother." She handed the letter to Eric. "Mrs. McCurdy wrote to a woman, Mrs. Malcomb, who took care of my grandmother when she first was brought in from the wilds. Mrs. Malcomb gave me so many details and enclosed a report by the policeman who was in charge of her case."

"I'd like you to read it to me, Molly. Would you?" She hesitated and then began in a soft voice.

Dear Molly,

I do not know you, but I knew your grandmother, Niboorana, quite well. She must be proud that you have become a nursing sister. I took care of her when she was first brought out of the desert. She was so frightened—everything was so alien to her. She had been naked until the policeman, Norman Marshall, gave her his shirt to wear before they came into town. He asked me if I would take her under my wing, but I was very dubious. She seemed like such a wild creature, and I had children of my own to protect. He assured me that she had been very obedient on the trip and that I should not anticipate any problems, other than communication. He was right. She never had taken a shower and couldn't comprehend that water could be wasted for such a purpose. I had my oldest girl get into our home-made hessian stall to show her how it worked, and from then on she delighted in having a daily wash. I gave her an old flowered dress of mine, which she cherished, but I could not induce her to sleep indoors. She insisted on sleeping on the ground outside our bungalow. Niboorana was a kind, gentle girl—no more than sixteen, I imagine. When Achmet, the Afghan camel driver, asked to marry her, I told Norman there would be complications. You see, she was pregnant.

The policeman told me the whole story of her rescue. A wandering tribe had reported seeing a body in the outback, a victim of a spearing. Marshall had to investigate, of course. He hired an Aboriginal tracker, Jackie, and Achmet, who took care of the camels. He found the body, almost stripped of its flesh by scavengers, and buried it.

Then they followed the trail for two more days. When they came to the top of a little rise, Jackie gestured for them to approach quietly, and they could see two Aborigines sitting by a small fire. The woman added a few twigs to the fire occasionally, but the man had not moved.

Molly, I'm going to enclose the policeman's personal account of what happened next. His official statement was to the effect that the woman evidently had been abducted and her rescuer killed. The kidnapper died as they watched, apparently of natural causes. There was no sign of food or water at the campsite. This enclosure was the unofficial account of this event as Norman wrote it over fifty years ago. He retired some time ago, and I was lucky that he still kept the story.

At this point Molly brushed tears from her eyes and said, "I'd like you to read this part, Eric. It's ... It's just too much for me."

"Of course, Molly." He unfolded the yellowed paper and began:

Achmet hobbled the camels and we crept toward the pair by the fire. Just before Jackie realized that the man was dead, an eerie cry poured from the woman. She rocked back and forth, hands tearing at her hair, her face contorted. I thought she was afraid because of our presence, but she hadn't seen us yet. She rushed around, gathering more material for the fire and then built a little shelter of brush. When I asked Jackie what she was doing, he said it was necessary for her to construct this little wurlie to house the spirit of the dead man, because if she didn't provide a place for it to rest, it would pursue her, and she would be cursed.

I asked Jackie if he thought she had killed the man, and he shook his head. 'No, boss,' he told me. 'Somebody pointed the bone at him and of course he died.' I knew this ceremony was the most feared of all Aboriginal rituals—it meant from a great distance terrible pains would enter the body of the afflicted one like a thousand knives, and the person simply died without a mark on him.

When the woman became conscious of us, she shrank back, poised to run. Then she realized that there was no escape and sank down on her knees, head bowed. Jackie said this was a position of complete submission and approached her. Through sign language, he made known my wishes. She raised her head, eyes widening in horror, and shook her head. Jackie tried to convince her that I would not hurt her and that she had to come with us. Her whole body trembled, and she would not look at me. When I asked Jackie to find out what had happened there, she refused.

Jackie told me, "Boss, it is taboo for her to speak the name of the dead. If she says his name out loud, she is afraid she will die."

Achmet and I dug a pit for the body. It would have been inadvisable to try to take the body back in such warm weather, and there was no one capable of performing an autopsy in our town.

Jackie refused to go near the dead man. Two burials in one trip! It was just too much. My official report would have to state 'apparent heart attack.' I could hardly report 'someone pointed the bone at him.'

The trip back was uneventful other than our being amused at the young woman's reaction to the camels. They frightened her at first. Probably the largest animal she had even seen was a red kangaroo. She kept a safe distance from them, and on no account, no matter how tired she was, would she ride on one. But she began to relax a little and managed to laugh when they groaned and protested getting to their feet. She was very thin. We had no idea how long she might have been forced to wander the desert, and we urged her to eat. She accepted the food but ate only when the three of us had finished, sitting back on her haunches and watching us with suspicious eyes.

"Men always eat first," Jackie explained. "Old men first, then young ones. Women eat last."

She could not comprehend when I lit a match to start a fire to boil the billy. Gradually she drew nearer to examine the matches and then drew back in fear. Finally, she seemed to accept this unusual experience and toward the end of the journey she smiled with delight each time I struck a match. I noticed that Achmet was secretly watching her. He had never seen an Aboriginal woman from the wild. In his home country the women her age would be veiled from the eyes of men, and here she was unclothed. I gave her my shirt to help cover her, but modesty was an unknown quality for her. She didn't know what to do with it, so I showed her how to button and unbutton it. She so enjoyed manipulating the buttons that she spent a good part of her time fastening and unfastening the shirt, revealing far more than she covered. She walked well, never faltering, determined to keep up no matter how rough the terrain or how exhausted she might be. I was relieved to finally reach the town where I turned the girl over to Mrs. Malcomb, the publican's wife. I felt Niboorana, for we learned that was her name, would be in good hands.

When Mrs. Malcomb told me her charge was pregnant and that Achmet had asked to have her for his wife, she gave me advice. She said that in Achmet's home country virginity was highly prized and no man there would consider a woman like Niboorana. But this was the outback and there were no other acceptable mates for him here.

Mrs. Malcomb told me, "I am more concerned for Niboorana than I am for Achmet. There are so many taboos that I am not familiar with. One deals with the belief that the father or mother must visualize the baby before it becomes a reality in the womb. If the man has not 'dreamed' the baby, he won't acknowledge it as his own. Some Aborigines think there is a place underground where baby spirits frolic about waiting to be called to their mother's body."

At this point I almost exploded. How could I tell Achmet he must tell Niboorana he had dreamed her baby? And what would he do when he was told she was already pregnant? Well, it worked out much better than I expected. Achmet thought a moment and then said, "At least she is fertile. The next one will be mine."

Mrs. Malcomb and I both were happy to see the problem resolved and watched with relief to see the pair walk down the road to Achmet's little dwelling.

Eric raised his eyes from the manuscript. "What a remarkable story!"

"What the policeman didn't tell was the end of the account," Molly said. "It's in the remainder of her letter to me." She read, "I watched Niboorana over the years and was pleased when Goonabi was born and then Mohammed. Last was your lovely mother, Ashira. I knew your grandmother longed to go walkabout with her tribe when they passed through this area, and she disobeyed Achmet to do it. When she returned with Ashira, she found a measles epidemic had taken the lives of her second son and husband.

I took her cold hands in mine and told her, "There was nothing anyone could do."

Suddenly the veneer of civilization vanished, and the wailing for the dead burst from her. She knelt in the dirt, flinging dust over her head, rocking to and fro, refusing all comfort, crying, "It was all my fault, my fault!" It was dreadful watching her grief and guilt. Ashira stood there like a little statue, not understanding. Then I lifted Niboorana up and led them both back to my house. I talked to her when her torment lessened. I said, "You could have done nothing if you had been here. Perhaps it is God's will that you and Ashira have been spared."

She raised her tear-streaked face to me and said, "How can that be? Men are more important than women."

I gave her a big hug and said, "Not always, Niboorana, not always. You don't know what lies ahead." Then I made arrangements for her and Ashira to go to Wiluru Station where she could work as a domestic for Mrs. McCurdy.

Molly, I'm so glad I had this opportunity to write to you. Norman Marshall sends his greetings to you and says he is happy that he could fill in some of the blanks.

Affectionately,

Martha Malcomb"

Molly wiped the tears from her eyes. "I can understand now why my grandmother never wanted to talk about this part of her life. I'm glad I know, but I will not tell her I found out. I will respect her desire for privacy. What a strong woman she is! I hope I have her will for survival."

"I'm sure you do, Molly. Now I'll leave you to your duties. We have a lot of time ahead of us, don't we?"

Yes, Molly thought. But you just won't make a commitment!

CHAPTER TWENTY-SIX

DURO HAD MADE TWO PAYMENTS and was deter-
mined to pay no more. When he received the second demand,
he knew then the blackmailer would never stop but would
gradually squeeze him dry. The fear that had so possessed him
when he read the first note stayed with him constantly. How
could anyone know? He had been so careful. Someone was
watching him now and had been watching him that night at
the Four Mile, but how could that be? He brooded night after
night about how to find the blackmailer. He began to drink
excessively and found he was becoming careless in the mine.

Dimitrios watched him critically and noted his sloppy
work but said nothing. The American wasn't pushing them to
work harder, it was Dimitrios who was the slave driver. Duro
reflected that he, too, wanted to get ahead fast so he could
leave Coober Pedy with a lot of money. He was willing to
work hard, but there was a limit. He knew he shouldn't drink
so much, remembering how Lucas had deteriorated, but the
nights were so long and finding the blackmailer was consuming him.

There must be a go-between, he thought. But who? The blackmailer can't risk picking up the money himself. He wouldn't dare risk being recognized. If Duro could find the intermediary, he'd be on the right track. He must first find the accomplice, and that would lead him to the blackmailer. And then what would he do? Duro stirred from his dark thoughts and stared at the knife on the table. He ran his finger over the blade and shook his head. With a small whetstone he honed the edge until it was razor sharp and smiled with satisfaction. He came to a decision—no one was going to make a fool of him, and whoever was trying to would live to regret it. Duro chuckled to himself. He had used the wrong word. His adversary would not *live* to regret anything. When an opportunity presented itself, he would be ready to act. He was still an expert with a knife.

He paused to consider a different plan. If we do well in the mine, the news will leak out when we sell the parcel. The blackmailer will ask for a larger sum then. Perhaps he could trip him up by stashing an empty envelope or one with just a little cash. Everyone has a weakness or acts carelessly sometimes. Careful observation would reveal something.

The days went by. There were no more letters. Work at the mine progressed well. Dimitrios had found a new vein and things looked promising. Duro began to relax. Maybe his blackmailer just needed some drinking money. In his heart he knew that was only wishful thinking.

CHAPTER TWENTY-SEVEN

BERT MCCURDY WAS HOT AND SULLEN after his talk with his father. He simply had asked if he could take the Land Rover and absent himself from chores for a couple of weeks. His father was adamant in his refusal—there was too much work to be done. He couldn't spare him now.

"I've never asked for a holiday before," Bert protested. "The equipment is all in good shape, and I've repaired the windmill at the far bore. I've finished all the things you've asked me to do. There's no real need for me to be here for awhile."

"Bert, I said, 'No' and that's enough." McCurdy's face reddened.

"It's because of Molly, isn't it?" Bert flared. "You don't want me to see her. You and Mum are both against me."

"Good Lord, boy, can't you see? Molly may be a nice girl—I've never said she wasn't, and I have nothing against her personally, but look at the facts, son. Can you picture us having her to dinner with our friends and her Aboriginal grand-mother helping in the kitchen? You can't do this to us, you can't! It will never work."

"Then I'll take her somewhere else!" Bert blazed. "I've always wanted to get away from here, anyway. All I ever do is work. I never have any fun, never have a voice in decisions. I'm tired of being under your thumb all the time!"

"That's enough!" shouted his father.

"You keep saying that, but I don't care any more. It isn't enough!" Bert shouted back. "This has been a long time coming. I'm sick and tired ..." He stopped abruptly when he caught sight of his mother standing in the doorway wringing her hands, looking distressed and pale.

"Tom ..." Mrs. McCurdy began.

"You keep out of this!" her husband yelled, his eyes glaring at the interruption.

"That's right, Dad. Order Mum around, too! You've got to control everyone, don't you? Well, I've had it!" Bert's voice shook. He was dangerously close to losing control. His father took two steps toward him, fists raised, when his mother's shrill voice pierced the air.

"Stop it!" she cried. "Stop it, both of you, right now!"

Tom McCurdy looked at her in amazement. Rarely had she ever interfered or counteracted his authority. Some of the fury passed from his face as she strode into the room and took him by the arm.

"Niboorana heard everything," she said. "How could you, Tom?" She looked at her husband with bitterness. "She's been with us so long, worked so faithfully with never a complaint, and now this! You've hurt her so. I don't approve of this romance either, but it should have been handled differently. Niboorana ran out the back. I don't know where she's gone. I've never seen her so upset."

"And just how differently can this be handled, eh? What great ideas do you have for solving this problem? Tell me!"

"Let Bert go," she said softly. "He's a man now. He has to decide for himself. It's not what I want, but he has to live his own life."

"Has Molly encouraged you to do this?" McCurdy demanded of his son.

"No!" Bert retorted. "She doesn't even ..." He broke off and glared at his father. "She's been so busy. She only writes to her grandmother through Mum ... But I know she'll want to see me, and I've got to see her. I've just got to." He looked desperately from one to the other.

"Bert, do you know how far it is to Coober Pedy?" McCurdy refused to give in easily.

"Yes, and I'll pay for everything. I've saved my money."

Mrs. McCurdy sighed and faced Bert. "Son, promise us you won't rush into anything," she pleaded. "Just go see her. I like Molly. I've watched her grow up. She's a sensible girl. Don't make any commitments yet. You're both so young."

"All right, Mum. She's obliged to stay a year on her assignment anyway. I just want to see her."

There was a coldness at the supper table that night. Niboorana had not returned, so Mrs. McCurdy served the meal. Mr. McCurdy maintained a stony silence, and Bert's older brothers were uncommunicative. After clearing his throat and commenting on the weather, for which there was no response, Bert lapsed into a self-conscious silence. The ticking of the big clock and the occasional clinking of silver on china were the only sounds that relieved the quiet. Bert, miserable, asked to be excused.

He left early the next morning, certain that Molly would welcome him with open arms, and appreciate that he would care for her in spite of her grandmother. Not many fellows would do that. She was a damned lucky girl!

There was a chill in the air when Bert drove up to the hospital. He had brought a jacket but had not expected to use it. He asked the supervising nurse, Sister Thomas, to relay a message to Molly that he had arrived and would like to see her. She smiled at the big, honest-faced young man with approval. She had been concerned by some of Molly's choices and her apparent naivety about men. While she thought Eric was nice, there was nothing better than a good hard-working Aussie. She went to Molly's room and relayed his message.

Molly, taken by surprise, fluttered her hands with indecision and then shrugged. "What am I waiting for?" she laughed. "He's come a long way. Of course I'll see him."

"Don't be too quick to send this one away," advised her co-worker. "He looks like a nice chap—good looks, good manners."

When Molly came into the waiting area, Bert stood and held out his hand. He had the Australian bushman's natural reticence of being demonstrative in public. She shook hands cordially and looked up at him with an impish grin.

"Did you fly? Your letter just came a couple of days ago!" She was determined to keep things light.

"I didn't fly, but there were times when the Land Rover almost did. That's some road!"

"I came up here by plane," Molly said. "I feel sorry for the poor people who have to travel by car."

Bert looked at her with shining eyes. "You're even prettier than I remembered you," he said. Then he added shyly, "I drop in to see your grandmother often, and I always look at your picture. Not that I'd forget what you look like," he added hastily. "It's just that I like to keep you fresh in my mind."

"Thank you for going to see her. How is my grandmother?" She thought she detected a slight hesitation before his answer.

"Oh, she's fine. She's looking good."

"I'm glad."

The conversation lapsed. Bert struggled for words. "I'm going to be here for a few days," he said finally. "I hope I can see a lot of you."

"I'm on duty most nights, but I can see you from four to eight in the evening. I have to sleep in the earlier part of the day, of course. Usually I work eight hours, but sometimes it's ten or twelve depending on the need. In an emergency it's around the clock if we're short handed. If a patient is critically injured, we have him flown to Adelaide, but we haven't had any bad accidents lately, thank heaven."

"You do get time off don't you?"

"Yes, Wednesday and Thursday nights, if I'm not needed. Of course I have those days free, too."

"What about dinner tonight? I'll get you back in time for your duty."

"I'd like that. There's a little Italian restaurant here. We're very cosmopolitan you know."

They had a pleasant meal, punctuated with little jokes and commentaries about life in general. Bert ate heartily—he was hungry after the long trip. Molly enjoyed seeing a man with a good appetite. The tension of his presence gradually left her, and she began to enjoy herself.

"How could your folks part with you for so long?" she asked innocently.

His face flushed uncomfortably, but he recovered quickly.

"It's a pretty slack time right now," he answered a little lamely. Then he grinned. "I've been working hard and deserve a break." She tucked his reaction and words away in the back of her mind.

When he saw her to the door of the nurses' quarters, he pulled her into the shadow of the building and planted a warm, moist kiss on her lips. It wasn't entirely unexpected, but Molly was not prepared for his growing passion, and when his tongue began to probe her mouth, she jerked her head away, resisting further advances.

"Don't push me away, Molly," he pleaded.

"I'm not ready for this, Bert! Don't rush me." Although Molly protested, her body tingled and sent her mixed reactions, her spirit of independence struggling with her natural desire. She was determined to take charge of the situation.

"That's enough, Bert! I mean it."

"Please, Molly, don't be this way."

"I'll see you again tomorrow. I can't be too befuddled when I go on duty." She smiled to soften the tension. "Goodnight, Bert."

He left reluctantly.

The next night was a repeat of the first. She found herself attracted to Bert but resisted his advances at the same time. They ran into Eric one night as they left the Opal Inn, and she flushed with embarrassment. He simply gave her a quick nod of recognition and walked on without speaking. She had missed his quiet competence and undemanding manner more than she had realized. Bert was fun to be with but he was shallow. She wished he hadn't come—she didn't like being confused.

On Wednesday, Molly's night off, Bert urged her to come to his hotel room. "I need to talk with you, Molly. We can't really discuss anything in a restaurant or on the street. I want some time with you alone before I leave. I'll need to go back in a few days. Please come. I'll be a real gentleman—I promise."

Uneasiness concerning her present situation catapulted her thoughts to Eric. She must see him before Bert left. She needed him to clarify their relationship and not leave her dangling, but he had ignored her since that evening she shared the story of her grandmother. Although his absence disappointed her, she understood that he didn't want to intrude while Bert was in town. But it was almost as if he was pushing her into the younger man's arms. Seeing Eric again would reveal whether there was any depth to his feelings for her or if she was just projecting her desires into false hopes. That he cared for her was evident, but how much did he care? She knew he'd been hurt deeply before, but why couldn't he realize that she was sincere?

In comparison, Bert was just a kid. She was sure of her feelings. Why wasn't Eric? The rendezvous with Bert that night made her uncomfortable, and she suspected it would mean putting him in his place again and saying goodbye. But if Eric was truly rejecting her, did she really want to close the door completely on Bert? After all, he did have some good qualities, and there would be another year for him to mature. She just had to talk with Eric again. She would borrow Sister Thomas' car and drive over to the caravan park.

CHAPTER TWENTY-EIGHT

TERROR ENVELOPED JANET like a dark shroud. She tried to keep her mind on her work, but the combination of depression and fright rendered her almost useless. Her boss commented on her inattention to details and sharply reprimanded her twice for spilling food. She knew if he didn't need a waitress so badly, she would undoubtedly have been discharged. She didn't have enough money for bus fare to go to another town where she could lose herself, and writing to her father for help was unthinkable. There was no one she could turn to. Occasionally Sergeant MacDonald came in for lunch or tea, but he was the last person she wanted to confide in. Although Janet tried to act natural, her hands were shaking so much it was certain he must detect her nervousness. He never indicated that anything was amiss, but she was sure he had noticed and filed that information away in his mind. He had the reputation for never forgetting details, however innocuous they might appear.

When Peter came in, she tried to ignore him but found his compelling eyes working like a magnet. She had decided she would refuse to act as his go-between no matter what he threatened. He would be putting his own head into a noose as well as hers if he talked. She convinced herself that he was all bluster, and she wouldn't be an accessory any more. But when he stared at her in that malignant way, she found herself losing courage. He could hurt her, and what protest could she make without implicating herself? He could even kill her, as he had inferred. Helplessness overwhelmed her.

Then she thought of Mick Barker. He used to come in for meals occasionally and was always pleasant. He had asked her out several times, but she had started dating Peter at that time and had turned him down. What a fool she had been! Mick had said something about working his way around Australia, that he hadn't planned on staying in Coober Pedy very long. There was too much to see in this beautiful land to be stuck in one place, he had told her. In desperation she decided to approach him. Maybe he would be willing to take her with him when he left.

When Eric returned to his caravan after work, he was surprised to see Janet wandering around, looking aimlessly from one vehicle to another. It was very warm, and the late afternoon sun was still an hour from setting. Pale dust hung like an aura in the air.

"Are you looking for someone?"

"I'm trying to find Mick Barker," Janet told him. "I don't see his caravan."

"Oh, Mick moved on a couple of weeks ago. Said he was

heading for Alice Springs and then maybe Darwin." Eric noted the stricken look on her face. "You look awfully tired. It's too hot out here. Why don't you come in for a cold drink?"

She nodded dumbly and followed him inside. He poured a glass of lemonade, which she accepted gratefully.

"Is there anything I can do for you?"

She shook her head. "I'd just like to sit awhile, if that's all right."

"Sure." He sat back and studied her speculatively, but did not speak. He assumed she'd been jilted and maybe was in trouble, and observed her sunburned face and disheveled hair with compassion. He thought back to various conversations he had with Mick, recalling that his neighbor had stressed how much he had wanted to take the new waitress out but when he failed to gain acceptance, he had stopped his pursuit. He said that Peter Bagley had "beat him out." Why was the girl looking for Mick when he'd never had a date with her?

"If you're having a problem, I'm a good listener," Eric suggested, but she shook her head.

The two sat quietly, Janet grateful for his consideration. Eric was disturbed at her apparent misery. He felt sorry for anyone who had been rebuffed by life. As twilight approached, she bestirred herself and prepared to leave. Trying to blink back her tears, she held out her hand and thanked him.

Molly hesitated as she pulled into the caravan park. She was unfamiliar with the area and didn't know which caravan was Eric's, until she recognized his truck. He would be pleasantly surprised to see her, she hoped. She never had done anything quite so spontaneously before and felt a trifle bold, but she earnestly needed his reassurance. As she started to park the car, Janet emerged from Eric's doorway. The girl, obviously distraught, brushed tears from her face and attempted to bring order to her tangled hair. Shock jolted Molly's body and she sat paralyzed for a moment. Janet! The little waitress at the Opal Inn! Molly had tended her burned hand the week before. She couldn't be more than sixteen years old! Molly felt her world crumbling around her. She drove away quickly, not risking recognition by either Janet or Eric, her own tears almost blinding her vision.

After Janet left, Eric began fixing supper. A loud thump on the caravan door startled him. He opened it to find Wilanya scowling up at him, his features contorted with hostility. Matted hair hung to his shoulders, and filth caked his naked chest and arms. He stank, and Eric could see that he was in an advanced state of intoxication.

"What do you want, Wilanya?" he asked in a quiet tone. The youth did not answer but stared with malevolent eyes. He was weaving, and Eric was afraid he would pass out right at his doorstep. "Do you need some help? Are you in trouble?"

Wilanya did not reply; he just continued staring, projecting an eeriness that made Eric increasingly uncomfortable. He didn't want a confrontation with the Aborigine, but it might be difficult to get rid of him.

"What is it, Wilanya?" he said a little sharply. "What's the matter?"

"You!" Wilanya answered in a high pitched voice, jabbing a skinny finger at Eric. "You are the matter!" Eric drew back and attempted to close the door, but Wilanya tried to push past him, shouting, "You leave Molly alone, you hear me? You leave Molly alone! She was here! I saw her!"

"That's not true," Eric said evenly. "Molly has not been here."

Wilanya's expression became savage in its intensity. Sweat ran down his body, making little furrows in the grime. His shorts, the only garment he wore, were damp from the perspiration. He wiped his trembling hands on the material and then ran his fingers through his unkempt hair, tugging at the greasy locks. Then he steadied himself and raised his fist in a threatening gesture.

"She was here! I saw her driving away. I saw her!"

"You're mistaken, Wilanya. She was not here tonight, and she has never come here." In spite of the possible violence facing him, Eric felt some pity for the misguided lad. It was sad that he cared deeply for Molly because it was so impossible for her to reciprocate his affection. Eric tried to soften the situation. "Wilanya, I don't own Molly. Nobody does. She's her own person. She's your friend and only wants good things for you."

The Aborigine raised his head with a primitive cry and spat into Eric's face. It took all of Eric's self-control not to send the youth sprawling to the ground. He knew it would be an uneven contest to tangle with this drunken boy, and he might actually hurt him seriously.

"You are a liar!" Wilanya cried. "You had her here ... you had her here ... I saw her ..."

"Wilanya," Eric's voice had steel in it. "I won't have you saying bad things about Molly. She hasn't been here. She has never been in my caravan. She doesn't even own a car. She's the best friend you'll ever have. Now please leave." He gave Wilanya a quick shove and closed the caravan door abruptly. He could hear the youth yelling incoherently for a few minutes, and then it was quiet. He washed his face and looked out a window, breathing a sigh of relief when he saw the grounds were empty. He had not relished a public brawl.

The whole episode unsettled him. He disliked any thought of an association between Molly and this half-civilized fellow, and then he wondered if he would put up as stiff a fight for Molly as this young lad did. Eric realized he had relinquished any special claim on her when he encouraged her to see Bert. In fact, he had almost propelled her in that direction. She was probably with him right now. Eric winced at the pictures that were developing in his imagination. The next few days would be a critical test for her. As a teacher, he knew how important tests could be.

CHAPTER TWENTY-NINE

AFTER MOLLY RETURNED THE BORROWED CAR, she began to walk toward the Opal Inn, her mind in turmoil. Each step taken was an unconscious revolt from what she had witnessed. When she reached Bert's room, she felt drained of emotion. She did not want to believe that Eric had entertained the young girl, but she could not deny what she had seen. There must be some explanation, and she frantically sought one, but none came to mind. The room reeked of Bert's cigarettes. He had smashed several half-smoked ones into the ashtray. His eyes shone as he tried to kiss her, but she wrinkled her nose and turned away from his bitter breath.

"Sorry, Molly. I guess you don't like smoking, but a guy's got to do something while he's waiting, and I've waited a long time for you, honey." He reached out again to embrace her, but she was unresponsive to Bert's overtures.

"You look pale, Molly. Are you feeling all right?'

"I'm okay. I guess I just feel a little uncomfortable coming to your room."

"Honey, I know you were strictly brought up at the mission since you were a little girl, but you're a big girl now. You can do what you want without feeling guilty." He gestured for her to sit down in the only comfortable chair in the room and tried to put her at ease.

"Molly, I promised I'd be a gentleman, and I meant it. We just haven't had much time to really be together, and this was the only way to do it. I'm not going to bite. Now how about a smile?" When a tenuous smile played about her lips, he relaxed. "Now that's better."

"Bert, don't rush me. I'm ... I'm confused ... I need more time to think things out ..."

"What do you mean 'you need more time'? You've had plenty of time," he blurted. "You must know how you feel. Don't tease me, Molly. I won't stand for that. I've come all this way to be with you, and by God, I'm going to be!"

He reached for her hand and drew her up, but when she remained reluctant, he grew impatient and took her in his arms, gave her a hard kiss. She heard his breathing become deeper, felt the increased warmth of his face and was keenly aware of his masculine scent. She started to pull back, but her doubt about Eric loomed larger and larger. Had he been lying to her all along, justifying his divorce and dismissal from his position in college? She wanted to believe him—everything about him cried out to be believed, but she knew she couldn't be here with Bert if she really trusted Eric. Everything had changed with her visit to the caravan park, and she couldn't think straight. Her resistance began to crumble. In spite of her resolve, she began to respond to Bert's kisses and felt herself being swept away. Then his words registered.

"I love you, Molly. You've got to believe that. I need you. I want you—now. Let's not wait. You know I'll marry you if I have to."

She froze. "If you have to?"

"Oh, you know what I mean."

"No, I don't know what you mean. You'll marry me 'if you have to'? Is that what you're offering me? What kind of marriage is that! That's an insult!"

"You don't understand!"

"I think I do. What would your parents say about those circumstances?"

"To hell with my parents! It's you I'm talking about. They don't approve of my marrying you. They didn't want me to come here in the first place, but I came anyway. Don't you see, Molly? I love you that much. I'm going against my parents' wishes. We don't have to go back to the station. There are a thousand places we can go where nobody knows us."

Momentarily befuddled, she braced herself against him. "I'm not sure what you're saying, Bert."

"Please, Molly. Don't mix everything up. I want to make love to you, don't you understand? I won't be able to see you again for a long time. You know I love you. Haven't I proved it by coming to you? What more do you want? You can trust me to take care of you, now and always. You know you can. I'll marry you in spite of—" He stopped short.

"Go on, Bert."

"All this talk is getting us nowhere. Let's cut out this fool-ishness and get down to business." He spoke brusquely, his encircling arms tightening around her.

"You'll marry me in spite of my background? Is that what you're saying? That I'm part Aborigine and have a full-blooded Aborigine grandmother?" Her dark eyes glittered.

"Don't be that way, Molly. I didn't mean that exactly."

"What 'exactly' did you mean, Bert?" His flushed face and pleading manner brought to mind her other encounter with Bert on the track from the Wiluru Station on her last visit there. She recalled the intrusion of raucous magpies that had brought her back to reality. She started to pull away.

"There's plenty of time in the future to work things out. Right now I just want us to be together. I said I'd marry you, didn't I? What more do you want?" he repeated, a surliness creeping into his tone. "Come on. We're wasting time." He pulled her over toward the bed.

"Stop it, Bert! It won't work! It just won't work."

"Now you're talking like my parents! They said it wouldn't work. I'm beginning to think you're on their side. I've driven a long way and—"

"You shouldn't have come here to Coober Pedy."

"Well, I am here, and you encouraged me, Molly. You know you did."

"Bert, I'm sorry if you feel that way. This whole thing is a mistake, a terrible mistake." She rushed toward the door.

"I'm sorry," she repeated. "Try to understand."

"I do understand! You've just been teasing me. I can't stand to be teased!" He grabbed her by the arm, trying to force her back into the room, but she jerked free. She ran out the door, down the hall and out to the open air. Bert started to follow her and then turned back. He picked up a glass and threw it against the wall with all his might.

CHAPTER THIRTY

As Molly STEPPED INTO THE STREET, she detected a slight movement behind her. She sensed Wilanya's presence even before she recognized his odor. Something sharp pressed into her back.

"What do you want, Wilanya?" she asked, without even turning around.

"Always you choose a white man. But I wasn't good enough for you," he growled.

"You're mistaken, Wilanya. There's nothing between Bert and me. He's just a friend. I visited him for a few minutes and then left. He's an old friend from Wiluru Station. He knows my grandmother."

"I don't believe you." The sharp point was hurting her back.

"It's the truth."

"I've been watching you."

She flared. "You have no right to follow me.'"

"I make it my right. I do as I please. I saw you at the caravan park today. One man isn't enough for you, is it?"

"Wilanya, I didn't even see Eric today. I didn't even stop," Molly protested.

"Liar! I saw you drive away."

At first Wilanya's diatribe annoyed her, and she began to tell him that her affairs were none of his business, but she stopped, no longer certain that she understood him. He was behaving in an irrational manner, and a shiver passed over her as he commanded her to walk ahead of him. She tried to turn around, but he pushed her ahead.

"Walk over to that Land Rover." She recognized the car as Bert's and realized that in his excitement he had left the keys in the ignition.

"I don't want to go any place with you," Molly protested. "I'm going to walk home."

"Get in, or I'll cut your throat right here." More than the words, horrifying as they were, was the cold, malevolent tone that made her realize that she was in extreme danger. For the moment the street was deserted, and unfortunately Bert had not followed her out. She decided it would be best to humor Wilanya until some kind of help appeared.

"All right, I'll get in. It's a nice night for a ride." She felt the sharp point released from her back, and she started to move to the side but he grabbed her arms and twisted them behind her. He had put the knife between his teeth to free his hands. He bound her wrists with a cord and gave her a shove. With a quick movement he thrust her onto the seat and locked the door. She saw his eyes for the first time—they were like a snake's, unfeeling and implacable. In spite of being incapacitated she spoke calmly, measuring each word as he started the engine.

"I know I've hurt you, Wilanya," she began. "I didn't mean to. Let's park some place where we can talk."

He jabbed at her leg with the knife. He was having great difficulty shifting gears with his left hand and keeping a grip on the weapon. Molly felt a warm trickle of blood oozing from the cut.

"You've cut me, Wilanya!" she cried.

"Good. I want to hurt you—a lot."

Molly said nothing, hoping someone would appear so she could shout out. Still there was no one in sight. She leaned against the door, as far away from him as she could and tried to think. She was sure he meant to kill her, but why hadn't he done it back there? They were headed for the desert now. What was his purpose? She fumbled with the cord binding her hands and found she could loosen it a bit. She worked gently with the knots.

"Don't try to untie the cord," he warned her. Although he reeked of alcohol, he did not appear to be drunk—his perceptions were too accurate, his voice too steady. She had hoped he was intoxicated and that he would revert to normalcy in time, but the change in him seemed to be deep and unalterable.

She lay still. The night was quiet but not completely dark. Usually the stars sparkled like Christmas tree lights in the sky, but tonight there would be almost a full moon, and there already was a glow hovering on the horizon. It would soon be quite light. They drove until they reached the turn-off to one of the more distant mining areas where Wilanya followed a faint track between some abandoned mines. He brought the vehicle to a stop and dragged Molly roughly across the seat through his open door. She staggered as she tried to find her balance.

"Walk ahead," he said curtly. She stepped forward gingerly. Her shoes were not adapted for desert walking. She could feel the sharp stones pushing through the thin soles She stumbled several times, almost falling, but Wilanya made no effort to help her. He seemed oblivious to her discomfort. After a mile he stopped and looked around. The moon had risen and a soft, creamy light reflected back from the white opal clay that lay in cones around the distant mine shafts. They crossed a small hill, and ahead of them was open country, mostly flat but with a few undulating ridges here and there that made it impossible to see clearly to the horizon. No one could see them, either. Molly's apprehension increased. She slipped and pitched forward, unable to break her fall. She bruised the side of her face and felt a rock tearing a gash in her leg. Her shoulder ached, and she lay for a moment, trying to recover from the shock. Wilanya prodded her with his foot, ordering her to get up. With her hands tied behind her, she could not raise herself, so Wilanya yanked her harshly to her feet. She looked at him appealingly, but his face was unmoving. They walked in silence for another hour. Molly's feet became sore and swollen.

"Couldn't we stop to rest?" she asked in a quiet voice.

"You're not a very good Aborigine, are you, Molly?" She was relieved that his voice sounded almost natural. For the first time she was hopeful.

"I'm not dressed for this kind of traveling." She tried to laugh, but the words sounded hollow.

"You're right. Now we'll be real Aborigines—none of this half-baked phony pretending. Take off your clothes." He cut the thong binding her hands. She chafed her wrists, bringing some circulation back into her numb fingers. "Take off your clothes," he repeated. Reluctantly she began to obey, fumbling unnecessarily with the buttons on her blouse.

"Hurry up. We've got a long way to go," he snapped.

"Where are we going?" Molly hoped to distract him for a few minutes. Maybe he would come to his senses and see how ludicrous the whole situation was.

"We're going back in time, Molly," he answered. "We're going to live like our ancestors, right back to our Dreamtime primordial existence. Doesn't that sound wonderful? You didn't know I could use words like that, did you? You thought I was stupid. But I listened, and I learned and I remembered. Do you understand what I'm saying?"

She shook her head. "No, Wilanya, I don't. I just want you to take me home, and we'll forget this whole evening."

"No, Molly. You have always belonged to me, and I'm going to take what is rightfully mine."

She had removed the last of her clothing, including her

shoes. The night still held some warmth, but she was shivering. He threw his clothes on top of hers and gestured to them. "Dig a hole and bury them," he commanded. "We will leave no trace of our former lives."

She bent over and with her bruised hands scooped a shallow hole in the sand and put the clothes into it. She covered the garments with sand and pebbles, hoping to leave a small piece visible, but Wilanya watched intently and smoothed the surface over with his foot when she finished. She decided to try a different approach.

"Wilanya, your behavior is a disgrace to your tribe," she chided him.

"We have no tribe, Molly. Remember, you said we are no longer a tribe, just a 'people'?"

For a moment he seemed to soften; then his face became hard again. He gestured ahead with his knife. "Start walking."

They trudged through the wasteland, each step an agony for her. She dared not complain. As long as they kept moving, there was some hope he might spare her. She wanted desperately to live—everything now was focused on survival. He had brought no water or food; she wondered how long they could last. She must conserve energy as much as possible. She could feel her feet beginning to bleed but tried not to think of them. The encrusted wound on her leg throbbed. How tough her forebears had been! She thought of Kabbarli and took heart. Her grandmother had struggled through a hostile landscape at the hands of her abductor and had survived. Molly would, too.

They continued walking until the moon set and the sky became inky black. Still Wilanya prodded her to continue, his eyes seeming to pick out barriers before them. She stumbled often, willing herself to rise as blood issued from fresh cuts. Her abductor did not slacken his pace. As dawn approached, she looked ahead in apprehension—only rises and hollows could be seen. No one would ever see her this far into the outback. She sank to her knees, but Wilanya pulled her up when she went limp and hit her across the face.

"Don't do that again," he snarled. "It won't do you any good."

Again they set out, aimlessly Molly thought, but Wilanya seemed to have some destination in mind. The day became warmer, and finally he stopped and gestured toward a bush.

"Get under the shade, and we'll wait until later to move on. Don't try to leave," he warned. His heavy breathing revealed that the exertion of the night's travel had not been entirely without cost. Molly collapsed into the sparse shadow, trying to control her frantic thoughts. When would she have been missed? Probably not until that very morning when Bert looked for the Land Rover. Without knowing which way they went, how could they possibly find her in these thousands of unchartered acres surrounding Coober Pedy? Even if the searchers did locate the vehicle, the rising wind must have obliterated their tracks.

Wilanya closed his eyes, and for a moment he appeared to sleep, but when she tried to shift her body to a more comfortable position, he was instantly alert. After a few hours rest he stood up and jerked her to her feet. "We have to move on."

He indicated the direction to take and pushed her ahead.

With the setting sun, the air took on a crispness that at first was welcome but then became ominous. A cold night without clothing or shelter would be a double hardship after the previous exhausting twenty-four hours. Autumn was merging into winter, but on the desert seasons knew no boundaries, and weather in the outback could be capricious. Molly would have rejoiced at the coolness of the lengthening shadows earlier, but now the twilight cast a foreboding spell. They continued to walk until moonrise. Suddenly without warning Wilanya hurled her to the ground.

She tried to get up, but he struck her savagely in the face. She felt her nose bleeding, the discharge running back into her throat. She put out a protective hand against this violator whom she could not recognize as someone she had once cared about. She felt herself beginning to slip into unconsciousness from the severe blow her head had taken in the fall.

"You are my wife and I shall have you," Wilanya said, his words chilling her into awakening. "I won you from my enemy, and you belong to me."

Molly willed herself to one last confrontation. "Wilanya, you are not a warrior who fought bravely against an enemy. You are nothing but a boy who never even went through the initiation ceremonies. You make a mockery of an Aboriginal man!"

Wilanya's inner spirit seemed to crumble before her eyes. She went on relentlessly. "Don't do this terrible thing. You know there is still magic in our people. My grandmother will put a curse on you, Wilanya!" Her words came out of her parched throat more like a croak than a human voice.

Wilanya stared as though seeing her for the first time, his eyes dark hollows in his contorted face. "There's been a curse on me from the day I was born, Molly! There is nothing that can hurt me any more. Nothing." He reached out and touched her bruised face in wonder and wiped away some of the blood. Then he sprang back with a strangled cry. He picked up his knife and began to run, long, loping strides until he was far over the next ridge.

Only when silence enveloped her did Molly try to stir. She attempted to sit up, but each movement was agony, so she lay back again. Several hours passed. The moon, which had illuminated the scene so brilliantly, now slipped away, and darkness covered her like a comforting cloak. She finally slept. When she awakened, the sun poured over a hilltop with a play of colors that at another time would have awed her, but now all her senses were numbed. She had been without water the entire day before. She used all the moisture that remained in her mouth to speak to Wilanya. She knew she could not last much longer if the day turned hot. Help would have to come. She looked up at the hill where the sun was making such a spectacular entrance, and a Bible verse from her childhood drifted into her thoughts: "I will lift up my eyes to the hills. From whence does my help come? My help comes from the Lord, who made heaven and earth." Her faith demanded that she believe. Help would come! She clung to that assurance. Now only one thought penetrated her mind—she must find more shade and protect herself from the sun. She crawled toward a larger bush, curled her aching body beneath it and prayed for the strength to survive.

CHAPTER THIRTY-ONE

BERT MCCURDY SAT ON THE EDGE OF THE BED feeling angry and defeated. He hadn't insulted Molly, had he? He'd promised her marriage in the future. Most girls would have jumped at the chance, and with her background she should have been especially grateful. He'd come all this distance and had accomplished nothing. She'd run out on him and humiliated him. His anger intensified, and he decided to go down to the pub to drown his sorrows. Maybe he'd find someone else who would be more willing and appreciative.

He started down the hall when he suddenly remembered that, with all his anticipatory excitement, he had left the keys in the Land Rover. He thought he'd better go down and lock up first. He was alarmed when he found the vehicle missing, then realized that Molly in her panic and haste must have taken the car back to the hospital to save herself the walk. He became even more angry. She had no right to do that. He should go over right now and demand it back. No, she'd be on duty now. No, she wouldn't! This was her night off—he had expected her to stay with him the whole time. Well, he rationalized, she probably had returned to the hospital anyway, and he'd get the vehicle back in the morning. He'd let it go until tomorrow and enjoy himself tonight. He was sure he'd have no trouble finding an agreeable partner.

In the morning he walked to the hospital and asked Sister Thomas to waken Molly—he needed his keys. The nurse shook her head. "She's not here." She flushed with embarrassment. "I thought she was with you. She didn't come in last night."

Bert frowned. "She has my Land Rover, and I need it. Where else would she be? Does she have any friends in town?"

Sister Thomas hesitated, not wanting to make things awkward for Molly by revealing personal information, but she was concerned. This was uncharacteristic of the girl, and she might be in trouble.

"Yes, Molly does know a few people here. Sometimes she goes to the Aboriginal Reserve, but I doubt if she'd go at night. I've seen her with Eric Christianson at times. He stays in the caravan park."

Bert turned abruptly, his sunburned face looking more flushed.

"It's a bit of a walk—you can borrow my car if you like." The nurse tossed him her keys. She felt sorry for the young man and hoped the Land Rover would not be there. It was a ticklish situation. Perhaps she shouldn't have told him, but it was so unlike Molly to be irresponsible. Her worry increased.

When Bert drove into the caravan park, he could see

immediately that the missing vehicle was not there. He started to drive away when Eric stepped out of his caravan and recognized him. He waited for a possible confrontation, but none came. Eric's eyes questioned Bert's intentions. It seemed an odd time for a rival to come calling. Bert got out of the car and walked over to him, his face betraying his discomfort.

"I was wondering if you'd seen Molly Riley," he began. "She borrowed my car last night, and she's not at the hospital and ..."

Eric's thoughts leaped forward with lightning speed. "She's been gone since last night?" he cried. "Good God! We'll get the police!"

Bert was taken aback. "Maybe she's just visiting someone," he protested. He didn't want to draw public attention to this situation. There undoubtedly was some logical reason she had taken off. "The sister mentioned something about an Aboriginal Reserve ..."

"She would never go any place at night alone," Eric told him. "We must get help immediately." Bert nodded reluctantly.

Eric followed Bert to the hospital to leave the borrowed car, and they proceeded together to the police station. Bert reported the Land Rover missing and hoped someone would spot it. He did not bring Molly's name into his account, but Eric was not so reticent.

"Molly Riley, one of the sisters, is missing. She's always dependable," Eric told Sergeant MacDonald.

The policeman nodded. "I know Sister Riley."

"She may or may not be involved with the missing vehicle," Eric continued, trying to keep panic from his voice, "but I know she had a very unpleasant encounter with a quarrelsome Aborigine a few weeks ago. I saw him again yesterday at the caravan park, and he was extremely belligerent. There may be a link."

The sergeant agreed. "I'll spread the word and have a look around myself. I'll report any news back here to the office if you want to wait."

"No," Eric said. "I want to search, too. I'll check in from time to time."

Bert asked to ride along with him, his palms sweating. "If anything's happened to the Land Rover, I'll have a hell of a time explaining it to my father." When Eric stared at him in disgust, Bert said quickly, "I don't think anything bad's happened to Molly," and then added with bitterness, "That's one woman who's really able to take care of herself."

The wind picked up as the morning advanced, and soon small particles of dust and sand were swirling about. Eric groaned. "This dust storm will wipe out any tracks pretty soon. They aren't anywhere in the vicinity—they must be some distance by now. Let's check in and find out if there's any information from the main road north or south."

Bert looked at him curiously. "You're fond of Molly, aren't you?" he asked.

"We're just good friends," Eric replied shortly.

By noon there was no news of the Land Rover, but at six

o'clock Sergeant MacDonald returned with a grim look. "We've located the vehicle way out past the last opal field. All the tires are slashed. We couldn't see any tracks leading away—the sand is blowing so hard. We walked in several directions but couldn't pick up a trail. It'll take a general search party tomorrow in the daylight. It doesn't look good."

"Oh, hell!" cried Bert. "The bloody bastard! I hope nothing more is wrecked. Four tires!"

"What else did you see?" demanded Eric. "Was there any sign that Molly had been there?"

The policeman looked at him with a steady gaze. "There was some blood on the passenger seat."

Eric felt as though he had received a body blow. He started to speak when a commotion at the door caused them all to turn around. A large Aborigine shouldered his way through the crowd that had gathered and walked directly to Eric.

"I will find her," he said simply. Eric was startled. Who was this man, and how did he know about Molly? Then the Aborigine faced the sergeant.

"Take me to the place where you found the vehicle. I'll need water and food," he said. "I can track them."

MacDonald did not recognize the newcomer, but he welcomed his arrival. He could use a reliable tracker to follow a poor trail in this storm.

"Are you from the Reserve?" he asked.

"No."

"Then how do you know this area?"

"I can track anywhere."

"All right. We'll leave first thing in the morning."

"No. Now."

The policeman had known many Aboriginal trackers and had great respect for their special talent, and this man's determination impressed him. He nodded. "Let's go. It will be dark soon and every minute counts."

"Let me come, too," Eric said.

The Aborigine shook his head. "No. You'll slow me down."

"Better wait at the hospital," the sergeant told Eric. A chill passed over him as he realized the implication of MacDonald's words. He started toward his ute, and Bert joined him.

"Who is that man? Do you know him?" Eric asked.

"I'm not sure. I've seen him on our station at times. I don't know why he's here, though. He may have just been passing through—on walkabout, you know."

"I understand they are very sensitive to people's reactions and thoughts."

"So I've heard." Bert did not pursue the conversation.

Bert paced restlessly. He didn't know what Eric meant to Molly and didn't care. She had played him for a fool, and he seethed with resentment. He wondered if Niboorana had sent Goonabi here to see how things were going with Molly. She must have overheard the quarrel with his parents and been concerned. That was over a week ago, though. Was it just coincidence that Goonabi turned up today? Bert glanced over at Eric occasionally, noting the pain etched on his face. He

finally sat down, spending the rest of the evening sitting awkwardly in the presence of a man whom he presumed was Molly's
boyfriend. Why hadn't she written about him in her letters to
her grandmother? It would have saved him a long trip and all
this worry. Slashed tires were bad enough, but if the Land
Rover was wrecked beyond repair, his father never would let
him hear the last of it. Somehow he could not believe that
Molly was in any great danger—the Aboriginal call in her blood
may have been stronger than he realized. She and this fellow
might have gone on a walkabout lark, and Bert's face would
be red when it was over. His mother had been right—this
relationship had been a fiasco from the beginning, and he'd
been too blind to see it. Molly was just another pretty face,
and as uppity as when she was twelve. She *looked* Aboriginal,
too. Why hadn't he noticed before? He began to fidget and
decided to stroll down to the town for a beer. More than
anything else he hated waiting.

Eric sat tight-lipped and tense. Sister Thomas came over
with a cup of tea. "A good strong cuppa makes everything a little
easier to bear," she said with a practiced, professional smile. "Why
don't you go back to your caravan? There's nothing you can
do here. We'll send you word as soon as we know anything."

"No, I want to be here. In the morning I'll drive my
partner to the mine and let the fellows know they'll be on
their own, and then I'll come back here. I'm just glad I hadn't
already left this morning. I want to stay close."

Eric curled up in one of the chairs. He was not superstitious, but he felt almost as though some vibration or message was trying to penetrate his consciousness. Finally he dozed off, and when his internal alarm clock awakened him, he found he had slept only two hours. After driving Duro to the mine early, he went directly to the hospital and continued his vigil.

When Goonabi alighted from the police vehicle, all his senses were alert. He stopped thinking like a white man and reverted to his most primitive instincts. He called upon all the knowledge he had ever acquired in his early training, the painful rites of circumcision and walkabout days with his tribe. He began searching the area around the Land Rover in a wide circle, getting down often on hands and knees, eyes close to the ground. He would grunt or make some other non-committal sound, moving farther on, looking for any mark or scratch that might be a clue. Sergeant MacDonald followed behind, marking the trail as they traveled. When dusk set in, he used his torch to light the way back to the vehicle, offering a second one to Goonabi. The Aborigine smiled and refused—he would continue on until it became too dark to track. At dawn the policeman and his assistant would return, following his trail in their four-wheel vehicle as far as the terrain would permit, then they would continue on foot.

Goonabi lost the trail several times, as the wind had obscured the tracks. He retraced his steps, picked up a faint indication and continued. As darkness prevented further tracking, he built a small fire and ate and drank. He smoothed out a place on the ground to lie on and fell asleep instantly. He must waste no energy. Before dawn he would be rested and ready to continue the search.

He continued following the trail, keeping as emotionally detached as possible, concentrating all his skills on observing telltale signs. He came across the place where Molly had fallen, noticing the blood on a sharp rock. He could see Wilanya's footprints where he must have prodded her. Farther on he detected a bit of cloth exposed by the wind, a tiny corner of her blouse that only sharp eyes would have noticed. He dug up the rest of the clothes and frowned when he saw blood on her skirt. He rolled the blouse and skirt into a small bundle and tied it around his waist. He walked at a steady pace, lengthening his stride when the trail marks became clear.

Hours passed. The sun reached its zenith, and while the heat was not intense, the rays would be far too harsh on unprotected skin. Without water, Molly would become dehydrated rapidly in this dry air. Goonabi kept his mind on tracking. Once when he came to a rise, he looked back but could see no vehicle or search party following.

The wind had not erased the final scene, and his piercing eyes took in the entire story. The sharp rocks splattered with blood made him wince, even though he made every effort to remain calm. He looked about carefully and saw where Molly had managed to drag herself to a bush that would provide some shelter. She was not moving when he found her. He knelt beside her, searching for signs of life, relieved when he felt her feeble pulse. He raised her head and dribbled a few drops of water on her parched lips. Her eyelids quivered, but the swelling was so great she scarcely could open her eyes. He gave her some more water. Her tongue protruded slightly as she tried to lick her cracked lips, and he gave her a few more drops. Then he gently covered her battered body with her blouse and skirt. She was badly sunburned. The hot sun had beaten down on her unprotected body for almost two days. He continued giving her a few drops of water at a time, and she began to revive.

"Goonabi," she whispered. "How did you ..."

He placed his big calloused hand gently over her lips and smiled at her. She was going to be all right. She was tough—just like her grandmother.

He looked at the setting sun. It would be too late to retrace his steps back to the search party. He would send up the flares to reveal his whereabouts, but he feared the terrain was too rough for even a four-wheel drive vehicle to reach them. Where the wind had deposited sand, the dunes were thick and treacherous, and where it had uncovered boulders, the big rocks would be an impediment. It would be best to stay where they were for the night and start back in the morning. He would continue administering water to her parched body. Perhaps she could eat something soft later. He spread some soothing salve on her sun-burned skin and smoothed out a place for her to lie on, placing his shirt under her for added comfort. She clutched his hand, unwilling to let go, and finally dropped off to sleep. He kept a silent vigil beside her all night.

At dawn, Goonabi stood up, looking toward the north where many large birds soared and circled. His eyes narrowed. He spoke gently to Molly until she acknowledged him—he did not want to alarm her by his absence. He left quietly and walked over two ridges before he found what he was looking for. A gruesome sight met his eyes as he stared down the slope. The birds pecking at Wilanya's body flew away as Goonabi approached. He studied the remains for a long time and then, shaking his head, turned away. No punishment he could have inflicted on the young Aborigine would have been worse than what Wilanya had done to himself. The uninitiated youth had passed through as many stages of the rituals of manhood as he could before he died. He had circumcised himself with his own knife, which lay at his side encrusted with blood. He had driven a stick through the septum of his nose and had knocked out one of his upper incisors. Finally he had opened the veins of his arms so the precious blood would run down and hallow his body. He had bled to death trying to prove himself.

Goonabi built a fire at each side of the body because Wilanya's spirit would still be there and could do him harm. He did not touch the body—death was an evil thing. Let the policeman take care of the burial. The scavenger birds hovered a little distance away, waiting for the fires to burn down. The ubiquitous ants already were swarming over the body. Goonabi, his sense of justice satisfied, started back to Molly.

His business now was with the living.

The policeman pulled into the parking lot at the hospital at two o'clock in the afternoon. Goonabi had carried Molly in his strong arms for fifteen miles before he heard the approaching vehicle coughing and churning its way through the rugged landscape. He cushioned her body with his own to protect her from the jarring as they bounced over rocks and gullies. When the Land Rover stopped, Goonabi lifted Molly tenderly and carried her up the steps to the hospital.

Bert looked at her swollen, battered face and cringed. "My God, what did he do to her? Do you suppose he ...?"

Sergeant MacDonald cut him short. "Whatever may or may not have happened to Sister Riley is her own business, not ours."

Eric, grateful for his unexpected sensitivity, nodded. He grasped her hand for a moment as she was carried past, speaking softly, "Thank God you're back, Molly. Everything is going to be all right."

She smiled weakly, and Goonabi carried her into the surgery and the doctor closed the door. Eric clenched and unclenched his hands in distress, consumed with thoughts of retribution. "If I ever get my hands on Wilanya, he'll wish he'd never been born," he vowed. "I should have finished him off that day at the caravan park. If I had, this never would have happened."

"Wilanya is dead," MacDonald said shortly.

"Really? I'm glad!" Eric burst out. "How did it happen?"

"By his own hand. Sister Riley's well-being is the only matter of importance now."

"You're right," Eric said. He felt his anger dissipating. Revenge and regret would serve no purpose.

The sergeant, relieved that the matter was now out of his hands, prepared to leave. When Goonabi told him Wilanya was dead, his first thought was that the big Aborigine had taken his revenge on the abductor. MacDonald would have had a difficult conflict between duty and justice if he'd had to arrest Goonabi. But his story rang true; the case was closed as far as he was concerned, and there would be little evidence left by the time they returned for the body even if there had been a reprisal. His first consideration had been to get the girl back to health as quickly as possible.

Bert still looked stricken. Then he asked, "What about my Land Rover? Can I make arrangements to get it back now?"

"Why don't you go down to the garage and talk to the mechanic?" suggested the sergeant, and then he added, "It will cost you a pretty penny." He left and Bert rose to his feet, running his hands nervously through his hair. He turned to Eric with a guilty expression.

"I'd better go down and see about tires," he said. "My dad will skin me alive if I don't return the Land Rover in good condition." He hesitated and then seemed to come to a decision. "Will you tell Molly I have to get it back to the station? I really can't wait any longer. Please tell her I'm sorry—real sorry." He started to hold out his hand, but after observing Eric's face, drew it back and made a precipitous exit.

The policeman watched him walk toward town. He did not offer him a ride. It rankled him that the Yank had showed more compassion towards Molly than this Aussie chap.

Molly was allowed no visitors at first. Eric had to content himself with talking to the nursing sisters and being reassured that she was showing improvement. He was finally allowed to see her on the third day following her rescue. He had steeled himself in advance for what he might see, but it took all his self-control not to visibly flinch when he saw Molly's face. He wasn't sure that she could see him because her eyes were swollen almost shut, and great purple bruises covered her cheeks. He spoke quietly as he approached the bed.

"It's Eric, Molly. I wanted to see you before, but they wouldn't let me."

She didn't answer and turned her head away. He carefully placed his hand gently over hers, wincing as he noticed the cuts and scrapes that had been medicated. She did not pull her hand away.

"You're going to be all right, Molly. I'm so thankful." He waited a moment and then continued. "Molly, I've not been a praying man for a long time, but the night we waited for word about you, I prayed that you would be given the strength to survive. I felt a great power surrounding that prayer. Somehow I knew that it was being answered."

She turned her hand over and gave his an almost imperceptible squeeze. Then with a raspy voice he scarcely recognized, she whispered, "Why did he do it, Eric? We were friends."

"I know. You tried so hard with him, Molly."

"I lay here hating him, Eric, hating him with every ounce of my being. I was so terribly angry. Then I learned what he did to himself." She began to cry. "Poor Wilanya. He wasn't himself, Eric, when he took me. He was a complete stranger, someone evil. I taunted him and shamed him into doing what he did. He's gone now. It's my fault!"

"No, Molly—none of this was your fault. Stop blaming yourself. You must not feel guilty about anything. Wilanya made his choices."

"But I said my grandmother would put a curse on him! I don't believe in curses! That's against my faith! How could I have said that?"

"I think you must have brought him back to reality at the end. Molly, you've been through a terrible ordeal. It's a miracle that you survived."

"Yes, if it hadn't been for Goonabi ... Somehow he knew ... But how did he know?"

Eric smiled. "I don't know how, Molly. God moves in mysterious ways."

"Yes."

"I'm just thankful Goonabi showed up. I don't understand the Aboriginal mental communication any more than I do how prayer works. I just know that it does. Perhaps there is some similarity because it relies on a power greater than ourselves. Oh, Molly, forgive me! Here I am being pedantic again, and you are feeling so miserable."

"I like to hear you talk, Eric." They both were silent for a moment, and then she continued, "I'm going to put all this behind me. I'll try to remember Wilanya the way he was in the past when we were children."

Eric nodded. He started to say, "Oh, Molly, if you just knew how concerned I was, how much I care ..." when the nursing sister entered in a brisk manner, saying, "That's a long enough visit for now."

Eric rose reluctantly. "I'll see you again tomorrow. Get well fast." He leaned over and kissed her swollen cheek with great tenderness.

"I must look awful!" Molly wailed.

"You're getting better already. Vanity is the first sign of healing!"

In the corridor Sister Thomas stopped him. "We offered Molly a transfer if she wanted one. We thought perhaps under the circumstances ..." Her voice trailed off. "There will be talk, of course."

"What did she say?"

"She refused. She said her place was here, and she was staying out her year. The Flying Doctor would have taken her to Adelaide, you know. She's got a lot of—what do you say in your country?—grit!"

"She sure has. I'm glad she decided to stay."

"We are, too." The nurse hesitated. "For both your sakes."

Eric felt the color rising in his face. He gave her a warm handshake and left with renewed spirits.

CHAPTER THIRTY-TWO

As THE DAYS WENT BY, Dimitrios wielded his pick with frenzied determination, driving himself every moment, weighing their discoveries against the time he had left. Although he and Duro were hard-working partners, they had no genuine liking for each other. Daily labor and prospective riches were all that comprised their relationship. Dimitrios still resented the American, but he had not had any choice in accepting his help. He had to admit, in spite of his animosity, that the Yank always did his share. Right now Eric was noodling through the last load of opal dust he had pulled up, hopefully finding a few pieces of choice opal the men below had missed. The new vein had crossed a vertical slide that was especially rich in color, and soon they would have a parcel, the first that had real quality. The others had kept them in food and petrol, but not much more.

Sometimes Dimitrios examined the large supporting pillar from which several drives radiated. Their torches revealed thin traces of bright opal, but to explore the leads in any depth might weaken the important column. Not that there had been many cave-ins over the years in Coober Pedy. The opal clay was tough and did not lend itself to deterioration. On some of the fields the layers of jasper above the clay had ruined several drill bits. Working in most mines was as safe as working up above, but of course, common sense dictated caution. Some mines were not nearly so deep, and others were worked entirely on the surface with backhoes. Each situation called for its own special knowledge and precautions. Dimitrios looked longingly at the opal that was so enticingly visible in the pillar.

Some days he spent in sullen despair. Sophia's letters became more infrequent, less passionate. He wrote glowing reports of their mining successes—things were looking good; better opal was being dug out; the next parcel would bring top price ... just wait. Wait for him! He would be coming home soon. Show this letter to her father ... ask him for a little more time ... just a little more time.

Sophia's next letter was brief. Her father would not extend his time. Old Papagopolous was getting impatient. A bargain was a bargain. Please find the money soon.

Dimitrios knew it was useless to ask Eric to work out the opal in the supporting pillar. He would say it was too dangerous. Dimitrios couldn't do it alone—he needed Duro to assist him. How would the Yugoslav feel about it? From all of his observations of his co-worker, he surmised that Duro really didn't care much about what he did. He appeared to work in a mechanical way, but there was a strange light in his eyes. Sometimes Dimitrios felt there was complete detachment and at others an animal-like ferocity. Once when he had referred to him as a Yugoslav, Duro turned on him venomously. "I am not Yugoslavian! I am Serbian! Don't lump me in with those Croatians!"

Dimitrios simply had imitated the general understanding the Australians had, not differentiating the two bitter enemies from the old country. Duro had remained sulky and withdrawn the rest of the day. Dimitrios was almost afraid of him. Still, it wouldn't hurt to ask his opinion about the pillar. Maybe he was hungry for money, too. Maybe he wanted to leave Coober Pedy and all the bad memories. Dimitrios would approach Duro in the morning. If they could dig out the opal and it was as good as it appeared, they could force Eric to sell early. The parcel would be big enough to attract a good price if they could get the right buyer. American buyers might even be in town if they were lucky. Although they bargained down to the last dollar, the Americans were fair.

Duro was unusually quiet the next day. His mind seemed far away. Dimitrios hesitated to approach him but time was pressing. He could not delay.

"Duro, I've been examining the seam in the pillar," he began.

"I know. I saw you looking at it many times. I have, too."

"Do you think we could place charges in such a way we could follow the lead without weakening the whole column?"

"I'm not sure."

"Have you thought about it?" Dimitrios pressed.

"I have thought about it."

"I want to get a parcel sold right away. I need money fast. Working by hand will take too long. We need explosives."

Duro stared at him. "With money, both of us could get away from here soon."

"Are you thinking of leaving, too?" Dimitrios asked. He was sure now that Duro would help.

"I have been thinking about leaving. Yes."

"Where would you go? Back to Sydney?"

Duro shrugged. "Just away. But I need much money to leave."

"I know Eric doesn't want us to blast into the column, but I think it can be done safely. He needn't know until it's over. Will you work with me?"

Duro nodded. They shook hands.

"Soon," Dimitrios said. "We won't tell Eric. We'll keep him on top. He doesn't come down much anyway, since he injured his leg."

Dimitrios had no intention of telling Eric anything. It all went back to that terrible day when he was made aware of the difference between his brother, Constantine, and himself. He was ten years old, his brother was seven—an age difference that did not preclude playing together and having some mutual friends. Sometimes they enjoyed each other's company, and at other times they scrapped, mostly verbally. Dimitrios had landed a few sharp blows on his brother when he had become too bothersome. They helped their father in the store after school and on Saturdays, but they managed to steal a few minutes here and there for their own recreation, especially when they ran errands.

Their father's small shop was a wonderful place that exuded pungent smells of spiced olives, pickles in vats, cheeses, dried meats, and fresh fruits and vegetables. The boys never objected to their chore of keeping the place swept, the counters cleaned and replacing stock because they often could sneak little snacks behind their father's back. Nicholas Mylonas was a heavy set, swarthy man whose eyes could change instantly from friendly and warm to angry and hot. Never were they indifferent—they were always filled with emotion, and Dimitrios had become skillful in interpreting the mood.

Constantine, with his dark, coarse features, resembled his father and was similar in disposition—hot tempered and intense. Dimitrios usually shrugged off his brother's pesky ways, but this day the youngster was especially annoying. After they made delivery they had stopped for a few minutes to play soccer with the neighborhood boys, and the younger child had been excluded. Constantine sulked by the stone wall nursing his grievance and then struck up a conversation with another boy also who had been rejected. They shared their mutual resentment against older siblings and grew more put upon as the game continued without their inclusion. As the talk diminished, they sat kicking up dust and throwing small pebbles at a target. Then the new friend pointed to Dimitrios, whispered something and snickered.

On their return to the shop, which was below their living quarters, Constantine provoked his brother beyond endurance. As they entered the shop, Dimitrios gave him a quick cuff, out of sight of his father, and started to go behind the counter to help. The young boy's shrill voice filled the room with its piercing accusation. He hoped the big words he didn't understand would give him a degree of importance.

"I'm not afraid of you! You're just an American bastard!"

Dimitrios was about to laugh as he usually did when his brother hurled obscenities at him that he had picked up from the street. He was not prepared for his father's reaction. The older man's face had blanched to a peculiar greenish color, and his eyes glittered with a crazy light. He roared out from behind the counter and struck Constantine savagely across the face.

"Don't you ever say that again!" he shouted. "You dishonor your mother!" He trembled violently.

A chill swept over Dimitrios—his breath caught in his throat, and he could not speak. He looked at his father dumbly, eyes pleading for an explanation, yet dreading it. Never had he seen his father so uncontrolled.

"Papa ..." he finally managed to stammer, "Papa ..."

His father sank onto a stool and buried his face in his hands, refusing to look at the boys. Constantine cowered in a corner, a great red welt on the side of his face. Dimitrios steadied himself against the counter, afraid that his shaking legs would not support him. He wanted desperately to get away but feared to leave because his father might lash out at him, too.

His father began to speak, so softly that Dimitrios could scarcely hear him. "It was after the civil war," he whispered. "The communists held the countryside. There was terrible hunger. We'd had the Italians first, then the Germans, and afterwards our own people started fighting each other." He removed his hands from his face and stared at the wall. "The Americans sent supplies and advisors. Your mother's family was starving ... She kept them alive. An American soldier brought food for many weeks. He said he would return later, but he never did. I met your mother a year after you were born, and we were married." He turned his head and looked directly into Dimitrios' eyes. "We moved away to this village where we hoped no one would know. I was wrong. Secrets always come to light somehow. She is a fine wife and mother, and you must fight to protect her good name, as I have done. No man would dare to say anything against her any more, either to my face or behind my back, but I have no control over the children." He stood up. "Now go upstairs. We will never speak of this again."

Nicholas went over to Constantine, who still lay huddled in the corner, and lifted him up. The child's body was racked with sobs which did not diminish until his father held him close and comforted him. "Don't cry, my son. I'm sorry! Don't cry. Papa is sorry." Constantine then stumbled up the stairs with Dimitrios close behind him. Their mother was standing at the stove preparing dinner and did not turn around. The boys knew she had heard the disturbance downstairs. They could not see her flushed face, but the pink cast was visible on her ears, exposed to view by the severity of her tightly bound hair. Dimitrios washed his brother's face and held him on his lap. Then he looked in the mirror and saw the evidence that set him apart from his brother—the finely chiseled features, the hazel eyes with golden flecks, the fair complexion. He had a handsome face, almost classic, but he hated it. And he hated his unknown American father and by extension, all American men.

No, they would not tell Eric anything. They continued to gouge out the opal seam from the freshly blasted area. They worked without speaking, each intent on his own thoughts.

CHAPTER THIRTY-THREE

MOLLY HAD BEEN BACK TO WORK for several weeks—
her bruises gradually fading from dark blue to pale yellow and
her cuts and abrasions healing well. Hard work had been her
greatest ally—helping others reduced her own physical and emotional pain. Her natural optimism and Eric's unwavering support gave her a resilience that kept her on an even keel. She
basked in the warm glow of his caring and dismissed Janet from
her thoughts. Mrs. McCurdy wrote her a short note informing
her of Bert's return to the station, her regret for Molly's 'accident' and her grandmother's loving concern. Niboorana was
getting on in years, she wrote, and had decided to journey to
the Yunarra Mission where Pastor and Mrs. Holmgren had reared
Molly. Goonabi would accompany her.

Molly read between the lines—it would embarrass the
McCurdys for Molly to visit her grandmother now. The breech
was too great. She knew a sense of relief must have descended
on Wiluru Station when Bert had returned with a contrite spirit
and no more damage than four ruined tires. The knowledge
that her grandmother now enjoyed the protection and advan-

tages of the mission gladdened her heart. She had long wanted her there, but Niboorana's resistance precluded any change.

The days passed quickly with little alteration in routine. She spent her free time at the Aboriginal Reserve when she wasn't with Eric, assisting the authorities with health checks and entertaining the children. Molly was disappointed when she saw people that she thought she had reached, lying in a stupor in town after receiving their dole and spending it on liquor. She appreciated the successes her foster father had accomplished at the mission, where spiritual guidance as well as sustenance was offered.

One lazy afternoon she and Eric ambled into town for a cool drink and a chance to share their activities of the week. An impish smile crossed her face, and she suddenly asked, "I've been thinking of the day we spent at the Breakaways when I told you about the Rainbow Serpent. Do you remember?"

"Of course! How could I forget?"

"I asked you a funny question: If given a choice between the power of the Rainbow Serpent or finding the pot of gold at the end of the rainbow, which one would you choose?"

He laughed. "As I recall, I said a little of each."

"But suppose you had to make a choice between them and could choose only one, which would it be?"

He gave her a quizzical look, sensing that her question was really not as frivolous as it sounded. He considered it carefully, wondering why she had asked. She often surprised him with the hidden depth of her observations. "I think I would choose the Rainbow Serpent," he said.

"But why would you choose it?" she persisted.

It had become more than a game of words, and he paused to reflect before answering. "You said the Rainbow Serpent brings renewal of life, and if you had that, you wouldn't need the pot of gold, would you? And if you had the gold and the same old life, it wouldn't do you much good, would it? We have to be willing to change and grow."

"I'm glad you said that."

They walked back to the hospital slowly, prolonging their time together, savoring what remained of the afternoon before Molly went on duty. He gave her a lingering kiss, which was warmly reciprocated.

When Eric returned to his caravan, he found a note slipped under his screen door and read it with misgivings.

I have absolute proof of the whereabouts of Sandy Blackwell. This is no con trick, and I can show you tonight. I want $500. No money, no Sandy. Meet me at the Opal Inn at 9:00 p.m. Peter Bagley.

It almost sounded legitimate, but how could he trust the con man after his earlier encounter? Surely the rogue wouldn't try anything stupid again! With nothing to lose, Eric considered the request. He would certainly pay no money without actually seeing the boy. But, he would satisfy his curiosity about this new information if Peter had found out something important. Eric suspected Peter had been the one who removed all of his former notes concerning Sandy. He had left a new brief one that very morning at the Greek market: "Anyone with information about Sandy Blackwell contact Eric Christianson at the caravan park." What more could he do? It had been so long now that hope had almost dwindled. He would make this last effort to see what Bagley was up to. He scanned the communication again and checked his watch. It was only six o'clock so he had plenty of time to shower and relax. Relax? When he might see his son for the first time? He was afraid to believe, and yet hope kept pushing away the doubts. If this proved true, he would gladly pay Peter and forgive him for his past underhanded scheme.

CHAPTER THIRTY-FOUR

DURO FROWNED in perplexity. When he had encountered the young waitress that day in the Greek store, he had
seen a flicker of recognition in her eyes, but to his knowledge
he had observed her only once before, when she had walked
out of the Opal Inn as he was passing by. She had not even
glanced at him then. He decided to drop by the restaurant for
a cup of coffee and test her reaction. As he entered, he saw her
look fixedly at him for a brief moment, then quickly away.
She avoided him until it was evident that the other girl was
busy and there was no one else to serve him. She walked over
to his table to take his order, with her eyes downcast and face
slightly averted. He stared at her, and the girl became discon-
certed, a slight flush spread over her face. She brought the
coffee and retreated to the other side of the room.

Sergeant MacDonald sat at his usual table. He had been
casually interested in the little by-play, but as he looked at the
waitress with some intensity, he realized the panic on her face
must be registering inner turmoil. He watched as she rear-
ranged bottles of sauce and condiments, adjusting their posi-

tions as though playing a game of chess. His sharp eyes missed nothing as he sipped his tea with apparent unconcern.

Duro finished his coffee and rose to leave. When he saw the policeman, his features became rigid and expressionless. He did not hurry but walked with measured steps to the exit, not acknowledging the officer's presence nor indicating in any way that he knew he was being scrutinized. Once outside, his frown deepened. The waitress knew something. He intended to find out what it might be. He jammed his fists into his pockets in frustration, wondering why the policeman had been so interested in him. He didn't want the authorities observing anything he did, tonight or any time.

The sergeant motioned for Janet to come to his table and she did so with noticeable reluctance. Guilt hung over her like a heavy cloud. He had seen that attitude before, when someone was desperately trying to deny complicity. MacDonald wondered what she was trying to hide. She was obviously trying to avoid Duro. Why? Something stirred in the back of his mind.

"Miss, if there's anything you wish to tell me, perhaps I can be of help to you." He smiled as he spoke to alleviate her distrust. "Sometimes people don't want to get involved with the police, but if you feel you need a friend, I'm a good listener."

Janet shook her head. "There's nothing. I'm just tired tonight." Then she added, "But thank you, anyway." The wariness in her eyes did not diminish.

When Peter Bagley appeared, the officer's body tightened with a primitive reaction. He despised the man. He wished he had enough hard evidence to put him away, but this adversary was too slippery. Peter had hesitated on the threshold as if weighing the advisability of making an entrance, and then with his customary bravado he sauntered by the sergeant's table and sat down near by. Now MacDonald saw real fear spring into the girl's eyes. She stared at Peter, as though transfixed. The policeman could not see Peter's expression but heard his voice, smooth and caressing.

"I must see you later tonight, luv. When do you get off?"

"I'm working late. I can't see you tonight."

"You must. It's important. I can wait for you. Don't disappoint me."

"I can't," she whispered.

He lowered his voice. "You will."

"No! Please!"

Bagley glanced at MacDonald and said in a loud tone, "I'll see you when you're through working, honey. I'm looking forward to it." After he left, Janet stood immobile.

"Miss." The sergeant beckoned.

She roused herself. "Yes, sir?"

"Choose your friends carefully. Remember, I can help." He wiped his mouth, and with the cloth over his lips he said quietly, "Don't be afraid to talk to me."

Janet looked at him speechlessly and then moved to another table. Before she had finished with her next customer, she felt tears welling up in her eyes. She dabbed at them with her apron, but they continued to flow. Beside herself, she flung the apron on the counter and rushed out the door. MacDonald poured another cup of tea and drank it thoughtfully.

Janet glanced both ways when she reached the street and then proceeded in the direction of the hospital. Some men who congregated outside the pub almost blocked her way and jostled her as she passed by them, giving her appreciative looks and making suggestive comments. She needed to see Molly out of desperation—hoping the nurse, having recovered from a terrible experience herself, would be receptive to her problem. She began to run, gasping for breath and unable to speak when she burst through the hospital entrance. Molly sat at the receiving desk and looked up in astonishment. She led the trembling girl to a chair and put her arms around her protectively.

"It's going to be all right," she soothed. "Try to relax. You can tell me about it when you're ready." Janet raised her despairing eyes to Molly, finding a calm assurance in the nurse's expression that quieted her anxiety. "Has someone hurt you, Janet? Shall I call the police?"

Janet shook her head. "No! Please. No police! I'm at my wit's end, and I don't know what to do!" She broke into uncontrollable sobs, and Molly recognized the rising hysteria. She gripped Janet's hands tightly and spoke firmly.

"You must tell me about your situation so I can help you. Is someone threatening you? What kind of trouble are you in?"

Janet's words tumbled out. "It's Peter Bagley—he's forcing me to do something illegal. You've got to believe me—I didn't know how bad it was until it was too late. He says I'm implicated, but I swear I didn't know I was doing anything wrong when I started. Oh, I'm so frightened, Sister Riley."

"Call me Molly, Janet. That is your name, isn't it? I've seen you often at the Opal Inn, and you always seemed so capable and happy. I'm sorry if you have a problem, but I don't understand how I can help. What have you done that's against the law?"

"I can't tell you. I just can't say any more. I'm scared to death, Molly. Peter's going to hurt me. I know he is, especially if he thinks I've talked to anyone. I have to get away, and I don't have much money. Please help me, Molly. I don't have anyone else to turn to. I can't ask Anastasia. Her parents wouldn't understand."

"Janet, before I get involved, I must know what you've done."

Janet raised a tear-stained face. "Peter had me pick up money he said was owed him."

"Who owed it to him?"

"I don't know for sure. When I realized it was blackmail, I was in too deep to get out."

"Blackmail is a dirty business, Janet. No wonder you're scared. Why was Peter blackmailing this man?"

Janet hesitated for a moment and then said, "He didn't

tell me, Molly, but I'm sure it was something bad."

Molly looked at her speculatively, trying to determine whether she had been told the entire truth. Finally she decided the story rang true. The girl obviously was terrified. "I can arrange for you to go to the Yunarra Mission where I was brought up. My foster parents will be glad to help you until you decide what you want to do. Would you like me to make arrangements?"

Janet smiled through her tears. "Oh, yes," she said. "I don't know how to thank you. I won't be any trouble for them. I'm a good worker. I'll do chores for my keep."

"I'll phone them tonight. The bus comes through on Thursday at noon. Today's Tuesday. You'll have a day to get ready."

"I'm so happy. I do have a little money saved. I hope it's enough for the bus fare."

Molly patted her hand. "If it isn't, you can pay me back later when you find work."

"Oh, Molly, I'm so grateful. Only please, please don't tell anyone where I'm going to be. Not anyone."

"All right, Janet." She watched the girl walk slowly down the steps. She was so young, and Peter was such a devil. She would have liked to accompany her back to town, but she could not leave her station. It wasn't safe for a young girl to be walking about alone at night, not that it was that late—just 8:00 o'clock, but even then it involved risk.

Janet did not see the figure watching from the corner of the building, and it was only when a small sound caused her to turn around that she recognized her stalker. She began to run, and with terror giving wings to her feet, outdistanced her pursuer. Just as she approached the first building with a light that illuminated the road, the man faded into the shadows. Her heart pounded, and she gasped for breath. All she wanted was to get back to the sanctuary of her room at the motel. Thankfully her entrance was from the outside walkway, and she didn't have to go through the lobby. Peter stepped out of the pub unexpectedly and grabbed her arm as she ran by. She shook herself free and continued to run, to the amusement of the miners standing near. He started after her, but she reached her room first and locked the door.

"Let me in, Janet," he pleaded.

"No! Go away!"

"The policeman was in the restaurant tonight. He was watching you. Have you talked with him?"

"No! I swear I haven't."

"You know what will happen to you if you do."

Janet didn't answer. She threw herself on the bed, her body heaving from exertion, close to collapse. In spite of the racing of her heated blood, her mind felt frozen.

"Honey," Peter's voice was soft now, provocative. "I've been too hasty. I lost my temper and I'm sorry. Let's get back to where we were. We had some good times together. You know I'm really crazy about you."

He listened. No sound came from the room. He rattled the doorknob. "Let me in. Please, honey. Something important came up, and I need you."

There was no answer.

"Janet, I'm coming in if I have to break this door down!"

"Then break it down!" she cried. "That's the only way you'll get in. And if you lay one hand on me ever again, I'll fight you, I'll scream, I'll kill you!"

Peter realized the futility of further argument and started to turn away when he saw Sergeant MacDonald. The officer looked down the walkway to where Bagley was standing at the end room, his face dark with concern. Peter assumed he had overheard her last words.

"You little fool," Peter whispered. "Keep your voice down. MacDonald's within earshot. If the police get involved, we're both in trouble. You don't want to go to jail, do you?" He could hear muffled sobs through the door. "Get some sleep, luv," he told her loudly. "You'll feel better in the morning." Then more quietly he added, "I'll see you tomorrow. I can't have you falling apart now." He walked away in the opposite direction from MacDonald.

Janet curled into the fetal position, her arms holding her body tightly, trying to insulate herself against panic. She lay that way for a long time until she thought she heard furtive footsteps and raised her head to listen, but all was silent. She heard the door knob turn ever so slightly and then stop. She buried her face in her pillow, taking some comfort in the pounding of her pulse, a steady pulse now, a welcome reminder of her strength. She could endure one more day, feigning illness, and then on Thursday she would travel to the mission. Eventually she would find work somewhere. She was young and willing, and she could always find a job. If Peter implicated her, he was making himself a target for investigation. She had been a fool to think he could hurt her with his blackmail.

She became conscious of an eerie stillness, the void that often was the precursor of the willy-willy, the whirling dust storm that could ravage a town without warning. She would welcome it, for then she would have an excuse to huddle in her room. No one would be out in such weather. As she gradually fell asleep, her last thoughts were about how much she had learned in a very short while.

CHAPTER THIRTY-FIVE

AT NINE O'CLOCK Eric strode into the Opal Inn and stopped. There was no Peter Bagley, and his heart sank. This was a cruel hoax indeed. He looked around for Janet. Although it was rumored that she had severed her relationship with Peter, she might know of his whereabouts. This time he would give the con man a drubbing he wouldn't forget. Janet wasn't on duty, he was told. She had left early that evening, and the boss was angry.

Sergeant MacDonald had returned to the restaurant after being confronted at home by a shrill, accusatory virago. He had ceased trying to defend his innocence. Let his wife think what she wanted. He had no intention of becoming involved with a local woman, although his heart softened when he thought of Janet. She was such a fresh, pretty girl, and somehow she was getting a raw deal from Peter Bagley. He sat at his usual table and watched the American curiously. What would the Yank be doing here alone? he wondered. He glanced at his watch, his precision-loving mind automatically registering the time the American left the inn. Eric hadn't stayed long, and his clenched fists registered irritation.

Duro had waited outside the Opal Inn with vigilance and patience, determined to resolve his problem. That the waitress was an accomplice he was sure; he was also sure that she would lead him to his blackmailer. Since he had nothing else to do, he would wait until she came out. It happened sooner than he expected, almost catching him off guard as she hurried by. Had he not been mingling with the other men, she might have recognized him. He followed at a discrete distance, hoping she would lead him to someone significant. He observed with interest that she headed toward the hospital. Now what, he wondered, would she be doing there? Janet's rushed departure from the restaurant in itself aroused his curiosity, and her destination was even more odd. He stationed himself around the corner from the entrance, ready to waylay her if possible. He would get some answers from her one way or another.

As she left the hospital to return to the inn, he moved and made a sound that alerted her. His pursuit proved futile, and he cursed himself for his carelessness. Then he spotted Peter Bagley trying to force his attentions on her and continued his stalking. He circled around behind the inn, keeping a discrete distance, but could hear Peter's threatening words outside her room. Peter the Con! Of course. He should have realized that someone slimy like Peter would be the perpetrator. He had discovered what he wanted to know, and now he would bide his time. Sooner or later Peter Bagley would place himself in a position advantageous to Duro, and then his blackmailing scheme would be terminated permanently. He peered around the corner and could see the policeman standing at the end of the walkway and quickly slipped into the alley behind the building. He would take a shortcut to his dugout.

A small noise attracted his attention. Peter was using the alley, too, his shoes crunching on the rough clay and gravel mixture, but he was walking in the opposite direction. Duro surmised that Bagley was avoiding MacDonald after his unsuccessful confrontation with Janet and realized that in the dim light Peter had not even seen him. What an opportunity! He stealthily followed him, his knife unsheathed.

"Peter," he called quietly, and Bagley turned around in surprise. Without a moment's hesitation Duro thrust his knife savagely into Peter's chest several times as the surprised victim raised his hands futilely to protect himself. An instant of recognition flashed in his eyes giving Duro immense satisfaction. As Peter crumpled to the ground, blood spurting out, Duro leaped back and then pushed the body over with his foot so the face was ground into the clay dust. Duro wiped the blood off his knife on the dead man's shirt and slid the weapon back into its holder. Reaching into Bagley's pocket he pulled out his wallet and extracted the few bills that it contained. It all had happened so quickly and so easily. The con man had not even cried out. Duro had not felt such satisfaction since the night he killed Lucas.

He peered about around the corner and found the policeman no longer standing at the side of the inn and no one was loitering in the street ahead. He pondered about whether to slip down the alley and get home as fast as possible, which would be the safest plan, or whether to finish the job. Exhilaration drove him now. He felt invincible. He decided he might as well bring the whole episode to a completion right then and there.

He approached Janet's room cautiously. There was no light visible from the waitress' room. He tried the door handle, and although it turned, the door was bolted on the inside. Duro drew back in anger. He considered the situation for a moment. Peter probably had not told her the whole story, and if he had, hopefully she would be too frightened to say anything. He would change clothes and go immediately to his club and mingle with his fellow Serbians. Members would testify that he had been there, and he could not be implicated in Peter's killing. Soon he would have enough money to get away and start a new life. Meeting Peter in the alley had been very fortuitous.

When he strolled into his club later, he sat unobtrusively at a back table. He ordered wine and waved to a couple of acquaintances, who were pleased to see him in jovial spirits again. He beckoned them to join him and drank thirstily, feeling less guilty than if he had swatted a fly.

Tomorrow he and Dimitrios would work on the seam of opal in the column. It appeared to be widening, and beautiful fire was beginning to show. He would suggest to the Greek that they not even inform the American of their find. They could arrange to sell their opal on the sly without Eric even knowing. They would fly on Opal Air to Adelaide immediately afterwards, and from there to Sydney.

No one could catch him, and no one could trace him. Very shortly he would be a free man.

CHAPTER THIRTY-SIX

BRIAN MACDONALD was at his desk early the next morning, as always. He often felt his wife went to extra pains to make herself unattractive at the breakfast table, so he regularly left before she was even out of bed. He seldom looked at her any more and tried to keep her strident voice away from his consciousness as much as possible. He pitied her, but the pity was mixed with contempt. He had seen many unfortunate invalids in his line of work who, in spite of severe handicaps, retained dignity and warmth. Elizabeth punished him more for his lack of love and complete indifference than for that tragic accident. If only she had met him halfway back then. Convulsed with grief and guilt, he would have tended her with compassion. They could have built some kind of life together; at least there could have been understanding and mutual respect. Now there was nothing but vituperation—hers vocalized, his internalized. Work was a blessed solace for MacDonald.

He was informed of the murder within minutes of his arrival at the office. A miner had almost stumbled over the body in the faint light of dawn, and after debating whether to report it and perhaps be considered a possible suspect, he decided to notify the police. The sergeant had taken charge immediately. He recognized the victim, as did all the curious bystanders who had gathered around with ghoulish curiosity. Peter the Con was well known and universally disliked, including more than one lady who had succumbed to his blandishments. The sergeant would have no lack of suspects in this town.

He examined the position of the knife wounds and calculated the height of the attacker. Someone rather tall and very strong had inflicted those fatal blows. The sergeant always let his mind remain like blotting paper, soaking up bits of information but never leaping to conclusions. Someone must have hated him indeed—or feared him—to waylay Peter in this manner so close to town, but then perhaps it was just a common robbery. An empty wallet lay in the dirt beside him. Could it be a ruse? There were many hotheads in town, and there was no telling at this time who the murderer might be. But this appeared to be no ordinary pub fight or a spur-of-the-moment killing. MacDonald examined the tracks in the soft dirt. The assailant had stalked Peter, caused him to turn around and then stabbed him. This bespoke a deep hostility, a furtive surveillance, a desire to be recognized before the fatal, well-aimed blows, and then a melting back into a commonplace background. This unique murder loomed as a challenge. Fortunately the people gathering to watch had kept their distance and not disturbed too many clues. No one wanted to be identified as having unseemly interest.

MacDonald questioned many of the onlookers and noted replies in his little book. The last person to be seen talking with Peter was the waitress at the Opal Inn. The sergeant pursed his lips. He recalled her despairing words last evening. A frown hung momentarily on his forehead and as quickly disappeared. Janet wouldn't have had the strength to wield the knife with the force it took to cause those wounds, but he was convinced that she would have some pertinent information. Would she willingly shed any light on the problem? If she proved reluctant, a scare would surely produce results. His softer feelings vanished, and the disciplined officer surfaced. He had Janet brought to his office. His deputy reported that her bag was packed, and apparently she planned to leave town. Her eyes, wide with apprehension, seemed even brighter blue against the pallor of her face. MacDonald noted her hands twisting and untwisting in her lap. It would not be difficult to break her down.

"Do you know why you have been brought here?" he asked sternly.

She shook her head, her lips trembling. "No," she whispered.

"I must first warn you that anything you say may be used against you in a court of law."

Janet sucked in her breath. "I haven't done anything," she protested, her voice cracking. "I don't know why I'm here."

"Do you know Peter Bagley?"

She stared at him, her lips trying to speak but her words

were pinned back in her throat. She looked across the desk like a trapped animal. He felt sorry for her but continued the relentless questioning.

"I saw you dash out of the restaurant last night, and later you were seen struggling with him on the street. Where had you been?"

She didn't answer.

"Someone saw you coming from the hospital—you were running. Why were you afraid, Janet? Was someone chasing you?" She shook her head. "I heard Bagley outside your door. You were threatening him." Her eyes pleaded with him to stop. "Peter Bagley was found dead in the alley this morning. Did you know?"

"I ... yes, I heard talk."

"He was murdered." Her mouth hung loose, but the sergeant observed a flicker of relief cross her face.

"You were the last person to be seen with him," he told her.

Comprehension dawned in her eyes. "I didn't do it!" she cried. "I swear I didn't! I was in my room all night. You've got to believe me. I wanted to, but I didn't!" She began to sob.

"Why did you want to, Janet?" MacDonald asked in a kind but persuasive voice. "Why did you want to kill him?"

She choked back her tears but said nothing.

"Had he hurt you? Threatened you about something?"

He noted an almost imperceptible response. He pursued his advantage. "Peter was holding something over your head?" She still didn't answer. He became firm. "You are a prime suspect, you know. You may well be charged with his murder if you don't aid us with whatever knowledge you have. If you have any information that will clarify this situation, it may well help you to exonerate yourself."

"I didn't see the murder. I don't know who killed him."

"Possibly not. But you could be an accomplice. You may know something about his activities that might lead us to his killer. Think about it."

She shook her head.

"Your suitcase was packed. Were you leaving town?" She just stared at him. He would have to shake her up. "Were you planning to go away with the American, Eric Christianson?" he demanded.

"Eric Christianson?" she repeated, startled. "No! No, of course not."

"He was here about the same time Bagley was murdered."

"Here? At the inn?"

"Yes. Now maybe you'll tell me where were you going."

"Just ... somewhere ... out of town," she stammered. She would not bring Molly into this after all her help.

"Why were you leaving, Janet?" There was no response. He slammed his fist on the desk. "I would suggest that you start cooperating, Miss. If you're shielding someone, it will be hard on you. You'd better think this over very carefully."

He decided to let her fret for awhile. He picked up his hat and drove to the hospital. Maybe the sister could shed some light on Janet's twilight visit.

"Sister Riley, you may have heard about Peter Bagley's murder."

"Yes, Officer. That kind of news travels fast in Coober Pedy." Molly tilted her head speculatively.

"I hoped you might shed some light on a problem. The waitress Janet came to you last evening?"

"Yes."

"She was disturbed?"

"Yes, Sergeant MacDonald, she was."

"About Peter Bagley?"

"Yes, but she wouldn't tell me why." Her eyes widened. "Surely you don't think—"

"Don't jump to conclusions, Sister. I'm just here for information. What did she talk about?"

"She didn't tell me much except she inferred that Peter was involved in some blackmail scheme. You'll have to talk with her."

"We are, but she's not cooperating. I think she's shielding someone. Do you know Eric Christianson?"

Molly, startled, dropped the report she was holding. "Of course, Officer. We're good friends. Why do you ask?"

"Do you know why he might have been at the Opal Inn about nine o'clock last night?"

"Eric? At the Opal Inn? I have no idea."

"We think perhaps he was going away with the waitress. Can you shed some light on their relationship?"

The remembrance of Janet stepping out of Eric's caravan the day she was kidnapped hit her like a blow. She thought she had erased all suspicion from her mind, but it hovered just enough below the surface to be retrieved with a few words from the policeman. She thought of the tenderness of his last kiss. Was it meant to be a goodbye kiss? She could not accept that. Then Cynthia's vindictive sneer about Eric's being involved in a morals scandal came back. He had explained it all to her satisfaction, but of course she had only his word. He always was circumspect in his conduct, but was it possible there were underlying facets of his character that he kept hidden?

After a moment's hesitation, she shook her head vigorously. "That is a preposterous question!" she flared. "I am certain you are mistaken in your assumptions. I cannot help you any further, Sergeant MacDonald, and I have duties to perform."

"Thank you, Sister. Maybe Mr. Christianson can explain his presence at the inn. We'll talk with him."

Molly watched him stride down the steps, her pulse racing, her thoughts in turmoil. How could she doubt Eric? Her hands were cold. What had Eric said about skating on thin ice? She had laughed then. She wasn't laughing now.

Janet stood with both hands pressed tightly against the desk to steady herself when the policeman returned. She looked at him in agony. "I don't want to go to prison," she whispered. "I don't know what to say."

"Just tell the truth." MacDonald knew if he gave her

enough time, she'd come around. "I cannot promise leniency—that is for others to decide. But if you are not directly involved, the law may not be too harsh with you." He relaxed. He knew the story would be unfolding shortly. "Sit down, Janet. Have a cup of tea and start at the beginning."

He hoped she would implicate the Yank. Eric had been on the scene at the right time, and from rumors around, he had no love for the con man. The sergeant had seen a disturbed fellow at the inn last night. Christianson was waiting for someone. It would be poetic justice if he could arrest that good-looking American and charge him with murder. But that was not what the waitress was disclosing.

As the tale unwound, he thought, Poor fool of a girl, but his face remained impassive. Finally she brought her story to its conclusion. She averted her eyes in embarrassment.

"I don't know where Duro works or where he lives. I only know what Peter told me about that night at the mine. He was afraid I would tell you. He threatened me."

"I wish you had come to me. It would have saved a lot of trouble. I asked you to, remember?"

She nodded dumbly.

"You are the only witness to the burial of the first man Duro killed, so your life is in danger right now. I'll see that you are protected."

Janet looked at him gratefully.

"Of course," he continued, "we only have your disclosure that all this happened, and we must substantiate it. Could you recognize the area where you say Duro disposed of the body?"

"I think so. It was at the Four Mile."

MacDonald had a watchman posted near Dimitrios' mine to be sure Duro did not leave unexpectedly, and then he and his deputy drove Janet to the Four Mile. He was impressed with her memory and convinced she had guided them accurately. When they stopped at the location she indicated, they unloaded a metal pipe and sections of a ladder. He scooped out a place for the pipe to lie across the opening to the shaft where it couldn't roll and attached the first section of ladder. Two more sections were added, and then MacDonald swung himself over the hole and started down the ladder. When he reached the bottom, he flashed his torch around and then climbed back up. He shook his head.

"There's nothing there."

Janet turned pale. "I know I saw his truck!" she cried out in disappointment. "This has to be the right place."

"Could it have been farther on? At night things look different."

"Maybe," she said reluctantly. She was beginning to feel panic. If they couldn't find the body, they would not believe her story. Then she would be the prime suspect in Peter's death.

The sergeant could see her rising anxiety. He did not wish to increase it. "Perhaps it's at the next opal heap. Was there anything that might serve as a landmark that you can remember?"

She shook her head and wrinkled her brow. "All the heaps look the same ...Wait! Peter took his shovel and smoothed out a little level place for us to sit." She flushed at the memory.

"Good show. We'll scout around."

The sergeant and his deputy roamed about, checking each opal heap in that area and branching out a little further. A shout from his assistant brought MacDonald running. There it was, a small space that had been dug and evened out. The men crossed the road to the opposite opal heap. There they could see faint tire tracks where a truck had turned in. In a few minutes they had repeated the ladder hook-up and MacDonald descended. In even less time he emerged.

"The body's there. It's so cool in the mine that there has not been too much decomposition. I'll send another crew to bring it up for identification. Jim will stay on guard here while we go back to the police station. I have to make out a warrant for Duro's arrest."

Janet put her face in her hands, and her shoulders shook with sobbing as relief replaced anxiety. MacDonald wanted to put his arms around her to steady her, but discipline held him back. He gave her a little smile.

"Have a good cry, and then you'll feel better. I don't think you have too much to worry about now—the inquest should be fairly simple. We'll pick up Duro at his mine. You don't need to be afraid any more."

CHAPTER THIRTY-SEVEN

THE POLICEMAN pushed aside the stack of papers on his desk. Fortunately they were the usual problems and could all wait until tomorrow. He worried as he looked at the warrant he had signed. If Duro was on the surface, it would not be too difficult to arrest him. He might put up a fight, but that was to be expected. The sergeant and his assistant could handle that. If he was down in the mine, that would be a different story. They would eventually corner him, of course, because there were only so many passages to run into, but it would be rather a nasty chase and someone could get hurt. It might prove difficult getting him out of the mine, too, if he resisted. If the Yank was on top, maybe he could go down and spell Duro without his suspicion being aroused. No, it grated on MacDonald to have to ask for the American's help, even if it would make things easier in the long run. They would just camp nearby and nab Duro when he came out at the close of the day. MacDonald was always flexible in his planning.

The thought crossed his mind, as he sat staring at the papers on his desk, that he had always been flexible in planning but inflexible in his relations with people. Reminiscing about his life, he realized that there had been very little warmth in his childhood. His father was firm and generally fair, but cold. Birthdays were not remembered; lip service only was paid to Christmas with meager gifts, if any. He never recalled his mother receiving a present of any kind from her husband, nor had he seen outward signs of affection. Demonstrative conduct demeaned a true man, his father always said. Life was harsh and one had to respond in kind. One did not bend, if possible, and never broke. One endured and expected others to do the same.

MacDonald thought of his wife. It was wrong for him to have married her when he didn't love her. Had he ever shown her any kindness, even in the early days? Had he been as cold and domineering as his father? He saw himself now in the shadow his father had cast, stern and unyielding. Is that what had happened to Janet? Had her father driven her from home with his inflexibility? He sighed. If he could have another chance with a different wife, someone warm and affectionate, maybe he could be different; maybe life could be different. He rejected the thought. Too late, too late!

Eric helped himself to water from the jug and let some slosh over his face and neck. The day was going to be warm again, but then, summer was near and each day promised to get hotter. His two partners had insisted he stay on top most of the time since his injury, but he had protested, and now that he was healed, he wanted to get back to their old arrangement of taking turns working below. Besides, it was a pleasure working in the cool underground. They had been particularly adamant today and advised him to stay above to haul up the buckets, which Dimitrios hinted, "might contain something special." He found that they did miss some good opal occasionally, so he understood the importance of inspecting each bucketful. Still, with the sun beating down, he would have preferred to be below ground. He smiled to think how long he had feared going down into the mine, and now it was second nature. He could not fathom why his strange nightmare persisted.

A ute stopped at the crossroads and parked behind an opal heap. Eric paid it no attention. Then a neighbor drove by and shouted out the window, "Big news! Peter Bagley's been murdered! Stabbed behind the Opal Inn. No great loss, eh?"

Eric slammed his fist on the windlass, stunned at the timing of this unfortunate death. What information about Sandy had the man taken to his grave? Now he would never know if Peter's message had been a hoax or not. He stood for a moment, consumed with bitterness and then decided to go down to tell the others. It would give him a break from the heat and take his mind off of his disappointment. Peter was so universally disliked that it would probably be difficult to find the killer. There must be dozens of suspects!

Eric swung himself over the framework, grasped the pipe firmly and began descending, hand over hand. He welcomed the coolness. He had descended more than halfway when suddenly a detonation shook him, and the closeness of the blast alarmed him. "They're taking chances," were his last thoughts as he felt his hands slipping from the ladder. Then his head smacked against the side of the shaft, and he felt earth collapsing around him. He was falling ... falling ...

MacDonald pulled himself out of his reverie. What good did it do to cry over spilt milk? The past was over and nothing could change it. Castigating himself over blunders best forgotten was futile. He had a warrant to serve, and he should get moving. If Duro suspected he was under surveillance, he might leave the mine early and escape. On the other hand, most miners stayed down the entire day to avoid the hot sun, so speed wasn't all that crucial. Nevertheless ... his attention was drawn to the screech of brakes and the sound of pounding feet outside. In another moment Bill Larson had burst through the door.

"Cave-in! Bad! At the Eleven Mile!" he shouted.

"Damn! Just when I've got a murder warrant to serve. Are there any survivors?"

"Too soon to tell. We've sent for the rescue squad."

"Which mine?"

"The Greek's. Next to ours."

"Where the Yank is? And Duro Sulecic?"

"Yes."

The policeman drew in his breath. "Who's still on top?"

"No one. All three are down in the mine. It looks bad."

"I'll follow you out." The policeman hesitated and then stuffed the arrest warrant into his shirt pocket. An accident may have solved the problem for him, but if Duro survived, the law would have to take its course. MacDonald would serve the paper, even if Duro were badly injured. Regardless of the circumstances, he had a duty to perform.

All work on the opal field stopped as the news of the cave-in spread. Men hastened to the shaft with ropes and shovels. Some brought torches, others water, several brought first-aid kits. The volunteer rescue squad was sent for, and one of the miners summoned the doctor. A blower was moved over to the mine opening and the pipes lowered to suck out fouled air and debris. Long air hoses were brought from neighboring mines. There was organized confusion with so many people trying to help. When the rescue squad arrived and took charge, everything became systematic. The recently organized volunteer team was composed of dedicated members. They were a welcome sight in such an emergency. A van that served as a temporary ambulance pulled up along-side the collapsed mine.

One of the rescue crew, after donning a hard hat and a mask, started the descent. Dust hovered, heavy and acrid, making it difficult to see and breathe. Loosened dirt and pebbles rattled down on him. No sound came from below.

"Anyone hear me?" he called. "Answer if you do." He listened. Nothing. He called again and heard a low moaning almost directly beneath him. He stepped down cautiously from the last rung of the ladder and flashed his torch. An inert figure lay a few feet away partially covered with chunks of opal clay. A second member of the rescue team appeared, and together they pulled away enough of the debris to expose the miner's face, which he had fortunately shielded with his hands. His labored breathing told them he still lived, but the pulse was weak. Blood from a deep gash in his forehead saturated the opal clay around him.

They flashed their light twice up the shaft as a signal of life, and the doctor began to climb down. A stretcher was lowered on which they could strap the injured man and hoist him up. The doctor checked him over cursorily, stopped the flow of blood and checked vital signs.

"The nursing staff can handle this one," he decided. "It's serious, but he'll make it." He looked at the pile of rubble blocking the drive that would have to be dug through to locate the other two men. "I'll stay a bit longer. The others will be in far worse condition, if they survive at all. We better alert the Flying Doctor Service."

The work went on for several hours. The rescuers pulled away at the rubble with slow progress, being relieved from time to time with fresh recruits from above. They had a small tunnel leading into the drive, but it wasn't big enough to crawl through. The doctor shook his head and started toward the ladder.

"I see a foot!" shouted the man in the lead. All began to dig with renewed frenzy. "It's moving! Hurry, for God's sake!"

The tunnel widened, but large chunks of rock still barred the way. The miners put slings around the biggest rocks and tugged them out of the way. A twisted, inert form lay in the small space beyond. The first man squirmed through the opening and flashed his torch at the body.

"He's breathing, but he's a real mess. There's a bit of room here. Can the doc squeeze through?"

Helping hands pulled away more debris and widened the opening enough for the doctor to drag himself forward. He examined the injured miner, shaking his head. The legs were twisted and torn, but miraculously the head was in a small hollow where air was available. The doctor felt for his pulse—it was weak and erratic, but it was there.

"This one is really bad. There are probably internal injuries as well." He gave him a shot. "We'll have to be very careful getting him onto a stretcher." He showed the man who shared the small space with him what precautions to take in helping to lift the battered body onto the stretcher that had been thrust through the narrow opening. After the miner was immobilized, many hands helped slide him through the narrow tunnel.

"I'll follow him up," the doctor said. "I'll be needed right away." The men on top raised the stretcher as carefully as possible but couldn't prevent the bound figure from hitting against the sides of the shaft. Once up, the injured man was placed quickly in the back of the makeshift ambulance, and the doctor accompanied him to the hospital, administering emergency treatment as best he could.

The rescue workers continued searching for the third minor for the rest of the day, alternate teams spelling each other. There was less optimism with each change of shift. By late afternoon a body was brought up, so covered with blood and dirt that identification was not immediately possible. That would have to come later. The policeman stared at the mangled corpse and turned away. He was not worried that his suspect would be escaping from the arm of the law. He had a gut feeling that his warrant never would be served.

The weary workers gathered their tools and walked quietly away, acknowledging that it was miraculous that anyone had lived through the cave-in. The ceiling of the drive had partially collapsed when the column had been blasted. They shook their heads. It had been a foolish move. More caution should have been used, but it was too late now. They returned to their dugouts and tin shacks and thought about the precariousness of life.

CHAPTER THIRTY-EIGHT

WHEN ERIC OPENED HIS EYES, the dark, quiet room seemed dreamlike, but he knew he wasn't dreaming. He attempted to raise his head but fell back on the pillow, feeling nauseated. He didn't understand what had happened. Where was he? Why was the room spinning? A figure in white moved quickly to his side.

"You're going to be all right now," a voice said softly. It sounded familiar. He tried to speak, but words stuck on the roof of his mouth. His lips, dry and swollen, refused to move and his throat burned. His head felt as though a thousand needles were sticking into it. He couldn't focus his eyes or move his body. He knew there was something he wanted to say, but the woman in white kept fading away. He gave up and fell asleep again. When he awakened, there was a clarity that had not been there before. He saw Molly bending over him, smiling. Slowly, like a drowning man coming up for air, he became aware of his surroundings.

He struggled to make his voice heard and finally was able to whisper, "What happened?"

He heard a strange voice say, "Thank God he's regained consciousness," and then Molly said quietly, "You've been in an accident, Eric."

"It happened in the mine?"

"Yes."

"Where are the others?" Dimly he knew his partners should be there. "How are they?"

"We don't know yet. We'll let you know."

He tried to nod in acknowledgment, but it was torture. He felt a cool hand on his forehead. Then he closed his eyes and slept. It seemed but a moment before he awoke again.

"How long have I been here?" he asked

"Three days, Eric. You've been unconscious until this morning. You had us worried for a while, but you're better now, thank God."

He tried to raise himself up but couldn't. "Lie back," she admonished him gently. "Don't exert yourself. It's too soon."

"You were right, Molly," he said in a thick voice. "I never should have gone into mining. This accident might not have happened except for me. Without my help Dimitrios would have abandoned the mine ..."

"Don't blame yourself."

"I must. Something drove me on and on ..."

"It's not your fault, Eric. You mustn't punish yourself this way."

He drifted off to sleep. His old nightmare returned with all its terrors. He was a child again with a malfunctioning rifle trying to save his father. But he knew his father was dead—he had died because he had to buy food and shoes for Eric. He had died in the mine. There was no way Eric could save him. Anne was there, too, somehow looking like his mother and saying, "Everything's going to be all right." He tried to hold her and felt his fingers slipping. The rungs of the ladder were cold and slimy. He was going to fall! Then he looked up and found Molly reaching down for him. She stretched out her arms, holding him fast. She was saying, "It's not your fault, Eric! It's not your fault!"

He didn't realize tears were running down his face until he felt Molly wiping them away. "You're going to be all right," she kept repeating. He knew that something wonderful had happened to him. The terrible, dark burden that had oppressed him for so many years no longer afflicted him, and an incredible lightness encompassed his whole being. He managed to put his arms around Molly, holding her as tightly as he could in his weakened condition. Then he sank back, falling into a deep, refreshing, dreamless sleep. He did not awaken for many hours.

When he opened his eyes again, he saw Molly checking his vital signs. He smiled weakly, and her returning smile was reassuring. She pressed his hand in a happy, impulsive gesture.

"You had us worried for awhile, but you're going to be fine, just fine," she said.

"What happened at the mine?"

"There was a cave-in."

"I remember now. I had climbed down to tell them about

Peter Bagley. That's the last thing I thought about ... It's all a blank now. Where are the others?"

"They are being taken care of," she answered. "Here's something for you to drink now, and later I'll bring you something to eat. You'll have to take it easy for awhile. You had a bad concussion and some fractured ribs. Lots of bruises, but no broken bones, thank heavens. You need lots of rest."

"It's easy to rest when you give the order," Eric replied.

"I can see that you're getting better already."

"Ouch. It hurts to move my head."

"Of course. It's going to take time." She left the room quietly and returned later with some soup. She spooned it into his mouth over his protests. "I'm the boss now," she smiled.

He felt the bandage on his head. "Did I have a bad wound?" he asked.

"Yes, a nasty one. Doctor took sixteen stitches. There's still a lot of swelling. You were lucky in spite of your injuries."

"Were the others as lucky?"

She didn't answer.

"Tell me. I can bear it. It will be worse if you don't."

"The Greek boy was flown to Adelaide. He is in serious condition. They're trying to save his legs."

Eric turned his face to the wall. "Poor kid." There was a moment's silence, and then he asked, "What about Duro?"

"He's dead."

"Oh, no."

Molly waited for awhile and then left. Some kinds of

grief cannot bear intrusion, and she sensed he needed time alone. She told him she had another patient to check on and left him staring at the ceiling. He tried to understand how the accident had happened. They had been so careful before. What had changed? They never had planned to cut into the column. Strong as the opal clay was, there was a limit to what could be removed without weakening the ceiling. What caused them to be so careless? He was indeed a fortunate man to have survived with relatively few consequences. Poor Dimitrios—such a good-looking young fellow, so full of life and drive. And Duro ...

When she returned, he said in an agonized tone, "Molly, it's really an ironic twist of fate that Peter Bagley was killed. He was my last chance to find out anything about Sandy."

"What do you mean?"

"I had an appointment to meet him at nine o'clock at the Opal Inn. He wrote that he had absolute proof of Sandy's whereabouts, and now he's gone."

"You were at the Opal Inn to meet with Peter?" She could scarcely keep the joy from her voice, then realizing Eric's disappointment, she reached out to him. "I'm so sorry, Eric."

He sighed. "I guess it just wasn't meant to be, but it's hard to be so close. It's a wonder the murder wasn't pinned on me! It evidently happened shortly after I left. Do they know who did it?"

Eric noted Molly's hesitation. "What's the matter? Is it someone we know?"

"Yes."

"Well, who?"

"It was Duro."

"Duro killed Peter Bagley?"

"That is the belief. It cannot be proved now, of course. Sergeant MacDonald had a warrant for his arrest the day of the accident."

"I just can't take it in! Why, I worked with him every day! He was always rather surly, but I thought nothing of it. He did his share of work and never complained. What could have driven him to such an act?"

"It appears that he was being blackmailed."

"Ah! That I can understand." Eric lay back, exhausted.

In a few days Eric was up and walking about. He read for short spells, but his attention wandered. He was a cooperative patient, but restless. There was so much he did not understand, and his head hurt so abominably. Molly said it would take time, but time soon would be running out. His visa had to be renewed in Adelaide for his final three months, and then he would have to leave Australia. The visa could not be extended. He needed time ... more time ...

Anastasia tiptoed timidly into his room and sat without moving until he felt her presence and opened his eyes. Such a lovely face, he thought. So serene. Her hair was darker than Molly's and straighter. She had it pulled back tightly into a bun, making her eyes look large and luminous in her pale face. In her normal hand she held a book.

"I thought you might like something to read," she said softly.

"How nice of you."

"How are you feeling?"

"Much better, thanks. How are things at the store?"

"Busy. The Aborigines got their dole, so they came in to pay their bills."

"I understand they do that first."

"Yes. Many of them will spend the rest on liquor, you know, and then charge food until their next check. It's so sad. I hate to see it happen. Oh!" She stopped in confusion, putting her hand to her mouth.

"What's the matter?"

"I shouldn't have said that about the Aborigines. Molly ..." Distress and embarrassment dimmed her eyes.

Eric replied slowly, "Molly understands both worlds she lives in. She wouldn't take offense."

"Molly is special," Anastasia said quietly.

"Yes, Molly is very special."

Nothing was said for a few minutes. Anastasia prepared to leave and then turned at the doorway. "Have you heard anything new about Dimitrios?"

"No, other than that he is recovering slowly. I want to go see him."

"Oh! Are you going to Adelaide?"

"Yes, I have to. I think I'll fly down next week. My stitches were taken out yesterday. Everything seems to be healing. I want very much to see him. I'm afraid he'll be quite depressed."

"Would you ... would you tell him 'hello' for me?—and for my parents, of course," she added hastily.

"I'll be glad to, Anastasia. It will cheer him up to know a pretty girl asked about him."

She blushed scarlet. She shook her head as she stammered, "Perhaps it is best to say nothing. Please don't." She implored him with her eyes as well as her words.

"I'll be discreet. I promise you."

She gave him a shy smile and slipped out of the room.

Eric thought about Molly constantly. He cared for her with all his heart, but he knew he could not take her from this land she loved and the people she had sworn to help. It would be best for them both if he began to distance himself from her emotionally and then the final separation would not be so painful. He would not sacrifice her happiness for his own selfish needs.

As the days passed, he tried to be casual with Molly, but his nonchalance did not deceive her. She sensed his withdrawal, and her dark eyes held concern. On several occasions she began to speak but changed her mind.

"I'm making arrangements to sell any equipment that can be salvaged," he told her when he was well enough to be discharged. "And I'll find a buyer for the parcel of opal we already have." There would be no attempt to re-open the mine. There was an unwritten law in Coober Pedy that no one ever worked a mine where there had been a disaster that resulted in death, but he would have had no intention of doing so anyway. "Then I'm going to fly to Adelaide to see Dimitrios and to renew my visa for the last time."

She did not ask the inevitable question, "And then, Eric?"

Eric's gradual distancing from her was without explanation until the day she put Janet on the bus. The inquest was over, and the girl had been exonerated, so Molly and Janet enjoyed a happy lunch together after the bus arrived. The driver had allowed an hour for refreshments before facing any additional bouncing on the road to Kingoonya. Janet was pleased to become acquainted with her seat companion, a gray-haired, motherly woman. Janet, her suitcase already stowed in the rack above her seat, excused herself at the last minute and ran into the Greek store to say one last goodbye to Anastasia. When she returned, the driver had signaled his passengers to board and was waiting impatiently. Janet's naturally pale face now appeared almost bleached, and her eyes were wide with fright. She grasped Molly's hands as tears cascaded down her cheeks.

"Janet, what on earth has happened?" Molly cried.

"Promise me you'll not tell Eric Christianson where I'm going," she pleaded.

"That's ridiculous, Janet! Why shouldn't he know?"

"You promised me at the hospital you wouldn't tell

anybody!"

"I haven't, Janet."

"Promise me again." She stepped into the coach and the driver closed the door. "Promise me!" the girl mouthed through her window, and Molly reluctantly nodded.

Dark suspicions assailed Molly's mind as she trudged back to the hospital. Eric's emotional withdrawal became clear to her now. Regardless of how he had courted her, it was clear that he had entertained Janet as well and must have had some sort of dalliance with her. The girl had told her she wanted to escape from Peter, but it was evident that it was really Eric from whom she was fleeing. She would distance herself from him also. Molly recognized that her restored faith in Eric had shattered, and she dreaded seeing him. Then she raised her chin as she strode into the hospital, determined not to show any feeling. Eric was still her patient, and she would do her duty.

CHAPTER THIRTY-NINE

As Eric prepared to board Opal Air, the screeching of brakes caused him to turn around. To his surprise Molly ran from Sister Thomas' car with her arms outstretched. Out of courtesy he had informed her of his departure time, but after her cool reception had not expected her to show up. "Give my best to Dimitrios," was all she had said. Now her flushed face and a paper crumpled in her hand told him this last minute appearance was not a planned one. He knew it was her day off, and there had been no need for such last minute haste.

"Eric, I must talk to you," she panted.

"I'm sorry, Molly, there's no time. Everyone's waiting." He took another step up, and she grabbed him by the arm. He had never seen her so distraught.

"Then promise me you'll go to see my parents at the mission."

"Molly, that's hundreds of miles from Adelaide!" He had one more step before he was inside the airplane. She clung to him, forcing him to wait.

"I beg of you, Eric! Please!"

He resented her unreasonable request but couldn't resist her impassioned eyes and nodded, baffled at her change of attitude. As he started to duck into the doorway, she stretched up and kissed him impulsively on the lips then dashed toward the car. He stared out at her retreating figure, and to the amusement of the other passengers a slow blush crept over his face. Public display of affection was considered bad form in Australia, and the other men plainly enjoyed his discomfort. What could have come over her?

Eric leaned forward to see better out the small window. He enjoyed the panorama below him. He never tired of looking at the vastness of the land—it was not monotonous to him, even though mile after mile was unchanging. He found a soothing quality in its sameness and thought of the Aborigines who had respected the land, faced its privations and endured. It looked as untouched below as it must have been when the first wanderers had crossed it, asking little from it but bare sustenance, never injuring the land that gave them life.

Greed has played havoc with the environment, Eric thought. It destroyed our mine and cost a life, while the natives took only what they could use. He gazed again at the endless stretch of undeveloped land below—scrubby bushes, gibber plains, occasional undulating sand hills. Now he could see the road on which he had traveled months before, undeviatingly straight at times and at others like a long snake writhing across the desert. Some day there might even be a bitumen road to

Coober Pedy. Travel might be swifter then, but the adventure would be gone.

He lay back in his seat and mused about Molly's unexpected behavior. Her warm kiss still tingled his lips. However, she just didn't realize the problems involved in asking him to go to the Yunarra Mission. He had expected to take a bus from the airport to the center of town, renew his visa and visit Dimitrios. He'd stay overnight in a hotel and fly back the following day. Now he would have to hire a car in Adelaide and drive several hundred miles in less than comfortable circumstances. His ribs were still sore, and his bruises held some residual tenderness. He couldn't believe her request was frivolous, but what could account for it? He regretted acquiescing to her frenzied appeal, but he had promised and would keep his word.

The legend of the Rainbow Serpent drifted into his thoughts and the strange choice Molly had presented to him. What an odd girl she was at times! As he visualized the story again, a peculiar, almost transcendental, experience took place. The Rainbow Serpent coiled and uncoiled herself in a parched, desolate area on the ground below. Deep, sun baked cracks reached down into the red earth. There was no sound except for the scales of the snake as she slithered over the dry ground. Wherever she had coiled herself, a hole appeared and filled with fresh, cool water that bubbled and sloshed against the sides. Then the serpent lay down and stretched herself until neither head nor tail could be seen. Where she had lain, a river began to flow, faster and faster, becoming a roaring current that overflowed its banks and inundated the land. Gradually the water receded until only a trickle remained in the river bed, but the deep water holes remained. All along the banks and around the water holes grass began to appear, the lushness spreading until the entire panorama changed. Colorful flowers bloomed, and small animals crept about. The land was regenerated! Eric sat still, wanting to retain as long as possible the unusual product of his imagination. He thought about it for a long time. In his primitive wisdom, the unlettered Aborigine had seen the spiritual relevance of the symbolism—a man did not have to search for this regeneration or even deserve it. It was just there for the taking. It was a gift to be used wisely.

He thought of what he had told Molly—he would choose the Rainbow Serpent and what it represented, a renewal of life. He knew now that he would not give Molly up. He had dared to look at the future again since he had met her. Their ideas might not always be identical, but their ideals were. He was drawn to her in a way he never had experienced before. It was more than physical—he wanted to share his feelings, his dreams, his life with her. He loved her and always would love her. He had been completely honest with her about himself, and now the choice would be hers.

CHAPTER FORTY

THE ANTISEPTIC SMELL assailed Eric's nostrils as he hesitated in the doorway of Dimitrios' room, steeling himself to enter. Three beds were positioned side by side, and for a moment Eric questioned which one held Dimitrios, but his uncertainty quickly vanished. An old man lay in the closest one, his eyes closed, mouth open, snoring. In the middle bed, a young man with facial lacerations, head swathed in bandages and a neck brace gave Eric a lopsided grin and said, "Motorcycle accident." Eric looked beyond him and recognized Dimitrios in the next bed. The bandages did not conceal the finely shaped nose, the generous lips, the strong jaw, but the eyes were lusterless. His legs were in traction, and a cast covered his upper body. Only one arm was free. Eric walked to the inert figure and touched his limp hand. The Greek youth looked at him dumbly, and then tears came into his eyes.

"We were fools, stupid fools!" he whispered.

Eric said nothing.

"I heard you were hurt."

"Not too bad." Eric shrugged off his injuries.

"I heard about Duro."

"Yes."

"I almost lost both legs, you know. The doctors saved them, but I'll never be the same. It's all over for me, Eric. Stupid, stupid, stupid!"

"When you get out of here, you'll feel better," Eric encouraged him. "Doctors do amazing things nowadays."

Dimitrios shook his head. "No, even at best I'll always have a terrible limp. I'll never be able to mine again, but who cares? I have nothing to live for. I can't go back to Greece broke and crippled. I don't want to live this way. I wish I'd died instead of Duro!" He turned his face away.

"Is there anything I can do for you?" Eric said, helpless in the face of such bitter grief.

"Yes. Get me some paper and pen. I have to write to Sophia. She can't keep waiting, wondering if I will return." Tears came into his eyes again. "I was so close, Eric. I almost had it made when I found the pipe, and then Ari ..." His eyes burned with hatred. "I hope he rots in hell!"

"Dimitrios, before I get the things for you, I want to tell you that one of the rescue team brought me a piece of the opal vein that fell during the explosion. It was on top of Duro's body. The quality is exceptional. I added it to our parcel and sold it before I came here."

"Well, I'm glad that at least *you* got something out of the mess," Dimitrios said darkly.

"Also," Eric continued, ignoring the barb, "I want you

to have all of Duro's share."

The younger man's eyes opened wide. "I don't understand."

"It's very simple. Instead of our splitting Duro's share two ways, I want you to have it all."

"What I don't understand is why you are doing this?" Dimitrios' voice was tinged with suspicion.

"It's hard to explain, Dimitrios. Just say the Aborigines had the right idea—take only what you need. This extra money may be of more use to you than to me. There'll be about $5,000 from Duro's share."

Dimitrios gasped. "Eric, with what I've saved and my own share of the parcel and now Duro's—it will be enough! Oh, my God! Do you understand? It will be enough!" He raised himself slightly from the bed in his excitement. "I can't believe it! I'll write Sophia that I'm sending the money now, and I'll come later when I'm well. I've done it! I've done it!" He lay back in bed, exhausted, but with his face glowing. "When I get these casts off my legs, I'll walk again. I'll exercise, and I'll keep at it until I'm able to return to Sophia almost my old self." He gripped Eric's hand with surprising strength.

As Eric rose to bring Dimitrios the writing materials, he felt the letters in his pocket. "I have some mail for you," he said. "A lot of people are thinking of you." He lay the letters on the bed within reach. He noticed the foreign stamp. "This one's from Greece."

Dimitrios took it in his hand as gently as the wafer in the sacrament. He felt the smoothness of the paper; he looked at the large, colorful stamp. A miniature work of art rested in his fingers; he felt that ripping it open was almost an act of defilement. He looked wistfully at Eric.

"I'm almost afraid to open it. Would you do it for me?"

"Sure. Then I'll go and let you read it alone."

"No, please stay. I ... I wish you would." His shy demeanor contrasted with his former diffidence. Eric realized that for the first time the enigmatic youth felt warmth toward him and desired his companionship. Eric sat down again to share this important moment while Dimitrios slowly extracted the letter and began to read. He felt rather like an intruder but it pleased him that the Greek lad wanted his company. He had never understood Dimitrios' former constrained, almost hostile attitude toward him. As Eric watched, he saw the light die in Dimitrios' eyes. The letter fluttered to the floor like a tired moth. Eric waited, not speaking, wondering what to do. The young man lay motionless, his face white and strained.

Finally Eric said, "I'm sorry if it's bad news. Can I help in any way?"

Dimitrios shook his head, as though confused. Then anger suffused his face, and an animal-like scream burst from his throat. His entire expression was one of pure hatred.

"She didn't wait!" he cried. "She didn't wait! She's already married! My God, what a fool I was! Damn her, damn her!" Dimitrios sobbed convulsively, tears soaking his pillow. As he looked at Eric with savage eyes he cried, "Why did you come here? You've brought me nothing but bad luck since I met you. I wish I'd never known you!" He crumpled the paper and threw it at Eric.

Hearing the voice reverberating down the hall, the nurse came running in, and Eric intercepted her before she reached the bed. "He's had bad news. Can you give him something?" She nodded and left the room. The sobbing wore itself out. Eric turned to go, but Dimitrios gestured for him to stay.

"It's not your fault. I'll not cry again. Never."

The nurse returned with a pill and glass of water. "Take this. It will help you sleep."

"I hope I never wake up."

"May I sit by him for awhile?" Eric asked the nurse. She nodded and moved to the other patients, who were agitated by the outburst. He sat for several hours, his own head feeling heavy and sore. He stretched out his legs and stared at the smooth, plastered ceiling. A tiny hairline crack was beginning in one corner—he traced it with his eyes and then lost it. How can a crack disappear? he wondered. It must go underground like a river and then surface again—or is it like a road that suddenly can disappear over a hill and then reappear?—or a life that seems to end and then becomes something new? Would Dimitrios' life ever be renewed? Would his own? Eric felt himself sinking into oblivion. When he felt someone gently shaking him, he opened his eyes with a start and found the nurse at his side. "I must have fallen asleep!" he exclaimed.

"Yes, for several hours. Your friend hasn't awakened, so it's best to go now. He may be in better spirits tomorrow. He's been under great stress here, and we've all been very worried."

"I wish there was something I could do. I don't know if he really wants me here."

"I'm sure he does. He needs someone to care about him right now. Come back in the morning."

Eric assented, although it would be a hardship on him. He would lose valuable time on his long trip to Yunarra Mission, but this was important. He wanted to make one last attempt to help the poor lad. He understood now what had driven him so relentlessly, and how love had turned to hate so quickly. He empathized with him—he, too, had experienced the same reversal of affection, though not in such a dramatic degree perhaps. No, that was not true. He thought of that traumatic scene with Cynthia after the phone call. There was little difference between their reactions. Only Eric had had no one to share his misery with. Dimitrios needed a friend.

As Eric walked down the hospital corridor the next morning, he wondered what kind of reception he would encounter. He braced himself for rejection but was pleased to see a faint smile greeting him. It was a positive sign; complete dejection could not but hinder any medical progress.

"It's good of you to come back, Eric. I made an awful fool of myself yesterday."

"'No worries!', as the Aussies say. You had a bad shock. It would have unnerved anyone," Eric assured him. "I'm glad to see you looking better."

"I can't really blame Sophia. What kind of life would she have had with me? Papadopolous has a lot more money and can give her an easy life. She never would have been happy here with me. Once I was foolish enough to suggest that she might come. This is a hard place for a woman unless you strike it rich. She had time to think things over and made her choice. It just came at a bad time for me. I guess I'll always be bitter, though. All that work, all those hours, the accident—it was all for nothing." Eric didn't break into his tirade. "It's probably just as well," Dimitrios continued. "I wouldn't have wanted to return to Greece as a cripple." He turned his face away.

"A lot of people sent their best wishes to you," said Eric, hoping to cheer him a little. "The postmaster said to say, 'Hello' and so did the miners at the Eleven Mile. Anastasia came to see me in the hospital. She's a lovely girl. She asked especially for me to greet you and wish you well."

"It's good of them. I don't remember much after the cave-in, except that I hurt terribly. I lay there a long time, and then there seemed to be a lot of people helping. I think I heard someone saying, 'You're going to be all right.' After that everything is hazy. The doctor must have given me something to knock me out."

"Do you know yet when you'll be out of bed?"

"Not for awhile. I'll be in the casts for weeks, and then maybe I'll need more operations. I guess I was pretty well smashed up. They're all good to me here. The sisters do their best to make me comfortable."

"I wish I could stay longer, but I'm on my way to Yunarra Mission this morning, and after my visit I'll be flying back to Coober Pedy. But I will stop and see you again before I leave."

"Thank everyone for me, will you?"

"Sure. I think Anastasia wanted to write to you, but she was afraid you'd think she was being forward."

"Tell her I'll be glad to hear from her. I'll welcome a letter. It's lonesome lying here." Eric was about to take his leave when Dimitrios continued. "You know, I hated you because you were an American, Eric. My American father deserted my mother, but you've been good to me." His eyes clouded. "I don't deserve what you've done for me. I wasn't going to tell you, but now I will. Duro persuaded me to keep the last opal we found and sell it secretly, and I went along with him, Eric. I wanted that money so badly I was willing to cheat you! And now you ..." He couldn't go on.

"I'm glad you told me. We've all had our temptations, Dimitrios."

"It's strange about you and Duro and me—we all came to Coober Pedy for a special reason. Poor Duro lost out, and neither of us got what we were hoping for, Eric. I heard about your search for your son."

"Maybe we found something different, and it may work out for the best," Eric suggested.

Dimitrios shook his head in doubt but held out his hand. Eric clasped it, pleased at its strength.

"Thank you, Eric. For everything."

"Goodbye, Dimitrios. I hope you go back to Coober Pedy. You have good friends there who care about you."

The young Greek's eyes were misty as he watched Eric leave.

CHAPTER FORTY-ONE

As HE DROVE over the potholed road, Eric marveled at the stark beauty of the landscape. The ever-present gum trees stretched into the hinterland as far as he could see, not thick enough to be impenetrable, just enough to block a clear view. Occasionally he saw a wallaby or two springing through the woods, apparently unafraid, minding their own business. He never tired of watching these graceful yet comical creatures. The Creator had a sense of humor, Eric thought. That made him feel good, and he laughed out loud. *I never could be at odds with a God who could design a kangaroo,* he thought. *But perhaps He personally set up the chain of evolution and was somewhat surprised at the result!*

In some places the gray-green leaves hung over the road and provided welcome shade. Although it was still technically late spring, the warm hand of summer already reached out making the air heavier, the dust a little denser. He watched the dust boil up in ochre-colored clouds behind him, relieved that no one followed. He had followed cars before when the dust was so thick, he found it caked in his nostrils at the end of a run. It was no wonder the pub had become a life-saver to men on the trail.

It took him almost seven hours to reach the mission. His ribs ached, and he was tired to the bone when he finally arrived. It looked just as he had left it, only now there was no crowd of young people on the steps of the main bungalow. He thought about that day when he had visited the mission so spontaneously. The kids had really put one over on him, and he chuckled at his naiveté. He had felt foolish then, but now he could enjoy the scene in retrospect. Molly had been so shy—partly natural, and partly intentional, he realized. She did have fire in her when sufficiently provoked, and he liked that about her. She could stand up for herself when she had to. Molly had come to terms with her two worlds, developing into her own person: competent, sensitive and strong. He wouldn't want her to be any other way. She's dedicated to her work, Eric thought, and wondered if he could ever be as dedicated to his profession again.

Molly's loving, frantic goodbye at the airplane still puzzled him. Her insistence that he go to the mission left him nonplused, and he would have demanded an explanation before he boarded the plane had there been time. Whatever the cause of her emotional turn around, he rejoiced in it.

Pastor Holmgren hurried toward him with an outstretched hand. His eyes sparkled as he greeted him. "Well, well, well! It's certainly an unexpected pleasure to see you again.

I'm glad you could drop by."

"Drop by! It's a five-hundred-mile round trip from Adelaide!"

"You mean you're not passing through? You're returning to Adelaide?"

"Yes, and I don't understand why Molly insisted that I come to the mission. It's a mystery to me."

"And to me, also. I am genuinely astonished. But I'm glad you're here ... We were sorry to learn of your accident. It's a long trip out here, and you must be exhausted. Come have some refreshment—a cup of tea and something to eat. We'll have a proper supper later. We have an extra room for you, of course. How long can you stay?"

"I'm leaving in the morning."

"In the morning! Oh, my! What could have gotten into Molly?"

"I'm sure I don't know."

They sat on the wide veranda and enjoyed the tea and scones that Mrs. Holmgren brought on a pretty tray. "We don't have many amenities out here," she told him, "but tea and nice china are two of the things that make a rather drab life a little more pleasant."

They chatted informally, and the tiredness seemed to fall away from Eric. "How are things going at the mission?" he asked.

The older man sighed. "Not as well as I hoped when I last saw you. Progress sometimes is two steps forward and one step backward, which is discouraging, but I should be grateful that it isn't vice versa!" He laughed. "When I find myself a little downhearted, I think of Molly and those other fine young-sters who left for higher education, and I know there is hope. The Aboriginals must come at their own pace; we cannot rush them into an alien culture. Some are receptive, some are not." He gazed reflectively into the distance. "I was thinking of Wilanya. A terrible experience for Molly."

"Yes." Eric didn't want to discuss it. The thought of her torment was more than he could bear. "But getting back to your statement about people being receptive to change or not, isn't that true of every culture? In the States we have an expres-sion, 'You can lead a horse to water' ..."

"But you can't make him drink!" completed the pastor. "We have that one here, too. If we can work with them when they are very young, we have greater possibilities. So much that I do is undone by the outside world, and yet that is where they must live eventually. We need more teachers who care—more committed people to help. We have a few, but not enough. Some come and work for awhile, get discouraged with the slow progress and move on. And let's face it, it's a pretty dull place for a young person who's used to city life."

Eric nodded. "When I first came to Australia I heard so many times, 'No worries, mate, she'll be right.' I guess that attitude is necessary in a land where the only thing you can count on is change. There's certainly a spirit of optimism in it, but it doesn't always lead to dedication."

"No." Pastor Holmgren looked at Eric with a benevolent but fixed stare. "I know you once were a teacher. Have you ever thought of returning to the profession?"

"Yes," Eric admitted. "I left in bitterness, but I've missed it. I enjoyed the challenge. Young minds are like quicksilver, and it helps keep you young. You develop a mental attitude of looking to the future instead of the past."

"Molly's looking to the future," observed Pastor Holmgren.

Eric looked at him sharply, startled. He said nothing.

"Molly is very special to me," continued the older man. "I have watched her mature into a fine woman with high ideals. I'm sure it's not always been easy to keep them. You know, she has not been without chances to marry."

Eric remained silent. What was the pastor trying to tell him—keep away from her, or ask for his blessing? He cleared his throat. "I'm sure she has had many opportunities. She's a lovely girl."

"She needs someone who will value her for herself. She needs to be cherished for what she is, what she has made of her life."

"I had hoped to be that person, Pastor, but now I don't know. There are so many obstacles. But I had a strange dream on the airplane—almost a revelation—that gave me hope." He proceeded to relate his experience. "It was so vivid, so real, Pastor Holmgren. I almost thought—" He broke off, embarrassed. "I shouldn't be talking to you about something so pagan."

"How well do you remember your scripture, Eric?"

Eric raised his hands defensively. "Please, Pastor, don't preach at me!"

"No worries! I'm not going to deliver a sermon. I'm just going to give you an analogy. Do you recall the place where the apostle Peter thought the Gospel should go only to a select group and not to the Gentiles? Then he had a vision of a great sheet let down by four corners upon the earth, and it was filled with all kinds of animals and reptiles and birds. Then he heard a voice saying, "Rise and eat," and he protested that he had never eaten anything unclean. It happened three times, and the voice said, "What God has cleansed, you must not call common.""

"I don't quite understand your point, Pastor."

"From this vision Peter recognized the Gospel was intended for all mankind, and he changed his outlook. You see, Eric, the Lord doesn't always send an angel singing "Hallelujah" to reach his errant sons! I think your dream has significance. How can the renewal of life be pagan?"

"I understand what you're saying, Pastor Holmgren." He smiled at the older man. "I haven't asked Molly to marry me yet, but I'm going to. There's a problem though—I just renewed my visa for three months, but at the end of that time it expires, and I shall have to go back to the States."

"It's not an insurmountable problem if you really want to stay." Eric lifted his eyebrows. "There are certain mitigating circumstances in specific occupations, you know. Visas have been known to be extended. I am not without influence here."

"You would want me to teach at the mission?"

"Yes."

"I specialized in history and English. That would hardly be of vital concern here."

"You might be surprised. I grant you that your pupils would have a different background from those with whom you associated in the States. The Aboriginals are a very clever, creative people—very artistic, very intuitive. A few demonstrate a deficiency in verbal skills, and some are not oriented toward reading, but you have had students with similar problems, I am sure. A good teacher improvises and works with a child's needs. You know that, Eric."

"Yes."

"And some are like the chaps you met at our bungalow on your first trip here, anxious to learn and capable of moving into higher education. I don't want to lose students like that."

Eric hesitated and then asked, "Does Molly know about this offer, Pastor? Has she ever suggested ..."

"No, son." The pastor grasped Eric's arm firmly. "I am not asking this for Molly's sake—I'm asking for mine, and for the youngsters here who deserve more than they're getting. We have several students now approaching high school age who show promise. I sometimes think it is of greater value to have made a deep impact on a few than a surface influence on many. I really need your help. All I ask is that you think about it."

"All right, Pastor. I will think about it."

"What is between you and Molly is your own business,

and you will have to work that out yourselves. Molly is a very spiritual person." His eyes twinkled. "I have an idea she has been praying mightily these last few days for her special reasons. Let's walk around the mission and I'll show you some of the areas we're working in—the classrooms, the workshops, the gardens. Rather primitive structures compared with your grand schools, I suspect. Here's the bungalow where our teachers stay. We have only two now with my daughter Beatrice gone, so my wife and I help, also." As they walked along he continued speaking of Molly. "Did she tell you about her background?"

"Yes. She said she was brought here when she was just a few days old."

"Did she tell you her mother was the daughter of a full-blooded Aboriginal woman and an Afghan? He was a camel driver brought in during the early days."

"Not in so many words," Eric said. "She shared a report about her grandmother's early days, and he was part of it. She told me about her grandmother—Kabbarli, she calls her. There's a deep bond there, I know. She said she went back to see her grandmother as often as she was able, but she never knew her grandfather."

"Was his ethnicity important to you?"

"What do you mean? That he was an Afghan?"

"Yes."

Eric raised his shoulders in bewilderment. "I don't understand your question."

"Well, you see, it made her much more white than

Aborigine. Would that have made her more acceptable?"

Eric flared. "No, of course not. It would not have made any difference."

"It would to many others." Pastor Holmgren smiled. "Niboorana is here now, at the mission, if you would like to meet her."

"I would indeed. Why didn't she come before?"

"She had promised Molly's father that she would not interfere if he would allow Molly to visit her. She kept her promise all these years, but after Molly's kidnapping it was ... awkward to stay at Wiluru Station."

Eric nodded, remembering Bert with distaste. "I want to meet Molly's grandmother."

"You shall."

As they rounded the corner of the bungalow, they met Janet face to face. Eric smiled, rather startled at finding her here. He hadn't seen her since that day she had been looking for Mick. He was unprepared for her vehement greeting. Her lips were drawn back in a grimace as she spat out her words. "You followed me here! Molly betrayed me, and I trusted her! She promised that she wouldn't tell anyone. You can't make me go back. I won't go!"

Eric, stunned, saw the girl's eyes flashing with anger. He took a step backward in the face of her hostility and tried to make some sense out of what she was saying. "I don't understand, Janet. What do you mean? I have no intention of trying to make you go back to Coober Pedy if you don't want to.

I didn't even know you were here. In fact, I thought you were still working at the Opal Inn."

It was Janet's turn to look bewildered. "But you had to know I was here! Molly was the only one who knew."

He shook his head. The girl wasn't making sense.

"If my father didn't send you, why are you here?"

"Molly asked me to stop by to see Pastor Holmgren. You might say we're old friends. We've been discussing education."

"You're a teacher?"

"Yes. Or at least I was." Eric stared at Janet, baffled. He could see that the girl was belligerent and resentful, but why he couldn't imagine. He continued speaking in a conciliatory manner. "If you don't want to return to Coober Pedy after all that mess, I wouldn't blame you. But who's trying to make you? Do the police still need more testimony? I was in the hospital following Peter's murder but I understand the case was closed."

Janet stood without moving, her face pale. Finally she asked, "Is this some kind of trick?"

Eric raised his hands in a gesture of helplessness.

She continued, "Only two people in Coober Pedy knew my nickname—Peter and you. It was in your message."

"I sent you no message, Janet. If I'd wanted to see you, I'd have gone to the Opal Inn. There's some terrible mistake here. What are you talking about?" Then he saw the pendant shining against her white blouse. "Where did you get that pendant?" he demanded, his voice strained.

She reacted defensively. "I didn't steal it, if that's what you're thinking!"

"I need to know where you got it!"

"Suppose I told you I bought it at a jumble sale!" Her pert tone belied the fear flickering in her eyes.

"Did you?" He reached out to examine it, and she jerked away. The chain broke, leaving the pendant in his hand, a mosaic opal koala superimposed on a silver heart. He stared at Janet—golden-auburn hair, blue eyes ... He grabbed her arms and held her fast. She looked so frightened that Pastor Holmgren stepped forward as if to intervene. "Where did you get this pendant?" Eric demanded again.

She began to cry. "My mother gave it to me! It's the only thing I have that was hers."

Eric tightened his grip. "Is your name Sandy Blackwell?"

"You know it is!" Janet cried. "My father sent you after me!"

Eric loosened his grip and backed off, still staring at her. Janet stared back, her eyes revealing something was wrong, terribly wrong.

"All this time I've been looking ... trying to find you ... that message ... I posted a new note when I got out of the hospital ..." His words tumbled out incoherently. "I thought you were a boy! I thought Sandy Blackwell was a boy!"

Janet shook her head in bewilderment, waiting for some kind of explanation. "I don't understand a word you're saying!"

"How can I explain this to you? It means that instead of a son, I have a daughter! Janet, I'm your father!"

The girl pressed her trembling fingers to her mouth, never taking her gaze from Eric's face. "I don't believe you," she whispered, and then her face clouded with uncertainty. "I wrote to Molly that my father had sent you, but I told her I didn't understand why you didn't recognize me when I came to the caravan park for help. My father must have given you a description of me."

"You wrote to Molly?"

"Yes, five days ago. I left Coober Pedy in such a state ... I wanted her to know ..." She began to tremble. "I saw your message just before I boarded the bus."

Pastor Holmgren looked from one to the other in amazement and then putting his arms around Janet, assisted her into the bungalow. Mrs. Holmgren helped her wash her tear-stained face and pressed a hot cup of tea into her shaking hands.

"Drink this, dear. A good strong cuppa will do wonders." She glanced at her husband, who stood helplessly by. The very presence of the older woman seemed to lend strength and comfort to the dazed girl, so the pastor motioned to Eric to join him in his study. The shock gradually wore off, and Janet began asking pertinent questions. Mrs. Holmgren shook her head—she knew nothing of Janet's background, only that Molly had entrusted her to their temporary care.

In the other room Eric looked at the pastor in disbelief. "I just can't take it all in. It happened so fast. I must talk with her after she calms down. Poor girl! What a terrible experience for her—a bolt out of the blue ..." He stared at the older man as if seeking some explanation for the incredible occurrence. "If Janet hadn't asked Molly for help ... if Molly hadn't arranged for her to stay here ... If she hadn't made me promise to come ..."

"Exactly. You never would have known."

"Molly must have received Janet's letter minutes before my flight and realized she and Sandy Blackwell were the same person. There was no time to tell me—all she could do was beg me to come here. She hoped Janet and I would confront each other and the truth would come out." He gazed out the window before continuing and said, "You know, my confirmation verse was, 'All things work together for good for those who love the Lord.' I believe that now."

Pastor Holmgren sat quietly, immersed in his own thoughts. Then he said, "Eric you quoted the first part of your confirmation verse accurately, but you didn't finish it— 'for those who love the Lord and are called according to His purpose.' What do you think His purpose is for your life?"

Eric looked the pastor straight in the eye. "You asked me earlier to think about teaching here." He held out his hand. "I know now. I don't need any more time to think about it. I accept your offer, Pastor."

Holmgren gripped Eric's hand firmly, his face reflecting both joy and relief. "This is a happy day for me, Eric." He stood up. "I hear Mother Holmgren calling us. I can't wait to tell her the good news." They walked to the dining room and Eric stopped at the doorway.

"When Janet's more at ease, I'll tell her the whole story, and it's an incredible one! I still can't believe it."

Mrs. Holmgren produced a lovely table for supper. The white damask cloth set off the delicate flowered china, reminding Eric of the flowers that poked their heads through a late snow in Iron Valley. Lighted candles added a festive air. She surpassed herself with a lamb roast and mint sauce that Eric never had tired of during his stay in Australia.

Pastor Holmgren's blessing was brief but conveyed everyone's thoughts. "We are grateful, Lord, for your bringing us all together and for your bounty. We ask for your continued guidance in our lives. In Jesus' name, Amen" He smiled as he carved the lamb. "I never believed in a long-winded grace when the food is hot."

Eric had not sat at a family meal preceded with a prayer since his boyhood. He discounted the years he slouched at Sven's table, fuming at the old man's hypocrisy, and remembered his father's strong voice, his mother's bowed head, his own stirring at the warm affection mixed inextricably with the aroma of the food. Janet smiled tremulously at him from across the table. Once she said, "I'm glad Ben Blackwell isn't my real father." At another time she offered a little compliment. "I'm pleased you cared enough about me to try to find me." How easy it was to see Anne in her now—he was amazed that he had not recognized the resemblance before. He had so much to tell Molly when he phoned her that night.

The call was slow in getting through. Molly was on duty—there was an emergency. Would he please try later? He hung up impatiently, then sat back and relaxed. He enjoyed just looking at Janet. He showed her the picture of Anne and himself a passer-by had taken of them at Circular Quay in Sydney during that momentous time. He was glad now he had extracted it from Hulda's old photo album before he left the States. He had destroyed all other pictures of her along with her letters after their last communication.

Janet looked at the photo curiously and then up at Eric. "You haven't changed much. Mum was pretty then, wasn't she? She had such a hard life ... After she died, everything just fell apart for me ... I'd like to keep this ... Why did you think I was a boy?"

"I just had that notion, and then your fath—Ben Blackwell—reinforced it, out of spite, I guess."

"Are you sorry I'm a girl?"

"I'm delighted, Janet. You don't know how happy I am to have a daughter. But how did Molly know you were Sandy Blackwell?"

"When I came to Coober Pedy, I was so afraid my father would try to bring me back that I used my Christian name and shortened my surname to 'Black'. I made the mistake of telling Peter Bagley that I always went by my nickname at home. When I saw your notice on the bulletin board, I panicked. I told Molly not to tell Eric Christianson where I was, but I didn't have time to tell her why until I wrote her five days ago. Then she realized who I was."

"She kept her promise to you, and she had faith in my promise to her. She's quite a woman, isn't she?"

Janet's eyes shone with happiness.

"What would you like to do now? I can help you in any way you need."

She considered the question. "I'd like to go back to school somewhere and learn a trade. I'm tired of being a waitress."

"You would be welcome to stay here and finish your education, Janet," said Pastor Holmgren.

She shook her head. "Thank you, but I need to be more independent." She turned to Eric, her eyes imploring his understanding. "This is all going to take some getting used to. I'm going to need a little distance ..." Her voice trailed off. "I can't quite think of you as my father, but I will think of you as my friend."

"That's good enough for me, Janet," Eric smiled. "We have a long time ahead to get better acquainted. I'm not going to rush you."

"Our daughter Beatrice could advise you about school," suggested Mrs. Holmgren. "She would be glad to have you stay with her in Adelaide while you get your life in order."

"And I hope you'll come back often and visit," Eric told her. "I'm going to be teaching here. After all, we're not strangers any more, are we?"

She looked relieved, and impulsively she held out her arms and gave him a big hug. Tears shone in her eyes.

"Everyone's been so good to me. I'll make you all proud of me, just wait and see."

Eric's telephone call finally got through. His first words were, "I've found Sandy!" and he related the entire story. He could hear the pleasure in Molly's voice as she asked questions and made comments. "And Molly, it's because you had faith in me that I'm here."

He heard a catch in her voice as she said, "Oh, Eric, I almost lost you ... I beg your forgiveness ... I didn't understand ... There's so much I need to explain ..."

"Molly, when people care for each other, no explanations are necessary, and forgiveness is automatic. Besides, I can't imagine your doing anything I'd need to forgive you for." He could detect a little sigh of relief. "I have something wonderful to tell you. I've decided to teach at the mission. Pastor Holmgren can get my visa extended."

"Oh, Eric, I'm so glad. I was almost afraid that ..."

"Did you send me here deliberately, hoping this might happen?" he interrupted.

"I ... yes, I did," she admitted. "I won't lie to you, Eric. My father knew nothing about it. I just hoped ... and prayed ... and ..." A crackling sound came over the line, and her voice grew faint. He waited for the line to clear.

"There's too much static," she said. "I think we have a bad connection."

"No, Molly!" he shouted. "We have a wonderful connection! Can you hear me? I love you!"

"I can't hear you very well. What did you say?"

"I love you, and I want you to marry me—if you'll have me!"

"I heard you, Eric! I heard you!" There was more interference on the line. He could barely make out her faint, "Yes," but it was enough.

Pastor Holmgren led the way to Niboorana's simple hut. She was sitting outside by a little campfire, her eyes closed and her hands lying idle in her lap. As they approached, she raised her head, as though instinctively sensing their presence. Her black eyes stared at the fair-skinned man before her, appraising him with embarrassing exactitude. Then she stood and said something in her Aboriginal tongue. Eric saw before him a wrinkled old woman with years of hardship and endurance etched on her face but with a kindness and compassion he had seen equaled only in Molly. She extended her hands to him in a display of benevolent acceptance, her skinny fingers clutching his with warmth and vigor.

"You are right for Molly," she said. "I am happy for you both."

"How did you know?" he asked, amazed. "I only spoke to her a few minutes ago."

She shook her head, indicating no rationale was possible. Joy radiated from her. "All your children will have a strong spirit," she said.

"Our children?" Eric drew back. He remembered so vividly that terrible bout with mumps and the dire prediction about offspring.

Her grip grew stronger. "Doctors do not know everything." Her dark eyes searched his face, willing him to believe. A rush of optimism engulfed him, and his arms went around her in a tight embrace.

"Kabbarli," he whispered.

EPILOGUE

SERGEANT MACDONALD had smiled at Janet in an avuncular manner the morning she left on the bus. Stringent self-discipline forbade him to show his true feelings. He hated to see her go. He had enjoyed her pretty, expressive face and her vitality, but he knew it was best for her to leave. The official investigation had been short, but she still was in a state of shock. He shook her hand in the restaurant dining room before she left.

"Goodbye, Janet. Best of luck." She looked so young and vulnerable. He wondered how long she would move around before she finally settled down—hopefully with some nice Australian chap who would take care of her. He speculated that with a little encouragement from him she might have stayed in Coober Pedy, but no encouragement was offered. How like Anne she was with her golden-red hair forming a halo around her head. What a fool he had been when Anne came to him long ago, begging for a reconciliation. While their relationship had been brief before she went to work in Tokyo, he had thought of Anne as his girl until some Yank replaced him. He had scorned her that night and shouted he wouldn't take another man's leavings. He never saw her again. He sighed. It was all over and done with now.

"Goodbye, Sergeant MacDonald. You've been very helpful. I must hurry now because I want to say goodbye to Anastasia." She went into the Greek store and before a minute had passed dashed out to board the bus, clutching a paper in her hand

He stepped outside when the bus departed and could see that Janet had put on dark glasses and settled far down into her seat. He waved as the bus disappeared down the main street. In the distance the sergeant could see where the pavement ended and the dirt track began. Clouds of dust swirled up and obscured the vehicle.

Now, three weeks later, he watched Eric Christianson drive his caravan down that same road. His romance with the nurse must have cooled, the policeman thought, and he would be heading for some place more receptive. The sergeant was glad to see the Yank go—even though he had given the American grudging respect, his presence here disturbed him. His visa must shortly be up, and he would have to return to the States where he belonged. Rumors flew about Molly Riley. She was not renewing her contract at the hospital for another year. He couldn't blame her—she must be longing for a new venue in a big city with bright lights and interesting activities. There sure wasn't much to attract Sister Riley in a town like this one. Poor girl—spending her free time at the Aboriginal Reserve for something to do.

MacDonald walked over to the Greek store. He noticed a new sparkle in Anastasia's eyes. He hoped some lout wasn't trifling with her or there would be another killing for sure. He bought some cigarettes, and then a flowered silk scarf attracted his attention. The bright blossoms reminded him of the luxuriant foliage in Sydney. He speculated for a moment and then laid it on the counter.

"Do you have any special wrapping paper?" he asked Anastasia. "I thought my wife might like this. It's her birthday tomorrow."

As he walked back to his office with the brightly wrapped parcel under his arm, he thought, in a mining town everything's a gamble. Things are always changing, people coming and going. I guess nothing ever stays the same.

The day promised to be a hot one. Summer wasn't far off.